Mike Ashley was born in Southall, Middlesex in 1948. His interest in science fiction was first kindled by his father who would read to him or tell him of sf stories he had read. Later he started to track down these stories, which began his research into science fiction and allied fields. Mr. Ashley now lives in Kent and works in Local Government from which, he says, writing is a welcome escape.

Also edited by Mike Ashley:

THE BEST OF BRITISH SF 1

To my Mum for her years of waiting.
Her encouragement was invaluable.

Edited by:
Mike Ashley

The Best of British SF 2

Futura Publications Limited
An Orbit Book

An Orbit Book

First published by Futura Publications
Limited in 1977

ISBN 0 8600 7913 9

Printed in Great Britain by
C. Nicholls & Company Ltd
The Philips Park Press, Manchester

Futura Publications Limited,
110 Warner Road, Camberwell,
London S.E.5.

CONTENTS

Volume II. 'The Years of Reaping'

		Page
	Prologue to Volume II	9
1.	Tableau by *James White*	13
2.	Starting Course by *Arthur Sellings*	42
3.	Advertise Your Cyanide by *Kenneth Bulmer*	58
4.	A Full Member of the Club by *Bob Shaw*	80
5.	The Jackson Killer by *Philip E High*	110
6.	The Emptiness of Space by *John Wyndham*	130
7.	The Teacher by *Colin Kapp*	148
8.	Transit of Earth by *Arthur C Clarke*	188
9.	Zoomen by *Fred Hoyle*	203
10.	Something Strange by *Kingsley Amis*	226
11.	Manuscript Found in A Police State by *Brian W Aldiss*	247
12.	Now: Zero by *J G Ballard*	278
13.	Pale Roses by *Michael Moorcock*	294
14.	The Signaller by *Keith Roberts*	337
	Epilogue to Volume II	376

THE BEST OF BRITISH SCIENCE FICTION

VOLUME TWO

ACKNOWLEDGEMENTS

TABLEAU by James White. © 1958 by Nova Publications Ltd. for *New Worlds Science Fiction*, May 1958. Reprinted by permission of the author and E. J. Carnell Literary Agency.

STARTING COURSE by Arthur Sellings. © 1961 by Nova Publications Ltd. for *New Worlds Science Fiction*, January 1961. Reprinted by permission of Mrs. Gladys Ley and E. J. Carnell Literary Agency.

ADVERTISE YOUR CYANIDE by Kenneth Bulmer. © 1958 by Peter Hamilton for *Nebula Science Fiction*, April 1958. Reprinted by permission of the author and E. J. Carnell Literary Agency.

A FULL MEMBER OF THE CLUB by Bob Shaw. © 1974 by UPD Corporation for *Galaxy Science Fiction*, July 1974. Reprinted by permission of the author and E. J. Carnell Literary Agency.

THE JACKSON KILLER by Philip E. High. © 1961 by Nova Publications Ltd. for *New Worlds Science Fiction*, May 1961. Reprinted by permission of the author and E. J. Carnell Literary Agency.

THE EMPTINESS OF SPACE by John Wyndham. © 1960 by Nova Publications Ltd. for *New Worlds Science Fiction*, November 1960. Reprinted by permission of Vivian Beynon Harris and David Higham Associates.

PROLOGUE

VOLUME II – THE YEARS OF REAPING

Volume one traced the development of science fiction in Britain from its birth to its blossoming in the early 1950s. Volume two continues with a more select representation of the post-war era. This is because so great a profusion of new science fiction writers appeared in Britain with the growth of the post-war market that it proved impossible for me to include all of them in this already large anthology. Therefore, in order to do some justice to a few of the missing names, I shall briefly look at some of the other important authors of the period.

Probably the best known name in British sf *not* included in this collection is Charles Eric Maine. Maine (born 1921) is the pen-name of Liverpudlian David McIlwain, who was another of the small clan of pre-war sf fans. He was a great friend of Jonathan Burke (of whom more in a moment) with whom he co-edited the amateur magazine *The Satellite* in 1938. He got his start in 1951 with a BBC radio play *Spaceways* which was broadcast in 1952. It was then made into a film and Maine converted it into a book. Ever since he has obtained as much mileage as possible from his work, another radio play *The Einstein Highway*, forming the basis for his second novel *Timeliner*. Since then some dozen or so novels have come from his typewriter several of which have been filmed, most recently *The Mind of Mr. Soames* (1970) starring Terence Stamp. Alas what short fiction he has written reads today rather dated, but his novels are all well worth tracking down.

His companion Jonathan Burke, or J. F. Burke (b. 1922) as his by-line usually reads, is best known today for the various *Hammer Omnibus* volumes he produced, but back in the early 1950s his name would be found in all the leading magazines as well as on a score of paperback novels. Whilst he was educated in Liverpool he was born at Rye in Sussex. He has held a number of jobs including the Public Relations Officer for Shell International. He won the Atlantic Award in Literature from the Rockefeller Foundation for his satire *Swift Summer* (1949). His first sf novel published was *Dark Gateway* (1954) although he had had a short novel *Old Man of the Stars* in the October 1953 *Authentic*. Two collections of his stories have been printed, but there are still plenty that could be revived. If only there was room. . . .

An extremely prolific writer is the Scotsman J. T. McIntosh, real name James Macgregor who was born at Paisley, Glasgow in 1925. He succeeded in selling some early stories to *Astounding* in 1950 before the British market really opened up. He has remained to this day a writer who appears mostly in American magazines, though his great output means that he does not entirely neglect the British market. He supplied *New Worlds* with its first serial *The Esp Worlds* (1952) and on the last count has made over one hundred appearances in magazines on both sides of the Atlantic. Even then he found time to be a professional musician, a school teacher and a photographer at one time or another.

Bryan Berry looked like being a bright new star in the 1950s when an early death robbed the field of his talent. He sold several novels to British paperback firms, and had the distinction of having three stories published in the same issue of the popular American pulp *Planet Stories*, all under his own name. Other writers who made a name for themselves in the magazine field in the early 1950s were Lan Wright, F. G. Rayer, Peter Hawkins and Alan Barclay. Alas these names are seen all too seldom these days.

Outside of the magazine field a few other names are worth mentioning. Nigel Kneale is famous because of his *Quatermass* series on television. Kneale (b. 1922) actually had a collection of his short stories published as far back as 1949, *Tomato Cain*, and it won the 1950 Somerset Maugham Award for short stories. The first Quatermass episode, *The Quatermass Experiment* was broadcast in 1953 and filmed in 1955, finally appearing in bookform in 1959. Two other Quatermass serials followed. Since then Kneale has scripted two other major sf television plays *The Year of the Sex Olympics* and the ingenious *The Stone Tapes*.

The radio equivalent of Quatermass was probably Jet Morgan who starred in the memorable *Journey Into Space* series scripted by Charles Chilton (b. 1927). Three separate series were broadcast throughout the 1950s and later issued in book form as *Journey Into Space* (1954), *The Red Planet* (1956) and *The World in Peril* (1960).

A name much overlooked today is that of Paul Capon (b. 1912) from Suffolk. Originally a writer of detective fiction he turned to sf in the 1950s and wrote several memorable novels starting with *The Other Side of the Sun* (1950) – the first of a trilogy about Antigeos, a planet that corresponds with the Earth on the far side of the Sun. A later novel was *Into the Tenth Millenium* (1956).

Then there is the mystery man of sf, John Lymington. His name first appeared in the sf field with *The Night of the Big Heat* (1959) about an alien invasion. It was subsequently made into a convincing film. Since then Lymington has written about a dozen novels including *The Coming of the Strangers* (1961), *A Sword Above the Night* (1962) and *Froomb!* (1964). *Froomb!* was in fact a rewrite of Lymington's very first novel *David and Goliath* written in the 1930s. It was not published as Lymington was told 'There is just no market for fantasy'. And so Lymington turned to writing thrillers for which he has become widely known under his real name of John Newton Chance. Most of his short stories are of a supernatural nature and thus not suited to this anthology.

And, finally, Edmund Cooper (b. 1926). Whilst he is best known today for his novels, he also first appeared in one of Britain's sf magazines with *The Jar of Latakia* (*Authentic*, September 1954). His first sf novel was *Deadly Image* (1958), and he has concentrated on books ever since, such as his more recent volumes *The Overman Culture* (1971) and *Prisoner of Fire* (1974).

And there I must draw the line at the risk of omitting many other names. It's time I opened up the second part of this anthology and let you read the rest of *The Best of British*.

1 – JAMES WHITE: Tableau

The January 1953 issue of *New Worlds* (its nineteenth) was quite a special one for several reasons. Besides carrying the first sf story in print by J. F. Burke (*Chessboard*) it also printed the debut story of Northern Irish writer James White, *Assisted Passage*. To keep White company in the issue were fellow Irishmen Walter Willis, who contributed an article about the 1952 World Science Fiction Convention held in Chicago, and artist Gerard Quinn who supplied the cover and several of the interior illustrations.

White, who had been born in Belfast in 1928 but spent much of his early life in Canada, would soon become one of the most popular writers in *New Worlds*. Many of his early stories, like *Assisted Passage* and *Tableau* which follows, revolved around a military setting, but White could be versatile. His first novel, *Tourist Planet* (1956), centred on the intriguing idea of what holidays in space would be like. A more recent novel, *All Judgement Fled* (1967), dealing with the discovery and exploration of an alien ship, won him the Europa sf Award.

White is also known for his 'Sector General' series, which began with the story of that title in the November 1957 *New Worlds*. The series revolves around an intergalactic hospital, which instantly gives endless plot possibilities. In all fourteen have appeared to date, up to and including *Spacebird* in *New Writings in SF 22* (1973).

Of all his stories it was *Tableau* White chose as his favourite. When asked to comment he said:

> '. . . this story combines two of my favourite themes, Man Meets Alien and Nobody Wants War – especially the people unfortunate enough to be fighting in one, whether they are extra-terrestrial or human beings or both. *Tableau* also makes the point that wars should not be won, just ended, and as soon as possible.'

TABLEAU

James White

The War Memorial in the planetary capital of Orligia was unique, but it very definitely was not a nice object. A great many people – beings of sensitivity and intelligence – had tried vainly to describe their feelings of shock, horror and anger which the sight of it had caused them. For this was no aesthetic marble poem in which godlike figures gestured defiance, or lay dying nobly with limbs arranged to the best advantage. Instead it consisted of an Orligian and an Earthman surrounded by the shattered remnant of a control room belonging to a type of ship now long obsolete, the whole being encased in a cube of transparent plastic.

The Orligian was standing crouched slightly forward, with blood matting the fur on its chest and face. A few feet away lay the Earthman, very obviously dying. His uniform was in shreds, revealing the ghastly injuries he had sustained – certain organs in the abdominal region normally concealed by layers of skin and muscle being clearly visible. Yet this man, who had no business being alive much less being capable of movement, was struggling forward to reach the Orligian. It was the look on the Earthman's face which was the most distressing thing about the whole, horrible tableau.

Night had fallen, but the Memorial was lit erratically by the flashes which repeatedly outlined the buildings at the edges of its surrounding park. From all over the city came the sounds of sharp, thudding explosions, while rockets grew rapidly on slender stems of orange sparks to flower crashingly into clouds of falling stars. The city, indeed the whole planet, was in festive mood. With the

Orligian love of doing things properly or not at all, this meant the letting off of a great many fireworks as well as the usual merry-making. Sleep was impossible, the populace was going wild.

It was, after all, a great occasion. Tomorrow the Orligians were getting another war memorial . . .

Like most single ship engagements it had proved to be a long-drawn out affair. Normally such a duel led to the defeat of the Orlig ship within a few hours, MacEwan thought with that small portion of his mind which was not engaged in throwing his ship about in violent evasive action. But there was nothing normal about this fight, he thought bitterly; the enemy had begun to learn things, to adopt Earth armament and tactics. They, too, had regressed to throwing rocks . . . !

'Closer! *Closer!*' Reviora's voice squeaked suddenly through his phones. 'We're too far away, dammit! They'll get us in a minute . . .'

MacEwan did not have to be reminded of the necessity for sticking close to the enemy ship, and many another Captain would have told the Ordnance Office so in no uncertain terms. But he had discovered long ago that young Reviora, whose voice had only recently changed and was prone to change back again at times of emotional stress, could exhibit all the outward signs of panic while continuing to use his weapons with incredible accuracy. MacEwan relegated the Ordnance Officer's jitterings into the realm of general background noise and continued to focus all his attention on the controls.

His idea in taking evasive action at extreme range – extreme for his ship, that was; it was nearly ideal range for the enemy – was to lull the Orlig skipper into thinking that he intended breaking off the action. Such a thing was unheard of, simply because trying to run away from an Orlig ship meant certain destruction from their primary weapon, but there was always a first time. Maybe the enemy officer would think that his ship was crippled, or out of ammunition, or that its Captain lacked sufficient intestinal fortitude to ram. Anyway, he would be puzzled and maybe just a little bit inattentive . . .

MacEwan said quietly, 'Reviora, ready?' He pulled the ship round in a tight turn, then with the Orlig ship centring his forward vision screen he pushed the thrust bar through the emergency gate and held it there. The target vessel grew slowly, then expanded so rapidly that the screen was suddenly too small to hold it. A dull, intermittent vibration told of Reviora, with the ship holding a steady course and the enemy dead ahead, using his forward turret to the best advantage. MacEwan thought he saw a spurt of fog from a hole freshly torn in the Orlig ship's hull, then the image flicked out of sight to reappear as a rapidly shrinking picture in the aft view-screen.

His hands were slippery and he had to blink sweat out of his eyes. *Check velocity!* his racing brain yelled at his slow, fumbling fingers. *Move! Jump around! And above all, keep close . . . !*

So as to give Reviora a chance to get in a killing burst, MacEwan had made a fast but unswerving approach. He had held his ship steady for fully five seconds. That had been an insane risk to take, but he had gambled on the Orlig ship not using its primary weapon on him for fear of his hurtling ship smashing into it even after MacEwan's ship and crew were written off. Now however, he was fast receding from the enemy ship and evasive action was again indicated. Still on emergency thrust he began weaving and corkscrewing, at the same time trying desperately to kill the velocity away from the enemy he had built up during the attack.

Evasive action at a distance was much less effective than close up because the Orlig primary weapon had a certain amount of spread. Maximum safety lay in sticking close and moving fast. Or had done until now . . .

It had been estimated that the radiation, or force, or field of stress which was the Orligian Primary Weapon took roughly six to seven seconds to build up, but once caught in that field a ship and its occupants were a total loss. Yet strangely the ships affected appeared unharmed. Provided one was extremely careful they could even be entered. But just scratch the metal of one of those ships, or stick a needle in one of the crew-men, and the result resembled a small-scale atomic explosion – but again, strangely, without any trace of immediate or residual radio-activity. Such ships were now left severely alone, their orbits not even being plotted as dangers to navigation because the first meteorite to puncture their hulls caused them to destroy themselves.

It was a super-weapon, only one of those which had forced Earth back, so far as tactics were concerned, to the bow-and-arrow level.

MacEwan only half noticed the shudderings of his ship as Reviora, using absurdly adolescent profanity, tried for a deflection shot with the remote-controlled waist turret, and the harsher, more erratic vibration of Orlig shots getting home. At the moment he was wishing desperately that there was some means by which he could simply cut and run – not, he hastened to assure himself, because he was overly interested in his own safety, but because this new development represented a change in Orlig strategy. It was a change which would have to be countered, and MacEwan hoped that the Brass back home would be able to find the answer – he couldn't see one himself.

If only Nyberg had never been born, MacEwan thought; or failing that, if only he had not grown up into a stubborn, courageous and idealistic Swede whose highmindedness had started an interstellar war. Such wishing was sheerest futility, he knew, but even in the middle of the hottest engagement he had yet experienced there was this weak, traitorous segment of his mind which tried to escape into the world of what might have been . . .

Five years ago the UN survey ship *Starfinder* – crew of fifty-eight plus seven civilian specialists, Captain Sigvard

Nyberg in command – had, at very nearly the limit of its prodigious range, made contact with a ship of an alien culture for the first time. A tape left by the late Captain Nyberg told of the excitement of the occasion, and a day-by-day summary gave some indications of the difficulties experienced in widening that contact.

Strangely, the vessel of what were later to become known as the Orligians did not seem to want to maintain contact at first, though neither did they show signs of hostility. *Starfinder*'s psychologist, admittedly working on little or no data, had suggested that such behaviour might be due either to a high degree of conservatism in their culture or to a simple case of cold feet. He had added that cowardice was not a strong possibility, however, considering the fact that the alien ship was four times the size of their own. But Captain Nyberg had maintained contact – just how he had done so was not known in detail because he was a man who disliked talking about his own accomplishments – and widened it to the point where simple sequences of radio signals were replaced by exchanges of message capsules containing technical data which enabled the two ships to match communication channels.

It was shortly after sound-with-vision communications had been set up between the ships that something went wrong. The last words on Captain Nyberg's tape were to the effect that, far from being horrible monsters the aliens were nice, cuddly little creatures and that their atmosphere and gravity requirements seemed to be close enough to Earth-normal for the two races to co-exist on either of their home planets without artificial aids. A few words, mostly of self-identification, had already been exchanged. But the Captain intended going across to their ship next day, because he had a hunch that the Orligians were beginning to shy away again.

When the nine men in *Starfinder*'s tender, who had been investigating a nearby solar system during these proceedings, returned they found that the mother ship had been the scene of a massacre. Not one of the ship's personnel had escaped, and the condition of the bodies seemed to indicate that they had been battered to death with the nearest available blunt instrument. The slaughter had been merciless, the humans being obviously taken by surprise because in only a few places was the deck stained with blood which matched no earthly group, and there were no Orligian dead at all.

The nine-man crew of the tender somehow managed to bring their mother ship home. The situation was, of course, highly charged emotionally – much more so than normal because of the fact that *Starfinder*'s crew had been mixed – so that Earth, which had known peace for three centuries, found itself at war with the culture of Orligia.

And the war, MacEwan was thinking as he frantically threw his ship all over the sky half a mile from the Orligian light cruiser, had been going on for far too long. The sense of immediacy, where the people back home were concerned, had been lost – and with it the horror and righteous anger which had started it all. Defence spending was heavy and teddy-bears were no longer stocked in kiddy's toy stores, but otherwise there was very little to indicate outwardly that a state of war existed at all. But maximum effort was being, and would be, maintained simply through fear. Earth, had she chosen to, could have withdrawn her spacefleet at any time, could simply have left and called the whole thing off. Neither side knew the positions of each other's home planets. But that course would have left the situation unresolved and eventually, whether in fifty years or five hundred, the Orligs were bound to discover Earth. The people of Earth were honest enough not to gain peace by dumping the problem in the laps of their many times great grandchildren.

But it was an untidy and very unsatisfactory sort of war. The 'front line' so to speak was in the general volume of space where the original contact had been made, and bases had been set up by both sides on planetary bodies in the region, and supplied by ships taking very great pains to conceal their point of origin. The distances involved made patrolling a joke and any battle a vast, disorganised series of dogfights. Except when raids were carried out on enemy bases it was nothing unusual for three weeks to go by without a single clash, and this at a time when both sides were prosecuting the war with maximum effort. Altogether it proved what had been known from the first, that the very idea of interstellar war was impractical and downright silly. But the chief reason for the feeling of dissatisfaction was the fact that, slowly but surely, the Earth was losing.

Superiority in offensive and defensive weapons belonged to the Orligs. They had a screen, probably originally intended for meteor protection, which englobed each of their ships at a radius of two miles and which melted anything approaching at a velocity likely to do harm - meteors, missiles, attacking ships, *anything*. This screen could be penetrated only by guiding the ship through it at what was practically a crawl. Once through, however, the missile's remote-control equipment immediately ceased to function and the missile drifted harmlessly past the target. On the one or two occasions when a nuclear warhead had accidentally drifted into an Orlig ship, nothing at all had happened.

Earth science had been able to duplicate this screen, but it was no good to them because the Orligs scorned the use of such crude methods of attack as atomic missiles: they had The Weapon.

This the Earth scientists could not understand, much less duplicate. They only knew that it was some kind of beam or field of force which required several seconds to focus, and that its maximum range was about thirty miles. There was no answer to this weapon. A ship caught by it became a lifeless, undamaged but untouchable hulk which needed only sharp contact with a meteorite or piece of drifting wreckage to blast itself out of existence. The Weapon was also thought to be the reason why atomic warheads refused to function in the vicinity of Orlig ships, but this was just a guess.

There had been panic in high places, MacEwan remembered, when the most advanced offensive weapons of Earth had been proved useless. What was needed was some form of weapon which was too simple and uncomplicated for the Orlig nullification equipment to be effective, and a tactic which would bring such a weapon to bear. An answer of sorts had been found. To find it they had to go back, not quite so far as the bow-and-arrow era, but to the Final World War period and the armour-piercing cannon, and chemically powdered rockets used in the aircraft of that period. The tactics which had been developed were the only ones possible with such weapons, but they tended to be wasteful of men.

'Sir! Sir! Can I have the ship?'

It was Reviora, excited but no longer swearing. The tiny, wandering portion of MacEwan's mind came back to present time with a rush. He said, 'Why?'

'Ammunition's running out, but we've three Mark V's in the nose rocket launcher,' Reviora babbled. 'It's working now – I found the break in the firing circuit. They won't be expecting rockets at this stage. We can use that trick of Hoky's –' He bit the sentence off abruptly, then stammered, 'I . . . I'm sorry, I mean Captain Hokasuri –'

'Skip it,' said MacEwan. He ran his eye briefly over the control panel, then switched everything to the forward conning position. 'Right, you have the ship.'

Hoky had had lots of tricks. Hokasuri and MacEwan were the Old Firm, the unbeatable, invincible combination who invariably hunted together. But then every team was invincible until one or the other failed to come back. MacEwan squirmed restively. His mind, temporarily freed of the responsibility for guiding the ship, flicked back over the opening minutes of the engagement. It could only have been through sheer bad luck that his partner had been Stopped, the mild-mannered little Japanese with the apologetic grin and the black button eyes was not the type to make mistakes . . .

Hokasuri and he had been searching the nearby planet for signs of an enemy base when they had surprised an Orligian presumably engaged on the same chore. Distance had been about two hundred miles.sThey had immediately separated and attacked.

The Orligs used fairly large ships; apparently the generators for The Weapon took up a lot of space. Earth craft were very small and fast, and hunted in pairs. Though not one hundred per cent successful, this had proved to be the only effective means of coming to grips with the enemy. The Weapon had a range of thirty miles and took six or seven seconds to focus. Two ships, therefore, approaching from different directions, the while taking violent evasive action, discharging 'window' and performing various other acts designed to confuse enemy aim, could be expected to run the gauntlet of The Weapon until the screen which surrounded enemy ships at a distance of two miles was reached. But to penetrate this the attacking ships had to check velocity, and it was at this point that the two attackers usually became one, the reason being that there was time for The Weapon to be focused on one of them. The surviving attacker then closed with the enemy – its very nearness and extreme mobility protection against the slow-acting Weapon – and slowly battered the Orlig ship into a wreck with solid, armour-piercing shells and rockets.

Once begun such a battle had to be fought to the death, because the Earth ship would be a sitting target if it attempted to escape through the screen again.

MacEwan had not been worried about Hokasuri getting through the screen, they had done it so often before despite all the laws of probability and statistics. They were the invincible ones, the pilots with that little something extra which had enabled them to return together after eighteen successful kills. But he had seen Hokasuri Stopped, seen his ship diving unwaveringly into the planet below them and watched it explode in the fringes of its atmosphere.

For the first time then MacEwan had experienced a sense of personal anger towards this Orlig ship. Indoctrination to the contrary, previous attacks had always seemed more like a big and very dangerous game to him. But then his anger had been pushed into the background by a sudden upsurge of fear that was close to panic. The Orlig ship, which should have been helpless now that he had closed in, was hitting back. What was worse, it was using the same type of archaic weapon for short-range defence that Earth ships had developed for attack, heavy calibre machine-guns of some sort. His ship was in nearly as bad a state as was that of the enemy . . .

Now he watched the Orlig ship spreading out in his forward view-screen again. The bow-launchers were fixed mount; to line them up on the target Reviora had to aim with the whole ship, and the Ordnance Officer had to do it because MacEwan's fire control panel was dead.

Hokasuri's trick had been to open up the enemy ship with his guns, saving the rockets until he could place them right inside the target. It was a process which called for accuracy of a high order. Perhaps Reviora could match it.

For an agonising four seconds Reviora held the ship on a collision course with the enemy while the fire of two Orlig blister turrets gouged at its hull. Suddenly the rockets were away, streaking ahead and plunging unerringly into the long, dark rent already torn in the Orlig's hull plating by an earlier attack. Everything happened at once, then. Metal fountained spectacularly outwards and the ragged-edged hole in the Orlig's hull lengthened, widened and gaped horribly. Simultaneously there was a sharp cry from Reviora which faded out in peculiar fashion. MacEwan wondered about it for perhaps a fraction of a second, decided that the peculiar sound was due to the sudden loss of the air which carried Reviora's voice from his mouth to the suit mike, then he was reaching frantically for the control panel again.

Reviora was dead. They were still on a collision course!

Desperately MacEwan stabbed control keys – forward and rear opposed lateral steering jets to swing ship, and full emergency thrust on the main drive to get him out of there fast. The ship began turning, but that was all. Controls to the main power pile were cut, probably by the recent Orlig gunnery, and the hyperdrive telltales were dead, too – the ship was a wreck. Now it was skidding in broadside-on and still closing rapidly with the other ship. MacEwan hit more keys, firing all lateral jets on that side in an attempt to check velocity. Uselessly, it was too little and too late. There was a close-spaced series of shocks as the ship ran through the metallic debris blown from the Orlig ship, climaxed by a tearing, grinding crash as the Earth vessel embedded itself exactly in the hole its rockets had blasted in the enemy hull.

The shock tore MacEwan, straps and all, sideways out of his chair and threw him on to the deck. His head hit something . . .

When he was in a condition to think straight again his first thought was for the spacesuit. Captains did not wear protective suits in action for the same reason that necessitated their safety webbing being thin, flexible and generally not worth a damn – too cumbersome, and besides, the control room was tucked away relatively safe in the centre of the ship. But now there was no longer any need for his hands to be unhampered and his body able to move freely; his control board was dead. Two view-screens were still operating for some peculiar reason but that was all. There were no indications of a drop in air pressure, his ears felt normal and respiration ditto, but it was too much to expect that the crash had not opened seams even here. He was about to open the suit locker when his mind registered what his eyes were seeing in the two view-screens.

One was focused inwards and showed where the lateral jets had practically fused the two ships together before cutting out; some of the Orlig's bulkheads still glowed red hot. The other screen gave a view outwards and showed the planetary surface only a few hundred miles off. As MacEwan watched his ears detected a whispering, high-pitched rushing sound.

There are no sounds in space. The Orlig ship, crippled, a near wreck and carrying the remains of the small ship responsible for its present condition, was trying for a landing. It was already entering atmosphere. MacEwan abruptly forgot about spacesuits and dived instead for the acceleration chair.

He was still scrambling weightlessly above the chair when the first surge dropped him face downwards into it. He had time to fasten just one safety strap, before suddenly mounting deceleration hammered him flat. Briefly, he thought that the Orlig ship must be in bad trouble to want to land in its present state. With the damage inflicted by the Earth ship the Orligian must be an aerodynamic mess, and that without taking into account the wreckage of the aforesaid ship jammed against it like some spacegoing Siamese twin. Then all thinking stopped as he strained every nerve and muscle to keep alive, to keep his creaking and popping rib cage from collapsing on to his straining heart and lungs and strangling the life out of him.

After what seemed an impossibly long time the deceleration let up somewhat, becoming steady, measured surges of one or two G's which he could take comfortably. Obviously the Orlig pilot had shed most of his velocity in the thin, upper air to minimise atmospheric heating, then was taking her down slow for the last few miles. Not too slow, though, or stratospheric winds might buffet her off vertical despite everything the gyros could do. This Orlig was *good*, MacEwan thought; he deserved to make it. MacEwan also thought that he would like to buy the Orlig pilot a drink, supposing such a thing was possible and that Orligs drank.

The control room was vibrating and heaving in a manner unnerving both to mind and body, as if jerking and swaying in time to the mad cacophony of shrieking air, bellowing engines and a banging, rattling percussion section as deceleration and air resistance tried to shake both ships to pieces. MacEwan was amazed that the wreckage of his ship had not torn itself free long ago.

Suddenly there was a last, violent surge of deceleration, a smashing, jarring shock, then the grinding scream of tearing metal. They were down – but not still. There was a sickening, outward swaying motion and more harsh crepitation of ruptured metal. MacEwan's eyes flew to the view-screen. It showed a stony, desert-like planetary surface swooping up to meet him. One of the Orlig's landing legs must have buckled, they were toppling . . .

The noise was like a pick driven into his brain, and he saw the ship coming to pieces all around him. Bits of sky showed in surrealistic geometric shapes which changed constantly with the shifting of the wreckage. There was a sudden bright explosion, and MacEwan had time only to remember their damaged midships launcher and the primed rocket still jammed in it, then flying, jagged-edged metal ripped all consciousness from him.

When MacEwan came to again there was surprisingly little pain; his strongest impressions were those of numbness and extreme, clammy cold. This must be shock, he diagnosed briefly. But there was a warm wetness overlying the chill of his body that seemed to be localised in the area where he felt the dull, shock-numbed pains. He looked down at himself then, and realised how very lucky he was to be in a state of shock. He knew at once, of course, that he was dying.

The blast had left only a few shreds of his uniform, there was a great deal of blood, and his injuries . . .

A man should not have to look at himself in a state like this, MacEwan thought dully. If he had met an animal in this condition he would have shot it, and had it been a member of his own species he would have turned away and been violently sick. As it was he gazed at the frightful wounds with a strange objectivity until his brain, not quite as numb as the rest of him, re-opened communications with his one good arm. He fumbled open the emergency medical kit that still hung from his belt and used the coagulant spray freely, ending by swallowing rather more than the prescribed dose of antipain against the time when the shock would wear off. With most of the external bleeding checked, MacEwan tried to lie as motionless as possible. If he moved at all he felt that he would burst open along the seams like some great big football filled with red molasses.

It was while he was trying to look around him – and endeavouring to decide why he had given himself this inadequate first aid – that MacEwan saw the Orligian.

By what freak of circumstances it came to be there it was impossible to say, but not three yards from MacEwan lay one of the Enemy. It was not a very impressive object, he thought, this small being which resembled nothing so much as a teddy-bear that had been left out in the rain. But it was not rain which matted the fur on the creature's chest and head, nor was it water oozing from the raw ruin of its face. It was in much better shape than MacEwan, however, it was breathing steadily and making odd twitching movements which suggested returning consciousness. The broad belt to which was attached MacEwan's holster and the pouch containing the medical kit was the only part of his uniform left intact. He carefully drew the little gun with its clip of thirty explosive bullets and waited for the Orlig to wake up.

While waiting he tried hating it a little.

MacEwan had always been an unemotional man – perhaps that was the secret of his success as a Captain, and the reason for his unusually long period of active duty. In his particular job MacEwan was convinced that emotion simply killed you off in jig time. A man making an attack approach with hate or any other emotion – whether directed towards the enemy, or something or somebody else – clogging his mind was leaving that much less of it for the vital business of evading The Weapon. In battle MacEwan felt no hatred for the enemy, no anger that his Ordnance Officer cursed and swore in a highly insubordinate fashion at him – Reviora was invariably full of apologies on their return to base – and none of the softer emotions that could leak over from the times when he was not in battle.

There had been a girl once, a tall, dark-eyed girl who had been attached to the base Plot Room. MacEwan had eaten with her a few times, seen how things were going, then avoided her. That had been the smart thing to do; good survival. Now he was realising what an unhappy man he had been.

Hokasuri had treated the whole thing as a game, too. MacEwan had had one of his rare moments of anger when his brother Captain's Stopped ship had exploded in this planet's atmosphere, and when Reviora had died. But now he felt only a dull regret. He reminded himself that the Orlig lying over there was responsible – in part, at least – for those deaths, but still he could not actively hate the thing.

It was his duty to kill it, whether he hated the Orlig personally or not. Why, then, was he being so squeamish about not wanting to shoot it when it was unconscious, and trying to work up hatred for it? Was his imminent demise making him go soft, had Iron Man MacEwan turned to putty at the end? Phlegmatic, unsmiling and distant, Captain MacEwan was looked upon back at base as the embodiment of the soulless, killing machine. Now he felt as if he was thinking like a woman. Now he was thinking that, just this once, he would like to do something on a basis of emotion rather than for cold, calculating, logical reasons. It would be the last chance he would have, he thought wryly.

But wasn't he fooling himself? Suppose he forgot logic for once, would he use the pistol to blow the Orlig into little pieces out of sheer hate or would he do something stupid? Yellow cowardice was a motivation as well as duty or hate, and MacEwan was coming near his end. He had never been a religious man, but nobody had been able to give him concrete data on what lay on the other side, though a great many believed firmly that they knew. Was he simply scared that doing a bad thing now would have serious consequences later, after he died – even though he did not really believe there was a later? MacEwan swore weakly, the first time he had done such a thing in years.

All right, then! MacEwan told himself savagely. This mind of mine, admittedly dopey from shock and antipain pills not to mention a generous measure of sheer blue funk, will for the first and most decidedly the last time reason on the purely thalamic level. He would not shoot the Orligian. Fear of the Hereafter was only part of the reason, there was the fact that this particular Orlig, or one of his crew mates, had made a very fine crash landing.

MacEwan said, 'Oh, go ahead and live, damn you!' and tossed the gun away from him.

Immediately the Orlig leapt crouching to its feet.

MacEwan only faintly heard the gun sliding down the inclined deck, falling between the ruptured seams of floor plating and clattering down through the wreckage below. He was watching the Orlig and realising that it had been playing possum, pretending unconsciousness and covertly keeping him under observation while he had the gun in his hand. A smart little teddybear, this Orlig, and now that he was unarmed . . .

He could not help remembering that the muscles under those soft-looking, furry arms were capable of tearing a man's head off, as the massacre on the *Starfinder* had shown.

'MacEwan,' he told himself sickly, 'you have done a very stupid thing.'

At the sound the Orlig started back, then it began edging nearer again. One of its arms hung limp, MacEwan saw, and very obviously it was having to force itself to approach him. Finally it got to within three feet and stood looking down. It growled and whined in an odd fashion at him and gestured with its good arm; the noises did not sound threatening. Then the arm reached out, hesitated, and a stubby, four-fingered hand touched MacEwan briefly on the head and was withdrawn quickly. The Orlig growled again and retreated. It disappeared behind a nearby tangle of wreckage and he heard it clambering awkwardly through to the remains of its own ship.

MacEwan let his head sink to the deck, no longer willing to exert the tremendous effort needed to hold it upright. The antipain was not working too well and his brain seemed to function in fits and starts, racing one minute and completely blank the next. All at once he was utterly, deathly tired, and it must have been at that point that he blacked out again. When he came to, MacEwan's first impression was of vibration striking up through his jaw from the deck plating. His second was that he had gone mad.

His eyes were closed yet he could see himself – all of himself, including the head lying on the deck with its eyes closed. And there was a constant gabbling in his mind which could only be delirium. MacEwan wanted to black out again but the delirium kept him awake. It was too loud, as if somebody were shouting in his head. But the words, though nonsense, were heard clearly:

. . . *It is wrong to do this. My Family would be ashamed. But my Family is dead, all dead. Killed by the Family of this loathsome thing which is dying. It is wrong, yet here is a chance to obtain valuable data about them, and with my Family dead the displeasure of other Families cannot hurt me. Perhaps my efforts are useless and the creature is already dead, its wounds are frightful* . . .

MacEwan shook his head weakly and opened his eyes. He blinked so as to focus on the odd mechanism which had appeared on the deck about a foot from his head. It was squat, heavy-looking and was dull grey except where clusters of fine, coppery rods stuck out at intervals. A thick power cable sprouted from its base and disappeared somewhere, and just behind the machine the Orlig sat on its haunches. The expression in its eyes, which were the only feature in that ruined face capable of registering any emotion, could only be described as intent.

In his present state it was hard for MacEwan to feel undue excitement or amazement. But he was not so far gone that he would not reason logically, so that he knew quite clearly what it was that he was experiencing.

The Orligs had telepathy.

In the instant of his reaching that conclusion the babble in his head ceased, but there was not silence. Instead there was a bubbling stew of half-thoughts, memory fragments and general confusion, the whole being overlaid by an extreme feeling of antagonism and instinctive loathing which the Orlig was trying unsuccessfully to control. But it *was* trying, MacEwan knew, and that was a good point in its favour. And the main reason for its confusion, he saw, was the fact that having opened communications with a species which was its deadly enemy, the Orlig was at a loss for words.

MacEwan thought that the right thing to do would be to mentally spit in its eye. But he had stopped doing the right things recently – he had gone all emotional. Instead he thought, *That was a very nice landing you pulled off A very fine landing.*

With the rapport existing between them MacEwan now *knew* that this was the Orlig pilot.

Surprise and increased confusion greeted this, then: *Thank you,* the creature's mind replied. *At the time I did not know I had a passenger to observe it.*

Maybe it was due to an accident of phrasing, but MacEwan thought that there was an undercurrent of surprisingly Human humour in the thought. But it was lost abruptly in an upsurge of the ever-present antagonism and revulsion, and the flood of sight, sound and pain impressions that, although shockingly clear in themselves, were roaring through the Orligian's brain at a speed too fast for words. The screaming hail of metal from the attacking Earth ship, searching out its Family one by one, ripping them into bloody ruin and continuing to churn horribly at what was left. As the most junior member of the Family with the fastest reflexes it had been in the pilot's position, and relatively safe. But it had felt and seen its brothers being cut to pieces, and when its father had left the control room to take over a firing position, the mentacom had sent him the feelings of its parent gasping frenziedly for air in a compartment which had suddenly been blasted open to space by MacEwan's guns . . .

You started this war not us! MacEwan broke in, suddenly angry because he shared identical feelings about Reviora and other acquaintances that he had been careful to avoid thinking of as friends. He was remembering the *Starfinder.*

The reply he got staggered him. It was his own race,

not the Orligs, who were responsible for the war, and looking at it from the other's point of view he could see that it was so.

What a perfectly ghastly mess! MacEwan thought. And Nyberg, poor, brave, ignorant Captain Nyberg. If only he had realised that a feeling of instinctive friendship towards these newly-discovered aliens - because they were so soft and furry and so reminiscent of a child's first non-adult friend, a teddy-bear - did not necessarily have to be reciprocated. On the Orlig's home planet there was a sqecies which resembled the Earthmen as closely as Orligs did teddybears. Its habits were dirty, it was vicious, cowardly and possessed just enough intelligence to be depraved. To the Orlig mentality that species was like fat, wet things under rocks, and things that itched and stank. One of their tricks was to play and cavort within sight of groups of Orlig cubs until one or more, intrigued and as yet not intelligent enough to know better, would wander off after them. The species was, of course, carnivorous . . .

And Captain Nyberg, impatient to broaden Earth's mental horizon by contact with an extra-terrestrial civilisation and puzzled by the alien's tendency to shy away, had crossed to the Orlig ship. He had been admitted by beings whose conditioning from earliest childhood towards things like him were diametrically opposed to his feelings for them. But that alone might not have led to war. If only Nyberg had not tried too hard to win friends and influence Orligs by the tactic so beloved of Earth politicians.

If only he had not tried to kiss babies.

The Orligs were a very emotional race and things had happened very quickly after that incident. There were not enough beings on the ship possessing the objectivity to realise that Nyberg's action might only have *appeared* threatening . . .

But why, MacEwan wondered, had not one of the mentacom gadgets been handy. Instead of halting words and actions, both of which were wide open to misunderstanding, there would have been full comprehension of the potentially explosive differences in the backgrounds of both races. The *Starfinder* incident would never have happened, there would not have been a war and he, MacEwan, would not be dying. Even at this late date he wondered what the Earth authorities might do if the true situation was explained to them. They, too, like Captain Nyberg, had been at one time anxious for contact with an intelligent extra-terrestrial species.

But the flood of the Orlig's thinking was pouring over him again. The main torrent roared through his brain, but not so loudly that the small, revealing side streams went unnoticed. Things like the fact that large-scale war had been unknown on Orligia – though small ones, something like feuds, tended to be rugged – because the Family system made them impossible. There were no nations on the planet, just Families, which were small, close-knit groups of up to fifteen who submitted willingly to the near-Godlike authority of the male parent until they showed sufficient aptitude to form a family group of their own.

It was an intensely conservative type of culture with very complicated and inflexible codes of manners, and Nyberg's misadventure proved the severity of punishments for offences against this code. And the mentacom, it seemed, had been recently developed from existing instruments in use by Orligian psychologists. Apparently the noise of a space battle played hob with the delicately modulated whines and growls which were the Orlig spoken language so that they had been forced to develop a method of mechanical telepathy to solve the communications problem.

Just like that, MacEwan thought dryly, then he concentrated on the mainstream of thought being radiated at him. It was so much easier to do that.

He was cold all over now, his mouth and tongue burned with a raging thirst and he could not believe that a human body could feel so utterly and completely weary and still remain awake. Had the conversation been in spoken words MacEwan knew that he could never have carried it on, he was too far gone. His brain felt funny, too, as if a cold, dark something was pushing at it around the edges. Fatigue, loss of blood and oxygen starvation were probably responsible for that effect, he thought, and wondered ironically what particular code he would break if he died on the Orlig in the middle of a conversation.

A sudden new urgency had come into the Orlig's thoughts. They were on the *Starfinder* incident again, and apparently there were those in that Orlig ship's crew who had felt themselves unduly constrained by their home planet's codes of behaviour and of thinking. In their opinion the planet was too hide-bound and conservative and contact with an alien culture was just what it needed if stasis and decadence were to be warded off. The Families in the Earth ship were, it was true, outwardly loathsome to an infinite degree, but perhaps the visual aspect, thought some, was not of primary importance . . .

MacEwan felt a sudden wild hope growing in him as he guessed the trend of the other's thinking. But an equally great despair followed it. What could *he* do, he was as good as dead?

Do I understand, he thought as distinctly as he could, *that you would like peace*?

The Orlig's thoughts fairly boiled out at him. Their centuries-old civilisation was being disrupted. Though warships were generally crewed by one or more complete Families, for technical reasons some Families had to be split up. The pain and tragedy of this process could only be appreciated by an Orligian. And hundreds of other Families, the very best Families who specialised in the various technologies, were being lost every year in the war. Most decidedly the Orlig, and quite a few of his acquaintances, would like peace!

We, also, thought MacEwan fervently, *would like peace.* Then suddenly he cursed. A door had been opened, just the barest crack, and it was heavy with the inertia of past guilt and blood and misunderstanding. How could a dying man push it wide and cross the threshold?

MacEwan felt that his mind as well as his body was packing up on him. It would be so nice and easy just to let everything stop. But he was Iron Man MacEwan, he reminded himself goadingly; MacEwan the Indestructible, the big bodied and even bigger headed Superman, the perfect killing machine. Now he had something which was really worthwhile to strive for, and all he wanted to do was give up because he felt tired. *Think, damn you!* he raged at himself. *Think, you stinking lousy quitter . . . !*

And he did think. Weakly, urgently he pleaded with the Orlig to relay his suggestions to the other's superiors. He thought in terms of an Armistice preparatory to peace talks, and explained how this might be brought about by using the Earth device of a flag of truce. A raid on an Earth base in which message containers only were dropped, followed by a single ship with a white flag painted prominently on the hull. The Earth forces would be suspicious, but MacEwan did not think they would blow the ship out of the sky . . .

At that point MacEwan blanked out. It was as if the peaks and hollows of his brain waves had suddenly evened themselves out, leaving him with the knowledge of being alive but with no other sensations at all. He didn't know how long it lasted but when he came round again the Orlig pilot was pleading with him desperately not to die, that medical help was on the way – together with a flotilla which was escorting the rescue ship – and that he must live until the other's superiors talked with him.

MacEwan was icy cold and sick and his thirst was a dry acid in his throat. The antipain was not working so well anymore, but he knew that he would never be able to keep a clear head – or even stay conscious – if he took another dose. He thought longingly of water; he knew the Orligs used it.

But the Orlig sent him a firm, sorrowful negative. He did not know much of Earthmen's physiology, but he was very sure that food or drink would do further harm considering the seriousness and position of MacEwan's injuries. There was a queer, guilty undertone to the thought. MacEwan fastened on it, prised it open, and felt a sensation of hurt which had nothing to do with his wounds. As well as the reasons stated the Orlig had been trying to hide the fact that he did not want to have to touch the Earthman again at any price.

Tell me of yourself, the Orlig went on hastily, *of your world, your background, your friends and Family. I must know as much as possible in case* . . . It tried to stop the thought there, but only succeeded in accentuating it: there can be no tact in a meeting of minds . . . *In case you die before my superiors arrive.*

MacEwan fought pain and thirst and soft encroaching darkness as he tried to tell the Orlig about Earth, his friends and himself. He was pleading a case, and a successful decision meant the end of the war. But he could not be eloquent, nor could he cover up the unpleasant aspects of certain things, because it was impossible to lie with the mind. Several times he slid into a kind of delirium wherein he fought out the last engagement which had killed Hoky and Reviora, right down to the crash, the explosion and the meeting with the Orlig pilot. He could do nothing to stop it, this recurrent nightmare which just might end on a note of hope.

The Orligian was horrified at MacEwan's personal score of kills, but at the same time he seemed to feel just a little sympathy for the loss of Hokasuri and Reviora. And there was a peculiar thought, which MacEwan did not catch properly because he was slipping into a delirious spell at the time, about the Weapon that was somehow tied in with the strange belief on the Orlig's part that no civilised being could attack knowing he had a fifty-fifty chance of being killed; such bravery was incredible.

But what impressed the other most was the knowledge that the long-dead Captain Nyberg's actions had been motivated by *friendship* towards the Orligians. And that there were creatures on Earth closely resembling the Orligians which the Humans liked and treated as pets, whereas positions were completely reverse on Orligia. It meant that the unfortunate Captain had been slain unjustly, and if it could convince its superiors of that, the groundwork for understanding and eventual peace might be laid.

A severe mental struggle became apparent in the Orlig pilot's mind at that point, so intense that the other seemed deaf to MacEwan's thinking even though he was in one of his rare lucid periods. The being rose to his feet and padded up and down the clear deck area of the wrecked control room. Its mental distress was extreme. Finally it stopped, crouching above MacEwan, and began to bend forward. It was fighting hard, every inch of the way.

A stubby, hairy hand found MacEwan's, held it and actually squeezed it for all of two seconds before being hastily pulled away.

My name is Grulyaw-Ki, it said.

MacEwan could not think of a reply for several seconds because there was a funny tightness in his throat - which when he came to think of it was silly.

MacEwan.

Things were hazy after that. They talked a good deal through the mentacom, mostly about the war and regarding tactics and installations in a way which would have had the security officers of both sides tearing their hair. It came as a shock to see that the control room suddenly contained three more Orligs, who eyed him keenly and touched him in several places without any particularly strong signs of repugnance. Obviously Medics are used to horrible sights since the war. They withdrew and immediately afterwards he noticed a large section of the control room wall being cut away, revealing a blue sky, the slender pillar of the rescue ship and a barren stretch of desert. An intricate piece of electronic gadgetry was being assembled in the gap, with power lines running from it to the wrecked Orlig ship. MacEwan could not ask about it because the power cable to the mentacom had been taken out and plugged into this new mechanism.

The Orlig medics had cleaned Grulyaw-Ki up but had not been able to do much for his face, and the being had steadfastly refused to leave MacEwan and go to the rescue ship for proper treatment. It seemed that the Orlig felt deeply obligated to MacEwan because of the Captain's earlier decision not to kill it when he had had the gun and the Orlig was lying helpless on the deck. The Orlig had got the memory of that little item from MacEwan when he had been delirious, apparently. He wanted to stay with the Earthman until . . .

The mentacom had been disconnected at that point.

Officers of ever increasing seniority arrived and talked with Grulyaw-Ki. Some hurried away again and the others stayed and looked down at MacEwan from positions behind the electronic gadget – still apparently arguing with the Orlig pilot, who seemed to be refusing to move more than a few feet from MacEwan's side.

There was something going on here, MacEwan knew suddenly, something which was not consistent with the things he had expected from reading the Orlig's mind. For instance why, after pleading with him to stay alive until the arrival of Orligian higher-ups had the pilot allowed the mentacom to be disconnected immediately after the arrival of the medical officers? Why weren't they asking him questions over the mentacom instead of whining and growling urgently at the Orlig pilot from behind the now apparently complete mechanism a dozen feet away? What *was* the blasted thing, anyway . . . ?

Tenuous as mist, with neither strength, directional properties or even clarity, an Orlig thought sequence seeped through his mind. The mentacom beside him was disconnected, but somewhere – at extreme range and probably on the rescue ship – there was another which was operating, and there was an Orligian near it who was thinking about him. There was an undercurrent of excitement in the thought, and hope, and the overall and everpresent problems of strategy and supply – the thought of a very important and responsible Orlig, obviously. MacEwan was a very brave entity, the thought went on, but even so it was better that the Earth-being should not be told what was to happen to him . . .

Rage exploded so violently in MacEwan that he forgot his wounds, and his anger was matched only by his utter self-loathing. He had been a blind, stupid fool! He had talked too much, betrayed his friends, his race and his world. He had told *everything* to the Orlig pilot, and with knowledge of the spatial co-ordinates of Earth a planet-wrecker or a few bacteriological bombs would soon end the war. Of course the Orlig had given him equally vital information, but with the difference that MacEwan was hardly in a position to pass it on. Now apparently, they were too impatient even to wait for MacEwan to die, because the mechanism which had been set up and which was now focused on his huddled, near-corpse was nothing less than The Weapon.

The sheer force of his emotions sent him crawling towards Grulyaw-Ki. Mounting waves of pain pounded and roared over the small, feeble core of purpose in his brain and he dared not look down at his injuries. But the Orlig pilot was looking, and his companions behind The Weapon, and a ragged, tortured whine of sympathy and horror was dragged from their throats at the sight. They had feelings; he had met one of them mind to mind and he knew. It didn't fit, what they were going to do to him – Grulyaw-Ki's mind had not even considered his being killed out of hand. Maybe that was why the pilot was electing to go with him, because he disapproved of the treachery of his brothers.

Out of the corner of his eye he saw certain coils within the complex mass of The Weapon glow brightly, and he hunched himself desperately forward. *We're not all bad,* his mind screamed, in a vain attempt to reach them without benefit of a mentacom. *Maybe you've tricked me, but there can be peace . . . peace . . .* He tried to reach out and grasp the Orlig pilot's hand, to show them that he meant what he was thinking, but his stupid, senseless lump of an arm refused to move any more for him, and off to one side The

Weapon was about ready to project its radiation, or force pattern, or field of stress . . .

. . . After two hundred and thirty-six years the Orligians were getting another War Memorial, were being forced to get another War Memorial. And the Orligians were a very emotional race.

It was after dawn when the noisy festivities died down and the crowd – silent now and strengely solemn – began to gather round the protective plastic of the old Memorial, the most gruesomely effective War Memorial ever known. They had remained far away from it during the night's celebrations, it would not have been proper to indulge in merrymaking in this place, but now they were gathering from all over the city. They came and stood silent and grave and still moving only to let through the ground vehicles of off-planet dignitaries or the numerous other technicians and specialists who had business at the Memorial. Some of them cried a little.

At midday the Elected Father of Orligia rose to address them. He spoke of both the joy and solemnity of this occasion, and pointed with pride at the ages-frozen figure of the mighty Grulyaw-Ki, the Orligian who, despite the urgings of his friends and the orders of his superiors, had determined to discharge his obligation towards this great Earth-being MacEwan.

The time stasis field projector, once an Orligian weapon of war but now in use in hospitals on every planet of the Union, had made this possible. With great difficulty the Stopped bodies of MacEwan and Grulyaw-Ki had been sealed up and moved to Orligia, there to wait while the first shaky peace between Earth and Orligia ripened into friendship and medical science progressed to the point where it was sure of saving the terribly injured Earthman. Grulyaw-Ki had insisted on being Stopped with his friend so that he could see MacEwan cured for himself. And now the two greatest heroes of the war – heroes because they had ended it – were about to be brought out of Stasis. To them no time at all would have passed between that instant more than two hundred years ago and now, and perhaps now for the first time the truly great of history would receive the reward they deserved from posterity. The technicians were ready, the medical men were standing by, the moment was *now* . . . !

The crowd in the immediate vicinity saw the figures come alive again, saw MacEwan twitching feebly and Grulyaw-Ki bending over him, saw the bustle as they were transferred into the waiting ambulance and – temporarily Stopped again until the hospital would be reached by a small and more refined projector – hurried away. The throng went wild then, so that the noise of the previous night would have been restful by comparison. Some of them stayed out of deference to the sculptor for the unveiling of the new memorial, a towering, beautiful thing of white stone that caught at the throat, but only a few thousand. And of these there were quite a few who, when the ceremony was over, went to look through the little peep holes set at intervals around its base.

Through them could be seen a tiny, three-dimensional picture in full detail and colour of the original war memorial, placed there to remind viewers that there was nothing great or noble or beautiful about war.

2 – ARTHUR SELLINGS: Starting Course

In Volume one I referred to the *Observer*'s short story contest *AD 2500*, that brought us Aldiss's *Not For An Age*. That competition led to the publication of a book of the twenty-one best entries, chosen by Angus Wilson. Besides the Aldiss offering, and a tale by Robert Wells (an author finally making his mark), it also included *The Mission* by Arthur Sellings.

Sellings was the pen-name of Robert Arthur Ley, born in Tunbridge Wells, Kent in 1921. He moved early to London where he had a vivid recollection of seeing both *Metropolis* and *The Girl in the Moon* – two classic early and influential German sf films – and soon after he discovered H. G. Wells and the US sf magazines.

He did not turn his hand to writing, however, until 1953, with the sale of *The Haunting* to *Authentic*. Thereafter, he sold regularly, predominantly to the United States, in particular to *Galaxy Magazine*. His appearances in the British magazines were few and far between but they were no less entertaining as *Starting Course* from the January 1961 *New Worlds* shows only too well. Two collections of Sellings' short stories exist as well as several novels including the powerful *Telepath* (1962) and the fascinating *The Power of Y* (1965).

Science fiction was dealt a tragic blow when Sellings died on September 24th, 1968, aged only 47. Several stories appeared posthumously, the last, prophetically entitled *The Last Time Round*, being published in the November 1970 *If*. I leave you with these words from his widow, Gladys Ley:

> 'As a friend said to me, never to converse with Arthur, share his enthusiasms and his love of life again; we have lost so much.'

STARTING COURSE

Arthur Sellings

'Good afternoon, sir. Mr Trendall? I'm from Android Bank.'

Trendall looked past the visitor, looking for – what? – a gyrotruck, a crate? Then he realised. *This* was it – him. He looked down at the neat bag in the young man's hand, then up past trim slacks and jerkin of dark grey to the fresh, strangely *new*, face.

'Uh – well, come in.'

He was conscious that his voice sounded hollow. Hell, it wasn't his fault. Just how did you welcome an android into your family?

He showed the young man into the lounge and called his wife in from the kitchen where she'd hidden herself. She entered nervously.

'Oh, May, this is our guest, Mr –'

Trendall felt suddenly even more awkward, and cursed both that and the fact that he'd been pressured into this. He was a solid twenty-second century citizen, integrated in his job and in his social sector, and unused to feeling awkward. The schmooze about that being the very reason he'd been selected! He hadn't swallowed that – no *sir*. But how about the thinly-veiled threats of penalties, down-grading of status? He had the kids to think of, hadn't he? But he was beginning now to regret desperately that he hadn't made a stand.

The young man spoke – in the same careful, rather flat, tone in which he had announced himself. 'Just call me Eddie. I do have a surname – A hyphen Smith. A for android, of course. But that's only for the records. A surname is rather superfluous in my case, don't you think?'

Trendall felt oddly grateful. That seemed to put the matter in perspective somehow. His wife said, 'Oh dear, yes, why of course –' He shot her a meaningful look.

'Well then – uh – Eddie. Take a seat.' He noticed now the curious correctness with which the visitor moved. They all sat down. There was an awkward silence.

'Perhaps you'd like to freshen up,' May blurted.

Was that the right thing? Trendall wondered. Did they? Have need to, that was?

'No, thank you, ma'am. I've come straight from the Bank.'

Heck, thought Trendall, he says it as if he had just stepped out of the vat! That was how they bred them, the man from the Bank had said. Up from single artificial cells, emerging as a human being – or a damn good copy. Forget that, the official had said – treat him just as an ordinary, if immature, human. They had given him a basic education. Now he had to live with a family for six months. A finishing course, the official had said with a slight smile.

May tried again. 'Would you like some tea?'

'Yes, thank you, ma'am,' said the young man, to Trendall's surprise. May heaved a visible sigh of relief and went out to the kitchen. Trendall felt less constrained now. He could talk to the other, man . . . as it were . . . to man.

'How many of you are there?'

'Of me? Oh androids, you mean? About fifty, I think. I was in a class of twenty-five. There was one other class. I think we're the only bank so far in the world.'

'What I can't understand,' Trendall confessed, 'is why –'

He faltered, realising that that was one question he couldn't ask – why there was need for androids, anyway. As well ask an ordinary man why he thought he had a right to live!

'Why the Bank sent me here?' the young man suggested.

'Why, *yes*, that's just it.' That was the second time the android – Eddie, he'd have to get used to calling him that – had helped him out. Perhaps it wouldn't be so difficult after all.

'Because my life has been all theory so far. The syllabus at our school would probably strike you as odd. We get the three Rs, naturally. But basic reflexes, that's one early course. Then advanced reflexes, speech modulation, social orientation, they're a few of the others. You see, we're fully intelligent when we – come out. An ordinary human as an infant learns as it develops, by experience, trial and error. We're *taught* everything, in capsule courses. With us there's no time for experience.'

This was a chance, a clue. 'Time? Why, what's the hurry?'

But the chance disappeared, or was it side-stepped? 'No hurry. It's just because of the way we're made. The point is, after the basic courses, we have to gain real human experience. We have to learn how to adjust to people, to learn the right thing to do or say.' His voice became suddenly earnest. 'So, please, if I say or do the wrong thing, please don't blame me too much. I'll try to learn.'

Trendall felt touched and embarrassed simultaneously.

'Why, sure, son . . . I – you —' Heck, ordinary human kids weren't as eager to please as this. *They* were on their own feet by eight, going their own way – too much their own way, he thought sometimes. And how old was this one – about eighteen, nineteen?

May came in with the tea and handed it round.

'By the way, son,' Trendall asked, 'how old are you?'

'Five,' the other said simply.

Trendall spluttered into his teacup. That was another one I shouldn't have asked, he thought ruefully. Eddie seemed quite unconcerned as he sipped his tea. But what could you say to follow that one? *Really?* Or *You're a big lad for your age?*

He didn't have to worry, because Kathy, sixteen and breathless, came bouncing in just then. She pulled up short when she saw their visitor. Eddie rose.

'This is Eddie, our guest I told you about,' Trendall said.

Kathy, in shimmering kneelength pants and cape, just stood there – and burst out laughing.

Eddie looked desperately from Trendall to his wife. He

saw no help there, only a scandalised look focused on their daughter.

But Kathy only went on laughing.

'I – I think I'll go and unpack,' Eddie said quietly.

'I'll show you your room,' said May. They went upstairs hurriedly.

'You'll have to excuse Kathy,' May said as she showed him into the little spare room. 'I don't know what's wrong with kids these days,' she added as she left him.

Eddie unpacked his change of clothes, his books, then sat down on the bed. Would he get to understand people? They were polite, as anxious obviously to accommodate themselves to him as he to them. Then this curious girl behaved the way she did. Ah well, he had a job to do. He mustn't let such things deflect him. He opened his books and got down to study.

A short while later there came a knock on his door.

'Come in,'

The door opened, just wide enough to admit a slim form. It was Kathy.

He smiled – yes, that was the required thing.

'I came to apologise.'

'That's all right.'

'Is that all? Is that what you're told to say?'

'I'm not told to say anything. I'm just told to try and fit in. Why, what should I say?'

'You're funny. You should be annoyed and ask me why I laughed.'

'Should I? Then, why *did* you laugh?'

'It was Dad calling you Eddie.'

'But that's my name.' He got the point. 'Why, do you think a number would be better?'

Quite suddenly and shockingly she burst into tears. He didn't have a clue what to do. He had never met tears before. All he could do was wait for her to stop.

She did, as suddenly as she had begun.

'Trust me! I never start off right with anybody. I was determined to with you. I made it a test, because – because you're different. There I go again!' She gesticulated with both hands above her smooth black hair as if tearing it up by the roots.

'It's all right,' Eddie said. 'I *am* different.'

'But don't you see?' she burst out. 'You can say that. But it doesn't make *me* right. And we're all of us different. It's everybody trying to make out that we're not that gripes me.' She shrugged her shoulders. 'But no amount of talking now can put it right. I'll try and make a fresh start – but not now. I'll have to wait.'

And, turning, she fled, banging the door after her, leaving Eddie standing there, utterly confused. After a long moment he went back to his books. Mathematical symbols he could understand; if he couldn't, they would yield to his searching. But human beings!

Despite his misgivings, Eddie gradually settled in. An absolute lack of communication reigned between him and Kathy, but since they only met at meal times that was no great problem. He thought it best to make no effort himself. In spite of her outburst in his room that first day, Kathy seemed well integrated and popular with a wide circle of friends. She was out every evening, to parties or tennis or to the Free Fall Drome – while he studied or watched TV with the family. Once Mrs Trendall suggested she take Eddie to the Drome with her party. He was pleased because it was one of several little indications that he was getting to be accepted. All the same he was relieved when Kathy ducked out by saying it was club night.

Mr and Mrs Trendall seemed much less complex characters than their daughter. TV, drinks, a few friends in, seemed the round of their life. Eddie was introduced to the friends, who seemed as easy-going – and faintly bored – as the Trendalls. He learned to differentiate between them, to laugh at their standard jokes, to serve them the drinks they preferred. None of them showed any curiosity about him or mentioned his background – and Eddie had an idea that his host had never told them. By now he had recognised Mr Trendall as a man who took the easy way.

With the other member of the Trendall family he got off on the right foot immediately. That was Steve, who had been away at the jetball finals in Paris the day he'd arrived. Steve was twelve and his hobby was making midget two-way TV sets. As Eddie was not only studying electronics but also possessed a keen eye and a deft hand, it was a natural.

Steve never asked him questions – not personal ones, anyway. But he asked him plenty on math and lattice equations and micro-junctions – and listened – and *talked.* That was the main thing. Eddie learned when to accept a statement straight, when to read the opposite, when to know it was in code for something entirely unrelated. Most important of all, he began himself to ask questions.

'What are you going to do, Steve, when you leave school?' he asked one day. He was over half-way through his stay with the Trendalls by then.

'Oh, join the ranks of the button pushers,' Steve said casually.

'Is that what you want to do?'

'That's all anybody *can* do, isn't it? Boy, it makes me cackle. We work our brains to the bone, getting our heads stuffed with a lot of facts – just so we can read what's on the right button!'

'But won't you go into electronics?'

Steve shrugged. 'Probably – but in industry it's all done by robot mechanisms – self-repairing ones. I'll be responsible – if I get that far – for one tiny bit that won't make much sense at all on its own. I *know*, brother.' He suddenly grinned. 'Hey, why'd you get me started on this? I'll settle for what I can. Didn't you learn history? People have been working for ages to get what we've got now. I'm not complaining.'

He sounded very mature for a twelve-year old, but his next words were more in keeping. 'Gosh, I'm just waiting for my first pay cheque. I'm gonna go straight out and get me a stereo tube. What are you going to do, Eddie?'

'When I get my first pay cheque?'

'No, crazy. When you finish studies.'

'I'm listed for colonisation.'

'Wha-at?' Steve waved a hand. 'You mean out there?'

'One or another of the outposts.'

'Rather you than me. I've been up to the moon. Great – for once. Real free fall and, boy, the stars! Fine for astronomers, I guess, but catch me living out there! Strictly twentieth century.'

'But there's some interesting stuff out there. Creatures, landscapes.'

'I can see it all on TV. Anyway, I wouldn't want to spend the best years of my life on some weird mudball back of nowhere. As I see it, there's the grind of school, then before you know where you are you get hooked by some dame and settle down in a dinky little box like this. You've only got a few years really to live.'

That seemed to settle that. But Steve suddenly looked at Eddie in a way he never had before. 'Is that why you people were made – to go out there?'

'I guess so. That's what we're being used for, anyway.'

'*Used* for!' Steve exploded. 'You take it lying down, just like that? But you've got rights, man. You're a human being.'

'Thank you, Steve,' Eddie murmured. Then, in a more normal tone, 'But I want to go. You see, people made me. Anything I can do is only a small repayment of that debt.'

Steve looked horrified. 'Nobody owes anybody anything. Hey, I bet they planted that feeling in you when they made you.'

'I don't think so. It seems natural to me. If your father was in danger, wouldn't you go to help him?'

'I guess so.' Steve grimaced. 'But heck, he's too careful. He'd never get in danger. But that's beside the point. I think you chaps ought to make a fight against being forced. Lead a revolt, that's it! Want any help?'

'No thanks,' Eddie laughed.

When he left Steve's den he went to his own room and got out his books. But he was in no mood to study. His chat with Steve had unsettled him. He went over to the window and looked out.

They *were* like boxes, the thousands of little houses stretching to the horizon, punctuated by skyscraper blocks pointing up to the sky. A few gyros flitted about in the twilight like dragon-flies. Everywhere, even in the graceful gyros, men made little boxes for themselves. And yet, out there, becoming visible now as the sky darkened, lay the stars.

He thought of what Steve had said – you could see it all on TV. And it seemed wrong, terribly wrong for a twelve-year old. Yet Steve was ready to help him revolt!

Eddie smiled sadly. Steve, and probably all the other young people like him, had plenty of spirit, but it seemed as if it was all . . . kind of turned in.

The midget TV bleeped then. He switched it on without turning from the window, and said, 'Hi, Steve.'

'It's not Steve, silly, It's me.'

He turned. It was Kathy, her big eyes appealing in the tiny colour screen.

'Can I come and see you?'

'Sure.'

The screen faded. A moment later she came dashing into his room.

'I just heard from Steve. I –'

Eddie smiled. 'Come and sit down. Or you'll fall over your feet again.'

'Thanks. I don't think I will this time. But is that right what Steve told me, that you're going into space?'

'Yes. Why, do you want to join Steve's revolt?'

She tossed her head and said, *'Steve,'* with all the contempt of a sixteen year old for a twelve. 'Man, is he wet behind the ears!' Her big eyes became grave. 'Eddie, can I come out there with you?'

He gaped at her.

'Why not? If it's good enough for you –' She winced. 'There I go again. But can I, Eddie, can I?'

'I don't know. But are you serious?'

'Never been more in my life. When Steve told me it all came flooding in on me. It's all wrong that it should be put on – people like you. Ordinary people should go.'

'I don't think enough ordinary people want to go. But, Kathy –' he reached out and took her hand – 'that's not the real reason, is it?'

She looked down at his hand.

'That's just for friendship,' he murmured.

She smiled. 'I know. You are nice, at that. No the reason I said, that's part of it. But the main thing is, I want like hell to get away.'

'Steve says it's the best year's of anyone's life.'

'Then why waste it here, mouldering? On this world you can't get away from people enough. I don't like people that much.'

'But, Kathy, are you sure – but this is difficult – I don't want us to get snarled up again. We seem to be understanding each other –'

'Please say it.'

'Well, are you sure this isn't just a phase? I mean, being young, having trouble adjusting?'

'Sure. I spend all my time adjusting. But is it worth it, adjusting to a lot of creeps?'

'I couldn't give an opinion on that. Nobody can be – what you call them – to me. Anyway, is that enough reason to want to go off to somewhere entirely new and strange, leaving everything behind?'

'It's the same for you, isn't it?'

'No. I don't have a home, for one thing, not a permanent one. Nor parents. In any case, Kathy, I'm sure you're too young to be allowed to go on your own.'

'Well, I'm going, you see. Watch out, you'll be coming round the mountain on Sirius Four and you'll bump right into little old me.'

Eddie got up next morning, feeling ten feet high. He was doing what he had been sent here to do – making contact with people, learning how they felt. And they knew now what his purpose was.

The feeling didn't last long. Steve was moody. As for Kathy, the barriers were obviously down between them, but now he seemed to be included with her in some conspiracy. She winked at him over the breakfast table and giggled and generally behaved in a fashion that seemed decidedly odd.

And seemed so not only to Eddie. He caught her parents looking at her and then at each other with perplexity. As for Steve, his sister's antics – or was it only that? – made him leave his breakfast and slam out of the house long before he had to catch the gyrobus for school.

The atmosphere lasted several days before things came to a head. Eddie was in his room, studying, when a knock came at the door.

'Come in,' he called, expecting Kathy. She had been a frequent visitor these evenings. She hadn't mentioned another word about space. She had just chattered and clowned – and he had found her highly amusing.

But it was Mr Trendall, looking untypically perturbed. He wasted no time coming to the point.

'Look here. What's going on between you and Kathy?'

'I – I don't understand, sir.'

'Don't you? Then what's all this nonsense about her wanting to go off with you into space?'

'That was her idea, not mine. I told her it couldn't be done.'

'No? Well, she's made an application. I can veto that. But what kind of hold have you got on the girl?'

'Hold? I still don't understand. I haven't influenced Kathy.'

'Maybe you don't think so, but it's pretty plain you have. Come on now, what have you and Kathy been up to?'

'Nothing. It wasn't forbidden for Kathy to come and talk to me, was it?'

'Only talk? You think I'd believe that? Kathy's an independent girl. I never question her choice of friends, but' – Trendall shook – 'I'm not having her messing around with a damn android.'

Eddie got to his feet slowly, but said nothing. He just stood there, looking at Trendall. Finally he said, 'I'd better leave.'

Trendall made no answer, nor did he meet Eddie's gaze. He had plainly said more than he had intended.

'But before I do,' Eddie said, 'let me tell you two things. First, I'm not leaving because I'm offended. I'm not, nor could I be allowed to leave on those grounds. I know I'm different, so you can call me what you like. And that's the second point, there couldn't be anything between Kathy and me.' He knew what Trendall meant – not because he'd had a course . . . that would have been superfluous – but because he'd learned a lot in the past few months, even if a lot of it had been secondhand, from TV.

'Why not?' Trendall said gruffly. 'Because you've got orders to behave yourself? I don't take much notice of that. And don't tell me you're too young – you said yourself your kind come out fully developed.'

'That's the point – not in that respect. Nor will I ever be. That's the only real difference between us and real humans – we don't breed.'

Trendall's eyes jerked up to meet Eddie's for a shocked moment. He looked away again, muttering something inaudible, then groped for the door. Eddie heard his footsteps descend the stairs.

He turned and began methodically to pack. There was nothing else to do, no stopping now to wonder just how he had failed. He didn't have instructions as to what to do in this case – it obviously hadn't been expected of him – but there was only one thing for it. Report back to the Bank.

But he had accumulated things since he had come here – more books, the little TV which Steve had given him, the jerkin Mrs Trendall had spun for him, things too personal to leave behind, even if he were leaving under a cloud. They added up to more than he could pack in the single small bag he had brought. He would have to go down and ask if he could borrow another one.

He heard footsteps on the stair again. Mrs Trendall came in.

'You can unpack,' she said firmly. 'Tom told me. I'm dreadfully sorry. So's Tom, more than he can say. It makes his accusations about you and Kathy seem pretty horrible.'

'All the same, Mrs Trendall, perhaps I ought to leave. I've caused you all too much upset.'

'You'll do no such thing. Perhaps we were due to be upset. Perhaps it will do us good. Perhaps it would do everybody a bit of good. We all go on our little way, thinking all's right with the world. Nobody asks any sacrifices of us. We think it's all handed to us on a plate.

'Then somebody like you turns up. You've been brought into this world just to do a job that nobody else wants to do – none of us ordinary people who've got everything to live for and be thankful for. And when one of our own kids realises that fact before we do and wants to take her share, all we can do is turn it into something nasty.'

This forceful speech was quite unlike the mild self-effacing manner that Eddie had come to regard as normal in Mrs Trendall. He certainly had started something!

'No, Eddie – you've opened *my* eyes. And Kathy's going into space, I can promise you that, and if she's too young to go on her own, then I'm going with her?'

May spoke truer than she knew, and certainly more than Eddie could have ever guessed.

A few days later it was Steve who was deputed to tell Eddie the news.

'We're *all* coming with you, Eddie! Dad just got the papers from the Colonisation Board. Procyon Three, leaving on the twenty fifth.'

'*Wha-at!* That's great! But – I can't believe it. Kathy – yes. And your mother. But your dad – I can't see him wanting to go.'

Steve grinned. 'Kathy and Mom are a combo even I couldn't resist. And Dad's not such a stick-in-the-mud after all, it seems. He's the keenest of any of us now.'

'But you, Steve, how about you? The best years of your life – remember?'

Steve grinned even wider. 'I've grown up since then. And I've been reading up on Procyon Three. It's got a very near satellite. We could have fun bouncing stuff off that!'

'You bet!' said Eddie.

After that, it was all rush, getting ready for the big day. Clearing up, choosing what to take and what to leave behind. A hundred things – forms to be filled in, shots to get. Eddie was told that shots weren't necessary for him. That should have made him suspect something, but he just accepted it as being due to his different physical make-up.

As it was, when the big day dawned and they took a gyrocab for the spaceport, he was unprepared.

They were about to leave the control building for the great ship, waiting in the middle of the ferroconcrete field, when an official in the grey of Android Bank stepped out of nowhere and took Eddie by the arm.

'Can I see you for a moment?'

'Of course.' Eddie gestured to the Trendalls. 'Go on. I'll see you on board.'

'Sit down, Eddie,' said the official. 'I've got a shock for you. You're not going.'

Eddie stared at him. 'Wha – what do you mean? How about those people?'

'This is only the first time,' the official said gently. 'We had to play it like this. It won't be so hard the next time and the time after that. You see, it's not you we want in space.'

He nodded in the direction of the four Trendalls, their figures tiny now against the huge bulk of the starship. 'It's them, and other people like them.'

'You mean – it was a kind of trick?'

'If you like – but one played in the best of interests. We've reached a danger point. It was bad enough when man had pushed out to the frontiers and there was nowhere left to push out to – on the eve of the Space Age. They had the opposite kind of problem then. But by the time the frontiers were open again – wide open – men had got too comfortable. And that was infinitely worse. Because it seemed there was nothing that could be done about it. If there's a pressure it will eventually break out. But how to create a pressure when none exists?

'They tried selling the idea of colonisation. That wasn't successful enough. Money, status, meant nothing to people because they didn't see the colony worlds as places where they could enjoy either. Oh, we could always get the wrong types, the ones who couldn't make a go of things here and couldn't on any other world. No, it was ordinary people like the Trendalls that were needed out there.

'Now, we had the know-how to make your kind – but to what end? Then somebody had the idea. *This* idea. You see, Eddie your job wasn't really to adjust to people – it was to *dis*adjust *them*. Not so much your finishing course as their starting course.'

Eddie got up and looked out of the plexiglass windows. The Trendalls had been swallowed up in the ship. Now the massive port was closing on them.

'But what will they think? Of me? My kind? Couldn't I even have said goodbye to them?'

The official laid a hand on his shoulder. 'Believe me, this is the best way. There's a note on board for them from the Bank, making excuses. They've only signed on for a three-year term to begin with, anyway. And they won't have any regrets, I know that.'

Bells rang stridently, once, twice. It was the departure signal. The ship began to glow greenly as the drive generators started up.

Eddie's throat felt suddenly tight. 'But why couldn't I have gone with them?'

The official smiled. The ship was lifting now.

'Because you're too valuable, son. Look at that ship. You cost considerably more than that did. And you're considerably more important. You've notched the first score in the campaign – one out of one, a hundred per cent so far. If we can keep up that record we'll soon have enough people out there to make the colonies self-sufficient. By that time your job will be done. You'll be free to join your friends out there if you want. And the ones that come after.'

The great ship was suspended fifty feet up now, supported in a green glowing web. Then, so fast that the eye could not catch it, it was gone, leaving only a red after-image that soon died.

Eddie stood there, feeling that a piece of him had died too, gone with the Trendalls out beyond the daylight of this world, out into the black distances. Would it always be like this, a piece of him dying every time?

The official had said that next time it would be better. But *would* it, now that he knew his purpose? Wouldn't it be all the harder? And he realised now just how much more he had to learn – that for him, as for the Trendalls, the starting course had only just begun.

3 – KENNETH BULMER: Advertise Your Cyanide

One of the mainstays of the British magazines throughout the 1950s was Kenneth Bulmer. As a rule Bulmer concentrated on the longer stories, in fact he does not consider himself a short story writer. He prefers the length of a novel which allows him space to develop his characters and his often bizarre themes.

Henry Kenneth Bulmer was born in London on January 14th, 1921, and was an avid sf fan from his early days producing seven issues of his own fanzine *Star Parade* during 1941. Then Bulmer became entangled in the war, in the Royal Corps of Signals, but afterwards returned to the sf fold. After an apprenticeship on the Panther series of sf novels for Hamilton's, Bulmer sold a short story, *First Down*, to *Authentic* and it appeared in the April 1954 issue. Thereafter he appeared regularly in the magazines, under his own name and a few aliases like Nelson Sherwood and H Philip Stratford. Also he collaborated on scientific articles with research chemist John Newman under the name Kenneth Johns.

In 1970 Bulmer edited a fantasy companion magazine to *Vision of Tomorrow*, called *Sword and Sorcery*, but after two issues were set in type the magazine was aborted because of the crippling distribution problems which also killed *Vision*. Most of the unused material was snapped up by other magazines and the experience stood Bulmer in good stead. Today he successfully edits the original anthology series *New Writings in SF*, which he took over after John Carnell's death in 1972.

Readers of *New Writings 24* will have noticed Ken Bulmer drew attention to a story *Advertise Your Cyanide* in his introduction. That story first appeared in the April 1958 *Nebula*, a magazine edited and published single-handedly by Glasgow fan Peter Hamilton. The drive and tenacity of Hamilton produced a highly memorable and exciting (if amateurish looking) magazine that often contained superior fiction to *New Worlds* and the other publications. Hamilton produced the magazine frequently if sometimes erratically, from 1952 to 1959 when, after 41 issues, everything finally became too much. Thereupon Hamilton disappeared from the scene, and I sincerely hope that if he is reading this he will contact me. *Nebula* is a suitable monument to the memory of what one man can do for science fiction and it is fitting that its shade should be invoked by *Advertise Your Cyanide*, undoubtedly one of the finest stories it ever published.

Ken Bulmer had the following to relate about the tale:

'The origins of this story may be traced back to Manhattan and a New York newspaper. It is one of the results of the USA's sledgehammer effect on my sensibilities. In addition the disquieting facts being turned up during the course of my work as 'Kenneth Johns' gave the background story to the foreground action racketing away. The newspaper claimed that as so many million more mouths would have to be fed, and bodies clothed and housed and provided with wheels, in the near future, mammoth building programmes were under way for the wholesale production of every conceivable product. The disquieting facts were showing that there was a limit to certain commodities.

'All this now screeches at us from every form of media, and in fact has almost been oversold. Back twenty years it was not fashionable.

'The form of the story is presented in a way that is now remarkably familiar to the many New Wave stories of a few years ago. This presentation was a conscious attempt, given that form and content are indivisible, to make the form work hard and punch home the content. The story was written in 1955 and took some time to sell. I concur with the preceding remarks about *Nebula*. One reader wrote to Peter Hamilton saying I was either a madman or a genius. Peter was considerate in his reply. Now, in these latter days, the form as well as the content has perhaps been oversold.

'One final thing: *Advertise Your Cyanide* – there may be a sequel one day called *Hoard Your Psionide* – remains firmly in the sf canon. It deals with specific problems that are within the province of sf. I also write funny stories, too. You may find many rewarding stories covering the whole gamut of sf within the pages of *New Writings in SF*. I like to think, had I been editing *NWinSF* then, I'd have had Peter Hamilton's courage and accepted *Advertise Your Cyanide*.

ADVERTISE YOUR CYANIDE

Kenneth Bulmer

Time: 2100.

The porage flooded into his forearm vein with its usual high-kick bloating impact. That was better! Now he could hit the sky! The needle dangled from his fingers.

Consider this man.

Index: T/A/77894S.

Name: Spencer Lord.

Age: 32. Height: 179 cms. Hair: Black. Eyes: Brown. Ex-Captain Terran Space Force. Athletic. First class shot. Twice wounded. Decorations: Gold Star, Space Cross. Security Risk Rating AAA. Terran Secret Service Operative.

The paper was yellow, thin, official. You ate it when you'd read it.

From: *Security Bureau.*

To: *Op.K.2.*

Subject: *Sahndran Ambassador. Coverage and Protection Advert. Convention.*

You will protect the life of His Excellency Josiah Gosheron at all times during the convention. His Excellency must not rpt not be aware of this protection. You will rpt will consider yourself expendable.

Bolz.

Lord put the needle back into its nest and thrust the plastic case on to the dressing table. The lightning pulsing through his body ironed out the shivers. He ate the yellow message form.

STAB WITH ME,
JAB WITH ME,
COME ON, BABY, *GRAB* WITH ME!

Lord blinked, pulled on his weapons belt, adjusted his anti-grav and flung his huge synthiermine cape over one arm. His stiff, jewelled guantlets snapped magnetically to the over-cape's garish hem, ready for use. Expendable, huh? So he was supposed to worry?

He opened the window.

Predatory jungle of light and noise and smell. Neons and lumivapour writhing intestinal convulsions across a slate dinosaur-back horizon. Inside out. Screeching beast-hum of the city; pulsing colour and movement; insistent scraping at nerves deadened and excrutiatingly excited by drugs in pain-pleasure cycles.

The world of logical licence. Culture-arid. Scrabbling up a side-avenue of time, self-cnsciously aware of know-how, worshipping it, refusing to face life and hurrying helter-skelter into experience

SCOOT WITH ME ON MY ATOMIC-SLED,
ROOT AND *TOOT* AND *SLIDE* TO BED!

Consider the past years.

The middle period of the twentieth century put the waste of the planet's resources on an organised footing. By that time America had used up in the preceding half-century more raw materials than had all of recorded history. One family – two cars. A spoonful of coffee – use a tree trunk to wrap it. A pack of cigarettes – use two tree trunks. Smooch in the Drive-In – burn a few gallons of gas, they're cheap. Mine the iron, mine the rare metals, process them, turn them into guns and planes and tanks. Let them rust into red wasteful ruin. Cut those trees, men; dig that ore. We won't freeze, men; there's plenty more.

Only there wasn't.

Lord stepped smartly off the windowsill, dropped a sheer hundred stories, then activated his anti-grav belt and swept up and away, relishing that first delirious plunge. He headed over the scarlet-lipped neon of a nude a block wide. She puffed smoke in sulphurous clouds, perfect ring after perfect ring. Her wooden framework was half charred away.

CLEAR THAT BLOCK AND BE A CLEAR,
BLOCK THAT CLEAR AND BE A DEAR.

Cut through the ring of smoke like a shot from a gun in Security HQ target range, spurn that dust, hit the clouds. His Excellency Josiah Gosheron. He savoured the name sourly. The damned old Terran hater. Another all night assignment and Katy on the loose. This convention promised to be dull, too – until you thought about it.

He was speeding above the city now, the wind slapping at his stator field and rushing past his ears. Other citizens sliced across on the downtown levels. Their lights were like frenetic dances of doom, writhing before some obscene idol in a torch-lit temple. Which reminded him of Katy.

She might make it to the convention, she'd said. She might be tippling with some half-crazy spacemen. She might be parading that body of hers on tridi. She might be doing anything. Lord bet a million credits she wasn't thinking of him. The knowledge was an ice-barb in his guts.

Time: 2114.

He slanted in towards the hotel rooftop, where uniformed lackeys stood with magnetoclamps, waiting for outer clothing and hand luggage from guests.

All across the horizon in an unvarying arc marched the squat gloomy bulks of the accumulator stations, waiting insatiably for the energy to quench their bottomless thirst. Now they were giving of their stored wealth, providing the sustenance for a night's squandering. Lord angled his downward plunge to miss the stacked solar mirrors on the hotel's roof and hoped that tomorrow would be fine: the city's power supply was down to danger level and if storm clouds banked heavily tomorrow it might cost more in weather control than would be got out of the sun when it reluctantly appeared.

His feet hit the wooden roof with a jolt. Damn porage wasn't spreading evenly yet: his reflexes were still slightly out of skew. If Katy was here he'd find her. Gosheron permitting. Lord began to walk across the roof towards the attendants.

Get the old Terran hater drunk; that was the idea. Souse him, douse him, light and louse him. Lord smiled and flung his cape at the attendants. His fingers twitched. He needed a drink.

HIT THAT SYNAPSE WITH A WHIZ,
DRAG THAT JAG WITH A NUCLEAR FIZZ!

'Your invitation card, sir?'

The attendant had a flame-rifle steadied across his fore-arm, aimed uncompromisingly at Lord's navel. The man's trigger finger was white around the knuckle, scar tissue gleamed in reflected light.

'Here, uncle.' Lord tossed a plastic card at the man, twitched his fingers and walked away towards the throng. Free-loading was becoming a tough proposition. But for all that the free-loaders would be here, eating and drinking and doping and experiencing. They were the people he'd have to watch. The regular police could handle most; but the odd man out, the hopped up fanatic, the one with the flash-grenade in his mouth talking quietly to the ambassador. . . .

Whooosh! Bang! Back to the stars, alien.

Back to the stars, where Q's were unimportant. Q's? A trifling item. Merely the amount of energy needed to raise one pound of water one degree fahrenheit – multiplied by one million million million. And how we'd used up our Q's! Two cars a family – but one simply must, my dear. Square-miles of incinerating dumps outside every city. A million years of carboniferous growth consumed in a minute – and no-one to feel the warmth in the room at the time. Empty cans tossed aside to rot.

Spencer Lord stopped at the tall plasti-glass doors to arrange his jacket more comfortably over his weapons belt.

Two brightly painted women, chattering like parakeets, passed him. He caught the magnificent glitter of the elder's ring, set with a solid piece of genuine coal, surrounded by diamonds. If he worked all his life, his soured mind nagged him, he still couldn't have bought a ring like that with his amassed salary. Katy'd just have to make goo-goo eyes and do without. Or seduce some fat old algae-mogul, more likely.

Dig deep for that coal. Rake down for that ore. A mile down. Two. Send robots. Honeycomb the Earth. Let the steel rust, plenty more. *Consumption is the god. Advertising is his prophet.*

And productivity is the money.

Only the prophet oversold his god and went bankrupt.

Smoke, smoke, smoke that cigarette. Burn, burn, burn up that old earth. Consume, friends, consume. Sit in your neat little, tight little, snug little house and waste a thousand man-hours every time you open a door. Transmute those elements. Two atoms for one. Big, buster, big! Something for nothing – only the something turned out to be hollow, and to have compound retroactive interest like tiger's claws, or the wind round the poles.

And the world woke up one morning and found itself poor.

Lord stood just inside the door to the crystal walled ballroom. He kept his inner tenseness bubbling inside and an idle, indifferent outward composure. He speared a drink from a passing robot. His mouth might have drooped cynically and he might have felt very tired if the porage wasn't coursing like a breeder reaction through his body. He stood in shadows and watched.

Costumes were everywhere. Almost as much as the absence of costume. Feathers waved above chalky faces, scented masks framed bold eyes. Lights glittered from jewellery and precious metals. Naked flesh, powdered and creamed and electro-treated, gleamed sybaritically against lush fabrics and alien furs. Gas-filled balloons drifted and, bursting, sent everyone around giggling hysterically. Lord caught a whiff of one that split near him and fought down treacherous headiness. He inserted his nasal plugs with a grimace.

Liquor spilt and stank and ran across the floor, soaking into priceless rugs. Streamers fluttered in artificial breezes. Flash bulbs plopped everywhere. People strutted and shouted, carmine lips opening and closing, unheard a pace away. Rockets soared to burst in shimmering stars against the roof. Somewhere massed bands were thumping and groaning and syncopating away almost lost in the gargantuan human uproar.

Everybody was having themselves a whale of a time.

Time: 2123.

Lord found Josiah Gosheron in the arms of a semi-clothed girl struggling in an alcove. The Sahndran Ambassador's two aides were standing by, grinning, unwilling to help the old guy. The girl was persistent. He was having fun, too; but his wind wasn't what it used to be.

Consider this alien.

Index: S/A/64389D.

Name: Josiah V. X. Gosheron.

Age: 83. Height: 151 cms. Hair: Red. Eyes: Brown.

Accredited Sahndran Diplomatic Corps. Responsible for treaty between Eridani and Sirius freezing Earth out. Elusive. Strong racial prejudices. Maintenance of his goodwill to Earth essential. A dangerous man (alien Int.).

SPEND THAT MONEY – BREAK THE GRAVE,
ONLY *SUCKERS* EVER SAVE!

Glib profiteering words, spilling from fat, rat-trap mouths: 'We believe in the future of this great country. There are more than twenty-five million people swelling the world population each year – a potential market of seventy thousand fresh individuals per day. We must feed and clothe and house and amuse and provide transportation for them all. This company's opening two new plants this year and three next . . . blah . . . production . . . blah . . . consumption . . .'

That's a perfectly good idea! It's a good thing to have children and provide for them and see they have all the things you didn't.

Dig that Earth, provide for all; There's no dearth, come one, come all!

A girl ran past, screaming, her hair trailing silver dust. Parts of her costume fell off as she ran. A youth pursued her, flushed, laughing. He held outstretched a hypodermic filled, ready to provide unworried dream horizons. She'd let him catch her when they were alone – or more or less alone.

Gosheron's two aides finally pulled the squawking girl off their boss. She pouted at them, her face a solid gold-dusted mask, unrecognisable. Her hair was bleached white, coiffed and curled into a spaceship with flaring venturis down ears, nose and nape. Every time she laughed a beacon lit up on the spaceship's prow. She was lit up, too. Her naked arms and legs showed dozens of pin-pricks through the clogging powder, like a miniaturised moonscape.

Gosheron guffawed, belly shaking. He flung the girl a credit note. He was dressed like an ancient Indian Rajah, spattered with jewels, turban cunningly wound round a stator field generator. His sword looked like it had been built round a flame-rifle. An alien. A Terran hater. A dangerous man.

Lord's life meant nothing measured against the need to keep this alien alive and happy.

This alien Ambassador represented solar systems where Q's were still unused. We'd had ours. We'd been using about .004 Q's a year up till 1850, taking it from the muscles of animals and men. The next hundred years we used four Q's. Then we had twenty-seven Q's of coal and oil left – but why worry? Atomic power, buster, use your noggin!

'Waste not, want not.' That was a laugh. Consume friends, consume. Oh, sure, salvage where you can. A little later: 'Salvage is a national effort.' Then, reluctantly: 'The scrap-iron industry is the largest in the world.' Panicking: 'Salvage is a major aim of all citizens.' Finally, terror-stricken: 'Salvage is the new god!' But – consume, friends, consume!

A robot waiter trundled by and Lord hefted another Nuclear Fizz. This was an Advertising Convention, advertising the world to the aliens – and Katy was off somewhere with a goon from beyond the stars. Lord gulped the drink.

DRINK! DRINK! WOOD AL-CO-HOL!

The Advertising Industry have their eye teeth invested. You can't suddenly cut off an entire industry, with ramifications extending into every part of the economic set-up, with a casual: 'Sorry, Mac.' Not a multi-billion credit organisation. Not with that power. Power to keep things running. Power to ensure that the advertising business stayed in power even when there was a worldwide shortage of nearly everything.

Gotta live, you know. Play you eighteen holes, George, then we can talk things over at the nineteenth. Sure you know how it is, old man, times are tough; but there's still the good old atomic power.

Yeah, there's still the good old atom.

All five hundred seventy-five Q's of it.

That didn't last long.

Someone had smuggled in an erotibomb. Lord heard it go off over by the conservatory. He turned to watch, fingering the filters in his nose, and from his position in the alcove was able to see over the milling heads below. Ushers rushed from all directions wearing gasmasks. They shepherded the crowds, surrounded the area. A number of entwined couples were carried out. Lord didn't smile.

He was searching the throng, looking for signs he knew he couldn't possibly see. You couldn't tell an assassin by his expression, not with all those plastic facials about. And, too, he was looking for Katy.

What colour hair would she have tonight? What face would she wear? What brand of porage had she hit?

SHOOT THAT PORAGE, SMOKE THAT TEA,
VROOM AND *ZOOM* ON A BLIND D.T.!

The Synthetics Industry had climbed to power. Inevitably, they'd taken over when resources ran thin. Them – and the solar-erg boys. But there was one ever-replenishing resource that had to be handled with kid gloves.

Trees.

Re-afforestation, afforestation, priority. Terran global super-priority. Grow those trees, uncle, else you'll shiver. Bubble that algae, buster, else you'll starve. Split those atoms, fella, else you'll freeze. Synthesize.

SYNTHI, SYNTHI,
I'M A LITTLE SYNTHI,
AREN'T WE ALL . . . . ?

Over in a corner, drawn apart from the coruscating bedlam, a group of men talked with the cigar-spurts of conscious authority. Moguls of the Trees. Forest Lords. Big browed, spectacled atom-jugglers. Chlorella Kings.

'. . . forest fire in Asia that . . .'

'Don't be obscene!'

'Fires exist, they snatch profits. Grow up, pal!'

'. . . . new hexo-laminated ply peeled off. The ship disintegrated. Need a new bonding resin . . .'

'. . . Wembley's plastic weld . . .'

'. . . finished 'er, George! Two hundred stories. Less than a hundred tons of metal. Should last fifty-seventy years before the weather breaks through . . .'

'I need a drink.'

DRINK, DRINK, WOOD AL-CO-HOL!

Down beyond the main ballroom the crystal walls seemed to bulge with the crowd, shimmering and reflecting colours and landscapes, moonscapes, alien scapes as a shadow mime in mood and feeling complementary with the music's thrum.

Lord felt confused looking in that direction. Someone shot an immense chandelier loose. It crashed down, scattering people like sparks. A girl's clothes caught fire. Extinguishers foamed automatically from the floor. She ran, naked, laughing, foam flecked, plucked three feathers from a fan, used them, rejoined the fray.

They'd formed a snake-hipped line, were singing and stomping, collecting more people, winding round the ice-columns soaring to the roof.

'We're doomed, doomed, pigging in the tomb.'

Time: 2136.

Noise and colour and heat made an almost solid cloud in the wide room. Make-up was running down painted faces. Can't afford a custom re-facial. But, darling, new plastic faces at giveaway prices! Last you twenty years. After that . . . You're a big girl, now. You're on your own, sister.

From the shouting crazy line a man reeled like a yo-yo spun off its thread. He stumbled towards the alcove. Lord drew back, tensing. The drunk's wide Chinaman's sleeves flapped and his imitation pigtail bobbed. Lord didn't know the guy.

Index: T/Y/876398/R.

Name: Grunewald Abduol Sloane.

Age: 29. Height: 168 cms. Hair: Brown. Eyes: Brown.

Known revolutionary. Prison record. Member of Earth for Terrans party. Cardio-dope addict. Security Rating XX. A dangerous man.

Beyond the alcove and Lord and the Chinaman the noise drained away in his senses, as though this razor-sharp scene were contained in a balloon, as though everything fined down. Rockets burst silently, hooters whistled and shrilled soundlessly and vacuous mouths opened and shut like fish trapped in four glass walls.

YOU'LL NEVER NEED A PADRE
WHEN YOU HIT THAT TICKER WITH THE ADRE

Lord could see the man was a cardio-dope all right. The blue cheeks, the rapid, shallow breathing, were a trademark. The wide, meaning, knowing smile, as though all the world were an oyster for this guy's own guzzlement. *Get your own ticker-sticker, uncle.*

Gosheron looked up, smiling vacantly, his be-ringed fingers, wet with wine, clutching a liquor dispenser. His aides seemed to tense up, like ropes dipped in water, their faces going stiff and hard and ugly. The man in Chinese costume staggered a few further unsteady paces, stopped and drew himself up in drunken solemnity. His face twitched. His feet were planted wide apart on the synthiglass floor, heels off. His knees were slightly bent and Lord could see the quiver running along the muscles of those legs.

The man wasn't drunk.

Noise and confusion came back into Lord's world. The groaning bedlam of the convention beat at him with frenzied hands.

Lord moved a fraction of a second before Gosheron's aides. He drew his needle-beam, holding it carefully under a lapel flap, sighted on the pseudo-drunk and shot his stomach out through his backbone. Then, sheathing the weapon, Lord moved swiftly down the steps on to the floor, his coat flaring, took the dead man companionably by the arm and murmured a polite phrase of greeting.

The man's eyes were still open. Mirrored there was no expression at all. Death had struck too fast for any purely physical reaction. Lord had used a needle beam fined down so the wound was small; there was a little blood and intestine on the back of the man's Chinese coat but the hole in his stomach was invisible. Lord flicked the coat across to make sure.

The cardio-dope was still standing balanced on those wide-apart betraying legs. As he began to fall, his legs buckling, Lord took the weight on his arm, held the corpse upright and started to manoeuvre towards the nearest exit to one side of the alcove. Half-dragging half-carrying the body he got outside attracting as much attention as a hypo-needle at a party. Dopes, drunks, mixers, they all came alike to the bouncers.

'Stab with me, Jab with me, Come on, baby, GRAB with –'

The man suddenly welled a spurt of blood down his trousers and Lord hastily thumbed a window slide and tipped the body over. It's a long way down, buster. Goodbye, uncle. He went back into the big room, changing faces as he went.

Gosheron would never know he had just had his life saved by a Terran. He musn't know, of course: all that he'd make out of it would be the attempted attack itself. A fine life. Terran Security Agent, a fine jim-dandy life.

Time: 2140.

A group was singing, loudly, discordantly, but in an iron mesh of rhythm.

I wanna GLOW
With a baby who's not SLOW
I wanna SHOT
Of porage that is hot, HOT, *HOT!*

He'd been out of sight of Gosheron for perhaps forty-five seconds. His sigh of relief was not pleasant. Everything looked the same. If Gosheron copped his blood-bucket tonight – exit Lord also, ungracefully.

Impossibly the noise and confusion grew. Sounds and colours rose and burst around him like fire-streaked porpoises breaking the surface of a turgid, boiling, lava-engorged sea.

That was one attempt that had failed. There'd be others – probably fanatics from the Earth for Terrans party. Just so long as the Sahndran Ambassador had a fine old time and was suitably impressed by Terran independence and wealth – wealth! that was as false a front as an anaemic fifteen year old hat-check girl's – then the big wheels of Earth might chisel a few contracts for materials.

He snatched a glass from a passing robot. *Wood al-co-hol!* Down the hatch, derriere's up – whatever a derriere was. His mind fretted again over Katy. Where in hell was the girl? She'd forgotten him, obviously, taking some boob of a spaceman and sucking him dry. To hell with all women.

I wanna GLOW . . .

Lord grimaced disgustedly and threw the empty glass at a dispenser. He missed and the crystal shattered into fragments. A girl's high-pitched laugh jeered at his nerves.

Gosheron was talking now with the arbiters of trade and industry and money. This was the crux of the whole jamboree. This little quiet casual conference was the reason this lavish display of worldly wealth and squandering extravagance had been staged. Gosheron represented Sahndran on Earth, and Sahndran had systems choc-full of raw materials, resources, metals, *Q's*, everything that Earth lacked. Be nice to him, Terran hater though he might be, pal, he holds the whip hand. Only – don't let him know. Put on a show, throw an Advert. Con. and let him see how we can whoop it up! Dazzle the old boy. Geriatrics kept him chipper at eighty-three. Fling in a woman or two. Talk nice.

And get those raw materials for Earth!

Drink, Your Excellency? Which porage would you prefer? Yes, Your Excellency. This is the latest –

I wanna WHIZ
Wanna ZIZ,
Drink my NU-CLE-O-NIC FIZZ!

There had been more than a hint of desperation in the way Earth had flung itself into the algae business. If algae and bacteria could not provide the protein and carbohydrates and fats needed and if the forests could not supply the raw materials for commerce and synthesis, then mankind was sliding to hell in a bucket. The enormous demand for energy had stripped the land of renewable Q's – the sun and wind and tides were left. And still the consumption racket went on, still the stentorian calls for more production and consumption boomed out. It was hysterico-religious mania by then, of course. Geriatrics added to the inferno. Improved methods of equipping the unfit for life sprang up, adding still more burdens. Birth control? Just try, uncle, just try. The whole crazy mess rolled on inevitably, with warfare an outmoded – and unmentionable – method of control.

The basics were perfectly correct. Just that something went wrong along the line, somewhere. Even space travel didn't turn out to be the panacea everyone had confidently expected.

We just weren't the only people in the Galaxy.

A tall, glistening, floodlit flagpole with the United Nations flag bravely fluttered, towering over a garbage can with a gaping ever hungry mouth. That was the symbol.

WE'LL DRINK AT *BARS*
SPREAD FROM HERE OUT TO THE *STARS*

A world bedlam of frenzied, sensation-seeking, hungry, frightened people.

Drink, drink, wood al-co-hol!

You couldn't really blame them.

Lord felt the shivers and pulled his nasal plugs out, took a rapid sniff of snow, and replaced the filters. He needed it, anyway, after that hop-headed Chinaman. He finished another Nuclear Fizz – this time his cast was accurate and the glass splintered down the dispenser to be carried into the city's complex reclamation system – and wandered into the shadows to the rear of the animated group around Gosheron.

They were busily building empires and tearing others out from under the clammy feet of friends. Lord felt a faint disgust.

The woman with the golden face mask and bleached rocket hair glided swiftly from some purple-lit alcove, seized his arm. Her eyes were yellow pits of fire.

'Spencer! Darling Spencer! Fancy seeing you!'

Index: T/F/354920/E.

Name: Katherine Coburn.

Age: Alleged 26. Chronologic: 40. Height: 160 cms. Hair: Mousy. Eyes: Blue (partial to yellow stain).

Professional tridi entertainer. Four hospitalisations on unspecified data. Possible connections with Earth for Terrans party. Security Risk Rating: BX – problematical. Appears on restricted 'arrest during emergency' list.

There burst a suffocating wash of sound and light from the ballroom carrying her throaty greeting on it like a surfboard, tearing into his guts and making him ache to crush her into his arms then and there.

'Katy – I'd not recognised you – Katy – why in hell didn't you visor me?'

'I recognised you easily, uncle. But, Spencer, darling – I've been so busy –'

'Yeah! I saw! With that fat slug Gosheron.'

'But he's important, darling. And he's got lots of you know what.'

'I can keep you in reasonable comfort, Katy, you know that –'

'Oh, don't propose again, there's a dear boy! I believe

passionately in Trial Marriage, and it's so much less fuss. We've been happy for a couple of years, uncle, why not let it go on that way?'

'We've been happy! I've been in hell!'

She shrugged, her naked shoulders agleam in the lights where finger marks had smeared away powder. Lord's tongue was a cinder in the dryness of his mouth. She smiled at him, the golden sheath around her mouth dimpling and folding over the flesh.

'I need a fix,' he said hoarsely.

'Atta boy, Spencer – I'll join you.' Her yellow eyes smouldered. She lifted her scrap of skirt, drew out a jewelled plastic box. 'What are you hitting these days?'

'Usual.' Lord's own box, his portable carry-case, opened clumsily under his trembling fingers, a hinge snapped with a sharp *ping!* and the lid hung askew.

'Hey, take it easy, uncle!' she laughed.

The needle filled smoothly. Lord bared his forearm, pinched up the flesh and slid the porage home where it was needed. Uncle! Hit that sky!

Katy's eyelids half closed, her body undulated and she rippled her hands in an abandoned temple dance, tiny bells tinkling on her ankles. She crooned softly.

'I need a tonic – Uncle;
I'm super-sonic – Uncle.
Don't get platonic,
You hep carbuncle.'

'You're mixing!' he accused her.

'Sure, uncle. Sure. I'm hot! I've been mixing coupla weeks now. Get wise, Spencer darling. Grab a jab and stab! The old mainline porage is strictly for the crumbs.'

The golden sheath around her mouth crimped in and her smile would have drowned the sunrise. Her teeth were very white.

'Do get me a drink, dear boy –'

He brought two Nuclear Fizzes and didn't realise he had finished his own in one gulp. Somewhere off to one side Gosheron was surrounded by the moguls of finance, safe for the moment, giving time to talk to Katy without nagging worry.

'I'll see you after this –' he began eagerly.

She cut him off, gaily, like a sunbeam falling unexpectedly across a candle flame.

'Spencer, darling – have you seen Gruney around?'

'Gruney?' he said vaguely.

'Yes, Gruney,' she laughed impatiently. 'Grunewald Sloane. Such a dear boy. He promised to let me grab a stick from his ticker-sticker. Do you think I should?' She finished archly.

'Stay away from cardio-dopes,' Lord said automatically, not really hearing what she was saying, seeing only the outline of her in the sheathing golden film. He had just realised that the film was all she was wearing, it had looked like a dress with the scrap of pocket-skirt. She looked like the torrid flame from some pagan temple torch.

'That's your trouble, Spencer,' she pouted, flinging her empty glass somewhere in the direction of a disposer. 'You never want any fun! Cardio-dopes are hepped whizzes. Especially Gruney. If you see him tell him I'm aching to have a word with him.' She laughed kittenishly. 'He's dressed like a Chinaman, really utter. Bye, bye, Spencer, darling.'

And she was gone, like a flame twisting round a wind tossed torch. Spencer's mind groped among blackening embers. He puzzled over familiar things with foul sooty fingerprints across them.

Chinaman's clothes? Cardio-dope?

What was Katy doing running with that bunch?

JIB JOB JAB – AGAIN,
HIT THAT VEIN – BRAIN!

Time: 2148

Katy knew a man who had tried to kill Gosheron. Katy didn't know Lord was Terran Security. Katy had been trying to make Gosheron. Spencer Lord's mind twisted like a burned out hyper-drive. His face went sickly grey under the false features and he laid an unsteady hand against the wall to support himself.

Training took over. He didn't feel or hear the relays clicking in his brain; but the icy wall compounded of complete calm, utter confidence and dedicated obedience clamped shut like the closing valves of an airlock.

Almost.

Jamming the smooth functioning of his Bureau indoctrinated reactions, a sibilant golden flame mocked the closing of that wall. The vivid image of Katy danced maddeningly before his eyes, filtering the coldly calculated trained sequence of actions he must now go through. He shut his eyes in agony for a space, then opened them by an effort of will and put one hand to his weapons belt.

Security Rating Risk: AAA. Terran Security Operative. *Left, right, left, right, left.* BIM! BAM! BOOM! There wasn't much inside him now except a vastly dark hole which sucked his guts through claws of white hot steel.

The song from the chanting line in the ballroom beat up in metronomic waves of hypnotic sound. The wooden floor glistened with spilt liquor. An abandoned needle splintered under his foot. He disregarded all that, walked steadily over to the group around Gosheron. He couldn't see Katy.

If she tried to kill Gosheron he must kill her. It was black and white. There'd be no time for a fast deal, a hand across her mouth dragging her away where he could talk, unfix the crazy notions and fanatic schemes she must have had drilled into her poor befuddled brain. Gosheron must not know, ever, that his life had been endangered. These fanatics would try a shot even if they were dying in pieces – and Katy was one of them!

It was a situation fully covered by various aspects of the training he had gone through – except that the assassin wasn't the girl he – Lord was too far gone even to curse. The Earth's continued sustenance depended on the deals that would be made tonight, and once Gosheron, the old Terran hater, got a whiff of any murder-plot against him he'd be off – whoosh – to the stars.

Lord was sweating now, the sleazy feel of it slick between plastic face mask and flesh. He felt sick, too.

Giggle-gas balloons were popping everywhere now and

Lord forced himself to smile foolishly, mouth drooling as the stuff billowed around him. He had half a mind to take out one filter – it was a hell of a job trying to giggle the way he felt. And, suddenly, it was too dangerously easy.

He checked himself savagely. Gosheron was laughing and chuckling, greasy fat tears rolling down his slobby cheeks. The group around the alien were back-slapping, chortling, having a whale of a time; Lord knew their keen brains were bent on one objective, talking Gosheron into ripe contracts for Earth.

Sharks and shysters they might be: but Earth's future depended on them – good luck to them. Katy – Katy was a moth, a gaudy, brilliantly empty flutterer, giving nothing to the world, only taking. Yet – she was Katy . . . Katy . . .

Time: 2151.

When Lord saw her flashing eyes and laughing mouth in the crowd around Gosheron, her leg rubbing familiarly against a flushed young roisterer, he knew it was too late. She had wormed her way through the crush towards the alien. Lord pushed through after, laughing, shouting, a drink seized from a lax hand held high. His other hand stayed on his weapons belt under the flaring coat. The girl was a sliver of quicksilver, gliding in among the guests, slipping closer and closer to Gosheron.

I'M RIZ
I'M HIZ
ON MY NU-CLEO-NIC FIZZ!

Lord pushed faster, hating himself, hating the world, wondering just what he dared to do. There was an icy band around his forehead that constricted and drew fire-hot sparks of pain from his temples. Glass smashed in a roar of laughter. Heat beat up in baking waves. People rolled drunkenly away from a couple locked in a torrid embrace. Balloons and rockets crashed and plopped. Gosheron was clumsily tilting a glass, an aide steadied it, moving between Lord and Katy.

He stepped casually fast to one side, reached out a rock steady hand for Katy. She eluded his grasp without appearing to see him. Then he saw the needle between her fingers.

That wouldn't be porage. That would be a killer.

YOU NEED A TONIC – UNCLE
YOU'RE SUPER-SONIC – UNCLE . . .

She had one impudent arm around the fat alien now, her ripe lips reaching for his flabby mouth. She was laughing screechingly, piercingly, and flakes of gold began to peel from her body. An aide glanced at her, chuckled, and reached out.

Lord was held suspended in a timeless vacuum. He thought he had stopped breathing and his heart-beats came in sluggish reverberations of sound that hurt his chest.

The aide saw the needle. His laughing face went grim. Katy, all her vibrant body a golden bow, moved the hand with the needle. The drop of liquid at the tip caught the lights and shone fragmentarily blinding like a nova.

'Porage, porage, have a shot of porage,' she chanted.

Gosheron wheezed and shook, his fat face creased in smiles, his eyes avid on the girl's slim body. The aide's hand raked down towards Katy. She thrust and in that instant the other aide, unseen by Lord, fired. His wide beam tore Katy's hand and wrist off. The needle vapourised. She stood looking dazedly at the stump, cauterised already and with no blood oozing.

Miraculously a clearing appeared around the drama. Women screamed. Men swore. There was a sudden, awful, engulfing silence.

Lord's face felt as though a granite crusher had used it for a dummy run. His brain told him that he mustn't allow the Sahndrans to think this an organised attempt on the life of their Ambassador. He had to cover up – fast.

He could not trust himself to speak yet. He shoved roughly into the cleared area, trampling splintered glasses, and took the girl's body on his arm as she collapsed in a dead faint. He faced Gosheron, forced his rigid lips to open.

'She meant no harm!' He whined the words as though

fear and horror stricken. 'She wanted to give you a shot of porage – give you a kick. And you blasted her arm off.'

Gosheron's smile was now all diplomacy.

'I am sorry for the impetuosity of my guards, but –' He shrugged and ripples of fat ran disgustingly along his shoulders. 'We cannot take chances. She should have known better.'

'I'll look after her,' Lord got out. 'My name's Kinroy Tracey, in case you want to pay any compensation.'

Then he was pulling away, carrying Katy, her nude gold filmed body cold against his arm. Cold?

He glanced down in panic. Her closed eyelids showed blue where the gold had worn away. She was barely breathing. He scraped a nail across her gold filmed flesh, saw the betraying blue tinge beneath.

The little idiot! She'd been cardio-doping, all right! The shock, with her in that condition . . .

Before he had left the great ballroom she was dead.

'The filthy aliens!' Lord mumbled blindly to himself, over and over. 'They used a molecular on her. The poor kid. Dead. They only needed to knock her hand away. Dead. A molecular. The dirty rotten twisted . . .'

He sat with her in his arms for a long while, whilst around him beat the insistent roar of the world, going to hell in a bucket and enjoying itself every inch of the way.

Time: 2200.

Spencer Lord laid Katy down gently and walked back into the ballroom to continue protecting the alien Ambassador.

Get a Jab – Get a *Grab*.
On a nu-cle-o-nic Fizz!
Drink, drink, wood al-co-hol!
Going to hell in a bucket.

4 – BOB SHAW: A Full Member of the Club

Like James White, Bob Shaw comes from Northern Ireland, although he now lives in Lancashire. A fan from the early days, he graduated to sf with the publication of a short story, *Aspect* in the August 1954 *Nebula*. This was followed by a half-dozen other stories over the next eighteen months. Then he virtually disappeared from the scene, re-emerging just enough to keep his name in readers' memories with *The Silent Partners* in the last issue of *Nebula* (June 1959) and the following year in America's *If*, in collaboration with Walt Willis with a tongue-in-cheek vignette *Dissolute Diplomat* (which you will find included in my forthcoming Orbit anthology *Splinters From the Mind*). This absence from the sf scene was deliberate policy on Shaw's part. He had felt he was not really ready to write, and accordingly spent three years abroad as part of his plan to 'study the inhabitants of Sol III'.

He returned to sf in 1965 with . . . *And Isles Where Good Men Lie* in *New Worlds*, then edited by Michael Moorcock. This was followed in the May 1966 issue with a brilliant novelette *Pilot Plant*. Then in August he took *Analog* by storm with a fascinating new concept – 'slow glass'. *Light of Other Days* told of the invention of a material which absorbed light and allowed it to pass through at a much slower rate, eventually releasing it, after so many days, weeks, months or years, depending on the glass. This meant a piece of slow glass could be placed at a scenic view for several years and then installed in a home allowing the occupants to look out on the 'captured' live scene, just as if they were there. It also put paid to crime, as a slow glass window in a room would reveal all after the given period. This angle was explored in a sequel story *Burden of Proof* (*Analog*, May 1967). Eventually Shaw wrote a slow-glass novel, *Other Days, Other Eyes* serialised in *Amazing* in 1972.

In fact the majority of Shaw's recent sales have been to the American market, due mostly to the blatant absence of any regular British market. He has averaged one novel a year since 1967, and 1974 was a special 'boom' year. A novel, *Orbitsville*, was serialised in the June to August issues of *Galaxy*, and whilst that was running the July *Galaxy* published *A Full Member of the Club*, which was picked by one anthologist as amongst the year's best short stories. Concurrently the July issue of *If* published *A Little Night Flying* which had previously appeared in the May issue of Britain's *Science Fiction Monthly* as *Dark Icarus*, and which was also picked by another anthologist as one of the year's best short sf stories.

From that group Shaw picked his own favourite. He said: 'I chose *A Full Member of the Club* because its plot is perfectly suited to one of my favourite literary techniques. Roughly speaking, there are two ways to handle the telling of a science fiction story and they both involve the element of strangeness. One method is to pitch the reader straight into an unfamiliar environment and proceed to overwhelm him with its strangeness; the other is to ease the reader into a familiar environment, and then gradually, drop by drop, introduce the alchemy of strangeness. As a practitioner of science fiction writing I have used both methods, but prefer the latter because it is – if I may use an unliterary term – sneaky. (The reason nobody likes a sneak is that his methods are effective). The challenge for the writer is to install the reader in a smoothly moving railcar and try to keep him looking straight ahead while a succession of points are quietly switched, thus sending him off in an unexpected direction. The challenge for the reader is to decide the exact moment at which he becomes aware of having left the mundane world and having entered that fantastic Other Universe, the building blocks of which are all the science fiction and fantasy stories ever written.'

'However, stories are for reading – not analysing – and I hope you enjoy reading *A Full Member of the Club*.'

A FULL MEMBER OF THE CLUB

Bob Shaw

It was a trivial thing – a cigarette lighter – which finally wrecked Philip Connor's peace of mind.

Angela and he had been sitting at the edge of her pool for more than an hour. She had said very little during that time, but every word, every impatient gesture of her slim hands, had conveyed the message that it was all over between them.

Connor was sitting upright on a canvas chair, manifestly ill at ease, trying to understand what had brought about the change in their relationship. He studied Angela carefully, but her face was rendered inscrutable, inhuman, by the huge insect eyes of her sunglasses. His gaze strayed to a lone white butterfly as it made a hazardous flight across the pool and passed, twinkling like a star, into the shade of the birches.

He touched his forehead and found it buttery with sweat. 'This heat is murderous.'

'It suits me,' Angela said, another reminder that they were no longer as one. She moved slightly on the lounger, altering the brown curvatures of her semi-nakedness.

Connor stared nostalgically at the miniature landscape of flesh, the territory from which he was being evicted, and reviewed the situation. The death of an uncle had made Angela rich, *very* rich, but he was unable to accept that as sufficient reason for her change in attitude. His own business interests brought him in more than $200,000 a year, so she knew he wasn't a fortune hunter.

'I have an appointment in a little while,' Angela said.

Connor decided to try making her feel guilty. 'You want me to leave?'

He was rewarded by a look of concern, but it was quickly

gone, leaving the beautiful face as calm and immobile as before. Angela sat up, took a cigarette from a pack on the low table, opened her purse and brought out the gold cigarette lighter. It slipped from her fingers, whirred across the tiles and went into the shallow end of the pool. With a little cry of concern she reached down into the water and retrieved the lighter, wetting her face and tawny hair in the process. She clicked the dripping lighter once and it lit. Angela gave Connor a strangely wary glance, dropped the lighter back into her purse and stood up.

'I'm sorry, Phil,' she said. 'I have to go now.'

It was an abrupt dismissal but Connor, emotionally bruised though he was, scarcely noticed. He was a gypsy entrepreneur, a wheeler-dealer, one of the very best - and his professional instincts were aroused. The lighter had ignited first time while soaking wet, which meant it was the best he had ever seen, and yet its superb styling was unfamiliar to him. This fact bothered Connor. It was his business to know all there was to know about the world's supply of sleek, shiny, expensive goodies, and obviously he had let something important slip through his net.

'All right, Angie.' He got to his feet. 'That's a nice lighter - mind if I have a look?'

She clutched her purse as though he had moved to snatch it. 'Why don't you leave me alone? Go away, Phil.' She turned and strode off towards the house.

'I'll stop by for a while tomorrow.'

'Do that,' she called, without looking back. 'I won't be here.'

Connor walked back to his Lincoln, lowered himself gingerly onto the baking upholstery and drove into Long Branch. It was late in the afternoon but he went back to his office and began telephoning various trade contacts, making sure they too were unaware of something new and radical in cigarette lighters. Both his secretary and telephonist were on vacation so he did all the work himself. The activity helped to ease the throbbing hurt of having lost Angela, and - in a way he was unable to explain - gave him of comforting sense that he was doing something towards getting her back or, at least, finding out what had gone wrong between them. He had an illogical conviction that the little gold artifact was somehow connected with their breaking up. The idea was utterly ridiculous, of course, but in thinking back over the interlude by the pool with Angela it struck him that, amazingly for her, she had done without smoking. Although it probably meant she was cutting down, another possibility was that she had not wanted to produce the lighter in his presence.

Realising his enquiries were getting him nowhere, he closed up the office and drove across town to his apartment. The evening was well advanced yet seemingly hotter than ever – the sun had descended to a vantage point from which it could attack more efficiently, slanting its rays through the car windows. He let himself into his apartment, showered, changed his clothes and prowled unhappily through the spacious rooms wishing Angela was with him. A lack of appetite robbed him of even the solace of food. At midnight he brewed coffee with his most expensive Kenyan blend, deriving a spare satisfaction from the aroma, but took only a few disappointed sips. *If only*, he thought for the thousandth time, *they could make it taste the way it smells.*

He went to bed, consciously lonely, and yearned for Angela until he fell asleep.

Next morning Connor awoke feeling hungry and, while eating a substantial breakfast, was relieved to find he had regained his usual buoyant outlook on life. It was perfectly natural for Angela to be affected by the sudden change in her circumstances, but when the novelty of being rich, instead of merely well off, had faded he would win her back. And in the meanwhile he – the man who had been first in the country with Japanese liquid display watches – was not going to give up on a simple thing like a new type of cigarette lighter.

Deciding against going to his office, he got on the phone and set up further chains of business enquiries, spreading his net as far as Europe and the Far East. By mid-morning the urge to see Angela again had become very strong. He ordered his car to be brought round to the main entrance of the building and he drove south on the coast road to Asbury Park. It looked like being another day of unrelieved sunshine, but a fresh breeze from the Atlantic was fluttering in the car windows and further elevating his spirits.

When he got to Angela's house there was an unfamiliar car in the U-shaped driveway. A middle-aged man wearing a tan suit and steel-rimmed glasses was on the steps, ostentatiously locking the front door. Connor parked close to the steps and got out.

The stranger turned to face him, jingling a set of keys. 'Can I help you?'

'I don't think so,' Connor said, resenting the unexpected presence. 'I called to see Miss Lomond.'

'Was it a business matter? I'm Millett of Millett and Fiesler.'

'No – I'm a friend.' Connor moved impatiently towards the doorbell.

'Then you should know Miss Lomond doesn't live here any more. The house is going up for sale.'

Connor froze, remembering Angela had said she wouldn't be around, and shocked that she had not told him about selling up. 'She did tell me, but I hadn't realised she was leaving so soon,' he improvised. 'When's her furniture being collected?'

'It isn't. The property is going on the market as it stands.'

'She's taking *nothing?*'

'Not a stick. I guess Miss Lomond can afford new furniture without too much difficulty,' Millett said drily, walking towards his car. 'Good morning.'

'Wait a minute.' Connor ran down the steps. 'Where can I get in touch with Angela?'

Millett ran a speculative eye over Connor's car and clothing before he answered. 'Miss Lomond has bought Avalon – but I don't know if she has moved in yet.'

'Avalon? You mean . . . ?' Lost for words, Connor pointed south in the direction of Point Pleasant.

'That's right.' Millett nodded and drove away. Connor

got into his own car, lit his pipe and tried to enjoy a smoke while he absorbed the impact of what he had heard. Angela and he had never discussed finance – she simply had no interest in the subject – and it was only through oblique references that he had been able to guesstimate the size of her inheritance as in the region of a million, perhaps two. But Avalon was a rich man's folly in the old Randolph Hearst tradition, the nearest thing to a royal palace that existed outside Europe, and surrounded by a dozen square miles of the choicest land in Philadelphia. Real estate was not one of Connor's specialties, but he knew that anybody buying Avalon would have had to open the bidding at ten million or more. In other words, Angela was not merely rich – she had graduated into the millionaires' superleague, and it was hardly surprising that her emotional life had been affected.

Connor was puzzled, nevertheless, over the fact that she was selling all her furniture. There was, among several cherished pieces, a Gaudreau writing desk about which she had always shown an exaggerated possessiveness. Suddenly aware that he could neither taste nor smell the imported tobacco which had seemed so good in his pouch, Connor extinguished his pipe and drove out onto the highway.

He had travelled south for some five miles before admitting to himself that he was going to Avalon.

The house itself was invisible, screened from the road by a high redbrick wall. Age had mellowed the brickwork, but the coping stones on top had a fresh appearance and were surmounted by a climb-proof wire fence. Connor drove along beside the wall until it curved inwards to a set of massive gates which were closed. At the sound of his horn a thickset man in a uniform of *café-au-lait* gabardine, and with a gun on his hip, emerged from a lodge. He looked out through the gate without speaking.

Connor lowered a car window and put his head out. 'Is Miss Lomond at home?'

'What's your name?' the guard said.

'I'm Philip Connor.'

'Your name isn't on my list.'

'Look, I only asked if Miss Lomond was at home.'

'I don't give out any information.'

'But I'm a personal friend. You're obliged to tell me whether she's at home or not.'

'Is that a fact?' The guard turned and sauntered back into the lodge, ignoring Connor's shouts and repeated blasts on the horn. Angered by the incident, Connor decided not to slink away. He began sounding the car horn in a steady bludgeoning rhythmn – five seconds on, five seconds off – but the guard did not reappear. Five minutes later a police cruiser pulled alongside with two state troopers in it, and Connor was moved on with an injunction to calm down.

For lack of anything better to do, he went to his office.

A week went by, during which time Connor drew a complete blank on the cigarette lighter, and was almost forced to the conclusion that it had been custom-built by a modern Fabergé. He spent hours trying to get a telephone number for Angela, without success. Sleep began to elude him, and he felt himself nearing the boundary which separates rationality from obsession. Finally, he saw a society column picture of Angela in a New York nightspot with Bobby Janke, playboy son of an oil billionaire. Apart from making Connor feel ill with jealousy, the newspaper item provided him with the information that Angela was taking up residence at her newly acquired home sometime in the following weekend.

Who cares? he demanded of his shaving mirror. *Who cares?*

He began drinking vodka tonics at lunchtime on Saturday, veered onto white rum during the afternoon, and by nightfall was suffused with a kind of alcoholic dharma which told him that he was entitled to see Angela and to employ any means necessary to achieve that end. There was the problem of the high brick wall but, with a flash of enlightenment, Connor realised that walls are mainly psychological barriers. To a person who understood their nature as well as he did, walls became doorways. Taking a mouthful of neat rum to strengthen his sense of purpose, Connor sent for his car.

Avalon's main entrance, scene of his earlier defeat, was in darkness when he reached it, but lights were showing in the gate lodge. Connor drove on by, following the line of the wall, and parked on a deserted stretch of second-class road. He switched off all lights, opened the trunk, took out a heavy hammer and chisel, crossed the verge and – without any preliminaries – attacked the wall. Ten minutes later, although the mortar was soft with age, he had not succeeded in removing one brick and was beginning to experience doubts. Then the first brick came free and others virtually tumbled out after it. He enlarged the hole to an appropriate size and crawled through onto dry turf.

A dwarfish half-moon was perched near zenith, casting a wan radiance on the turrets and gables of a mansion which sat on the crest of a gentle rise. The building was dark and forbidding, and as he looked at it Connor felt the warm glow in his stomach fade away. He hesitated, swore at himself and set off up the slope, leaving his hammer and chisel behind. By bearing to the left he brought the front elevation of the building into view and was encouraged to see one illuminated window on the first floor. He reached a paved approach road, followed it to the Gothic-style front entrance and rang for admission. A full minute later the door was opened by an archetypal and startled-looking butler, and Connor sensed immediately that Angela was not at home.

He cleared his throat. 'Miss Lomond . . .'

'Miss Lomond is not expected until mid . . .'

'Midnight,' Connor put in, expertly taking his cue. 'I know that – I was with her this afternoon in New York. We arranged that I would stop by for a late drink.'

'I'm sorry, sir, but Miss Lomond didn't tell me to expect any visitors.'

Connor looked surprised. 'Didn't she? Well, the main thing is she remembered to let them know at the gate lodge.' He squeezed the butler's arm democratically. 'You know, you couldn't get through that gate in a Sherman tank if your name wasn't on the list.'

The butler looked relieved. 'One can't be too careful these days, sir.'

'Quite right. I'm Mr Connor, by the way – here's my card. Now show me where I can wait for Miss Lomond. And, if it isn't imposing too much, I'd like a Daiquiri. Just one to toy with while I'm waiting.'

'Of course, Mr Connor.'

Exhilarated by his success, Connor was installed in an enormous green-and-silver room and supplied with a frosty glass. He sat in a very comfortable armchair, sipped his Daiquiri and judged it to be the best he had ever tasted. The sense of relaxation prompted him to reach for his pipe but he discovered it must have been left at home. He prowled around the room, found a box of cigars on a sideboard and took one from it. He then glanced around for a lighter. His gaze fell on a transparent, ruby-coloured ovoid sitting upright on an occasional table. In no way did it resemble any table lighter he had ever seen, but he had become morbidly sensitive on the subject, and the ovoid was positioned where he would have expected a lighter to be. Connor picked it up, held it to the light and found it was perfectly clear, with no works visible inside. That meant it could not be a lighter. As he was setting it down, he allowed his thumb to slide into a seductively shaped depression on the side.

A pea-sized ball of radiance – like a bead fashioned from sunlight – appeared at the top of the egg. It shone with absolute steadiness until he removed his thumb from the dimple.

Fascinated by his find, he made the tiny globe of brilliance appear and disappear over and over again, and proved its hotness with a fingertip. He took out the pocket magnifier he always carried for evaluating trinkets and examined the tip of the egg. The glass revealed a minute silver plug set flush with the surface, but nothing more. Following a hunch, Connor carefully guided one drop of liquid from his drink onto the egg and made sure it was covering the nearly invisible plug. When he operated the lighter it worked perfectly, the golden bead burning without wavering until the liquid had boiled off into the air.

He set the lighter down and noticed yet another strange property – the ruby egg was smoothly rounded at the bottom yet it sat upright, with no tendency to topple over. His magnifier showed an ornate letter P engraved in the base, but provided no clue as to how the balancing act was achieved.

Connor gulped the remainder of his drink and, with eyes that suddenly were sober and watchful, took a fresh look around the room. He discovered a beautiful clock, apparently carved from solid onyx. As he had half-expected there was no way to open it and the same elaborate P was engraved on the underside.

There was also a television set which had a superficial resemblance to an expensive commercial model but which bore no maker's name plaque. He checked it over and found the now-familiar P inscribed on one side where it would never be noticed except by a person who was making a purposeful search. When he switched the set on, the image of a newscaster which appeared on the screen was so sharp and perfect that he might have been looking through a plate glass window into the man's face. Connor studied the picture from a distance of only a few inches and could not resolve it into lines or dots. His magnifier achieved no better results.

He switched the television off and returned to the armchair, filled with a powerful and strange emotion. Although it was in his nature to be sharp and acquisitive – those were attributes without which he could never have entered his chosen profession – it had always remained uppermost in his mind that the world's supply of money was unlimited, whereas his own allocation of years was hopelessly inadequate. He could have trebled his income by working longer and pushing harder, but had always chosen another course simply because his desire for possessions had never taken control. However, that had been before he discovered the sort of possessions real money could buy. He knew he was particularly susceptible to gadgets and toys, but the knowledge did nothing to lessen the harsh raw hunger he now felt. And there was no way that anybody was going to stop him from joining the ranks of those who could afford future-technology artifacts. He would prefer to do it by marrying Angela, because he loved her and would enjoy sharing the experiences, but if she refused to have him back he would do it by making the necessary millions himself.

A phrase which had been part of his train of thought isolated itself in his mind. *Future technology*. He weighed the implications for a moment then shrugged them off – he had lost enough mental equilibrium without entertaining fantasies about time travel.

The idea was an intriguing one, though, and it answered certain questions. The lighters he coveted, partly for their perfection and partly because they could earn him a fortune, were technically far in advance of anything on the world's markets, yet it was within the realms of possibility that a furtive genius was producing them in a back room somewhere. But it was hard to see how the impossibly good television set could have been manufactured without the R & D facilities of a powerful electronics concern. The notion that they were being made in the future and shipped back in time was only slightly less ridiculous than the idea of a secret industry catering exclusively for the super-rich . . .

Connor picked up the cigar and lit it, childishly pleased at having a reason to put the ruby egg to work. His first draw on the cool smoke gave him the feeling that he had been searching for something all his life and suddenly had found it. Cautiously at first and then with intense pleasure he filled his lungs with the unexpected fragrance. He luxuriated. This was smoking as it was idealised in tobacco company commercials – not the shallow disappointing experience commonly known to smokers everywhere. He had often wondered why the leaf which smelled so beguiling before it was lit, or when someone nearby was smoking, promising sensual delights and heart's ease, never yielded anything more than virtually tasteless smoke.

They promise you 'a long cool smoke to soothe a troubled world', Connor thought, *and this is it*. He took the cigar from his mouth and examined the band. It was of unembellished gold and bore a single ornate P.

'I might have known,' he announced to the empty room. He looked around through a filigree of smoke, wondering if everything in the room was different to the norm, superior, better than the best. Perhaps the ultra-rich scorned to use *anything* that was available to the man-in-the-street or advertised on television or . . .

'Philip!' Angela stood in the doorway, pale of face, shocked and angry. 'What are you doing here?'

'Enjoying the best cigar I've ever had.' Connor got to his feet, smiling. 'I presume you keep them for the benefit of guests – I mean, a cigar is hardly your style.'

'Where's Gilbert?' she snapped. 'You're leaving right now.'

'Not a chance.'

'That's what you think.' Angela turned with an angry flail of blonde hair and cerise skirts.

Connor realised he had to find inspiration and get in fast. 'It's too late, Angela. I've smoked your cigar, I lit it with your lighter, I have checked the time with your clock, and I've watched your television.'

He had been hoping for a noticeable reaction and was not disappointed – Angela burst into tears. 'You fool! You had no *right!*'

She ran to the table, picked up the lighter and tried to make it work. Nothing happened. She went to the clock, which had stopped going; and to the television set, which remained lifeless when she switched it on. Connor followed her circuit of the room, feeling guilty and baffled. Angela dropped into a chair and sat with her face in her hands, huddled and trembling like a sick bird. The sight of her distress produced a painful churning in his chest. He knelt in front of Angela.

'Listen, Angie,' he said. 'Don't cry like that. I only wanted to see you again – I haven't done anything.'

'You touched my stuff and made it change. They told me it would change if anybody but a client used it . . . and it has.'

'This doesn't make sense. Who said what would change?'

'The suppliers.' She looked at him with tear-brimmed

eyes and all at once he became aware of a perfume so exquisite that he wanted to fall towards its source like a suffocating man striving towards air.

'What did you . . . ? I don't . . .'

'They said it would all be spoiled.'

Connor tried to fight off the effects of the witch-magic he had breathed. 'Nothing has been spoiled, Angie. There's been a power failure . . . or something . . .' His words tailed away uncertainly as he remembered the clock and the television set were cordless. He took a nervous drag on the half-smoked cigar and almost gagged on the flat acrid taste of it. The sharp sense of loss he experienced while stubbing it out seemed to obliterate all traces of his scepticism.

He returned to Angela's chair and knelt again. 'They said this stuff would stop working if anybody but you touched it?'

'Yes.'

'But how could that be arranged?'

She dabbed her eyes with a handkerchief. 'How would I know? When Mr Smith came over from Trenton he said something about all his goods having an . . . essence field, and he said I had a molecular thumbprint. Does that make sense?'

'It almost does,' Connor whispered. 'A perfect security system. Even if you lost your lighter at the theatre, when somebody else picked it up it would cease to be what it was.'

'Or when somebody breaks into your home.'

'Believe me, it was only because I had to see you again, Angie. You know that I love you.'

'Do you, Philip?'

'Yes, darling.' He was thrilled to hear the special softness return to her voice. 'Look, you have to let me pay for a new lighter and television and . . .'

Angela was shaking her head. 'You couldn't do it, Philip.'

'Why not?' He took her hand and was further encouraged when she allowed it to remain in his.

She gave him a tremulous smile. 'You just couldn't. The instalments are too high.'

‘Instalments? For God’s sake, Angie, *you* don’t buy stuff on time.’

‘You can’t buy these things – you pay for a service. I pay instalments of $864,000.’

‘A year?’

‘Once every forty-three days. I shouldn’t be telling you all this, but . . .’

Connor gave an incredulous laugh. ‘That comes to about six million a year – nobody would pay that much.’

‘Some people would. If you even have to think about the cost Mr Smith doesn’t do business with you.’

‘But . . .’ Connor incautiously leaned within range of Angela’s perfume and it took his mind. ‘You realise,’ he said in a weak voice, ‘that all your new toys come from the future? There’s something fantastically wrong about the whole set-up.’

‘I’ve missed you, Philip.’

‘That perfume you’re wearing – did it come from Mr Smith, too?’

‘I tried not to miss you, but I did.’ Angela pressed her face against his and he felt the coolness of tears on her cheek. He kissed her hungrily as she moved down from the chair to kneel against him. Connor spun towards the centre of a whirlpool of ecstasy.

‘Life’s going to be so good when we’re married,’ he heard himself saying after a time. ‘Better than we could ever have dreamed. There’s so much for us to share and . . .’

Angela’s body stiffened and she thrust herself away from him. ‘You’d better go now, Philip.’

‘What is it? What did I say?’

‘You gave yourself away, that’s all.’

Connor thought back. ‘Was it what I said about sharing? I didn’t mean your money – I was talking about life . . . the years . . . the experiences.’

‘I could never be sure of that.’

‘I loved you before you even knew you would inherit a cent.’

‘You never mentioned marriage before.’

‘I thought that was understood,’ he said desperately. ‘I

thought you . . .' He stopped speaking as he saw the look in Angela's eyes. Cool, suspicious, disdainful. The look that the very rich had always given to outsiders who tried to get into their club without the vital qualification of wealth.

She touched a bellpush and continued standing with her back to him until he was shown out of the room.

The ensuing days were bad ones for Connor. He drank a lot, realised that alcohol was no answer, and went on drinking. For a while he tried getting in touch with Angela, and even drove down to Avalon. The brickwork had been repaired at the point where he had made his entry, and a close inspection revealed that the entire wall was newly covered with a fine mesh. He had no doubt that tampering with it in any way would trigger off an alarm system.

When he awoke during the night he was kept awake by hammering questions. What was it all about? Why did Angela have to make such odd payments, and at such odd intervals? What would men from the future want with twentieth century currency? On several occasions the thought occurred that, instead of concentrating on Angela, he would do better to find the mysterious Mr Smith of Trenton. The flicker of optimism the idea produced was quenched almost immediately by the realisation that he simply did not have enough information to provide a lead. It was a certainty that the man was not even known as Smith to anybody but his clients. If only, while shocked into talking, Angela had revealed something more – like Smith's business address . . .

Connor returned each time to brooding and drinking, careless of the fact that his behaviour was becoming completely obsessive. Then he awoke one morning to the discovery that he already knew Smith's business address, had known it for a long time, almost from childhood.

Undecided as to whether his intake of white rum had hastened or delayed the revelation, he breakfasted on strong coffee and was too busy with his thoughts to fret about the black liquid being more tasteless than ever. He formulated a plan of action during the next hour, twice lighting his pipe – out of sheer habit – before remembering he was finished with ordinary tobacco for ever. As a first step in the plan he went out, bought a five-inch cube of ruby-coloured plastic and paid the owner of a jobbing shop an exorbitant sum to have the block machined down to a polished ovoid. It was late in the afternoon before the work was finished, but the end product sufficiently resembled a P-brand table lighter to fool anyone who was not looking too closely at it.

Pleased with his progress thus far, Connor went back to his apartment and dug out the .38 pistol he had bought a few years earlier following an attempted burglary. Common sense told him it was rather late to leave for Trenton and that he would be better waiting until morning, but he was in a warmly reckless mood. With the plastic egg bumping on one hip and the gun on the other, he drove westwards out of town.

Connor reached the centre of Trenton just as the stores were showing signs of closing for the day. His sudden fear of being too late, and of having to wait another day after all, was strengthened by the discovery that he was no longer so certain about locating Mr Smith.

In the freshness of the morning, with an alcoholic incense lingering in his head, it had all seemed simple and straightforward. For much of his life he had been peripherally aware that in almost every big city there are stores which have no right to be in existence. They were always small and discreet, positioned some way off the main shopping thoroughfares, and their signs usually bore legends – like 'Johnston Bros' or 'H & L' – which seemed designed to convey a minimum of information. If they had a window display at all it tended to be nothing more than an undistinguished and slightly out-of-style sport jacket priced three times above what it had any chance of fetching. Connor knew the stores were not viable propositions in the ordinary way because, not surprisingly, nobody ever went into them. And yet in his mind they were, in some indefinable way, associated with money.

Setting out for Trenton he had been quite sure of the city block he wanted – now at least three locations and images of three unremarkable store fronts were merging and blurring in his memory. *That's how they avoid attention*, he thought, refusing to be disheartened, and began cruising the general area he had selected. The rush of home-going traffic hampered every movement and finally he decided he would do better on foot. He parked in a sidestreet and began hurrying from corner to corner, each time convincing himself he was about to look along a remembered block and see the place he so desperately wanted to find, each time being disappointed. Virtually all the stores were closed by now, the crowds had thinned away, and the reddish evening sunlight made the quiet dusty facades look unreal. Connor ran out of steam, physically and mentally.

He swore dejectedly, shrugged and started limping back to his car, choosing – as a token act of defiance – a route which took him a block further south than he had originally intended going. His feet were hot and so painful that he was unable to think of anything but his own discomfort. Consequently he did a genuine double-take when he reached an intersection, glanced sideways and saw a half-familiar half-forgotten vista of commonplace stores, wholesalers' depots and anonymous doorways. Connor's heart began a slow pounding as he picked out, midway on the block, a plain store front whose complete lack of character would have rendered it invisible to eyes other than his own.

He walked towards it, suddenly nervous, until he could read the sign which said GENERAL AGENCIES, in tarnished gold lettering. The window contained three pieces of glazed earthenware sewer pipe, beyond which were screens to prevent anyone seeing the store's interior. Connor expected to find the door locked, but it opened at his touch and he was inside without even having had time to prepare himself. He blinked at a tall gaunt man who was standing motionless behind a counter. The man had a down-curving mouth, ice-smooth grey hair, and something about him gave Connor the impression that he had been standing there, unmoving, for hours. He was dressed in funeral director black, with a silver tie, and the collar of his white shirt was perfect as the petals of a newly-opened flower.

The man leaned forward slightly and said, 'Was there something, sir?'

Connor was taken aback by the quaintness of the greeting but he strode to the counter, brought the ruby egg from his pocket and banged it down.

'Tell Mr Smith I'm not satisfied with this thing,' he said in an angry voice. 'And tell him I demand a repayment.'

The tall man's composure seemed to shatter. He picked up the egg, half-turned towards an inner door, then paused and examined the egg more closely.

'Just a minute,' he said. 'This isn't . . .'

'Isn't what?'

The man looked accusingly at Connor. 'I've no idea what this object is, and we haven't got a Mr Smith.'

'Know what *this* object is?' Connor produced his revolver, confident he had seen and heard enough to justify taking a harder line.

'You wouldn't dare to shoot me.'

'No?' Connor aimed the revolver at the other man's face and, aware that the safety catch was on, gave the trigger an obvious squeeze. The tall man shrank against the wall. Connor muttered furiously; clicked the safety off, and raised the gun again.

'Don't!' The man shook his head. 'I beseech you.'

Connor had never been beseeched in his life, but he did not allow the curious turn of speech to distract him. He said, 'I want to see Mr Smith.'

'I'll take you to him. If you will follow me . . .'

They went through to the rear of the premises and down a flight of stairs which had inconveniently high risers and narrow treads. Noting that his guide was descending with ease, Connor glanced down and saw that the tall man had abnormally small feet. There was another peculiarity about his gait but it was not until they had reached the basement floor and were moving along a corridor that Connor realised what it was. Within the chalk-stripe trousers, the tall man's knees appeared to be a good two-thirds of the way down his legs. Cool fingers of unease touched Connor's brow.

'Here we are, sir.' The black-clad figure before him pushed open a door. Beyond it was a large brightly-lit room and at one side was another tall cadaverous man dressed like a funeral director. He too had ice-smooth grey hair and he was carefully putting an antique oil painting into the dark rectangular opening of a wall safe.

Without turning his head, he said, 'What is it, Toynbee?'

Connor slammed the door shut behind himself. 'I want to talk to you, Smith.'

Smith gave a violent start, but continued gently sliding the gold-framed painting into the wall. When it had disappeared he turned to face Connor. He had a down-curved mouth and – even more disturbingly – his knees, also, seemed to be in the wrong place. *If these people come from the future,* Connor thought, *why are they made differently to us?* His mind shied away from the new thought and plunged into irrelevant speculations about the kind of chairs Smith and Toynbee must use . . . if any. He realised he had seen no seats or stools about the place. With a growing coldness in his veins, Connor recalled his earlier impression that Toynbee had been standing behind the counter for hours, without moving.

'. . . welcome to what money we have,' Smith was saying, 'but there's nothing else here worth taking.'

'I don't think he's a thief.' Toynbee went and stood beside him.

'Not a thief! Then what does he want? What is . . . ?'

'Just for starters,' Connor put in, 'I want an explanation.'

'Of what?'

'Of your entire operation here.'

Smith looked mildly exasperated. He gestured at the wooden crates which filled much of the room. 'It's a perfectly normal agency set-up handling various industrial products on a . . .'

'I mean the operation whereby you supply rich people with cigarette lighters that nobody on this Earth could manufacture.'

'Cigarette lighters? I'm afraid . . .'

'The red egg-shaped ones which have no works, but they light when they're wet and stand upright without any support.'

Smith shook his head. 'I wish I *could* get into something like that.'

'And the television sets which are too good. And the clocks and cigars and all the other things which are so perfect that people who can afford it are willing to pay $864,000 every forty-three days for them – even though the goodies are charged with an essence field which fades out and converts them to junk if they fall into the hands of anybody who isn't in the club.'

'I don't understand a word of this.'

'It's no use, Mr Smith,' Toynbee said. 'Somebody has talked.'

Smith gave him a venomous stare. '*You* just did, you fool!' In his anger Smith moved closer to Toynbee, so that his body was no longer shielding the wall safe. Connor noticed for the first time that it was exceptionally large, and then it occurred to him that a basement storeroom was an odd place for that particular type of safe. He looked at it more closely. The darkness of the interior revealed no trace of the oil painting he had just seen loaded into it. And, far into the tunnel-like blackness, a bright green star was throwing off expanding rings of light, rings which faded as they grew.

Connor made a new effort to retain his grasp of the situation. He pointed at the safe and said, casually, 'I assume that's a two-way transporter.'

Smith was visibly shaken. 'All right,' he said, after a tense silence, 'who talked to you?'

'Nobody.' Connor felt he could get Angela into trouble of some kind by mentioning her name.

Toynbee cleared his throat. 'I'll bet it was that Miss Lomond. I've always said you can't trust the *nouveau riche* – the proper instincts aren't sufficiently ingrained.'

Smith nodded in agreement. 'You're right. She got a replacement table lighter, television and clock – the things this . . . person has just mentioned. She said they had been detuned by someone who broke into her house.'

'She must have told him everything she knew.'

'And broken her contract – make a note of that, Mr Toynbee.'

'Hold on a minute,' Connor said loudly, brandishing the revolver to remind them he was in control. 'Nobody's going to make a note of anything till I get the answers I want. These products you deal in – do they come from the future or somewhere?'

'From somewhere,' Smith told him. 'Actually, they come from a short distance in the future as well, but – as far as you are concerned – the important thing is that they are transported over many light years. The time difference is incidental, and quite difficult to prove.'

'They're from another planet?'

'Yes.'

'You, too?'

'Of course.'

'You bring advanced products to Earth in secret and sell or rent them to rich people?'

'Yes. Only smaller stuff comes here, of course – larger items, like the television sets, come in at main receivers in other cities. The details of the operation may be surprising, but surely the general principles of commerce are well known to you.'

'That's exactly what's bothering me,' Connor said. 'I don't give a damn about other worlds and matter transmitters, but I can't see why you go to all this trouble. Earth currency would be of no value on . . . wherever you come from. You're ahead on technology, so there's nothing . . .' Connor stopped talking as he remembered what Smith had been feeding into the black rectangle. An old oil painting.

Smith nodded, looking more relaxed. 'You are right about your currency being useless on another world. We spend it here. Human culture is primitive in many respects, but the race's artistic genius is quite remarkable, even by interstellar standards. Our organization makes a good trading surplus by exporting paintings and sculptures. You see the goods we import are comparatively worthless.'

'They seem valuable to me.'

'They *would* seem that way to you – that's the whole point. We don't bother bringing in the things that Earth can produce reasonably well. Your wines and other drinks aren't too bad, so we don't touch them. But your coffee!' Smith's mouth curved even further downwards.

'That means you're spending millions. Somebody should have noticed one outfit buying up so much stuff.'

'Not really. We do quite a bit of directing buying at auctions and galleries, but often our clients buy on our behalf and we credit their accounts.'

'Oh, no,' Connor breathed as the ramifications of what Smith was saying unfolded new vistas in his mind. Was this why millionaires, even the most unlikely types of men, so often became art collectors? Was this the *raison d'être* for that curious phenomenon, the private collection? In a society where the rich derived so much pleasure from showing off their possessions, why did so many art treasures disappear from the public view? Was it because their owners were trading them in against P-brand products? If that was the case, the organisation concerned must be huge and it must have been around for a long time. Connor's legs suddenly felt tired.

He said, 'Let's sit down and talk about this.'

Smith looked slightly uncomfortable. 'We don't sit. Why don't you use one of those crates if you aren't feeling well?'

'There's nothing wrong with me, so don't try anything,' Connor said sharply, but he sat on the edge of a box while his brain worked to assimilate shocking new concepts. 'What does the P stand for on your products?'

'Can't you guess?'

'Perfect?'

'That is correct.'

The readiness with which Smith was now giving information made Connor a little wary, but he pressed on with other questions which had been gnawing at him. 'Miss Lomond told me her instalments were $864,000 – why that particular figure? Why not a million?'

'That *is* a million – in our money. A rough equivalent, of course.'

'I see. And the forty-three days.'

'One revolution of our primary moon. It's a natural accounting period.'

Connor almost began to wish the flow of information would slow down. 'I still don't see the need for all this secrecy. Why not come out in the open, reduce your unit prices and multiply the volume? You could make a hundred times as much.'

'We have to work underground for a number of reasons. In all probability the various Earth governments would object to the loss of art treasures, and there are certain difficulties at the other end.'

'Such as?'

'There's a law against influencing events on worlds which are at a sensitive stage of their development. This limits our supply of trade goods very sharply.'

'In other words, you are crooks on your own world and crooks on this one.'

'I don't agree. What harm do we do on Earth?'

'You've already named it – you are depriving the people of this planet of . . .'

'Of their artistic heritage?' Smith gave a thin sneer. 'How many people do you know who would give up a Perfect television set to keep a da Vinci cartoon in a public art gallery five or ten thousand miles away?'

'You've got a point there,' Connor admitted. 'What have you got up your sleeve, Smith?'

'I don't understand.'

'Don't play innocent. You wouldn't have talked so freely unless you were certain I wouldn't get out of here with the information. What are you planning to do about me?'

Smith glanced at Toynbee and sighed. 'I keep forgetting how parochial the natives of a single-planet culture can be. You have been told that we are from another world, and yet to you we are just slightly unusual Earth people. I don't suppose it has occurred to you that other races could have a stronger instinct towards honesty, that deviousness and lies would come less easily to them than to humans?'

'That's where we are most vulnerable,' Toynbee put in. 'I see now that I was too inexperienced to be up front.'

'All right, then – be honest with me,' Connor said. 'You are planning to keep me quiet, aren't you?'

'As a matter of fact, we do have a little device . . .'

'You don't need it,' Connor said. He thought back carefully over all he had been told, then stood up and handed his revolver to Smith.

The good life was all that he had expected it to be, and – as he drove south to Avalon – Connor could feel it getting better by the minute.

His business sense had always been sharp, but whereas he had once reckoned a month's profits in thousands, he now thought in terms of six figures. Introductions, opportunities and deals came thick and fast, and always it was the P-brand artifacts which magically paved the way. During important first contacts he had only to use his gold lighter to ignite a pipeful of P-brand tobacco – the incredible leaf which fulfilled all the promise of its 'nose', or glance at his P-brand watch, or write with the pen which produced any colour at the touch of a spectrum ring, and all doors were opened wide. The various beautiful trinkets were individually styled, but he quickly learned to recognise them when they were displayed by others, and to make the appropriate responses.

Within a few weeks, although he was scarcely aware of it, his outlook on life had undergone a profound change. At first he was merely uneasy or suspicious when approached by people who failed to show the talismen. Then he became hostile, preferring to associate only with those who could prove they were safe.

Satisfying though his new life was, Connor had decided it would not be perfect until Angela and he were reunited. It was through her that he had achieved awareness and only through her would he achieve completeness. He would have made the journey to Avalon much sooner but for the fact that there had been certain initial difficulties with Smith and Toynbee. Handing over the revolver had been a dangerous gambit which had almost resulted in his being bundled through their matter transmitter to an unknown fate on another world. Luckily, however, it had also convinced them that he had something important to say.

He had talked quickly and well that evening in the basement of the undistinguished little store. Smith, who was the senior of the pair, had been hard to convince; but his interest had quickened as Connor enumerated all the weaknesses in the organisation's procurement methods. And it had grown feverish when he heard how Connor's worldly know-how would eliminate much of the wasteful financial competition of auctions, would streamline the system of purchasing through rich clients, would institute foolproof controls and effective new techniques for diverting art treasures into the organisation's hands. It had been the best improvisation of his life, sketchy in places because of his unfamiliarity with the art world, but filled with an inspired professionalism which carried his audience along with it.

Early results had been so good that Smith had become possessive, voicing objections to Connor's profitable side dealings. Connor smoothed things over by going on to a seven-day work schedule in which he also worked most evenings. This had made it difficult to find the time to visit Angela, but finally his need to see her had become so great that he had pushed everything else aside and made the time . . .

The guard at the gate lodge was the same man as before, but he gave no sign of remembering his earlier brush with Connor. He waved the car on through with a minimum of delay, and a few minutes later Connor was walking up the broad front steps of the house. The place looked much less awesome to Connor but, while ringing for admission, he decided that he and Angela would probably keep it, for sentimental reasons as much as anything else. The butler who answered the door was a new man, who looked rather like a retired seaman, and there was a certain lack of smoothness in his manner as he showed Connor to the large room where Angela was waiting. She was standing at the fireplace with her back to the door, just as he had last seen her.

'Angie,' he said, 'it's good to see you again.'

She turned and ran to him. 'I've missed you so much, Phil.'

As they clung together in the centre of the green-and-silver room, Connor experienced a moment of exquisite happiness. He buried his face in her hair and began whispering the things he had been unable to say for what seemed a long, long time. Angela answered him feverishly all the while he spoke, responding to the emotion rather than the words.

It was during the first kiss that he became aware of a disturbing fact. She was wearing expensive yet ordinary perfume – not one of the P-brand distillations of magic to which he had become accustomed on the golden creatures he had dated casually in the past few weeks. Still holding Angela close to him, he glanced around the big room, and a leaden coldness began to spread through his body. Everything in the room was, like her perfume, excellent – but not Perfect.

'Angela,' he said quietly, 'why did you ask me to come here?'

'What kind of a question is that, darling?'

'It's a perfectly normal question.' Connor disengaged from her and stepped back suspiciously. 'I merely asked what your motives were.'

'*Motives!*' Angela stared at him, colour fleeing from her cheeks, then her gaze darted to his wristwatch. 'My God, Philip, you're *in!* You made it, just like you said you would.'

'I don't know what you mean.'

'Don't try that with me – remember I was the one who told it all to you.'

'You should have learned not to talk by this time.'

'I know I should, but I didn't.' Angela advanced on him. 'I'm out now. I'm on the outside.'

'It isn't all that bad, is it? Where's Bobby Janke and the rest of his crowd?'

'None of them come near me now. And you know why.'
'At least you're not broke.'
She shook her head. 'I've got plenty of money, but what good is it when I can't buy the things I want? I'm shut out, and it's all because I couldn't keep myself from blabbing to you, and because I didn't report the way you were getting on to them. But you didn't mind informing on me, did you?'
Connor opened his mouth to protest his innocence, then realised it would make no difference. 'It's been nice seeing you again, Angela,' he said. 'I'm sorry I can't stay longer but things are stacking up on me back at the office. You know how it is.'
'I know exactly how it is. Go on, Philip - take yourself out of here.'
Connor crossed to the door, but hesitated as Angela made a faint sound.
She said, 'Stay with me, Phil. Please stay.'
He stood with his back to her, experiencing a pain which slowly faded, then he walked out.

Late that afternoon Connor was sitting in his new office when his secretary put through a call. It was Smith, anxious to discuss the acquisition of a collection of antique silver.
'I called you earlier but your girl told me you were out,' he said, with a hint of reproach.
'It's true,' Connor assured him. 'I was out of town - Angela Lomond asked me down to her place.'
'Oh?'
'You didn't tell me she was no longer a client.'
'You should have known without being told.' Smith was silent for a few seconds. 'Is she going to try making trouble?'
'No.'
'What did she want?'
Connor leaned back in his chair and gazed out through the window, towards the Atlantic. 'Who knows? I didn't stay long enough to find out.'
'Very wise,' Smith said complacently.
When the call had ended, Connor brewed some P-brand

coffee, using the supply he kept locked in the drinks cabinet, and the perfection of it soothed from his mind all the last lingering traces of remorse.

How on Earth, he wondered idly, *do they manage to make it taste exactly the way it smells?*

5 – PHILIP E HIGH: The Jackson Killer

Philip Empson High was born in Biggleswade, Bedfordshire, on April 28th, 1914. Shortly after, the family moved to Kent, where he still lives. It was there during his school holidays in the August of 1927 that he discovered the sf magazines, and a whole new world opened to him. Thereafter he devoured all he found, and, eventually, despairing that his favourite authors seemed to be ignoring various aspects of the genre, he started to write himself. The first story to sell, *The Statics*, appeared in the September 1955 *Authentic*. Unlike his fellow authors, High came late to writing sf, and his fiction reflects the years of experience behind him. He has been a commercial traveller, an insurance agent, a reporter, a salesman and is now a bus driver, which, he says, suits him admirably. During the war he served in the Royal Navy.

Fiction appeared with increasing regularity over the ensuing decade, although the diminution of the British market in the late 1960s meant fewer of his stories appeared. As a consequence he sold several novels to the American paperback market, some of which have since appeared in this country. Most notable amongst them are *The Prodigal Sun* (1964), *No Truce With Terra* (1964), *Reality Forbidden* (1967), and his most recent *Speaking of Dinosaurs* (1974).

For High's own favourite short story we go back to the May 1961 *New Worlds* and *The Jackson Killer*. High says:

> 'No writer worthy of his salt is ever satisfied with his own work. This story, however, almost hit the target from my own personal standard. Further, I enjoyed writing it and can still read it without wincing.'

THE JACKSON KILLER

Philip E High

Lassen spun the glass slowly in his hand, watching the tiny whirlpool in the wine. He did not really care for alcohol, local or imported, but it served a purpose. One sipped, one looked lonely and one waited.

He glanced casually at the noisy party at the nearby table. One of the women was beginning to wear the look, the kind of look Colonial women wear when they see a lonely stranger.

Colonial hospitality, God bless it, it saved a lot of work.

He caught the woman's eye and smiled. A careful smile which was neither suggestive or arrogant but reserved, friendly and a little shy. He had practised it successfully on many occasions and it would serve his purpose now.

He waited, staring at his glass, his face intent as if lost in thought.

Lassen was handsome in a taughtly aristocratic kind of way, smooth, well groomed and the bleakness in his eyes was only visible in a certain light at a certain angle. A vaguely repellent quality is something an Eliminator acquires and must learn to hide successfully.

'Excuse me,' said a voice at his elbow.

Lassen started slightly as if surprised. 'Yes?' *One of the men, a big red faced specimen in a shiny suit.*

'Thought you might like to join us.' *The fellow was grinning like an ape, close relative, no doubt.* 'Saw you were a stranger. Hate you to think the people of Kaylon were unfriendly, plenty of room at our table.'

Lassen looked pleasantly surprised, a little emotional but still faintly reserved. The correct reactions in the correct order for a given situation.

'How kind, but I would not dream of intruding on a purely private –'

'Private, hell, on Kaylon nothing is private. Come on, join us.'

'Well, if you are quite sure –'

He permitted himself to be led to the table and introduced. They found a vacant chair, filled a glass and pressed food upon him.

He gave a clever impression of slowly unbending and even laughed moderately at some of the jokes but he was sighing inwardly. Colonials were always the same, brash, crude, hungry for an Earth they had never seen and infected with a vague sense of inferiority. Nonetheless he had to bear with them, they were part of the job, just as this alleged place of amusement was part of the job. What better place to start the rot than the principle night spot of a Colonial city. Long experience had taught him that rumour, *his* kind of rumour, would spread like wildfire on a pioneer planet. It was more effective than the most modern forms of communication and far quicker; in a few hours even the remotest posts in the Backlands would have it in detail.

One chose the spot, started the rumour and waited. It was as simple as that.

His orders assured him that the prey was on this boisterous half-developed planet. It was just a question of dropping the right word in the right place and smoking him out.

He had to endure nearly two hours of banal merriment and pioneer 'shop' before the chance came.

'Staying on Kaylon long, Mr Lassen?' It was Dirk, the red-faced fellow in the shiny out-dated evening dress.

'Not long, Mr Dirk. Once my business is cleared up I shall be on my way.'

'Oh, you have business here? I thought you were waiting ship connections.'

'No, definitely business and very important.'

'What kind of business, if that's not a leading question?' Hunter, a wizened little man with a limp moustache.

'I am an Eliminator, Mr Hunter.'

'Eliminator!' They stared at him.

'I suppose you mean pests,' said Hunter finally. 'But we don't have much here, apart from the tiger-rats which will take another hundred years to control.'

Lassen pushed his empty plate to one side. 'I don't kill pests, Mr Hunter – I kill men.'

Their open mouths and wide eyes echoed the words soundlessly. 'Men – he kills *men*.'

A coldness seemed to fall on their faces, the red lips of the women thinned and, without moving, they seemed to draw away from him.

'Bluntly you are a paid assassin?' The words were spoken by a slender, dark-haired man who had been introduced to him as David Kearsney.

'Not an assassin, sir, a government agent from the Eliminator Corps.'

'A flowery title for the same thing, isn't it?' Kearsney's face was cold. 'You kill men.'

Lassen sipped his wine. 'Only a certain type of man – I'm a Jackson killer.'

There was a strained silence then someone laughed a little nervously. 'My name's Jackson.'

Lassen made a deprecating gesture. 'You confuse a name with a social malaise.' He looked about him. 'The work of the Corps is necessary, just as the elimination of pests is necessary.'

'Governments, and their agents, can always justify their excesses on reasonable grounds,' said Dirk bitterly. 'But as far as you rate with us here, you're a paid gun-slinger.'

'I have my duty, I do it.'

'Oh, spare us *that* one. That was the plea of war criminals back in pre-space days. Today a man must answer to his own conscience, his own conceptions of right and wrong, or did you eliminate those first?'

Lassen looked at them coldly. 'I see by your expressions you are unfamiliar with the Proxeta Uprising. I would respectfully suggest that an outline of Galactic history should be added to your school curriculum before passing judgment. As reasonable men, you must see that capital punishment cannot exist without an executioner.'

'You enjoy your work presumably.'

Lassen frowned. He had not expected a question like that on a pioneer world. It was altogether too penetrating and savoured slightly of interrogation.

'I object to that remark, Mr Kearsney.' Lassen rose and bowed slightly. 'Thank you for your hospitality and good-night.' He turned and strode towards the door.

For some time after he had gone, no one spoke.

'An assassin,' said Dirk, finally. He looked miserably about him. 'I'm sorry, I never suspected –'

'It was my idea,' said his wife quickly.

'No one is to blame – God!' Hunter tugged angrily at his moustache. 'We all made a fuss of him.'

'I think,' said Dirk, 'someone should see the ladies home, this is something we should talk over.'

When they had gone, Hunter sat down and said: 'Well?' He looked slightly perplexed.

Dirk scowled at him. 'Don't say "well" like that. The obvious question is – what are we going to *do*?'

'Do?'

'Do about *him*. He's come to Kaylon to kill someone, one of us, we've got to stop him.'

'Easy, now.' Hunter looked alarmed. 'Don't go rushing into things, he's a trained killer. Further, he's a government agent and the law is on his side.'

'Did you see him produce anything to prove it?' Dirk was almost shouting. 'In any case why did he relish telling us so much?'

'I should think that was fairly obvious.' Kearsney was leaning back in his chair, frowning slightly. 'He *wanted* us to talk about it. You know how quickly such a story would spread, eventually Jackson – whoever Jackson is – would hear about it. A normal man – and we assume Jackson is a normal man – would either run or betray himself by trying to eliminate the eliminator. It's no good keeping silent about it, in the first place we may not be the first people he's told and in the second the women know. The story will probably reach Jackson before we leave the room.'

Hunter rose. 'A call to Central Information wouldn't be out of place, would it?' He pushed his chair angrily under the table. 'I've never *heard* of the Proxeta Uprising.'

'Check on Jackson while you're at it,' Dirk called after him.

Hunter entered the booth frowning. Dirk was a good fellow, a reliable friend and all that sort of thing but too damned impetuous. His type of reaction could get them all killed, there were limits to Colonial loyalties. Not that he didn't understand, it was just Dirk's way of rushing things.

He dialled CI and scowled at the mouthpiece of the caller. Lassen's words had implied an ignorance they had been unable to refute. How the hell could they be expected to know about an uprising in another part of the galaxy? Terran history and their own ten generation colonisation programme had been all their educators had considered necessary. True, the CI memory banks contained the entire knowledge of the Empire but there just wasn't the *time* to use it. Despite a ten generation colony, three large cities and a twelve million population, Kaylon was *still* a beach-head. You had to *fight* to stay on it. Beyond the cities and the roadways, there were still the jungles and, of course, the tiger-rats. In the Backlands you lived behind the barrier screens and if you went out, you used an armoured vehicle.

'Central Information,' said a pleasant recorded voice. 'Subject, please.'

When he returned to his table they looked at him expectantly.

'I got some but not all.' Hunter lowered himself into his chair and reached for the whisky. 'The Proxeta Uprising was an attempt by ten worlds in sector 72 to set up an independent autonomy outside the Empire. The attempt was opposed for the obvious economic and military reasons and developed into major war which lasted nearly five years.' He paused and sipped his drink. 'If it's any help, the instigator and self-style leader of the insurgent forces was a man named Howard F. Jackson.'

'Jackson, eh?, Dirk pulled at his chin, frowning. 'Where does that get us?'

'Nowhere. What we're looking for is not classified under the Jackson heading. When I tried, CI simply referred me back to the uprising. As the original Jackson was executed for war crimes over sixty years ago, Lassen, obviously, is looking for someone or something else.'

'He could be looking for a symbol,' said Dirk in a thoughtful voice. 'Something which the original Jackson embodied or represented.'

'I formed the same opinion.' Hunter drained his glass and lit a cigarette. 'Jackson was regarded by his followers as a superman.'

'Superman!' Dirk scowled at the other without seeing him. 'Here on Kaylon! Surely we should have got wind of him?'

'If I were a superman,' said Kearsney in a soft voice, 'I'd lie low until I was ready to make myself felt.'

Hunter nodded quickly. 'Makes sense that, damn good sense.'

Dirk reached for the nearest bottle. 'And what do we do about our superman, assuming of course, our guess is right?'

'What the hell are we supposed to do?' Hunter's voice was suddenly challenging.

Dirk flushed angrily. 'Damn it, he's one of us isn't he?'

'Easy, easy.' Kearsney's voice was soothing but firm. 'We want to know why Lassen wants him first.'

'I couldn't agree more.' Hunter was looking angry and nervous. 'You can carry this pioneer-unity-stuff too far. It's all very well talking of covering or aiding him just because he's one of us but we've got to *think* first. In the first place we'd be putting ourselves on the wrong side of Galactic law. In the second – and to be frank – I don't fancy tangling with a trained killer. I've done my share of fighting in the Backlands but this is something we might not come out of alive if we don't use our heads.'

'You make a good point,' Dirk admitted grudgingly. 'But it goes against the grain, very much so.' He frowned at his empty glass and refilled it. 'I suppose this eliminator business is on the level?'

Hunter nodded slowly. 'I'm afraid so, yes. I checked CI. There is, definitely, a government, or more correctly, a military organisation known as the Elimination Corps.'

Dirk shook his head slowly. 'A murder squad – you can call it that, can't you? In this day and age it doesn't seem possible – what the hell do they *do*?'

Hunter smiled at him twistedly. 'The same as Lassen told us – they kill Jacksons.'

Lassen lay on his bed, the thin handsome face intent and thoughtful. He was almost fully dressed but his body in the neat, one-piece suit was completely relaxed.

The Eliminator was waiting. He had removed his shoes and loosened his collar but these were the only mild relaxations he permitted himself.

The hotel room, like the man, was neat and uncluttered, with personal belongings in their proper places. The smart carry-case open at the foot of the bed suggested only that he was about to pack and only an astute observer would have noticed the slight bulge beneath the sheet and close to his right hand.

Lassen was thinking about Jackson. Sooner or later the rumour would reach him and the man would react. His name might be Smith, Hereward, Brown, anything, but he would know what the news meant instantly. Only a Jackson would know he was a Jackson because only a Jackson would spend day after day in CI absorbing knowledge like a sponge and, in so doing, would learn about *himself*.

When Jackson heard there was an Eliminator on the planet, there were only two courses open to him, fight or run because he would know straight away that hiding from an Eliminator was out of the question. Neither solution was a happy one, however clever you were, fighting a trained man backed by the scientific know-how of an entire Empire was not a job with the odds in your favour.

Escape, on the other hand, was even less attractive. Every planet, however advanced, has only one escape route – the ferry ports. To get off the planet, you had to take the ferry, there was no other way and preventing such attempts was almost too easy. All one needed was a stellar shipping list, the ferry wouldn't blast off until a ship was in orbit. No, in point of fact, a planet had only one escape route, one rat-run, which was too easy to plug.

The alternative, therefore, was to kill the Eliminator and then run; hoping to put light years behind you before his successor took up the chase.

In his time, Lassen had experienced a variety of attacks, most of them ingenius and all doomed to failure. A single individual pitting his skill against the scientific knowledge of an Empire was a task even a Jackson couldn't handle.

Lassen smiled to himself. That was the trouble with Jacksons, they were too smart for their own good and, worse, most of them were only half-Jacksons. A *real* Jackson would place himself in a position where the chance of detection and subsequent elimination was almost an impossibility.

The neat carry-case at the foot of the bed purred softly and instantly he was tense. His right hand slid beneath the sheet, gripping the butt of the Pheeson Pistol, his left hand twisted the buckle of his belt activating the personal deflector screen.

'Postal service,' said a pleasant recorded voice. 'A parcel for Mr. Lassen.'

Something thudded into the delivery basket.

Lassen eyed the small package warily and without moving. The automatic postal system was more than thorough and would automatically reject explosives but there were quite a number of lethal devices requiring no explosives whatever. He had seen deadly little clockwork mechanisms firing poison needles by compressed air, 'treated' papers which killed the careless by impregnation through the skin . . .

'Postal service,' said the voice again. 'A parcel for Mr Lassen.'

There was a second plop in the delivery basket.

Lassen stiffened. A tiny pin-point of brilliant light had appeared which began to expand like a minor sun.

At the foot of the bed, the carry-case hissed and began to vibrate slightly. Forces rushed from it, blanketing the heat and the light and crushing them backwards. There was an impression of suffocation and growing weakness. The brilliant light seemed to fall in on itself, turned to a dull red which faded to blackness and a few grey whisps of smoke.

Lassen rose slowly and crossed the room. The delivery basket still dripped hot metal but the charred mass within it was completely dead.

He shook his head thoughtfully. Clever, quite clever, two parcels, probably despatched from widely different points but timed to arrive within seconds of each other. Each parcel was, of course, harmless in itself but deadly when brought together. Altogether it was an ingenious method of getting reactives into critical contact through the carefully vetted postal system.

He nodded to himself with satisfaction. This one was a *real* Jackson. Further, and far more important, the reaction had been swift which meant only one thing, he was in the city. He might even have been in the same room, possibly among those at the table to take counter action so swiftly.

Lassen shrugged. The auto-senders recorded details of their users as a protection against loss or fraud; tracing Jackson or his stooges required only an examination of the records.

He stroked his chin thoughtfully. Routine, once the prey reacted he betrayed himself and that was the end. Not that this fellow wasn't far above average, his reactions had been swift but with precise and careful planning but, like all Jacksons, there was the inevitable weakness. It was characteristic that they would concede a technical superiority because it was the product of a joint effort but never, no *never* the superior intelligence of the operator and that was where they lost the fight.

Lassen lit a cigarette and crossed the room. Having made the first move, Jackson would, at the same time, be preparing for escape. All he, Lassen, had to do was plug the rat hole.

He touched a button. 'Hello? Ferry port? Can you give me the date and time of the next stellar liner, please?'

Hunter opened the door of his apartment half-way and hesitated. 'Oh, hello, Dirk,' he said a little ungraciously. 'Something important?'

'It's about Jackson.'

'Now look – if you've got some crazy scheme, count me out, we'll have that cleared up from the start.'

Dirk scowled at him. 'It's merely information – information which I don't intend to talk about in the passage. Do you mind?'

'Oh, very well.' Hunter stood aside with obvious reluctance. 'Come in.' He waved his hand at the nearest chair. 'Make yourself at home, I'll dial you a drink – whisky as usual?'

'Thanks.' Dirk dropped into the chair and fumbled for a cigarette. 'Careful aren't you?'

'I prefer to call it sensible.' Hunter passed the drink. 'A difference of opinion, that's all.' He sat down. 'What is this information?'

Dirk puffed at the cigarette. 'I know about Jackson, all there is to know, everything, that is, except his identity.'

'The hell you do – where did you get it?'

'CI,' Dirk sipped his drink with faint complacence. 'I checked the psychiatric section, the master-selector soon cottoned on to what I wanted after a few questions.' He gulped his drink and put down the empty glass. 'A Jackson is a mutant primary.'

Hunter, who had just finished dialling for another drink, nearly dropped the glass. 'Mutant! I thought all those yarns about monsters was an exploded myth? This is on the level?'

Dirk looked at him directly. 'Absolutely.' He picked up

the second drink and scowled at it absently. 'As Lassen reminded us, we don't avail ourselves of CI enough and now that I have I rather wish I hadn't – we're *all* mutants.'

Hunter was suddenly a little pale. 'How come?'

Dirk shrugged. 'The early days of atomics, the unshielded ships when we began to challenge space.' He sighed. 'According to CI eighty-seven per cent of the human race are mutant.' He found another cigarette and lit it quickly. 'Naturally the most complex part of the body suffered first – the brain. Nearly all of us have – what shall I call it? – abnormal additions.'

'I don't feel any different.' Hunter laughed weakly and without humour.

'You shouldn't, your abnormality is latent, you are not a primary, that's the difference between you and – Jackson.'

'And just what is a Jackson?' Hunter was patently relieved.

'A human being with an incomprehensible IQ – in short, a superman.'

Hunter frowned at him. 'What's wrong with having a few supermen around?'

Dirk shrugged. 'Unfortunately and, it seems, inevitably, they're all raging paranoics. The original Jackson had a staggering IQ, incredible qualities both of leadership and organisation and the unshakable conviction he was the Chosen Saviour of Mankind.' Dirk shook his head, frowning. 'He nearly succeeded in proving it too, his ten planet autonomy nearly licked the Empire.'

'And there's no cure?'

'None. Conditioning leaves a drooling idiot which is crueller than execution, putting them in prison is too uncertain to be worth risking.'

Hunter picked up his drink, frowned at it, and put it down again without drinking it. 'That justifies Lassen or does it?'

Dirk made a helpless movement with his hands. 'I'm neither moralist nor philosopher – ten million died in the Proxeta Uprising.'

Hunter sipped the drink without tasting it. 'So somewhere on Kaylon is a Jackson; now we know the truth I think that lets us out.'

Dirk gulped his drink and banged down the glass. 'Of course, you'd love that kind of loyalty if *you* were Jackson, wouldn't you? And who the hell am I to argue with you.' He strode to the door which opened at his approach. 'I can see I've been wasting my time here, perhaps elsewhere I can find a colonist with guts and –'

The door slid shut behind him cutting off the final words.

Hunter frowned briefly, then shrugged. Poor old Dirk, in ten minutes he would calm down and begin to think for himself. Tomorrow, no doubt, he would be back, red faced and apologetic. Somehow you couldn't help liking him despite his tantrums and impetuosity.

Hunter's thoughts turned to more important matters. Dirk's information explained a lot of things, particularly the compulsory time-wasting psychiatric checks which one suffered twice every year. The authorities were not only checking for Jacksons but were determined to nip them in the bud before they developed. Was that why Lawson, Meeker and several more had been taken away for specialist treatment immediately after their checks? He rather thought it might be.

There were still important questions unanswered. What turned a normal into a primary, a potential into an active?

Thoughtfully he pressed the caller button and dialled Central Information.

The answers were detailed but obscure and boiled down to two factors comprehensible to the layman – intense emotional shock and *conditions and environment conducive to paranoia.*

Hunter thought about it. Did the peculiar social order of short-term office applicable to the whole Empire depend on that one factor. One could become a President, Mayor, Minister, General or Executive but *only for six months.* After which the constitution and galactic law demanded that one stepped down for another leader to assume the mantle of power.

It was said that absolute power corrupts and a sustained position of absolute power might be considered as conducive to paranoia. A man entrusted too long with power might come to believe in his own God-like qualities and so develop into a Jackson.

The explanation, of course, might not be the right one but certainly went a long way to account for a dithery administration and infuriating policy changes. The short-term-office was beginning to make sense at last.

Hunter sighed and sat down. He supposed, in due course, he'd hear what had happened and who the Jackson had been. He hoped to God it was not one of his friends. The thought made him warm slightly towards Dirk who, no doubt, was at this moment, trying to bamboozle some other unfortunate into some impractical rescue scheme.

It was a good guess. Dirk was working hard on Kearsney.

'I'm sorry, Dirk.' Kearsney shook his head slowly. 'I don't think this business really concerns me. Remember, I'm not a colonist I'm an immigrant, I've only been here two years.'

'You're splitting hairs, we took you in, made you one of us, you're just making –' Dirk's rather hectoring voice trailed suddenly into silence, he was staring past Kearsney and into the small bedroom. When he spoke again his tone was friendly and almost too casual. 'Going on a holiday?'

Kearsney glanced at the half packed cases and said, easily, 'Oh those – No, not a holiday, old chap, a Backlands job, some sort of administrative muddle at Salzport.'

Dirk lit a cigarette. 'The floater for Salzport,' he said in a detached voice, 'left eight hours ago. There won't be another for ten days.'

'Really?' Kearsney's teeth gleamed briefly in an unreal smile. 'I shall have to wait then, I must have got hold of an old timetable by mistake.'

'Yes, you must.' Dirk leaned against the wall and stared

into the bedroom. 'You don't pack stellar cases for the Backlands.'

'I do – any objection?'

Dirk exhaled smoke. 'Panzer-grubs will eat everything but the locks before you've been there thirty minutes.'

'That's *my* worry.' Kearsney crossed the room and removed a suit from a wall cupboard. 'We'll have a chat some other time, eh? I'm rather busy just now – do you mind?'

Dirk detached himself from the wall. 'Sure, even *I* can take a very broad hint.' At the door he turned. 'Good luck, Dave. He'll get no help from us and, if we can find a way of obstructing him, we'll do a damn thorough job.' The door slid shut behind him.

He left Kearsney staring unseeingly before him. So Dirk knew, or thought he knew, exactly how things stood. Under the bluster and impetuosity was an astute and singularly observant man, not many would have spotted those cases and drawn the right conclusions. His loyalties too, although misplaced, were not only understandable but peculiar to colonies in general. He understood clearly how easy it must have been for Howard F. Jackson to weld ten planets into formidable unity. Colonies were fertile soil for insurrection, not because they disliked Earth but by circumstance. Fighting to stay put on a hostile world bred more than ordinary ties of unity, you fought with and for your neighbour and learned that unless you did you both perished. This, of course, bred an attitude of my-neighbour-right-or-wrong and the outsider took the can back.

The 'Prodge' rang, interrupting his train of thought and he flicked the receptor switch irritably. What now?

'Taking a trip, Mr Kearsney?' The projected three-dimensional image of Lassen looked meaningly at the cases.

Kearsney shrugged, bluff was obviously out of the question. 'You didn't waste any time,' he said, evenly.

'Tracing your stooges was not difficult.' The projection paused to light a cigarette. 'That was quite a neat trick with the reactives but I'm afraid you won't get another chance. No time. Will you give yourself up or do you prefer to do things the hard way?'

Kearsney made a small movement with his hand. 'The hard way.'

Lassen smiled faintly. 'Excellent, I was afraid you might disappoint me. Where will it be?'

'I'll meet you in the hills somewhere along Eastern Highway at noon, tomorrow.'

'And you hope to rid yourself of me in a duel?'

'That is the general idea.' Kearsney's voice was expressionless.

'Time and date could be significant.'

Kearsney shrugged. 'You've probably worked that one out for yourself. The ferry lifts at 3 pm standard time, if I win I have time to make the ferry.'

'And you believe you'll win?'

Kearsney's jaw set stubbornly. 'I can hope.'

The other stared at him for a long second before speaking. 'Hope is a luxury you cannot really afford, Mr Kearsney.'

There was a faint click and the projection vanished.

Lassen climbed into the ground car without haste and re-checked the dials on the additional facia. He had spent six hours on the vehicle and was satisfied that the changes he had made were sufficiently comprehensive to take care of most contingencies.

This Jackson was well above the average and it was unlikely that he would depend solely on his own skill with weapons. An Eliminator thought ahead and was prepared for eventualities before they arose.

Lassen touched the starter button, pressed the thrust pedal and felt the wheel-less vehicle roll smoothly forward on its cushion of air.

After ten minutes driving, his instruments told him that he was being followed. A second vehicle was hanging doggedly on his tail a cautious two miles to his rear.

He shrugged. Colonists, probably labouring under the delusion they could help the fugitive when the shooting started. Well they would not be the first natives to obstruct the course of justice and get themselves killed along with the fugitive they were trying to aid.

The car jerked suddenly as his additional braking system took over and slithered to a halt.

A bare hundred feet in front of him a needle of white flame leapt a hundred feet into the air leaving a wide shallow crater.

Lassen switched the braking system to normal and approached the point of the explosion cautiously. It had been close, his instruments had detected and detonated the booby trap only just in time, another second . . .

Through the window of the car he studied the crater, frowning. The device itself was obsolete but the means gave one pause for thought. Only one explosive would leave a burnished effect in the crater and that was Trachonite.

Lassen frowned. It was difficult to imagine an unstable substance like trachonite being manufactured outside a fully equipped laboratory, yet this Jackson had not only constructed it but compressed the unstable elements into a pill-size device which could be tossed casually from a car window.

Lassen's wariness, if not his respect, increased considerably.

After another three minutes driving, he stopped the car and cut the motor.

He was now deep into the brown boulder-strewn slopes of the hills and a good forty miles from the city. Somewhere within the next two or three miles he decided, Jackson would be lying in wait.

Lassen leaned forward and began to manipulate his search instruments. Within three minutes he picked up a heart-beat and, a few seconds later, a respiration pattern.

Carefully he triangulated the position, picked up the rada-binoculars and studied the rising slopes to the left of the highway. Hum, yes, prone between the two large boulders at the top of the slope. Not a very subtle position really, open ground yes, but a more experienced fighter would have chosen a position with limited approaches which could be booby-trapped. Open ground, although providing no cover, made such devices worthless.

Right, distance one mile, two hundred and sixty-four feet, he'd walk out and take this on his two feet.

Lassen prepared himself without haste. He strapped on the thigh holster, adjusted the buckles of the deflector belt and stepped out of the car, carefully locking it behind him.

He gave no thought to the car which had been trailing him. He had already dismissed them mentally as 'natives'. As such they would not possess weapons worth worrying about, a Corps deflector screen would take care of any type of portable weapon. They might, of course, attempt to sabotage his car. Well, they could try. Kicking aside the charred bodies when he returned would not worry him unduly.

There was a sudden thud and some sort of missile kicked up a spurt of dust at the side of the road.

Lassen shrugged indifferently, left the road and began to walk up the rocky slopes. There was no hurry and in any case he had to wait. The Pheeson pistol, although limited in range, could be fired effectively from inside a deflector screen. At five hundred feet the weapon would make short work of the Jackson and the huge rock behind which he thought he was hiding.

A bullet slapped suddenly into the screen and went whining away into the distance.

Lassen smiled with faint contempt and paused to light a cigarette. He always rather enjoyed this part. In a few minutes no doubt Jackson would switch his weapon to automatic and fire long frantic bursts in a futile effort to stop him.

Another bullet slapped into the screen, then another and another.

At the tenth direct hit a compact mechanism strapped to his wrist began to chatter shrilly urgently.

A little stiffly Lassen raised his left arm and stared at the instrument, a coldness seemed to be rising upwards from the pit of his stomach. It wasn't possible, it just wasn't *possible.*

The tiny finger of the dial refuted the denial with precise indifference, it was already quivering uncertainly on the red danger line.

The coldness in Lassen's stomach seemed to rise upwards and embrace his heart. The bullets were 'rigged', they carried some minute energy-sapping device which drew power away from the screen every time they hit.

With dull resignation Lassen realised he had passed the point of no return. The prey was still beyond the range of his Pheeson pistol and he would be cut down before he could run back. There were no rocks behind which to take cover while he made adjustments and circuit changes to strengthen the screen –

He broke into a stumbling run towards the distant rocks, knowing that with this Jackson he had lost.

Dully his mind tried to find reasons. There was *nothing* capable of breaking a Corp deflector screen, if there was . . .

He was only beginning to understand when the twentieth bullet penetrated the weakening screen and exploded in his lungs.

Kearsney walked slowly down the slopes and stood staring down at the still body.

In death Lassen seemed to have lost his arrogance and the face was calm and peaceful like that of a sleeping child.

Kearsney shook his head slowly, only half aware of shouts in the distance.

'Wake up, Dave, over here.'

He turned slowly. On the distant road a figure stood waving by a dilapidated ground car.

'Over here – over here. We can get you to the ferry with minutes to spare.'

When he reached them, he saw that Hunter was crouched over the wheel and that Dirk was holding the door open in readiness.

'You killed him.' Hunter's voice was awed. 'You took an Eliminator.'

'We'll destroy both cars later,' said Dirk. 'If someone follows up on the next ship they'll have a hard job deducing the real facts. No one on this planet will volunteer information, you can sleep easy on that point.'

Kearsney heard himself say: 'You'll have to blow up Lassen's car, it's probably booby trapped.'

'We'll fix that – get in.'

Kearsney glanced back once as the car rolled swiftly down the winding road. 'You couldn't arrange a quiet burial for him, could you?'

'Burial!' Dirk stared at him, his expression almost outraged. 'What the hell for? We don't want to draw attention to this business when another killer comes. In any case, panzer-grubs will have had the body, including the bones, inside twelve hours. Burial!' He snorted. 'What *for*?'

'He died in the line of duty, isn't that enough?'

Dirk laughed harshly. 'When I start thinking of last rites for murderers I'll be going soft in the head.'

Kearsney shrugged. He wasn't getting through and never would. He supposed in a way it was understandable, the outsider saw only one side of the coin. Yet, could they but realise it, up there in those hills lay the body of a dedicated man or, if you preferred it, a hero.

A man whose dangerous business it had been to hunt down the intellectual wild beasts who had somehow evaded the careful psychiatric checks and risen later to threaten the structure of society.

Wild beasts which local authorities were ill-equipped to handle and could not subdue without the loss of many good men and countless innocent people.

Wild beasts who, in the last eight hundred years, had presented an account for eighty-seven million lives.

He realised suddenly that the car had stopped and Dirk was helping him out.

'Told you we'd do it, you've got sixteen minutes.'

Kearsney glanced back at the distant hills. Yes, a hero, selected, as all Eliminators were selected, not for their cold blooded capacity for killing but for their *dedication to the race of man*.

An Eliminator knew he was doomed from the moment he signed the necessary papers.

There was no short-term-office in the Eliminator Corps for, after the first few killings, he was too mentally shocked to retire with his own conscience.

After a few more, he had passed the point of no return and become to believe in his own God-like immunity.

Throughout the Empire there was no task so demanding and no walk of life *so conducive to paranoia.* Inevitably the agent moved from latent to positive and became as those he was ordered to destroy.

The Corps, who kept a tight check on its personnel, knew when an agent's usefulness was past and he was given what appeared to be a routine assignment.

Dully he heard his own voice say: 'Thank you both, thank you.'

Yes, an assignment which seemed routine but was actually a decoy job. A job like this one with someone waiting at the other end.

'Yes, yes, goodbye – goodbye –'

The Jackson killer turned slowly and walked towards the waiting ship.

6 – JOHN WYNDHAM: The Emptiness of Space

Brian Aldiss's story *Old Hundredth* that closed Volume one of this collection came from the centenary issue of *New Worlds*. It really was a colossal target for a British sf magazine, to have reached one hundred issues (and for that matter *any* sf magazine – only nine US sf magazines have exceeded 100 issues). To celebrate this event, editor John Carnell assembled a really star-packed issue with all the major names. In fact for the record, here are the titles of the stories in that edition: *Sitting Duck*, William F. Temple; *The Glass of Iargo*, Colin Kapp; *The Emptiness of Space*, John Wyndham; *Unfinished Sympathy*, John Hynam; *Old Hundredth*, Brian W. Aldiss; *Prerogative*, John Brunner; *Greater Than Infinity*, E. C. Tubb; *Countercharm*, James White.

There was also a guest editorial by Eric Frank Russell and a film review by Arthur Sellings. Only two of the contributors are not included in this anthology: the late John Hynam, under which name many may remember him for his BBC radio plays, although he usually wrote sf under the alias John Kippax; and the late John Rackham – who contributed an article *The Science Fiction Ethic* – and who besides his numerous stories in the British magazines has made a name for himself in *Analog* in America under his real name of John T Phillifent.

As you see, one of the stories in the contents list was John Wyndham's *The Emptiness of Space*, which is included here. During 1958 *New Worlds* published a series of four connected stories by Wyndham about the generations of the Troon family in expanding the frontiers of space. Specially for the one hundredth *New Worlds*, Wyndham wrote a fifth story, to my mind the best of the group.

The first book editions of this saga, titled *The Outward Urge*, only covered the first four episodes, but the fifth was included in a special Book Club edition in 1961, and then in the Penguin paperback edition in 1962. Readers were perplexed that the book was attributed to John Wyndham and Lucas Parkes. Who was Parkes? The interior blurb said that Parkes had confined himself to supplying technical data. But if you look back at Wyndham's full name as I gave it in Volume One, you'll notice there the name Parkes Lucas. In *The Outward Urge*, Wyndham had craftily collaborated with himself!

By the early 1960s, Wyndham's output was diminishing. A new novel, *Trouble With Lichen*, appeared in 1960. In July 1963 he married for the first time, a few months after the March 1963 *Amazing* had carried his new novelette *Chocky*, later expanded into the novel of the same title, published in 1968. That was to be Wyndham's last novel. The December 1968 *Galaxy* carried a new short story, *A Life Postponed*, and that was the last of Wyndham's output. He died on March 10th, 1969, aged 65.

Wyndham's contribution to science fiction is incalculable. His acceptance by all general readers made him a household name, and the word 'triffid' passed into the English language. His books have attracted to sf thousands of readers that might otherwise have avoided the genre altogether. When sf historians of the next century look back on the 1900s worldwide, the name of John Wyndham will be high up amongst the leading names on their lists. His work will never be forgotten.

THE EMPTINESS OF SPACE
THE ASTEROIDS A.D. 2194

John Wyndham

My first visit to New Caledonia was in the summer of 2199. At that time an exploration party under the leadership of Gilbert Troon was cautiously pushing its way up the less radio-active parts of Italy, investigating the prospects of reclamation. My firm felt that there might be a popular book in it, and assigned me to put the proposition to Gilbert. When I arrived, however, it was to find that he had been delayed, and was now expected a week later. I was not at all displeased. A few days of comfortable laziness on a Pacific island, all paid for and counting as work, is the kind of perquisite I like.

New Caledonia is a fascinating spot, and well worth the trouble of getting a landing permit – if you can get one. It has more of the past – and more of the future, too, for that matter – than any other place, and somehow it manages to keep them almost separate.

At one time the island, and the group, were, in spite of the name, a French colony. But in 2044, with the eclipse of Europe in the Great Northern War, it found itself, like other ex-colonies dotted all about the world, suddenly thrown upon its own resources. While most mainland colonies hurried to make treaties with their nearest powerful neighbours, many islands such as New Caledonia had little to offer and not much to fear, and so let things drift.

For two generations the surviving nations were far too occupied by the tasks of bringing equilibrium to a half-wrecked world to take any interest in scattered islands. It was not until the Brazilians began to see Australia as a possible challenger of their supremacy that they started a policy of unobtrusive, and tactfully mercantile, expansion into the Pacific. Then, naturally, it occurred to the Australians, too, that it was time to begin to extend *their* economic influence over various island-groups.

The New Caledonians resisted infiltration. They had found independence congenial, and steadily rebuffed temptations by both parties. The year 2144, in which Space declared for independence, found them still resisting; but the pressure was now considerable. They had watched one group of islands after another succumb to trade preferences, and thereafter virtually slide back to colonial status, and they now found it difficult to doubt that before long the same would happen to themselves when, whatever the form of words, they should be annexed – most likely by the Australians in order to forestall the establishment of a Brazilian base there, within a thousand miles of the coast.

It was into this situation that Jayme Gonveia, speaking for Space, stepped in 2150 with a suggestion of his own. He offered the New Caledonians guaranteed independence of either big Power, a considerable quantity of cash, and a prosperous future if they would grant Space a lease of territory which would become its Earth headquarters and main terminus.

The proposition was not altogether to the New Caledonian taste, but it was better than the alternatives. They accepted, and the construction of the Spaceyards was begun.

Since then the island has lived in a curious symbiosis. In the north are the rocket landing and dispatch stages, warehouses and engineering shops, and a way of life furnished with all modern techniques, while the other four-fifths of the island all but ignores it, and contentedly lives much as it did two and a half centuries ago. Such a state of affairs cannot be preserved by accident in this world. It is the result of careful contrivance both by the New Caledonians who like it that way, and by Space which dislikes outsiders taking too close an interest in its affairs. So, for permission to land anywhere in the group, one needs hard-won visas from both authorities. The result is no exploitation by tourists or salesmen, and a scarcity of strangers.

However, there I was, with an unexpected week of leisure to put in, and no reason why I should spend it in Space-Concession territory. One of the secretaries suggested Lahua, down in the south at no great distance from Noumea, the capital, as a restful spot, so thither I went.

Lahua has picture-book charm. It is a small fishing town, half-tropical, half-French. On its wide white beach there are still canoes, working canoes, as well as modern. At one end of the curve a mole gives shelter for a small anchorage, and there the palms that fringe the rest of the shore stop to make room for a town.

Many of Lahua's houses are improved-traditional, still thatched with palm, but its heart is a cobbled rectangle surrounded by entirely untropical houses, known as the

Grande Place. Here are shops, pavement cafés, stalls of fruit under bright striped awnings guarded by Gauguinesque women, a state of Bougainville, an atrociously ugly church on the east side, a *pissoir*, and even a *mairie*. The whole thing might have been imported complete from early twentieth-century France, except for the inhabitants – but even they, some in bright sarongs, some in European clothes, must have looked much the same when France ruled there.

I found it difficult to believe that they are real people living real lives. For the first day I was constantly accompanied by the feeling that an unseen director would suddenly call 'Cut', and it would all come to a stop.

On the second morning I was growing more used to it. I bathed, and then with a sense that I was beginning to get the feel of the life, drifted to the *place*, in search of apéritif. I chose a café on the south side where a few trees shaded the tables, and wondered what to order. My usual drinks seemed out of key. A dusky, brightly saronged girl approached. On an impulse, and feeling like a character out of a very old novel I suggested a pernod. She took it as a matter of course.

'Un pernod? Certainment, monsieur,' she told me.

I sat there looking across the Square, less busy now that the *déjeuner* hour was close, wondering what Sydney and Rio, Adelaide and São Paulo had gained and lost since they had been the size of Lahua, and doubting the value of the gains. . . .

The pernod arrived. I watched it cloud with water, and sipped it cautiously. An odd drink, scarcely calculated, I felt, to enhance the appetite. As I contemplated it a voice spoke from behind my right shoulder.

'An island product, but from the original recipe,' it said. 'Quite safe, in moderation, I assure you.'

I turned in my chair. The speaker was seated at the next table; a well-built, compact, sandy-haired man, dressed in a spotless white suit, a panama hat with a coloured band, and wearing a neatly trimmed, pointed beard. I guessed his age at about thirty-four though the grey eyes that met my own looked older, more experienced, and troubled.

'A taste that I have not had the opportunity to acquire,' I told him. He nodded.

'You won't find it outside. In some ways we are a museum here, but little the worse, I think, for that.'

'One of the later Muses,' I suggested. 'The Muse of Recent History. And very fascinating, too.'

I became aware that one or two men at tables within earshot were paying us – or rather me – some attention; their expressions were not unfriendly, but they showed what seemed to be traces of concern.

'It is –' my neighbour began to reply, and then broke off, cut short by a rumble in the sky.

I turned to see a slender white spire stabbing up into the blue overhead. Already, by the time the sound reached us, the rocket at its apex was too small to be visible. The man cocked an eye at it.

'Moon-shuttle,' he observed.

'They all sound and look alike to me,' I admitted.

'They wouldn't if you were inside. The acceleration in that shuttle would spread you all over the floor – very thinly,' he said, and then went on: 'We don't often see strangers in Lahua. Perhaps you would care to give me the pleasure of your company for luncheon? My name, by the way, is George.'

I hesitated, and while I did I noticed over his shoulder an elderly man who moved his lips slightly as he gave me what was without doubt an encouraging nod. I decided to take a chance on it.

'That's very kind of you. My name is David – David Myford, from Sydney,' I told him. But he made no amplification regarding himself, so I was left wondering whether George was his forename, or his surname.

I moved to his table, and he lifted a hand to summon the girl.

'Unless you are averse to fish you must try the bouillabaisse – *spécialité de la maison*,' he told me.

I was aware that I had gained the approval of the elderly man, and apparently of some others as well, by joining George. The waitress, too, had an approving air. I wondered vaguely what was going on, and whether I had been let in for the town bore, to protect the rest.

'From Sydney,' he said reflectively. 'It's a long time since I saw Sydney. I don't suppose I'd know it now.'

'It keeps on growing,' I admitted, 'but Nature would always prevent you from confusing it with anywhere else.'

We went on chatting. The bouillabaisse arrived; and excellent it was. There were hunks of first-class bread, too, cut from those long loaves you see in pictures in old European books. I began to feel, with the help of the local wine, that a lot could be said for the twentieth-century way of living.

In the course of our talk it emerged that George had been a rocket pilot, but was grounded now – not, one would judge, for reasons of health, so I did not inquire further. . . .

The second course was an excellent coupe of fruits I had never heard of, and, overall, iced passion-fruit juice. It was when the coffee came that he said, rather wistfully I thought:

'I had hoped you might be able to help me, Mr Myford, but it now seems to me that you are not a man of faith.'

'Surely everyone has to be very much a man of faith,' I protested. 'For everything a man cannot do for himself he has to have faith in others.'

'True,' he conceded. 'I should have said "spiritual faith". You do not speak as one who is interested in the nature and destiny of his soul – or of anyone else's soul – I fear?'

I felt that I perceived what was coming next. However if he was interested in saving my soul he had at least begun the operation by looking after my bodily needs with a generously good meal.

'When I was young,' I told him, 'I used to worry quite a lot about my soul, but later I decided that that was largely a matter of vanity.'

'There is also vanity in thinking oneself self-sufficient,' he said.

'Certainly,' I agreed. 'It is chiefly with the conception of the soul as a separate entity that I find myself out of sympathy. For me it is a manifestation of mind which is, in its turn, a product of the brain, modified by the external environment, and influenced more directly by the glands.'

He looked saddened, and shook his head reprovingly.

'You are so wrong – so very wrong. Some are always conscious of their souls, others, like yourself, are unaware of them, but no one knows the true value of his soul as long as he has it, it is not until a man has lost his soul that he understands its value.'

It was not an observation making for easy rejoinder, so I let the silence between us continue. Presently he looked up into the northern sky where the trail of the moon-bound shuttle had long since blown away. With embarrassment I observed two large tears flow from the inner corners of his eyes and trickle down beside his nose. He, however, showed no embarrassment; he simply pulled out a large, white, beautifully laundered handkerchief, and dealt with them.

'I hope you will never learn what a dreadful thing it is to have no soul,' he told me, with a shake of his head. 'It is to hold the emptiness of space in one's heart: to sit by the waters of Babylon for the rest of one's life.'

Lamely I said:

'I'm afraid this is out of my range. I don't understand.'

'Of course you don't. No one understands. But always one keeps on hoping that one day there will come somebody who does understand and can help.'

'But the soul is a manifestation of the self,' I said. 'I don't see how that *can* be lost – it can be changed, perhaps, but not lost.'

'Mine is,' he said, still looking up into the vast blue. 'Lost – adrift somewhere out there. Without it I am a sham. A man who has lost a leg or an arm is still a man, but a man who has lost his soul is nothing – nothing – nothing. . . .'

'Perhaps a psychiatrist –' I started to suggest, uncertainly. That stirred him, and checked the tears.

'Psychiatrist!' he exclaimed scornfully. 'Damned frauds! Even to the word. They may know a bit about minds; but about the psyche! – why they even deny its existence . . . !'

There was a pause.

'I wish I could help . . .' I said, rather vaguely.

'There was a chance. You *might* have been one who could.

There's always the chance. . . .' he said consolingly, though whether he was consoling himself or me seemed moot. At this point the church clock struck two. My host's mood changed. He got up quite briskly.

'I have to go now,' he told me. 'I wish you had been the one, but it has been a pleasant encounter all the same. I hope you enjoy Lahua.'

I watched him make his way along the *place*. At one stall he paused, selected a peach-like fruit, and bit into it. The woman beamed at him amiably, apparently unconcerned about payment.

The dusky waitress arrived by my table, and stood looking after him.

'O le pauvre monsieur Georges,' she said sadly. We watched him climb the church steps, throw away the remnant of his fruit, and remove his hat to enter. *'Il va faire la priére,'* she explained. *'Tous les jours* 'e make pray for 'is soul. In ze morning, in ze afternoon. *C'est si triste.'*

I noticed the bill in her hand. I fear that for a moment I misjudged George, but it had been a good lunch. I reached for my notecase. The girl noticed, and shook her head.

'Non, non, monsieur, non. Vous êtes convive. C'est d'accord. Alors, monsieur Georges 'e sign bill tomorrow. *S'arrange. C'est okay,'* she insisted, and stuck to it.

The elderly man whom I had noticed before broke in:

'It's all right – quite in order,' he assured me. Then he added: 'Perhaps if you are not in a hurry you would care to take a café-cognac with me?'

There seemed to be a fine open-handedness about Lahua. I accepted, and joined him.

'I'm afraid no one can have briefed you about poor George,' he said.

I admitted this was so. He shook his head in reproof of persons unknown, and added:

'Never mind. All went well. George always has hopes of a stranger, you see: sometimes one has been known to laugh. We don't like that.'

'I'm sorry to hear that,' I told him. 'His state strikes me as very far from funny.'

'It is indeed,' he agreed. 'But he's improving. I doubt whether he knows it himself, but he is. A year ago he would often weep quietly through the whole *déjeuner*. Rather depressing until one got used to it.'

'He lives here in Lahua, then?' I asked.

'He exists. He spends most of his time in the church. For the rest he wanders round. He sleeps at that big white house up on the hill. His grand-daughter's place. She sees that he's decently turned out, and pays the bills for whatever he fancies down here.'

I thought I must have misheard.

'His grand-daughter?' I exclaimed. 'But he's a young man. He can't be much over thirty. . . .'

He looked at me.

'You'll very likely come across him again. Just as well to know how things stand. Of course it isn't the sort of thing the family likes to publicize, but there's no secret about it.'

The café-cognacs arrived. He added cream to his, and began:

About five years ago (he said), yes, it would be in 2194, young Gerald Troon was taking a ship out to one of the larger asteroids – the one that de Gasparis called Psyche when he spotted it in 1852. The ship was a space-built freighter called the *Celestis*, working from the moon-base. Her crew was five, with not bad accommodation forward. Apart from that and the motor-section these ships are not much more than one big hold which is very often empty on the outward journeys unless it is carrying gear to set up new workings. This time it was empty because the assignment was simply to pick up a load of uranium ore – Psyche is half made of high-yield ore, and all that was necessary was to set going the digging machinery already on the site, and load the stuff in. It seemed simple enough.

But the Asteroid Belt is still a very tricky area, you know. The main bodies and groups are charted, of course – but that only helps you to find them. The place is full of outfliers of all sizes that you couldn't hope to chart, but have to avoid. About the best you can do is to tackle the belt as near to your objective as possible, reduce speed until you are little more than local orbit velocity, and then edge your way in, going very canny. The trouble is the time it can take to keep on fiddling along that way for thousands – hundreds of thousands, maybe – of miles. Fellows get bored and inattentive, or sick to death of it and start to take chances. I don't know what the answer is. You can bounce radar off the big chunks and hitch that up to a course-deflector to keep you away from them. But the small stuff is just as deadly to a ship, and there's so much of it about that if you were to make the course-deflector sensitive enough to react to it you'd have your ship shying off everything the whole time, and getting nowhere. What we want is someone to come up with a kind of repulse mechanism with only a limited range of operation – say, a hundred miles – but no one does. so, as I say, it's tricky. Since they first started to tackle it back in 2150 they've lost half a dozen ships in there and had a dozen more damaged one way or another. Not a nice place at all . . . On the other hand, uranium is uranium. . . .

Gerald's a good lad though. He has the authentic Troon yen for space without being much of a chancer; besides, Psyche isn't too far from the inner rim of the orbit – not nearly the approach problem Ceres is, for instance – what's more, he'd done it several times before.

Well, he got into the Belt, and jockeyed and fiddled and niggled his way until he was about three hundred miles out from Psyche and getting ready to come in. Perhaps he'd got a bit careless by then; in any case he'd not be expecting to find anything in orbit around the asteroid. But that's just what he did find – the hard way. . . .

There was a crash which made the whole ship ring round him and his crew as if they were in an enormous bell. It's about the nastiest – and very likely to be the last – sound a spaceman can ever hear. This time, however, their luck was in. It wasn't too bad. They discovered that as they crowded to watch the indicator dials. It was soon evident that nothing vital had been hit, and they were able to release their breath.

Gerald turned over the controls to his First, and he and the engineer, Steve, pulled space-suits out of the locker. When the airlock opened they hitched their safety-lines on to spring hooks, and slid their way aft along the hull on magnetic soles. It was soon clear that the damage was not on the air-lock side, and they worked round the curve of the hull.

One can't say just what they expected to find – probably an embedded hunk of rock, or maybe just a gash in the side of the hold – anyway it was certainly not what they did find, which was half of a small space-ship projecting out of their own hull.

One thing was evident right away – that it had hit with no great force. If it had, it would have gone right through and out the other side, for the hold of a freighter is little more than a single-walled cylinder: there is no need for it to be more, it doesn't have to conserve warmth, or contain air, or resist the friction of an atmosphere, nor does it have to contend with any more gravitational pull than that of the moon; it is only in the living-quarters that there have to be the complexities necessary to sustain life.

Another thing, which was immediately clear, was that this was not the only misadventure that had befallen the small ship. Something had, at some time, sliced off most of its after part, carrying away not only the driving tubes but the mixing-chambers as well, and leaving it hopelessly disabled.

Shuffling round the wreckage to inspect it, Gerald found no entrance. It was thoroughly jammed into the hole it had made, and its airlock must lie forward, somewhere inside the freighter. He sent Steve back for a cutter and for a key that would get them into the hold. While he waited he spoke through his helmet-radio to the operator in the *Celestis*'s living-quarters, and explained the situation. He added:

'Can you raise the Moon-Station just now, Jake? I'd better make a report.'

'Strong and clear, Cap'n,' Jake told him.

'Good. Tell them to put me on to the Duty Officer, will you.'

He heard Jake open up and call. There was a pause while

the waves crossed and re-crossed the millions of miles between them, then a voice:

'Hullo, *Celestis*! Hullo *Celestis*! Moon-Station responding. Go ahead, Jake. Over!'

Gerald waited out the exchange patiently. Radio waves are some of the things that can't be hurried. In due course another voice spoke.

'Hullo, Celestis! Moon-Station Duty Officer speaking. Give your location and go ahead.'

'Hullo, Charles. This is Gerald Troon calling from *Celestis* now in orbit about Psyche. Approximately three-twenty miles altitude. I am notifying damage by collision. No harm to personnel. *Not* repeat *not* in danger. Damage appears to be confined to empty hold-section. Cause of damage . . .' He went on to give particulars, and concluded: 'I am about to investigate. Will report further. Please keep link open. Over!'

The engineer returned, floating a self-powered cutter with him on a short safety-cord, and holding the key which would screw back the bolts of the hold's entrance-port. Gerald took the key, placed it in the hole beside the door, and inserted his legs into the two staples that would give him the purchase to wind it.

The moon man's voice came again.

'Hullo, Ticker. Understand no immediate danger. But don't go taking any chances, boy. Can you identify the derelict?'

'Repeat no danger,' Troon told him. 'Plumb lucky. If she'd hit six feet farther forward we'd have had real trouble. I have now opened small door of the hold, and am going in to examine the forepart of the derelict. Will try to identify it.'

The cavernous darkness of the hold made it necessary for them to switch on their helmet lights. They could now see the front part of the derelict; it took up about half the space there was. The ship had punched through the wall, turning back the tough alloy in curled petals, as though it had been tinplate. She had come to rest with her nose a bare couple of feet short of the opposite side. The two of them surveyed her for some moments. Steve pointed to a ragged hole, some five or six inches across, about half-way along the embedded section. It had a nasty significance that caused Gerald to nod sombrely.

He shuffled to the ship, and on to its curving side. He found the airlock on the top, as it lay in the *Celestis*, and tried the winding key. He pulled it out again.

'Calling you, Charles,' he said. 'No identifying marks on the derelict. She's not space-built – that is, she could be used in atmosphere. Oldish pattern – well, must be – she's pre the standardization of winding keys, so that takes us back a bit. Maximum external diameter, say, twelve feet. Length unknown – can't say how much after part there was before it was knocked off. She's been holed forward, too. Looks like a small meteorite, about five inches. At speed, I'd say. Just a minute . . . Yes, clean through and out, with a pretty small exit hole. Can't open the airlock without making a new key. Quicker to cut our way in. Over!'

He shuffled back, and played his light through the small meteor hole. His helmet prevented him getting his face close enough to see anything but a small part of the opposite wall, with a corresponding hole in it.

'Easiest way is to enlarge this, Steve,' he suggested.

The engineer nodded. He brought his cutter to bear, switched it on and began to carve from the edge of the hole.

'Not much good, Ticker,' came the voice from the moon. 'The bit you gave could apply to any one of four ships.'

'Patience, dear Charles, while Steve does his bit of fancy-work with the cutter,' Troon told him.

It took twenty minutes to complete the cut through the double hull. Steve switched off, gave a tug with his left hand, and the joined, inner and outer circles of metal floated away.

'*Celestis* calling moon. I am about to go into the derelict, Charles. Keep open,' Troon said.

He bent down, took hold of the sides of the cut, kicked his magnetic soles free of contact, and gave a light pull which took him floating head-first through the hole in the manner of an underwater swimmer. Presently his voice came again, with a different tone:

'I say, Charles, there are three men in here. All in space-suits – old-time space-suits. Two of them are belted on to their bunks. The other one is . . . Oh, his leg's gone. The meteorite must have taken it off . . . There's a queer – Oh, God, it's his blood frozen into a solid ball . . . !'

After a minute or so he went on:

'I've found the log. Can't handle it in these gloves, though. I'll take it aboard, and let you have particulars. The two fellows on the bunks seem to be quite intact – their suits I mean. Their helmets have those curved strip-windows so I can't see much of their faces. Must've – That's odd . . . Each of them has a sort of little book attached by a wire to the suit fastener. On the cover it has: "Danger – Perigoso" in red, and, underneath: "Do not remove suit – Read instructions within," repeated in Portuguese. Then: "Hapson Survival System." What would all that mean, Charles? Over!'

While he waited for the reply Gerald clumsily fingered one of the tag-like books and discovered that it opened concertina-wise, a series of small metal plates hinged together printed on one side in English and on the other in Portuguese. The first leaf carried little print, but what there was was striking. It ran 'CAUTION! Do *NOT* open suit until you have read these instructions or you will KILL the wearer.'

When he had got that far the Duty Officer's voice came in again:

'Hullo, Ticker. I've called the Doc. He says do NOT, repeat NOT, touch the two men on any account. Hang on, he's coming to talk to you. He says the Hapson system was scrapped over thirty years ago – He – oh, here he is. . . .'

Another voice came in:

'Ticker? Laysall here. Charles tells me you've found a couple of Hapsons, undamaged. Please confirm, and give circumstances.'

Troon did so. In due course the doctor came back:

'Okay. That sounds fine. Now listen carefully, Ticker. From what you say it's practically certain those two are not dead – yet. They're – well, they're in cold storage. That part of the Hapson system was good. You'll see a kind of boss mounted on the left of the chest. The thing to do in the case of extreme emergency was to slap it good and hard. When you do that it gives a multiple injection. Part of the stuff puts you out. Part of it prevents the building-up in the body of large ice crystals that would damage the tissues. Part of it – oh, well, that'll do later. The point is that it works practically a hundred per cent. You get Nature's own deep-freeze in space. And if there's something to keep off direct radiation from the sun you stay like that until somebody finds you – if anyone ever does. Now I take it that these two have been in the dark of an airless ship which is now in the airless hold of your ship. Is that right?'

'That's so Doc. There are the two small meteorite holes, but they would not get direct beams from there.'

'Fine. Then keep 'em just like that. Take care they don't get warmed. Don't try anything the instruction-sheet says. The point is that though the success of the Hapson freeze is almost sure, the resuscitation isn't. In fact, it's very dodgy indeed – a poorer than twenty-five-per-cent chance at best. You get lethal crystal formations building up, for one thing. What I suggest is that you try to get 'em back exactly as they are. Our apparatus here will give them the best chance they can have. Can you do that?'

Gerald Troon thought for a moment. Then he said:

'We don't want to waste this trip – and that's what'll happen if we pull the derelict out of our side to leave a hole we can't mend. But if we leave her where she is, plugging the hole, we can at least take on a half-load of ore. And if we pack that well in, it'll help to wedge the derelict in place. So suppose we leave the derelict just as she lies, and the men too, and seal here up to keep the ore out of her. Would that suit?'

'That should be as good as can be done,' the doctor replied. 'But have a look at the two men before you leave them. Make sure they're secure in their bunks. As long as they are kept in space conditions about the only thing likely to harm them is breaking loose under acceleration, and getting damaged.'

'Very well, that's what we'll do. Anyway, we'll not be using any high acceleration the way things are. The other poor fellow shall have a space burial. . . .'

An hour later both Gerald and his companions were back in the *Celestis*'s living-quarters, and the First Officer was starting to manoeuvre for the spiral-in to Psyche. The two got out of their space-suits. Gerald pulled the derelict's log from the outside pocket, and took it to his bunk. There he fastened the belt, and opened the book.

Five minutes later Steve looked across at him from the opposite bunk, with concern.

'Anything the matter, Cap'n? You're looking a bit queer.'

'I'm feeling a bit queer, Steve. . . . That chap we took out and consigned to space, he was Terence Rice, wasn't he?'

'That's what his disc said,' Steve agreed.

'H'm.' Gerald Troon paused. Then he tapped the book. 'This,' he said, 'is the log of the *Astarte*. She sailed from the Moon-Station 3 January 2149 – forty-five years ago – bound for the Asteroid Belt. There was a crew of three: Captain George Montgomery Troon, engineer Luis Gompez, radio-man Terence Rice. . . .

'So, as the unlucky one was Terence Rice, it follows that one of those two back there must be Gompez, and the other – well, he must be George Montgomery Troon, the one who made the Venus landing in 2144 . . . And, incidentally, my grandfather. . . .'

'Well,' said my companion, 'They got them back all right. Gompez was unlucky, though – at least I suppose you'd call it unlucky – anyway, he didn't come through the resuscitation. George did, of course. . . .

'But there's more to resuscitation than mere revival. There's a degree of physical shock in any case, and when you've been under as long as he had there's plenty of mental shock, too.

'He went under, a youngish man with a young family; he woke up to find himself a great-grandfather; his wife a very old lady who had remarried; his friends gone, or elderly; his two companions in the *Astarte* dead.

'That was bad enough, but worse still was that he knew all about the Hapson System. He knew that when you go into a deep-freeze the whole metabolism comes quickly to a complete stop. You are, by every known definition and test, dead. . . . Corruption cannot set in, of course, but every vital process has stopped; every single feature which we regard as evidence of life has ceased to exist. . . .'

'So you are dead. . . .'

'So if you believe, as George does, that your psyche, your soul, has independent existence, then it must have left your body when you died.'

'And how do you get it back? That's what George wants to know – and that's why he's over there now, praying to be told. . . .'

I leant back in my chair, looking across the *place* at the dark opening of the church door.

'You mean to say that that young man, that George who was here just now, is the very same George Montgomery Troon who made the first landing on Venus, half a century ago?' I said.

'He's the man,' he affirmed.

I shook my head, not for disbelief, but for George's sake.

'What will happen to him?' I asked.

'God knows,' said my neighbour. 'He *is* getting better; he's less distressed than he was. And now he's beginning to show touches of the real Troon obsession to get into space again.

'But what then? . . . You can't ship a Troon as crew. And you can't have a Captain who might take it into his head to go hunting through Space for his soul. . . .

'Me, I think I'd rather die just once. . . .'

7 – COLIN KAPP: The Teacher

As science fiction has developed over the decades, science has, in fact, taken a back seat. The emphasis has swung from scientific endeavour to the effects of science upon society. But there always will be a place for the hard-core *science* fiction story, and one of its most popular aspects is that of the scientific problem: namely a mystery that can only be solved by logical application of strict scientific principles. One of the best British exponents of this theme is Colin Kapp.

For many years a technician working on chemical aspects of electronic research and manufacture, Kapp is now an independent consultant in the printed wiring field, and brings all his vocational knowledge to bear in his fiction. His first story, *Life Plan* (*New Worlds*, November 1958) was widely praised, and his follow-up, *Survival Problem* (April 1959) cemented his position as an author to watch. The theme of that tale, inter-dimensional travel, reappeared with even more stunning effect in *Lambda One* (December 1962) which has since been adapted for television.

With *The Railways Up On Cannis* (October 1959) Kapp introduced us to his team of Unorthodox Engineers, scientists who have unconventional ways of solving seemingly impossible problems. They reappeared in *The Subways of Tazoo*, a fairly natural sequel, and then in the particularly fascinating *The Pen and the Dark*, the apparently insoluble *Getaway From Getawehi*, and the cleverly original *The Black Hole of Negrav*, all in *New Writings*.

The lack of a regular British market drove Kapp to the American magazines, where fortunately his work appears frequently. His special technique for realism has brought him much success especially with his two recent novels, *Patterns of Chaos* (1972) and *The Wizard of Anharitte* (1972), both originally serialised in *If*. Several shorter pieces have also appeared in America as did his own favourite choice, *The Teacher*, the cover story for the August 1969 *Analog*. Kapp says:

'*The Teacher* has two themes. Firstly, when – not if – man meets the other inhabitants of the stars, our technical sophistication will, hopefully, be matched by an equal expertise in the social sciences. We know that contact of a lower order of culture with a higher invariably destroys the former. This is a principle we may need to keep firmly in mind in order to preserve ourselves or to protect others from our influence.

'Secondly, *The Teacher* makes the point that the discovery of the wheel and the development of "hammer and fire arts" are not necessarily a pre-requisite for the development of a civilization. An electro-chemical based civilization is a perfect possibility. If you doubt it, remember that even on Terra the chemical primary cell came well before the dynamo, and the unique abilities of metal forming by electrolysis (electroforming) provide many of the highest-precision parts needed by our own technology. Also a crown for the Prince of Wales.

'Curiously, though, when starting to write *The Teacher* I had none of this in mind. I was having fun with descriptions of doing what were – for me – familiar things in an alien place and in an alien way. I think this is the way a story should be conceived – the exploration of the intriguing simply because it is intriguing. If *The Teacher* also had something to say, that was serendipity. The real purpose of writing it was trying to share a little of that private place where only I may enter – the realms of my own imagination.'

THE TEACHER

Colin Kapp

'Scorpid! Scorpid!' The cry of alarm echoed the panic back from the rock-slime of the roof. 'Scorpid in ten tank!'

There was good reason behind the fear. The scorpion's body was as long as a man's forearm and equally as thick. And it was deadly. Its savage mandibles snapped open and shut like the snicker of a machine tool, with the capacity of cutting through a centimetre of steel. Its tail, equipped with a murderous post-anal sting, lashed about in frenzy, splashing the vat acids many metres into the air.

Undeterred by the poisonous liquor into which it had fallen, the scorpid began to swim lunging circles around the great vat, looking for a way of escape. Its body arched dangerously as it attempted to project itself over the overhanging edge or to gain a hold on the protrusions. The workmen edged back, knowing the instantaneous death which could follow the creature's liberation on to the floor. The winchman, waiting his opportunity, quickly drew the plating mandrels from the tank to prevent the scorpid's escape by climbing the rope or cathode connections. The circular anode yoke was axed from its supporting cables, and slid quietly with its burden of anode metal into the depths of the vat. Now the creature was confined, unless it could manage to leap the overhang on to the vat surrounds. With practice and with the spur of hunger it would learn to do even that.

The workmen were soon prepared. New stocks of oil-soaked brands were hauled up from the oil pits and laid with ends adjacent round the perimeter. A fire-boy touched the brands into flame with long strokes from his firing sticks.

Soon the circle of fire ringed the entire vat, allowed no crevice through which a scorpid might penetrate. A further supply of brands was arranged to replenish the first when they became exhausted. Then the shouting, sweat-soaked men did all that they now could do – wait and hope.

OrsOrs, the overseer, checked to make sure the emergency arrangements were complete before he gave the next instruction:

'Find someone fetch the Gaffer.' This was very much a job for a volunteer. Although the divisions between day and night on the surface of Tanic made no difference in the deep caverns, daytime on the surface drove all manner of creatures into the shielding dark of the higher galleries. To fetch the Gaffer at this time of surface noon would be a difficult and dangerous assignment. It was a job suited only to a fleet runner and one who knew exactly the blackspots of the noon caves. OrsOrs would have gone himself, but his responsibilities tied him to the deep levels. In any case, to fetch the Gaffer at such a time was a job for a younger man and one without dependants.

JoJo was the obvious choice. The name was not his own. When working, all of them used given names invented by the Gaffer, whose alien tongue could never handle the forked aspirations of the ritual language from which all keep names were derived. JoJo was less of a volunteer than a nominee, but he raised no complaint when hands thrust him forward. His normal duties were those of fire-boy, and he was used to running the caverns with a flaming brand. Divested of his apron and rubber boots, he stood with all the nakedness of his forefathers. OrsOrs judged the boy had the physique and the stamina necessary. Whether he also had the courage and the skill needed to make the noon journey was something that only time would show.

'Find the Gaffer, JoJo. Tell him there scorpid in tank ten. The making of rocket projector tubes is stop. He mus' come at once.'

The youth looked uncertain.

'Are you sure he'll be willing come through noon caves?'

OrsOrs frowned. 'He's a Terran. He's not likely meet with anythin' more formidable than himself.' This was a stony jest, which raised a murmur of agreement from the onlookers. 'Anyway, he's never failed us yet. Say OrsOrs sent you. He will find way to come.'

JoJo nodded. He took three oil brands, fastened two at his waist with rope, and lit the third. He took also a short axe. Standing at the tunnel's entrance he turned and raised his torch in farewell. The fine muscles of his naked body were so accentuated by the angle of the light that he looked more god-image than a man. Then he was gone, the swift flame receding into the tunnel as he ran.

Once he was alone, JoJo began to re-examine his own feelings about the trip and his ability to survive it. For the most part, the lower tunnels and galleries were rock-strewn and damp and inclined to slime – treacherous to running feet. A man falling here could easily break a limb or his head, and once he had fallen it could well be days before he was discovered. JoJo slackened his pace and began to concentrate on footholds. Better to arrive slowly than not to arrive at all.

Twenty minutes took him to the foot of the air shaft, where the great ropes drew iron cages to the other levels and where the giant leathern bellows strained in their shackles like the guts of some gigantic reptile. The caves near the air shaft were places that JoJo feared. They were chemical rooms and mixing rooms, newly installed since the Gaffer's coming. The men who sweated in the black heat of these foul holes were prone to strange diseases and shortages of breath and tumours of the skin. JoJo hurried past as though the very draught entering the corridor might have the power to contaminate him. Because of places such as this, JoJo felt a strong resentment against the Gaffer even though, as OrsOrs was constantly reminding, without the Gaffer they could never hope to win the war against the reptiles.

He came to a rising passage. JoJo lit the second brand from the first, and threw the latter away still only half consumed. Although such wastage was a crime, he knew that in the galleries ahead he would need a steady light. He might get the chance to kindle one more brand on the journey, but he could scarcely hope for time to kindle two.

The passages became drier as he ascended, and the slight natural draft against his skin told him of the random chimneys connecting to the surface. At this point his main danger lay in the shards of fragmented quartz which lay like daggers in the sandy floor. To pass them uninjured called for skilled footwork and precise muscle control. He held his torch high to catch each bright reflection, placing his feet miraculously on to softness with each running step. But he knew that to make a mistake and sever a tendon, or even to cut a foot and bleed severely, could be fatal in the hours until surface darkness when OrsOrs would come this way himself to fetch the Gaffer.

It took him half a painful hour to reach the first of the noon caves. With aching thigh muscles and his back coated with dust and running sweat, he paused for a moment at the threshold. The galleries before him were too vast to be lit by a torch. Only his foreknowledge of the route could guide him to the tunnel's entrance at the other side. Now he would be forced to go slower in order to avoid collision with the bushes of razor crystal, yet not too slowly lest a *footburner* be drawn from its lair and wait with phosphoritic breath to burn his legs into stumps downward from the knee. At the same time he must travel watchfully, lest he rake his scalp on the stalactites descending from the roof – yet the noise and light of his passage would attract to his path all manner of *scorpids* and *snappers* and ghosts and things with wings and claws and webs of acridness and fright.

Before him, the things in the gallery sensed his presence and saw his light and began to mutter and flutter and move before him. He knew he must not stay to consider further. Holding his torch aloft, he began to run.

The beasties in the cave were more than usually active. Caught in the suddenly advancing light, the majority of them scattered from his path. Some, like the *spiny needleball*, curled into defensive knots, so well camouflaged on the sandy floor that he had to concentrate in order to differentiate between them and safe footrests. Here and there a *snapper* chattered at his heels with jaws that would have stripped the flesh from the bone had he not been able to outrun the fortuitously stumpy legs that carried them.

At the crystal forest he was forced to slow in case his arms brushed the razors hanging like leaves on the silvern crystal trees. Here the fleshy beasts, like *snappers*, kept well clear of the silicon barbs. Only the horn-shelled and armoured animals dared to form lairs in the deadly glades. Of these few could move fast save for the scorpids, who never hesitated to attack anything which crossed their paths, although they seldom bothered to pursue. In common with this kind, JoJo feared scorpids more than he feared the reptiles on the surface. If none were in his path, he might get through. But if he came across one directly . . .

With trepidation he made his way through the silvern glades, fearfully thrusting his torch at every moving shadow. He kept his eyes alert for the proximity of the glassy leaves, the mere touch of which could sever an artery or gash the flesh beyond repair. In this way he encountered only a couple of armoured *night-pods*, relatively harmless, who scattered with heliophobic haste from the illumination of the torch. He was almost out of the forest before great danger struck.

From a rock waist-high amidst the crystal bushes a scorpid launched itself directly at his side. Although he had his axe, JoJo had no time to use it. He struck at the scorpid wildly with his torch arm in a simple reflex action. At the normal velocity with which a scorpid moved he would have stood no chance. By pure accident the heavy fibre of the torch caught the moving scorpid body in midflight and deflected it in a long arc into the middle of a crystal bush. The bush erupted in a flurry of fractured blades. JoJo caught his breath and waited for the scorpid to re-emerge. Something hit the ground at his feet, and he panicked and beat at it with his torch several times before he gained the realization that the body which had fallen was already in the throes of death. By some miracle the razor leaves of the tree had penetrated the interstices in the scorpid's protective plates and severed its throat. Now it lay in a fluid pool of its own life blood, twitching with nervous reaction but incapable of attack.

JoJo raised his torch again, and ran.

Within minutes he gained the end of the first gallery and was in the tunnel which connected with the second. Here the dryness and barrenness of the rock gave poor living to the beasties from the surface. Apart from the *cave-crawlers* and the occasional stinging *bumble-bugs*, he was safe from attack. Neither the *crawlers* nor the *bugs* could stand the sight of fire, and he took advantage of the respite to light his third torch from the second and to carry both before him while the second remained alight.

The next gallery was larger than the one through which he had passed, and contained no crystal forest. Here, however, both stalactite and stalagmite turned the path through many wild contortions and thereby slowed the pace. This was a favourite haunt of the *footburners*, who played tag around the rocky columns and waited to snort their phosphorous-laden breath on any unwary flesh which happened to pass within their compass. To some extent to bear a light here was a disadvantage, because a footburner's phosphorescent snout was more clearly seen in darkness. But there were other beasties, some even as yet unnamed, against whom light was the only protection.

Warily JoJo threaded his way around the mineral pillars; occasionally running when a snapper chased his heels; occasionally slowing to avoid raking his head on an unexpected stalactite. Always his eyes were alert for a footburner's snout. Though he saw several in the distance, he was fortunate that none came close.

Then crisis! Breaking through a natural arch he was concentrating on the ground and nearly walked into an *acidtail*. Only the slight hum of wings warned him of the danger in time. Poised on a hundred delicate wings, the acidtail was directly in front of him, its tail of marvellous, corrosive lace draped fully across his path. OrsOrs had shown him how the threads of an acidtail's plumage could etch deeply into the glaze on earthen pots and was used by potters as an instrument for making decorations. He knew also that the acid liquors exuded from the threads gave rise to deep and painful wounds and sought through the flesh to rot the bones beneath.

He stopped, uncertain suddenly of what move he ought to make. To retreat back into the line of disturbed creatures behind him was unthinkable; to circumnavigate the acidtail was impossible without a long detour from known paths; to attempt to advance was to invite a peculiarly painful form of death. It was then that he became aware of the footburner closing in behind him. His only relevant weapon seemed to be his firebrand, though he had never heard of its use against an acidtail. However, this was no time to be bound by custom. Almost without thinking he thrust the flame into the acid lace. There was a brief flare, accompanied by a shriek such as the ghosts of ancestors were held to give. The crippled acidtail fell like a wounded bumble-bug, covered with lines of fire. Unthinkingly JoJo leaped straight over the fallen beastie into the darkness beyond. Almost at the same time the path behind him grew brilliant with the flare of the exhalation of the footburner.

JoJo landed on soft sand, amazed to find himself unhurt. Unexpected contact with a stalagmite knocked the torch from his hand, but he did not dare return to retrieve it. Then he distantly saw the yellow light of the annex which led to the Gaffer's tower. Heedless of anything which might now lie in his way, JoJo fled through the darkness in a tide of panic.

Then he was safe. The floor and walls of the annex tunnel were slightly corrugated, and stung his feet with invisible needles. No creatures would follow him into this place, so this was a pain he did not mind. The golden-yellow illumination was so intense it hurt his eyes, but no dangerous flying thing or bumble-bug would brave its radiation. Nothing more than stupid sun flies ever reached the screens. It was somehow characteristic of the Gaffer that he would play a creature's foibles against itself and yet leave unimpeded access to his quarters for those he wished to see. On all Tanic, JoJo could think of no other place so easily entered by a man yet so repellent to the beasties.

The Gaffer must have had warning of his coming because he was waiting at the end of the annex tunnel, his small, browned, terran face crossed with inquiry.

'JoJo? What the devil brings you through the noon caves?'

For once JoJo forgot to be overawed by the Gaffer's presence. Finding the man alone, he was very obviously human and, therefore, fragile. This threw a new light on the god-man from the stars. In fact, he was more approachable than OrsOrs, who was permanently worried by production problems and had not the kindly wisdom of the master technician from Terra.

'If you please, Gaffer, OrsOrs send me. There's scorpid in ten tank.'

The Gaffer scowled with sudden displeasure, his lean Terran face creasing across the tops of his eyes. 'So there's a scorpid in number ten. What of it?'

'Please, OrsOrs wants you come.'

The Gaffer pursed his lips as though in sudden anger. Then he checked himself. 'I was damnwell afraid of that!'

'Afraid of scorpid?' The surprise slipped through in JoJo's voice. He knew from birth that Terrans were afraid of nothing.

'No, not of scorpids . . . Of dragons rather.'

He caught JoJo's piteous, questioning look and smiled. 'You don't understand me, JoJo. Perhaps one day you will. But let me ask a question: Of OrsOrs and I, who has had the most experience in killing scorpids?'

JoJo struggled with his answer, not wishing to offend. The Terran rescued him from his embarrassment.

'Yes, you're right, JoJo. The answer is OrsOrs, of course. So why did he send for me?'

When he thought about it, JoJo found the second question unanswerable. On the face of it, sending for the Gaffer had seemed such a logical thing to do that no one had questioned it. But when he tried to examine the logic, the point escaped him.

Meanwhile the Gaffer fussed about his instruments as though loath to leave them, then began to prepare himself for the journey. When he was ready he turned back to JoJo.

'Where are your boots?'

'In deposition cave, where I left them.'

'But why did you leave them?'

'Because wearing-boots-man cannot run the noon galleries.' JoJo answered this as though the point was self-evident.

'But JoJo,' said the Gaffer patiently, 'wearing-boots-man doesn't need to *run* through the noon galleries. He can walk.'

Thinking about this, JoJo had to admit that the Gaffer was probably right. Most of the dangers in the galleries – the footburners, the snappers, the shafts of quartz, and the needleballs, were dangers to the feet. Given a pair of long yellow boots such as the Gaffer always provided, a man could choose his own pace according to the emergency. Of the things that were of harm to the body directly, almost all could be warded off with a blazing brand if you had the leisure to turn and face it out.

The Gaffer threw him a new pair of boots and put on a pair himself. He took a powerful handlamp from the clip by the door. After a moment's thought he also took up a sticklike instrument with a metal spike at one end and a black box beneath the handle.

'Come, JoJo! Let's see what we can do for OrsOrs.'

'You want torches?'

'No, I have the lamp.'

JoJo put his hand in front of the lens. 'It isn't burn,' he objected. 'You can' defend yourself with tha'.'

'No,' said the Gaffer. 'But I don't expect to have to.'

The Terran's manner showed none of the tension which JoJo felt about returning across the disturbed noon galleries. The Terran carried little about him other than his stick, and it was obvious that he intended to make the journey at no more than walking pace. It was an example of the terrible assurance that the universe must adapt to suit the Terrans, since they did not intend to adapt to it. The endpoint of this philosophy should have been arrogance, but the Gaffer was more of a father-figure, always with the iron hand well concealed in a leathern glove. JoJo sometimes wondered just how terrible the iron hand of a Terran could be, seeing what he could accomplish with a mere stroke of the leather.

Seeing that for once he had the Gaffer to himself, JoJo felt bold enough to ask some of the questions which had been puzzling him. At the first widening of the way he forsook his deferential position at the rear, and drew up to the Gaffer's side. Having gained this vantage point he became suddenly afraid of his own audacity. He blurted out his first question in a way he instantly regretted.

'Are you God?' asked JoJo.

The Terran footsteps faltered for a moment, then continued.

'Far from it, JoJo.' The Gaffer's voice was kind.

'Do you work for him then?'

'Again, no. In fact, from some of the jobs I get, I sometimes wonder if I'm not an agent for the opposition.'

The answer was inscrutable to JoJo, but the Terran seemed to be a little amused, so the youth continued in a bolder vein.

'Is a rocket terrible?'

'To those who have no defence against it, yes.'

'Would a rocket be terrible against Terran?'

'Providing he knew you had one, no.'

'If he knew, what would he do?'

'Laugh until his pants fell down, I guess. Then, if he thought you were a danger to him, he'd kill you. If you weren't, he'd just go on laughing.'

'Why?' This was a leading question, and the crux of JoJo's perplexity.

'Why? Because a Terran has access to weapons many millions of times more powerful. He could, if he wished, destroy this whole world in a second, the sun in minutes, and most of the stars you see in a matter of hours or years.'

'Is that what it means to be Terran – have the power to kill everything?'

'I've never thought of it that way,' said the Gaffer. 'We

always think of ourselves as builders and creators. But now I come to think of it, you do have a point.'

The focused beam of the Gaffer's handlamp was probably a thousand times more powerful than the illumination from JoJo's torch had been. With wide sweeps of arc, the Gaffer explored the roof of the gallery, revealing features which JoJo was sure no member of his own race had ever seen before. The entire cave was surmounted by banks of stratified crystal which shone with a thousand faceted mirrors, like transient stars. As the beam probed the far regions, JoJo became aware for the first time of the true proportions of the gallery. It was far smaller than his imagination had painted it. Thus gaining perspective, he lost a considerable amount of his fears.

JoJo realised with something of a shock that the Gaffer was more interested in the physical characteristics of the gallery than he was in the presence of the beasties. Such naïvety seemed to verge on the insane. JoJo constantly leaned to deflect the lamp back to their immediate path so as to reveal the terrors underfoot. This exercise seemed to amuse the Terran somewhat, and he finally handed the lamp to the fire-boy.

'You carry the lamp for me, will you, JoJo?'

JoJo accepted the offer proudly, marvelling at the solid, compact feel of the apparatus which was pressed into his hand. Like a child with a new toy he surveyed the path before them, delighted with the way the beasties fled from the intense beam into the cradling darkness. He could appreciate, now, that so bright a source of light was a very effective weapon against would-be attackers. It was suddenly no mystery to him that the Terran could walk through the noon caves with relative impunity, whereas Tanic's natives trod here in fear of their lives.

Before them snappers and needle balls fled into the shadows, and bumble-bugs and ghosts and acid-tails stirred in a scurry of wings out of the range of the revealing brilliance. Only a footburner squatted doggedly in their path, squinting its small eyes malevolently and slavering its gross, corrosive juices. The Gaffer extended his pointed stick close to the creature's face. From the spiked tip a long tracery spark appeared, searching out the footburner's eyes with a thin, tinkering discharge. The footburner screamed with agony and fled from the scene, leaving bright phosphorescent pools as witness to its involuntary spasm.

Treading warily over the phosphoritic excretion, JoJo became convinced of the Gaffer's wisdom in insisting on the wearing of boots. He anxiously probed the shadows with the lamp, expecting the footburner to have retreated into a position of ambush, but the beastie had fled far, and was probably in hiding.

'You didn't kill him then?' he asked.

'Heavens, no!' The Gaffer's reproof was mild. 'Live and let live unless you both need the same territory. It's a good motto. I merely tickled him with a high-tension electrical discharge. Plenty of volts but no current. Painful but not deadly.' He raised the stick and let the sparks play idly on to his fingers. 'It seeks out the softer, moister parts of the body because the spark goes for the point of lowest electrical resistance. There's no beast alive that could stand and face it, yet it couldn't kill anything. Simple, humane, and very inexpensive.'

'Are you always so worried for your enemies?'

'Usually.' The Gaffer's voice was alive with amused cynicism. 'It's mainly our friends who tend to get hurt.'

Something in the Gaffer's manner made JoJo feel suddenly afraid of the species who were so confident of their power to destroy that they could afford to show compassion for those who might destroy them. What the Terran had said about their friends was more difficult to understand.

With the handlamp it was easy to pick a more direct route through the columnar jungle and easy to avoid a colony of footburners, who scattered from the advancing light. The occasional snappers who rushed at them were almost casually turned by the Gaffer with his stick. Despite the Terran's apparent assumption that traversing the noon gallery was no more than an interesting stroll, they reached the connecting tunnel in record time.

In the tunnel JoJo resumed his questions.

'Gaffer, you came here to help us fight reptiles?' 'Yes.' 'Why do you help us?'

'Firstly, because you're a species so like Terran humanity that it's impossible to believe we have not come from common stock – though we've no idea how this could be so. Secondly, although you are technically the dominant species on Tanic, an ecological imbalance has given crucial advantage to the reptiles. Either we help you, or we allow you to become extinct in a century or so. We hate species to become extinct – especially when they're human like ourselves.'

'But what you gain from helping us?' JoJo still felt his earlier question was unanswered.

'Gain?' The question obviously took the Terran by surprise. 'I don't think we gain anything – except perhaps a mild feeling of satisfaction. But when you set that against the cost of an operation like this, it's a pretty expensive way of gaining satisfaction.'

'How expensive?'

'All the wealth of all your elders and chiefs who have never lived couldn't buy the power needed to drive one of our ships from Terra to Tanic.'

'Ships? You have more than one, then?'

'There are six in orbit around Tanic at the moment. The three survey ships will soon go home. The others, two supply ships and a cruiser, must wait for me.'

At the entrance to the second gallery they came across a scorpid. Sixteen incredibly agile legs, mandible that could break steel, and a mobile's sting capable of dispatching a dozen men. It sat malignantly in their path, its eye stalks undeterred by the brightness of the handlamp.

JoJo found his mind suddenly crossed with a hint of heresy. Though he feared the scorpid, he was almost glad to see it contest the Terran for right of way. While he had a strong regard for the god who was becoming human, he was beginning also to develop a sense of affinity with the creatures of his own world – and a growing apprehension about the race who were so confident of themselves that they could afford to be kind to their enemies.

The scorpid was wary but unmoving. Not normally nocturnal in its habits, its eyes were equipped with irises well able to compensate for the brilliance of the handlamp. It reared up, its breath hissing through its terrible beak, its sting whipping the air with increasing agitation. The Gaffer stood stock still, regarding his pretentious foe with a look more of admiration than of concern.

'Move along, old feller! I don't want to hurt you, but I've a great respect for that sting of yours. Besides which, you're standing in my way.' Experimentally he pointed his stick at the scorpid's head and moved forward. The long electric arc struck towards the scorpid's eye stalks. The scorpid, reacting faster than they could follow, hurled itself in fury at the spike, tearing it from the Gaffer's hand and severing the electrode with one single crush of its beak. Then it reared up, spitting fury, its legs clawing the air, preparing to launch itself at the handlamp and the quaking JoJo who held it.

There was a whip of leather as the Gaffer's hand drew something from his belt. This was followed by a blaze of light and a rapid series of explosions which were so powerful and unexpected that JoJo was deafened and robbed of the power of speech for many seconds after. The scorpid literally exploded in front of them. Fragments of its flesh hit the tunnel at all angles and fell ridiculously back to the floor.

The Gaffer returned an instrument to his waist and turned to the shocked fire-boy, whose nerveless hands still held the lamp as though he were a wooden image.

'Sorry, JoJo! I should have warned you. Not something I like doing, no indeed! A bit hard on the ears in a confined space like this.'

In JoJo's shocked mind two points were paramount – the absolute decimation of the scorpid, and the facile reason for the Terran's reluctance to use his fearful instrument. The latter factor was so greatly at variance with the Gaffer's odd notions of humane defence that the fire-boy's mind took an intuitive leap which brought him suddenly face to face with the terrible iron hand of Terra. For a moment the knowledge filled him with terror.

'What did you use on the scorpid?' he asked at last.

The Terran hand produced the instrument again.

'Only an old-fashioned automatic pistol. Bit of a museum piece really – but it has its uses.'

'Is that what Terrans use kill animals?' JoJo examined the blued-steel artifact without comprehension.

'Not very often.' The Gaffer was frowning as he returned the pistol to its holster. 'More often they use it to kill each other.'

JoJo retreated into silence then. The Gaffer retrieved his stick and tested it. Although the end had been completely severed by the scorpid's jaws, the metal core still obliged with its characteristic spark. They moved on into the crystal forest. Snapper and needle-ball scuttled hastily to either side, still apparently reacting from the shock of the firing of the Gaffer's weapon. The occasional snappers who dared enter the forest to rush at their heels received a discouraging shock from the electric stick and fled on stumpy legs slapping their stumpy tails behind them.

In the bright illumination of the handlamp the razor bushes were even more marvellous than JoJo had supposed. Millions upon millions of crystal platelets shimmered on ranks of skeletal trees, moved by an unseen unfelt wind. The regular track, he soon discovered, was by no means the safest route to follow. The Gaffer pointed new ways through which a man could pass without fear of accidentally brushing against the barbarous blades. JoJo reflected that the Terran in months had gained a better knowledge of the noon caves than his own people had acquired in their entire history.

This prompted JoJo to consider his people's place in the scheme of things. Certainly they were above the beasties, yet below the Terrans. The Terran was a humanitarian – providing it did not conflict with his own safety and convenience. But when something stood in his way he was terrible and ruthless. So how far up the scale did the Terran rate the natives of Tanic? If they displeased him, would he not be equally terrible with them? And, if he could command destruction on any scale, why did he not direct it against the reptiles if he was sincere in his intent to help?

'Do your ships have rockets?' asked JoJo suddenly.

'Far more powerful weapons than rockets, I'm afraid.'

'But no use against reptiles, eh?'

The Gaffer began to frown. 'So many questions, JoJo. What's bothering you?'

'I was thinking that if you already had plenty rockets up there, why don' you use them on the reptiles? Then we need no' to have make-men-work in the chemical rooms in order to make our own.'

'It's not that easy, JoJo. I could win your war for you in a week. But I don't dare do so.'

'Why no'?'

'Because for your own sakes you have to win it yourselves. I am already doing far more than I should.'

For a long time JoJo trudged in silence, trying to resolve the meaning of this curious phrase. Then: 'I don' understand tha', Gaffer.'

'No,' said the Terran. 'I scarcely expected that you would.'

JoJo seemed to lose interest then. He fell sullenly behind all the way down the descending passages which led to the air shaft. Only when the acrid vapours from the mixing rooms made the air sting their nostrils, did he speak again.

'I still don' see why we have let-men-kill themselves in there, when you could give us all the weapons we need.'

'I could give you everything but self-respect,' said the Gaffer quietly. 'That you can only give to yourselves. It isn't the winning that counts. It's the fighting that fits a species for survival. If I killed all the reptiles tomorrow, you don't know how utterly it would destroy you also. There are far worse things to tear a man apart than the claws of a lizard.'

'Like what, Gaffer?'

'Like the spawn of the dragon, for instance,' said the Terran, and refused to answer more.

When they reached the deposition cave the air was thick with smoke from the burning brands. So far the scorpid had been contained, but its growing desperation had lent it amazing turns of strength. Twice it had gained the tank rim and twice been forced back into the process liquor. Such was its frenzy that next time it reached the rim it would probably escape, despite the fire.

Swiftly the Gaffer summed up the situation, then seized a metal net on the end of a long pole, used for recovering fallen anode metal from the tank. Savagely he kicked a path through the fire ring and made his way through to stand on the vat surround. OrsOrs followed him, plainly perplexed by the Gaffer's action. Realisation brought a sharp cry of alarm.

'Don' be dumbchild, Gaffer! You know wha' tha' devil capable of.'

The Terran did not answer. Thoughtfully he watched the scorpid orbit on the surface of the liquid. When he judged the time to be right, he struck. The net took the scorpid fairly, and lifted it from the tank. Somebody screamed. OrsOrs cursed and rushed for a machette. The Gaffer held the pole resolutely horizontal, apparently uncertain what to do with his prize now it had been gained.

The scorpid had its own ideas on the situation. With machinelike rapidity its jaws tore the metal net apart. Then, with an agile flick of its tail, it leaped up and grasped the pole. Without pause it twisted, and like a streak of fury it raced towards the Gaffer's hands.

It did not complete its journey. A man's pace away from the Gaffer both scorpid and pole were severed by one blow from OrsOrs's descending knife. The bisected scorpid fell beside the vat, its muscles still moving but incapable of any action save that of dying. OrsOrs watched it warily for a long time, knife poised, as though he believed in resurrection. Then he straightened himself and turned to face the Gaffer. His brow was streaming with sweat.

'That was very dumbchild thin' you do, Gaffer. Not even fire-boy attemp' catch scorpid in net.'

'I did.' The Terran remained unmoved. His eyes were watching OrsOrs closely.

'Then you're no' afraid of death?' OrsOrs was critical.

'It was a calculated risk.'

'If I had not been quick, it would have killed you.'

'That was part of the calculation. Why did you ask me here, OrsOrs?'

'To kill scorpid.'

'Yet you have better skill with a knife. You're more familiar with the ways of a scorpid. It's your natural enemy.'

'When I want light I call fire-boy. When somethin' need liftin' I call winchman.'

'And when something has to be destroyed, you call a Terran – is that it, OrsOrs?' The Gaffer was sternly questioning. 'Is that how you think of us? As destroyers? As interstellar rat catchers and louse removers?'

'I did no' say tha', Gaffer,' OrsOrs protested.

'But wasn't that the way you *thought* about it?'

Machette in hand, OrsOrs drew himself up to his full height, towering above the Terran's head. 'No disrespect you, Gaffer, but I did expect you come with thunder and kill scorpid. Tha' way is easy.' His voice and tone were thick with the disrespect that his words claimed to negate.

'Why?' asked the Gaffer directly. 'I could have done it, certainly, but I'm damned if I can see why you should expect it.'

'Have you no' proven to us tha' whatever we can do, Terran can do better?'

The Gaffer blazed with sudden anger. 'If that's the lesson you've learned, then you've deceived yourselves. I came here to help you to stand on your own feet – not to have you ride on mine. I've better things to do with my life than to play wet nurse to a bunch of cravens.'

OrsOrs face clouded with wrath and disillusion. His machette hand moved involuntarily, almost as though it wished to cleave the Terran as it had the scorpid.

'By the ghosts of ancestors! If you were no' the Gaffer I would have killed you for far less an insul'.'

The Gaffer was unconcerned. 'You might have tried, OrsOrs, but I don't think you would have succeeded. Now get those mandrels back into the tank and the anodes reconnected. We need those projector tubes. The mixing rooms have already delivered the filled rockets, and we're anxious to start testing.'

OrsOrs tried to contain his fury. 'I know schedule, Gaffer. You don' need give me detailed instruction – nor would I ask now even if I did need. I think we understand each other?'

'I hope so.' The Terran reclaimed his electric stick and carefully inspected his boots which had been overmuch exposed to the heat from the ring of flames. He stooped for his handlamp, then walked away into the tunnel's entrance without a further word. JoJo followed him anxiously, uncertain which side of the schism his loyalties lay.

'You want a guide, Gaffer?'

'Thank you, JoJo, but I think I know the way.'

'Then may I walk with you little?'

'Be my guest.' The Terran's anger had subsided completely. Unexpectedly, he seemed to have come out of the encounter in remarkably good spirits.

'May I ask question?'

'You never stop asking, JoJo. But I'll answer if I can.'

'Why did you treat OrsOrs like tha'? Don' you know he almost worships you?'

'It was because of that I had to turn on him. I've already told you I'm no god. Neither you, OrsOrs, nor anybody must treat me as if I am. Whatever you can do, I can do. And the other way about. You can do whatever I can do – given a little time, a little patience, and a little learning. Only by seeming a little stupid could I make OrsOrs angry. And only when he was angry did he even try to match himself to me.'

'But you risk your life. You could have kill tha' scorpid as you did the other.'

'How the scorpid died was unimportant. What mattered was breaking OrsOrs's dependence on me. Unless I can do that, it would be better if I hadn't come.'

'You mean better had you left us be eaten by reptiles?' JoJo was incredulous.

'As I have said, JoJo, there are worse fates than being eaten by reptiles.'

'I think I shall never understand the Terran mind,' said JoJo.

'Then I'll let you into a secret. There's no difference between a Terran mind and yours, except that our expertise in death has forced us to acquire a somewhat painful sort of maturity.'

The assembly and testing of the first projector was carried out in one of the smaller noon caves which had been specially cleared for the purpose. At one end the cave narrowed to a horizontal shaft, which widened suddenly into daylight and ended at a ledge some thirty metres above the valley floor.

In all directions the high, purpled crags of the mountains rose up to enclose the valley within a bowl, with here and there a pass or fault giving tantalising glimpses of the wild vistas beyond. The floor of the valley was clothed with a thick forest of vegetation and sprinkled with the tracery of many rills and streams fed from the ice-capped heights. At the lowest point, a great yellow river moved sluggishly against the intrusions of the palmaceous weed which threatened to choke it into a swamp.

It was to this river and to the many others like it that the reptiles came to breed and to drench away their flaking scales. Their domain was centred on the watercourses and on the ecologically rich pastures which lay above the forest and below the sterile peaks. From his aerial surveys the Gaffer probably knew more of the local scene and topography than did any of Tanic's natives. His cameras and telescopes had pried into territory undisputedly the province of the reptilian kingship. He knew each reptile nest and breeding place on the river. He even knew where one of the old, forgotten cities bf Tanic still protruded its ruins through the clay waters of the river's course. Thus he alone could accurately measure the regression of Tanic humanity and the growing dominance of the reptile form.

From the ledge, even by eye, they could see a pack of hunting reptilian heads. The creatures were walking erect on two feet and a tail, their long necks probing over the vegetable screens searching for sight of prey. Their size and apparent ungainliness were deceptive. When running on all four limbs, a mature reptile could attain speeds of sixty kilometres an hour. Their jaws could cut a man in half with one bite.

The Terran was strangely silent. Through his powerful lenses he viewed an unknown yet familiar scene. Unlike his aerial survey pictures, his present position, barely above the tree ferns and cycads, gave him a sudden sense of perspective and presence. With very little imagination he might have been looking at Earth in Jurassic times. The hunting reptiles were disturbingly reminiscent of the Terran brontosaurus, except that they were fully carnivorous, had the teeth of tyrannosaurus, and a brain cavity approaching that of man himself.

Perhaps for the first time since the exploit had begun, the Gaffer began to feel afraid. The creatures before him belonged to an era predating the evolution of mammals on Terra. His own stance placed him at variance with his environment by about two hundred million terrayears, and the natives of Tanic who pressed his shoulder were scarcely far behind him. It was they, perhaps, who had developed aeons before their time - or was it *homo sapiens* who had been a late developer in the inexorable march of life from the primeval sea to some unknown mammalian evolutionary end?

From this consideration stemmed the Gaffer's unshown but almost reverent respect for OrsOrs and his people. With a culture almost ten times as old as Terra's they had missed the accident of the invention of the wheel, yet still progressed into a mature electrochemical-based civilization despite the fantastic odds of a gross ecological imbalance. The Gaffer was painfully aware that his own technological intervention must cause a radical change in the future development of the entire planet. It was a situation he did not relish, and one which tormented his imagination with possible end points he could never hope to see. His role was purely that of a catalyst in a potent evolutionary reaction.

He turned back to where the rocket projector tube was

receiving a loving final polish from the men who made it. Despite the dimensional accuracy inherent in the electro-forming technique, he had spent the night gauging it, uncomfortably aware of the dangers of being a one-man arsenal and armaments instructor. True to form, he had found the critical dimensions of the tube accurate to within several millionths of a centimetre, despite the apparent crudeness of the conditions under which it was made. These tolerances were well beyond the accuracy necessary for the jòb, and he knew that Tanic's own rough metrology would suffice when it came to the job of replication without Terran supervision.

The rockets themselves had been completed previously, but not testfired. He took one, fitted it into the projector tube, and returned to the ledge overlooking the valley. With a mixture of fear and anticipation, the Tanic warriors and OrsOrs's technicians followed him at a safe distance. The Gaffer hoisted the heavy projector over his shoulder and warned those behind to stay well clear of the rocket exhaust. He sighted on a standing shard of granite-like rock, and with a half prayer, pressed the trigger.

An unexpected recoil pressure threw him off balance and warned him of a miscalculation of propellant charge. The rocket, tail spiraling as it carved its way through the still air, passed over the rock shard and continued for another kilometre before it plunged into a rocky grotto.

The impact explosion was gratifying in its effect. Literally tons of rock and detritus were lifted into the air, fragmenting and scattering over a considerable area. Fern trees and cycads were uprooted, snapped and broken. The noise of the explosion split the air like thunder and rolled and echoed many times among the startled mountains. Afterwards the rent earth showed a great bruised scar where Tanic's first missile had landed.

It was the Gaffer's conservative estimate that both the propellant and the explosive charge had been at least three times as potent as the modest weapon he had set out to build. He looked back to OrsOrs to see his reaction, and was met by a look of shocked incredulity.

'What's the matter, OrsOrs? Wasn't that what you wanted to see?'

'Nothin' like tha'! There should never be anythin' as fearful as tha'. Suddenly I feel almos' sorry for devil-reptile . . .'

OrsOrs rubbed his ears, still hurting from the unaccustomed shock. He shook his head and turned away in the manner of one who is aware that a page of history is turning under his feet yet can not move nimbly enough to avoid being crushed between the leaves. His companions held no such reservations. Whooping with joy, some were busily swarming down the climbing ropes on the cliff face, running to see the crater. Others were inspecting the projector, marvelling that it had not itself been destroyed in the process. A few, like JoJo, clustered with many questions around the Gaffer, like children round a father whom they are still naïve enough to believe omnipotent.

Soon the ones who had run out into the valley came running back. There was fear in their shouting voices: 'Reptiles – see! Reptiles come!' They bunched in panic at the foot of the cliff, fighting for a place on the climbing ropes. Behind them, reptilian movements in the dense green jungle spoke of a hunting pack scenting man-meat and hungry for a killing. Then disaster struck. A climbing rope, overtaxed with the stress of half a dozen climbing men, snapped near the top. It shed its burden on to the clustered group below. In the midst of the shouting and the screaming one further voice broke the panic into a death-quiet reality.

'Reptile near! Reptile near!'

Instantly the Gaffer had the projector on his knee, clearing to reload. He had intended to dismantle and inspect for damage prior to re-firing, but the present emergency forced him to take a chance. From the edge of the forest no less than three reptiles broke cover. To judge by the tumult in the brush, at least three more were heading in their direction.

Swiftly the Gaffer hoisted the projector over his shoulder, took careful aim, and fired. Again the rocket went too high and too far, missing the first two creatures completely. By sheer off chance it plunged towards the third. The explosion ripped the reptile to shreds and hurled fragments of carcass back to the very edges of the forest fronds.

The Gaffer reloaded and considered his tactics. With such a widely erroneous instrument he could scarcely hope for this luck to continue. Far better to try to frighten away the two attackers who were still in the field. He aimed deliberately very short of his target in the hope of creating a crater and a blast area which would turn the creatures from their paths.

The projectile fell approximately where he had planned. In the meantime the two reptiles, running parallel, had increased their speed to escape whatever fate had engulfed their rear mate. They topped a slight rise just as the rocket exploded in the hollow before them. Although neither could have been materially hurt by the blast, both must have been affected by concussive shock. They fell against one another while still running, and toppled into the crater. Maintaining his range, the Gaffer managed to put a second rocket on top of them for good measure.

But this was no moment for respite. The knot of injured men at the cliff-foot still remained, despite several relief ropes which had been thrown down to them. Two other reptiles had broken cover and were apparently estimating the carnage of their kind before proceeding. Such was the magnitude of the reptile brain that they established, quite rightly, that the danger lay directly to the front. To avoid this they made first for the cliff edge well to one side, and began a wary sortie under the shelter of the rocky overhang. Attracted by spilled blood, several great toothed-birds took to the air on pteranodon wings, and patrolled the battle area waiting for a chance to settle in the injured.

The Gaffer swore. He had no chance even to see the reptiles advancing under the ledge, let alone destroy them. It was only a matter of time before they reached the group of men trapped at the cliff-foot. With quick decision, he shouted for OrsOrs.

'Lower me down with the projector and some rockets. I have to get below the ledge to get at them.'

OrsOrs, who had already given the majority of his fallen comrades up for lost, looked at him dubiously. 'Too late, Gaffer.'

'Not if you hurry. Get some men here fast.'

'No!' OrsOrs stood squarely in his way. 'Nobody goes down now. Risk too great. Especially we can' risk you.'

'Then stand out of my way!'

Angrily he thrust past OrsOrs to the warrior group at the edge of the cliff drop. JoJo and some of his associates ran to help. Within a minute, with the projector and six rockets roped to his body, the Gaffer was being lowered through space to the rocky floor.

Almost immediately he regretted the decision. As he spun helplessly on the descending thread the dark shadow of huge leathern wings closed the sunlight from him. An aerial bulk comparable in size with a small airplane screeched across the face of the cliff, creating a draught that swung him and his high-explosive load dangerously close to the rock walls.

Fortunately he was too close against the wall for the avian creature to try to seize him in flight. Below him he could hear quite plainly the blood-cry of the attacking reptiles making slow progress along the broken territory footing the cliff. Then his feet touched the ground. Knife ready, he slashed the yoke which had carried him, and freed his weapon for action. He had scarcely primed and loaded when a reptile broke round the edge of a bluff and came at him full charge. Without the luxury of sighting, the Gaffer swung the projector in the general direction and squeezed the firing trigger. Nothing happened.

Although the firing mechanism tripped, the rocket remained inert. In an instant of panic the Gaffer observed the charging reptile and searched frantically for a way of escape into or back up the cliff. There was none. Savagely he shook the reject rocket from the firing chamber and rammed another one in. By now he was working at point-blank range, and was as much in danger from the blast of his own fire as he was from the reptile's jaws. He fired at the thundering bulk which seemed almost upon him, then flung himself face down and waited for whatever fate would do to him.

Fortunately the major force of the explosion was taken by six tons of decimating reptile. Even so, the shock was severe enough to concuss him for several minutes. When he was fully conscious he found he was bleeding freely from a scalp wound and had over a dozen cuts and abrasions. Nevertheless he counted himself lucky.

A sudden eclipse of the sun reminded him that the battle was not yet over. Scrambling hastily to his feet he drew the pistol from his hip as the huge, winged creature dropped low over him with all the finesse of a crashing helicopter.

Nerved now to the prehistoric terrors which the day contained, he put two shots into the flying nightmare at places where logic suggested the wing muscles ought to be. The fantastic cry of pain which this act produced was something he knew he would carry to his grave. The creature slipped sideways to the ground in a mortally horrifying crash landing. Then, with a frightening movement consisting of claw-hops assisted by beats with broken leathern wings, the frantic wounded creature rushed at him, its beak lined with sharp, yellowed teeth. He let it come to within six paces before one further shot shattered its cranial cavity. The creature flopped to a reluctant death amid the fragments of the shattered reptile.

A noise behind him on the rock face made him wheel in sudden alarm. It was OrsOrs at the bottom of a rope, with a dozen warriors armed with machettes following him. OrsOrs surveyed the carnage uncomprehendingly at first, then his face became crossed with a sardonic smile.

'Not bad morning's work, even for Terran, I would imagine.'

The Gaffer smiled wanly. 'What happened to the other one? There were two under the cliff when I came down.'

OrsOrs shrugged. 'I expect he knew the Terran killer here. He stand off until res' of pack catch up. I know you've kill five times as many creatures in hour as mos' men in lifetime, but I still can' advise you fight full pack from the ground.'

'How are the men who fell?'

'Mos' recovered to cave, thanks to you. Two are dead, but the survivors will want to thank you for themselves. I've no doubt the Council of Elders will also be wantin' feast your name this evenin'. So much bloodshed needs rewardin'.'

'You sound bitter, OrsOrs. Don't you want the reptiles killed?'

'If I had several lives, I'd give them all win tha' fight. Don' think I don' appreciate what you doin'. There would have been twenty widows tonight had you no' risked your life stop tha' reptile.'

'Then what's your objection?'

'I seen nearly whole generation slaughtered by no more reptiles than you kill today. Tha' generation die because we no' able do what you do usin' our materials and our techniques. My objection no' to what you do, but the fact you seem to do it all too easy.'

It was several weeks later that the Gaffer found a sheet of Tanic bark paper on his desk in the annex when he came down in the morning. He was quite certain it had not been there the previous evening. He turned it over, not really expecting that he would find a message on it. He found a scrawl in Tanic formal script which he had difficulty in deciphering.

Gaffer

I shout you danger tall as biggest mountain. I cannot spell lest others come and read – which would stir gigantic beasts of trouble. Tomorrow I must tell you anything of help.

There was a hiatus here, as though the writer realised that to identify himself could lead to detection. Instead of a signature, a further phrase was penned at the bottom of the sheets:

I know dragons spawn.

The latter phrase brought a smile of cryptic amusement to

the Gaffer's lips. He transmitted a microstat of the document to the computer files, then dropped the original into the disposal unit. Shrugging his shoulders, he sought his boots, handlamp, and electric stick, and set out for the deposition caves.

The past few weeks had been fruitful. OrsOrs had demonstrated his ability to control the manufacture of both projectors and rockets, and seven Tanic warriors had been trained to use them. The crude effectiveness of the weapons had been demonstrated many times, and the sheer coverage of the blast pattern more than compensated for their inaccuracy when used against such large targets as the reptiles.

The Gaffer's latest task had been to encourage OrsOrs to divide his chemical and mixing rooms into small, well separated units, so that an accident in one would not destroy the whole facility. He had thus provided, at least in theory, for the continuity of his efforts in Tanic hands. Having been given the weapon and an understanding of its principles and potential, it was essential that the people of Tanic now accept the responsibility for its development and use. It was time for the Gaffer to pull out. One day the weapon was going to be used against men instead of reptiles, and Terra already had too much blood on its conscience.

With this thought in mind, the Gaffer traversed the noon caves. The galleries were relatively empty of beasties at this hour, since the outer darkness was only just lifting and the nocturnal residents were still braving the rising tides of dawn.

On the lower levels all the activity was human. The chemical and mixing rooms were draughting acrid fumes into the corridors, and pallid-faced men were appearing at the entrances like swimmers surfacing for air. The men in the deposition caves were working furiously. Two more vats were being commissioned for the electro-deposition of rocket cases, and one more dedicated to the forming of trigger mechanisms and fuse components.

The Gaffer searched for a long time before locating JoJo in the battery cave. The fire-boy was replenishing the torches over the cable run which carried the power to the deposition shop. Here over six hundred giant batteries, each one a chemical primary cell over two men's length in diameter and ten men deep, contributed their current to the giant acid-vat accumulators. From the accumulators the stored and balanced power was distributed via the giant cables to the deposition vats which lay in the several caves beyond.

The battery cave was the oldest installation which Tanic knew – so old that nobody could tell who had dug and lined the wells or first designed the system. It was said that some of the cells had been in operation for two thousand years or more, unchanged save for the yearly dig-out and re-furbishing. Only the cables, thick, random black snakes across the floor of the cable run, needed renewal and constant attention. It was necessary frequently to inspect their cracking hides and correct the slow but inexorable deformation of the bitumen insulators, which unchecked would allow the conductors to meet and result in a catastrophic short circuit.

The Gaffer appeared not to notice JoJo. Both waited until they could come together unobserved before they spoke.

'You got my message, Gaffer?'

'I did. Why all the mystery?'

'The elders held council yesterday. OrsOrs was there speaking against you violently. He thinks your influence is going destroy us.'

'He's probably right – it would, if I stayed. Fortunately in a day or two I shall be leaving for Terra.'

'They won't allow i'. If you leave you will become a legend – something which grows on re-telling to children. They want prove you are no more near a god than any other man on Tanic.'

'That's an easy thing to want, but a difficult thing to do.'

'Nothing makes more even than blow from long knife.'

'I see!' The Gaffer was speculative for a moment or so. 'Do you know who is going to do this, and when?'

'OrsOrs. He will ask to take you to our sacred place. All grea' things on Tanic end there.'

'How do you know this, JoJo?'

'I am fire-boy for council chamber. I was there.'

'Then it's privileged information. What will the council do to you if they find out what you've told me?'

'I would be sent out of the caves into the valley.'

'Death by reptile, eh? Very well, JoJo, knowing this, why did you risk telling me?'

'Because I can' agree with i'. The only thing you have done to us is give us a future. Tha's why you must no' go with OrsOrs. And –'

'And what, JoJo?'

JoJo told him what was on his mind. The Gaffer was silent for a long time afterwards. Then: 'If I can arrange that, can I count on your help when the time comes – no matter what I ask?'

'No matter wha', Gaffer.'

'Very well! Say nothing of this to anyone. I will tell you what I want you to do.'

'Do you need do anythin'? Can't you just go tonight?'

'I could, but it would solve nothing. You see, basically, OrsOrs is right. So we are going to prove his point for him – but in a way he won't quite be expecting.'

But even then it seemed as if JoJo might be wrong. Two weeks passed without incident, and OrsOrs, though taciturn, was in no way actively hostile. Then came the day of farewell, the day on which council elders received the Gaffer and showered him with gifts and wishes for his future, and the day many of his friends were in tears at the thought of parting. Late that day OrsOrs approached him.

'Before you leave us, Gaffer, there somethin' I would like show you – something may help you understand us better.'

'If you say so, I should be delighted to come.' The Gaffer looked at his watch. 'But it is getting late and there will not be much time left after. Before I come I must say a few more good-byes. If you can meet me by the air shaft in an hour, I shall be pleased to come then.'

OrsOrs nodded his assent, and parted. The Gaffer moved swiftly, and within the hour he had made his preparations and was back to meet OrsOrs waiting at the air shaft. OrsOrs was silent as he led the way through the almost unused south caves to a point where a sudden turn of rock concealed a door.

'This is place I wanted show you,' said OrsOrs. 'Mos' men come here only once in lifetime, as part of the ceremony admitting their manhood. Rememberin' wha' i' means to us, I ask you treat i' as temple.'

'And refrain from acts of destruction, eh?' The Terran was cynically amused.

'Your phrase, no' mine.' OrsOrs avoided his eyes. 'I merely ask you treat i' reverently. For instance, no' bear arms in these walls.'

'I wonder you bother to bring me here if you think me such a barbarian.'

'You have earned the right come here. Your innovations have given new meanings to our old crafts. You have shown us how make rockets which can kill reptiles, so tha' we can kill all on Tanic. In fac', nothin' after your comin' can ever be same again. Your ideas have taken over our history.'

'I was aware of that danger. It's the reason I kept my intervention to a minimum.'

'But you didn' succeed in i'. The old values are crumblin' – replaced by nothin' but uncertainty.'

'Would you have preferred that I hadn't come?'

'Your comin' was necessary for our survival. But i's mixed blessing. Before you go I wan' you also see wha' you've destroyed.'

Instead of querying the accusation, the Gaffer compressed his lips. He undid the broad belt at his waist and allowed it to drop its burden of weaponry to the floor. They entered a foyer where OrsOrs went through a dumb symbolistic ritual with two guardians before they were permitted farther. Then great ornate doors were opened and they were allowed into the gallery beyond.

Here the Gaffer stopped in sudden wonder. In his experience Tanic had essentially a utilitarian culture. Save for the chiefs and some of the prime elders, few possessed articles of great intrinsic value. The concept of riches was virtually unknown, and the most valuable items were invariably the most useful or the most necessary for survival. In this cave, however, lay a true concentration of valuable and artistic artifacts which would have been unique even upon Terra.

The gallery was rare in having a smooth wall structure,

and its decoration was fabulously rich and ornate. Its walls were entirely covered with a random lace of metal veins which had obviously been formed *in situ*, since it followed and emphasised the polished marvels of the rock structure. Even the roof, lit by probably five hundred torches, carried the tender tracery across the vaulted heights to meet and blend with that from the far side. Elaborate canopies, the detailed metalwork of which would have defied Terran sources to duplicate, protected the onlooker from burning oil drips from the high flames. But it was in the alcoves themselves that the true wonders began.

The chalices, trays, furniture, weapons and works of pure art, fabricated in a dozen different metals, were supreme examples of the electroformers art. Almost all were incapable of being reproduced by any of the more conventional techniques of manufacture. Locked solidly into the metal matrices, mineral crystals and precious stones lay in entrapped harmony with their settings in a way which appeared so supremely natural that all other art forms would have seemed contrived and artificial when set beside them. As works of craftmanship, each exhibit could have made its possessor a wealthy man on any home-world. As works of art, they were completely beyond any scale of price.

Dazed by the magnificence of such form and artistry, the Gaffer followed OrsOrs, alcove by alcove, along what appeared to be a descending chronological sequence of exhibits. OrsOrs offered no comment, but waited patiently while the Gaffer absorbed the miracles of one collection before proceeding to the next. In this way they covered the whole cave area. Near the end of the sequence most pretences to artistry had gone. The utilitarian aspect of pots and platters, many somewhat misshapen, was predominant.

The last exhibit was a simple copper bowl.

'Do you realise wha' you've seen, Gaffer?'

'I think so, OrsOrs. The history of Tanic in terms of its achievements in the forming of metal.'

'Then let me add time scale. Tha' copper bowl is ten times as old as earliest stone-age fragmen' found on Terra.'

'It makes me feel humble.'

'Nowhere near humble as you make us feel. Before you came we *believed* in ourselves, Gaffer. We kept this museum as record of our doings. Each generation came here to measure themselves up to their forefathers and aim little higher. Think what mockery tha's become now. The new generations will want only measure up to omnipoten' Terran.'

'I'm sorry, OrsOrs. You don't know how much I've tried not to overwhelm you with Terran technology.'

'By which you made things damnsight worse!'

'I don't follow your reasoning.'

OrsOrs looked away. His face was nearly impassive, yet his lips trembled with emotion. 'If you'd cast no reflection on us. If you'd been a god, we could have accepted what you've done. If you'd come with army, we could have told ourselves that our savin' was due to greater weight of fight. If you'd confused us with science, we'd have been amazed but grateful. But your comin' here alone gives us no excuse. Tha's a spiteful arrogance we can' forgive.'

'Arrogance?' The Gaffer was genuinely surprised.

'Wha' else you call i'? One man comes, and by showin' how use our tools in new way, turns battle that had brought us the edge of extinction. Because Terrans are so arrogantly sure of themselves that one man and a tool kit is all is necessary for salvation of Tanic. Am I right?'

'You're not right, OrsOrs. We know from experience that when a relatively undeveloped culture is forced into close contact with a technically advanced one, the lesser one is almost invariably destroyed. To stop that happening to you I had to come alone. I had to do everything by means of word and example, man to man. I had to interfere with your history without setting myself up as a deity. That took a bit of doing, OrsOrs. Even you tended to lean on me.'

'Because you prove to us how dumbchild we were. Your trouble, Gaffer, you can' even see yourself as we see you. You so confident you don' even need the luxury of seemin' superior. Have you any idea wha' tha' doin' to us?'

'I have a very good idea. That's why I'm leaving you now. Given a few years you'll have forgotten me.'

'You don' know your influence. You leave now, your name grow with the blood of every reptile we kill. Like or not, you already out-tower our gods. In a generation you will *be* our god, an' people in trouble will pray for the Gaffer to come again. The only thing can save our way of livin' is prove you are very much a man.'

'And how do you propose to do that?'

'I mus' kill you, of course.'

OrsOrs turned suddenly, the machette concealed in a corner appearing abruptly in his hand as if it possessed a life of its own. 'I'm sorry about this, Gaffer. But you see why has to be done.'

'You're not half as sorry as you'll be if you try it.'

OrsOrs advanced, the long knife carving patterns of reflected light around him.

'Isn' this the lesson you wanted us learn – do as Terrans do? Kill for pleasure? Kill for expediency and principle – not jus' for necessity?'

'I warn you, OrsOrs, don't try it. There's another way out of this.'

'Another Terran way?' OrsOrs spat. 'No! This is time do something Tanic way.'

He raised the knife and prepared to strike, but his attention was diverted by an unusual movement of the Gaffer's wrist. Something appeared in the Terran's fingers – a small capsule. Before OrsOrs could identify his danger a cloud of choking vapour hit his face. His eyes were blinded by a hail of stinging droplets which brought him excruciating pain. Through an anguished haze he still tried to hack at the Terran form, but the Gaffer had deftly slipped from his position. OrsOrs' descending knife hit some unseen edge of rock, and the shock drove it from his fingers.

The Terran finished the fight with a deft blow of his hand on the back of his opponent's neck. OrsOrs fell unconscious to the floor, his face a mask of pain and surprise even though his mind no longer registered emotions. The Gaffer straightened and looked round.

'JoJo,' he said softly, 'where the devil are you?'

'Here!' JoJo emerged from behind a canopy support where he had been hiding.

'Is everything all right?' The Gaffer noted the troubled look on the boy's face.

'I had trouble gettin' past guardians. One went down when I hit him, but other I had to beat many times before he fall. He bleeds quite a lot.'

'You'll learn to do it tidily in time. You've got the bags?'

'Four, as you said.' JoJo threw some soft bundles on to the floor. 'Will be enough?'

'Enough for us to carry. Take two and fill them with the best small items from the other side – especially the ones with jewel inlay. I'll take this side. Work towards the door. Now hurry, or we could get caught.'

For a second JoJo looked into the Gaffer's face with grave speculation, then he turned and began filling the bags with items from the collection with a rapidity that outstripped his mentor. The Gaffer was more selective. He chose his pieces in strict chronological order and ended with a simple copper bowl. They met again at the doorway. As JoJo had said, the guardian was indeed bleeding heavily.

'Where's the handlamp?'

'In the crevice to the lef'.'

'Good! I have it. Now we have to leave fast.'

'Suppose they follow us?'

'I'm prepared for that. I have some small explosive charges. If necessary we can create a rockfall behind us. Once we get to the ship we'll be safe.'

The Gaffer retrieved his weapon belt and they began to run the ascending passages, moving awkwardly because of the weight of the bags. As the incline lessened the Gaffer stopped occasionally and looked round. At first there were no sounds of pursuit, and only their own heavy breathing spoiled the silence. Then came a faint noise of many voices shouting, and a rising clamour in the farther tunnels.

The Gaffer caught at JoJo's arm. 'We seem to have been discovered.' He began to study the rock formation of the tunnel, and retreated a short distance before taking the metal cylinders from his belt.

'Go ahead, JoJo, past the next bend. Take the lamp and wait for me there.'

With rising apprehension, JoJo did as he was bid. Shortly he was rejoined by the Gaffer, who motioned that they must run swiftly. Then had not gone far before a great explosion rocked the ground around them. A wave of sound and pressure engulfed them and forced them onwards along the path. On all sides the walls and roof seemed to vibrate and resonate with a heavy internal thunder, and large pieces of rock fragmented from the walls and split from the roof. Behind them the cavernous shock of a major rockfall continued its echoes, and certified that the route was closed behind them.

Neither of them spoke, each being too full of his own thoughts and too intent on safely negotiating the difficult paths ahead. With their new knowledge of the noon caves, they passed swiftly through what had previously been a trail, and even the beasties seemed to sense their urgency and their desperation and stayed well clear. Then, after what seemed to be an eternity of running, the welcome yellow light of the Gaffer's annex showed through the disturbed darkness. Thankfully they flung themselves across the corrugations of the entrance grid and dropped their precious bags inside.

The Gaffer closed the door and did something to the walls which made them hum. Shortly the door opened again of its own accord. Instead of opening into noon-cave darkness, it opened to glazed sunlight. JoJo realised with something of a shock that they had been transported from deep in the ground to the top of the beautiful tower which the gaffer called his ship.

The Gaffer pointed out a soft pallet on which the boy might lie, and JoJo thankfully sank to rest.

'Are we safe now, Gaffer?' He was still worried by the proximity of the noon caves beneath.

'Quite safe, JoJo. As soon as the computers have found us an orbit we'll be leaving.' With quiet assurance the Terran busied himself with his instruments. JoJo watched him interestedly for a while, then caught up with the significance of the rendezvous with the ships waiting above.

'Are you sure it will be right for me come with you?'

'Of course. They'll send you to school for a while, so that you can learn to live as Terrans do. Then you'll be free to try for whatever kind of life you wish.'

'I want be what you are.'

'It's a thankless task, JoJo. You finish up making enemies even of your friends. When you wield the big stick of Terran technology, you're riding a pretty potent weapon. You have to develop a sense of responsibility which extends way beyond yourself. You have to do things that you know are wrong in order to make things go right.'

'Like stealing Tanic sacred things to make them hate you?'

'Just that. They had to hate me, because in hating me was the only way I could stop them despising themselves. They had to come to despise the Terran image. Otherwise contact with me would have damaged them far more than the reptiles could ever hope to do.'

'You think you made success?'

'For a couple of generations, yes. Unfortunately it's only a palliative. Once they get on top of the reptiles they'll start to look closely at the weapons and process I left. That exercise will lead them into the scientific method, and from there ten generations or less should get them into space. But the important thing is that they'll have done it themselves. But it won't alter the final endpoint. By the time we meet them in space their culture will be virtually indistinguishable from our own. It all becomes so inevitable. That's the kind of dragon spawn a Terran sows whenever he meets another culture in space.'

Somewhere on the ship a two-note gong was sounding. The Terran went back to his controls and started to key instructions for the ship computer. Glancing out of the window screens he smiled wanly and beckoned to JoJo.

'You see what I mean. OrsOrs's comrades trying to bring a rocket projector to bear on us. Probably the first time on Tanic that a group of men have co-operated in the attempted destruction of others. Yet in Terran terms it's the most logical thing to do. Already the dragon spawn begins to ripen. It should only take them about fifty years to get round to their first major war. As I said, there are worse things to tear a man apart than the claws of a lizard – and contact with Terra before a race is ready for it is about the very worst I know.'

A second alarm sounded, more urgent than the first. The Gaffer secured JoJo on his hydraulic pallet, then ran to his own. Slowly the chemical drive came in, building up an incredible intensity of sound and pressures. Majestically the beautiful tower which had been the Gaffer's home lifted skyward, bearing a startled JoJo on the first leg of a fantastic journey which was, in reality, only an acceleration of an already established trend which one day the rest of his race would follow.

Below them another missile, fired by Tanic hands, smashed their erstwhile launching-pit to dust, as the spawn of the dragon ripened in the rays of the Tanic sun.

8 – ARTHUR C CLARKE: Transit of Earth

Like Colin Kapp, Arthur Clarke is a great exponent of the scientific problem yarn. He is not adverse to attempting the impossible – such as the scene in *2001* where his protagonist finds he has to cross from the capsule to the Mother Ship without a space helmet. That episode, in fact, formed the bulk of his short story *Take a Deep Breath* (1957). Other such problems occur in his recent award-winning novel *Rendezvous With Rama*. Since then Clarke has completed his 'big' VEL; *Imperial Earth*, a project on which he was involved for some twenty years!

In the meantime we can content ourselves with the second Clarke selection in this anthology (the first, *Jupiter V* may be found in Volume One). Since the mid-1960s most of Clarke's short fiction has appeared outside the regular sf market, notably in the far better-paying *Playboy*, which published this current story, *Transit of Earth*, one of Clarke's own favourites. Here the protagonist faces a really insoluble problem, and accepts that fact. The story echoes all the skill associated with Clarke when weaving an emotional network, and the ending is an inevitable yet as unpredictable as anyone could wish.

TRANSIT OF EARTH

Arthur C Clarke

NOTE: *All the astronomical events described in this story take place at the times stated.*

Testing, one, two, three, four, five. . . .

Evans speaking. I will continue to record as long as possible. This is a two-hour capsule, but I doubt if I'll fill it.

That photograph has haunted me all my life; now, too late, I know why. (But would it have made any difference if I *had* known? That's one of those meaningless and unanswerable questions the mind keeps returning to endlessly, like the tongue exploring a broken tooth.)

I've not seen it for years, but I've only to close my eyes and I'm back in a landscape almost as hostile – and as beautiful – as this one. Fifty million miles Sunward and seventy-two years in the past, five men face the camera amid the Antarctic snows. Not even the bulky furs can hide the exhaustion and defeat that mark every line of their bodies, and their faces are already touched by death.

There were five of them. There were five of us and, of course, we also took a group photograph. But everything else was different. We were smiling – cheerful, confident. And our picture was on all the screens of Earth within ten minutes. It was months before *their* camera was found and brought back to civilization.

And we die in comfort, with all modern conveniences – including many that Robert Falcon Scott could never have imagined when he stood at the South Pole in 1912.

Two hours later. I'll start giving exact times when it becomes important.

All the facts are on the log, and by now the whole world knows them. So I guess I'm doing this largely to settle my mind – to talk myself into facing the inevitable. The trouble is, I'm not sure what subjects to avoid and which to tackle head on. Well, there's only one way to find out.

The first item: In twenty-four hours, at the very most, all the oxygen will be gone. That leaves me with the three classical choices. I can let the CO_2 build up until I become unconscious. I can step outside and crack the suit, leaving

Mars to do the job in about two minutes. Or I can use one of the tablets in the med kit.

CO_2 buildup: Everyone says that's quite easy – just like going to sleep. I've no doubt that's true; unfortunately, in my case it's associated with nightmare number one.

I wish I'd never come across that damn book – *True Stories of World War Two*, or whatever it was called. There was one chapter about a German submarine, found and salvaged after the war. The crew was still inside it – *two* men per bunk. And between each pair of skeletons, the single respirator set they'd been sharing.

Well, at least that won't happen here. But I know, with a deadly certainty, that as soon as I find it hard to breathe, I'll be back in that doomed U-boat.

So what about the quicker way? When you're exposed to a vacuum, you're unconscious in ten or fifteen seconds, and people who've been through it say it's not painful – just peculiar. But trying to breathe something that isn't there brings me altogether too neatly to nightmare number two.

This time, it's a personal experience. As a kid, I used to do a lot of skin diving when my family went to the Caribbean for vacations. There was an old freighter that had sunk twenty years before, out on a reef with its deck only a couple of yards below the surface. Most of the hatches were open; so it was easy to get inside to look for souvenirs and hunt the big fish that like to shelter in such places.

Of course it was dangerous – if you did it without scuba gear. So what boy could resist the challenge?

My favourite route involved diving into a hatch on the foredeck, swimming about fifty feet along a passageway dimly lit by portholes a few yards apart, then angling up a short flight of stairs and emerging through a door in the battered superstructure. The whole trip took less than a minute – an easy dive for anyone in good condition. There was even time to do some sight-seeing or to play with a few fish along the route. And sometimes, for a change, I'd switch directions, going in the door and coming out again through the hatch.

That was the way I did it the last time. I hadn't dived for a week – there had been a big storm and the sea was too rough

– so I was impatient to get going. I deep-breathed on the surface for about two minutes, until I felt the tingling in my fingertips that told me it was time to stop. Then I jackknifed and slid gently down toward the black rectangle of the open doorway.

It always looked ominous and menacing – that was part of the thrill. And for the first few yards, I was almost completely blind; the contrast between the tropical glare above water and the gloom between decks was so great that it took quite a while for my eyes to adjust. Usually, I was halfway along the corridor before I could see anything clearly; then the illumination would steadily increase as I approached the open hatch, where a shaft of sunlight would paint a dazzling rectangle on the rusty, barnacled metal floor.

I'd almost made it when I realised that this time the light wasn't getting better. There was no slanting column of sunlight ahead of me, leading up to the world of air and life. I had a second of baffled confusion, wondering if I'd lost my way. Then I realised what had happened – and confusion turned into sheer panic. Sometime during the storm, the hatch must have slammed shut. It weighed at least a quarter of a ton.

I don't remember making a U-turn; the next thing I recall is swimming quite slowly back along the passage and telling myself, 'Don't hurry – your air will last longer if you take it easy.' I could see very well now, because my eyes had had plenty of time to become dark-adapted. There were lots of details I'd never noticed before – such as the red squirrelfish lurking in the shadows, the green fronds and algae growing in the little patches of light around the portholes, and even a single rubber boot, apparently in excellent condition, lying where someone must have kicked it off. And once, out of a side corridor, I noticed a big grouper staring at me with bulbous eyes, his thick lips half-parted, as if he were astonished at my intrusion.

The band around my chest was getting tighter and tighter; it was impossible to hold my breath any longer – yet the stairway still seemed an infinite distance ahead. I let some bubbles of air dribble out of my mouth; that improved matters for a moment, but, once I had exhaled, the ache in my lungs became even more unendurable.

Now there was no point in conserving strength by flippering along with that steady, unhurried stroke. I snatched the ultimate few cubic inches of air from my face mask – feeling it flatten against my nose as I did so – and swallowed it down into my starving lungs. At the same time, I shifted gear and drove forward with every last atom of strength.

And that's all I remember until I found myself spluttering and coughing in the daylight, clinging to the broken stub of the mast. The water around me was stained with blood and I wondered why. Then, to my great surprise, I noticed a deep gash in my right calf; I must have banged into some sharp obstruction, but I'd never noticed it and even now felt no pain.

That was the end of my skin diving until I started astronaut training ten years later and went into the underwater zero-g simulator. Then it was different, because I was using scuba gear, but I had some nasty moments that I was afraid the psychologists would notice and I always made sure that I got nowhere near emptying my tank. Having nearly suffocated once, I'd no intention of risking it again.

I know exactly what it will feel like to breathe the freezing wisp of near vacuum that passes for atmosphere on Mars. No, thank you.

So what's wrong with poison? Nothing, I suppose. The stuff we've got takes only fifteen seconds, they told us. But all my instincts are against it, even when there's no sensible alternative.

Did Scott have poison with him? I doubt it. And if he did, I'm sure he never used it.

I'm not going to replay this. I hope it's been some use, but I can't be sure.

The radio has just printed out a message from Earth, reminding me that transit starts in two hours. As if I'm likely to forget – when four men have already died so that I can be the first human being to see it. And the only one for exactly one hundred years. It isn't often that Sun, Earth and Mars line up neatly like this; the last time was in 1905, when poor old Lowell was still writing his beautiful nonsense about the canals and the great dying civilisation that had built them. Too bad it was all delusion.

I'd better check the telescope and the timing equipment.

The Sun is quiet today – as it should be, anyway, near the middle of the cycle. Just a few small spots and some minor areas of disturbance around them. The solar weather is set calm for months to come. That's one thing the others won't have to worry about on their way home.

I think that was the worst moment, watching *Olympus* lift off Phobos and head back to Earth. Even though we'd known for weeks that nothing could be done, that was the final closing of the door. It was night and we could see everything perfectly. Phobus had come leaping up out of the west a few hours earlier and was doing its mad backward rush across the sky, growing from a tiny crescent to a half-moon; before it reached the zenith, it would disappear as it plunged into the shadow of Mars and became eclipsed.

We'd been listening to the countdown, of course, trying to go about our normal work. It wasn't easy, accepting at last the fact that fifteen of us had come to Mars and only ten would return. Even then, I suppose there were millions back on Earth who still could not understand; they must have found it impossible to believe that *Olympus* couldn't descend a mere 4000 miles to pick us up. The Space Administration had been bombarded with crazy rescue schemes; heaven knows, we'd thought of enough ourselves. But when the permafrost under landing pad three finally gave way and *Pegasus* toppled, that was that. It still seems a miracle that the ship didn't blow up when the propellant tank ruptured.

I'm wandering again. Back to Phobos and the countdown. On the telescope monitor, we could clearly see the fissured plateau where *Olympus* had touched down after we'd separated and begun our own descent. Though our friends would never land on Mars, at least they'd had a little world of their own to explore; even for a satellite as small as Phobos, it worked out at thirty square miles per man. A lot of territory to search for strange minerals and debris from space – or to carve your name so that future ages would know that you were the first of all men to come this way.

The ship was clearly visible as a stubby, bright cylinder against the dull grey rocks; from time to time, some flat surface would catch the light of the swiftly moving Sun and would flash with mirror brilliance. But about five minutes before lift-off, the picture became suddenly pink, then crimson – then vanished completely as Phobos rushed into eclipse.

The countdown was still at ten seconds when we were startled by a blast of light. For a moment, we wondered if *Olympus* had also met with catastrophe; then we realised that someone was filming the take-off and the external floodlights had been switched on.

During those last few seconds, I think we all forgot our own predicament; we were up there aboard *Olympus* willing the thrust to build up smoothly and lift the ship out of the tiny gravitational field of Phobos – and then away from Mars for the long fall Sunward. We heard Commander Richmond say, 'Ignition,' there was a brief burst of interference, and the patch of light began to move in the field of the telescope.

That was all. There was no blazing column of fire, because, of course, there's really no ignition when a nuclear rocket lights up. 'Lights up' indeed! That's another hangover from the old chemical technology. But a hot hydrogen blast is completely invisible; it seems a pity that we'll never again see anything so spectacular as a Saturn or a Korolov blast-off.

Just before the end of the burn, *Olympus* left the shadow of Mars and burst out into sunlight again, reappearing almost instantly as a brilliant, swiftly moving star. The blaze of light must have startled them aboard the ship, because we heard someone call out, 'Cover that window!' Then, a few seconds later, Richmond announced, 'Engine cutoff.' Whatever happened, *Olympus* was now irrevocably headed back to Earth.

A voice I didn't recognise – though it must have been the commander's – said, 'Good-bye, *Pegasus*,' and the radio transmission switched off. There was, of course, no point in saying, 'Good luck.' *That* had all been settled weeks ago.

I've just played this back. Talking of luck, there's been one compensation, though not for us. With a crew of only ten, *Olympus* has been able to dump a third of her expendables and lighten herself by several tons. So now she'll get home a month ahead of schedule.

Plenty of things could have gone wrong in that month; we may yet have saved the expedition. Of course, we'll never know – but it's a nice thought.

I've been playing a lot of music – full blast, now that there's no one else to be disturbed. Even if there were any Martians, I don't suppose this ghost of an atmosphere could carry the sound more than a few yards.

We have a fine collection, but I have to choose carefully. Nothing downbeat and nothing that demands too much concentration. Above all, nothing with human voices. So I restrict myself to the lighter orchestral classics; the *New World Symphony* and Grieg's piano concerto fill the bill perfectly. At the moment, I'm listening to Rachmaninoff's *Paganini Variations*, but now I must switch off and get down to work.

There are only five minutes to go; all the equipment is in perfect condition. The telescope is tracking the Sun, the video recorder is standing by, the precision timer is running.

These observations will be as accurate as I can make them. I owe it to my lost comrades, whom I'll soon be joining. They gave me their oxygen so that I can still be alive at this moment. I hope you remember that, 100 or 1000 years from now, whenever you crank these figures into the computers.

Only a minute to go; getting down to business. For the record, year 1984, month May, day eleven, coming up to four hours, thirty minutes, Ephemeris Time . . . *now*.

Half a minute to contact; switching recorder and timer to high speed. Just rechecked position angle to make sure I'm looking at the right spot on the Sun's limb. Using power of 500 – image perfectly steady even at this low elevation.

Four thirty-two. Any moment, now. . . .

There it is . . . there it is! I can hardly believe it! A tiny black dent in the edge of the Sun, growing, growing, growing. . . .

Hello, Earth. Look up at me – the brightest star in your sky, straight overhead at midnight.

Recorder back to slow.

Four thirty-five. It's as if a thumb were pushing into the Sun's edge, deeper and deeper – fascinating to watch.

Four forty-one. Exactly halfway. The Earth's a perfect black semicircle – a clean bite out of the Sun – as if some disease were eating it away.

Four forty-eight. Ingress three-quarters complete.

Four hours, 49 minutes, 30 seconds. Recorder on high speed again.

The line of contact with the Sun's edge is shrinking fast. Now it's a barely visible black thread. In a few seconds, the whole Earth will be superimposed on the Sun.

Now I can see the effects of the atmosphere. There's a thin halo of light surrounding that black hole in the Sun. Strange to think that I'm seeing the glow of all the sunsets – and all the sunrises – that are taking place around the whole Earth at this very moment.

Ingress complete – four hours, fifty minutes, five seconds. The whole world has moved onto the face of the Sun, a perfectly circular black disc silhouetted against that inferno, ninety million miles below. It looks bigger than I expected; one could easily mistake it for a fair-sized sunspot.

Nothing more to see now for six hours, when the Moon appears, trailing Earth by half the Sun's width. I'll beam the recorded data back to Lunacom, then try to get some sleep.

My very last sleep. Wonder if I'll need drugs. It seems a pity to waste these last few hours, but I want to conserve my strength – and my oxygen. I think it was Dr Johnson who said that nothing settles a man's mind so wonderfully as the knowledge that he'll be hanged in the morning. How the hell did *he* know?

Ten hours, thirty minutes, Ephemeris Time. Dr Johnson was right. I had only one pill and don't remember any dreams.

The condemned man also ate a hearty breakfast. Cut that out.

Back at telescope. Now the Earth's halfway across the disc, passing well north of centre. In ten minutes, I should see the Moon.

I've just switched to the highest power of the telescope – 2000. The image is slightly fuzzy but still fairly good, atmospheric halo very distinct. I'm hoping to see the cities on the dark side of Earth.

No luck. Probably too many clouds. A pity – it's theoretically possible, but we never succeeded. I wish. . . . Never mind.

Ten hours, forty minutes. Recorder on slow speed. Hope I'm looking at the right spot.

Fifteen seconds to go. Recorder fast.

Damn – missed it. Doesn't matter – the recorder will have caught the exact moment. There's a little black notch already in the side of the Sun. First contact must have been about ten hours, 41 minutes, 20 seconds, E.T.

What a long way it is between Earth and Moon – there's half the width of the Sun between them. You wouldn't think the two bodies had anything to do with each other. Makes you realise just how big the Sun really is.

Ten hours, forty-four minutes. The Moon's exactly halfway over the edge. A very small, very clear-cut semicircular bite out of the edge of the Sun.

Ten hours, forty-seven minutes, five seconds. Internal contact. The Moon's clear of the edge, entirely inside the Sun. Don't suppose I can see anything on the night side, but I'll increase the power.

That's funny.

Well, well. Someone must be trying to talk to me. There's a tiny light pulsing away there on the darkened face of the Moon. Probably the laser at Imbrium Base.

Sorry, everyone. I've said all my good-byes and don't want to go through that again. Nothing can be important now.

Still, it's almost hypnotic – that flickering point of light, coming out of the face of the Sun itself. Hard to believe that even after it's travelled all this distance, the beam is only one hundred miles wide. Lunacom's going to all this trouble to aim it exactly at me and I suppose I should feel guilty at ignoring it. But I don't. I've nearly finished my work and the things of Earth are no longer any concern of mine.

Ten hours, fifty minutes. Recorder off. That's it – until the end of Earth transit, two hours from now.

I've had a snack and am taking my last look at the view from the observation bubble. The Sun's still high; so there's not much contrast, but the light brings out all the colours vividly – the countless varieties of red and pink and crimson, so startling against the deep blue of the sky. How different from the Moon – though that, too, has its own beauty.

It's strange how surprising the obvious can be. Everyone knew that Mars was red. But we didn't really expect the red of rust – the red of blood. Like the Painted Desert of Arizona; after a while, the eye longs for green.

To the north, there is one welcome change of colour; the cap of carbon-dioxide snow on Mt Burroughs is a dazzling white pyramid. That's another surprise. Burroughs is 25,000 feet above Mean Datum; when I was a boy, there weren't supposed to be any mountains on Mars.

The nearest sand dune is a quarter of a mile away and it, too, has patches of frost on its shaded slope. During the last storm, we thought it moved a few feet, but we couldn't be sure. Certainly, the dunes *are* moving, like those on Earth. One day, I suppose, this base will be covered – only to reappear again in 1000 years. Or 10,000.

That strange group of rocks – the Elephant, the Capitol, the Bishop – still holds its secrets and teases me with the memory of our first big disappointment. We could have sworn that they were sedimentary; how eagerly we rushed out to look for fossils! Even now, we don't know what formed that outcropping; the geology of Mars is still a mass of contradictions and enigmas.

We have passed on enough problems to the future and those who come after us will find many more. But there's one mystery we never reported to Earth nor even entered in the log. The first night after we landed, we took turns keeping watch. Brennan was on duty and woke me up soon after midnight. I was annoyed – it was ahead of time – and then he told me that he'd seen a light moving around the base of the Capitol. We watched for at least an hour, until it was my turn to take over. But we saw nothing; whatever that light was, it never reappeared.

Now, Brennan was as levelheaded and unimaginative as they come; if he said he saw a light, then he saw one. Maybe it was some kind of electric discharge or the reflection of Phobos on a piece of sand-polished rock. Anyway, we decided not to mention it to Lunacom unless we saw it again.

Since I've been alone, I've often awaked in the night and looked out toward the rocks. In the feeble illumination of Phobos and Deimos, they remind me of the skyline of a darkened city. And it has always remained darkened. No lights have ever appeared for me.

Twelve hours, forty-nine minutes, Ephemeris Time. The last act's about to begin. Earth has nearly reached the edge of the Sun. The two narrow horns of light that still embrace it are barely touching.

Recorder on fast.

Contact! Twelve hours, fifty minutes, sixteen seconds. The crescents of light no longer meet. A tiny black spot has appeared at the edge of the Sun, as the Earth begins to cross it. It's growing longer, longer. . . .

Recorder on slow. Eighteen minutes to wait before Earth finally clears the face of the Sun.

The Moon still has more than halfway to go; it's not yet reached the mid-point of its transit. It looks like a little round blob of ink, only a quarter the size of Earth. And there's no light flickering there anymore. Lunacom must have given up.

Well, I have just a quarter hour left here in my last home. Time seems to be accelerating the way it does in the final minutes before a lift-off. No matter, I have everything worked out now. I can even relax.

Already, I feel part of history. I am one with Captain Cook, back in Tahiti in 1769, watching the transit of Venus. Except for that image of the Moon trailing along behind, it must have looked just like this.

What would Cook have thought, 200 years ago, if he'd known that one day a man would observe the whole Earth in transit from an outer world? I'm sure he would have been astonished – and then delighted.

But I feel a closer identity with a man not yet born. I hope you hear these words, whoever you may be. Perhaps you will be standing on this very spot, 100 years from now, when the next transit occurs.

Greetings to 2084, November 10th! I wish you better luck than we had. I suppose you will have come here on a luxury liner – or you may have been born on Mars and be a stranger to Earth. You will know things that I cannot imagine; yet somehow I don't envy you. I would not even change places with you if I could.

For you will remember my name and know that I was the first of all mankind ever to see a transit of Earth. And no one will see another for 100 years.

Twelve hours, fifty-nine minutes. Exactly halfway through egress. The Earth is a perfect semicircle – a black shadow on the face of the Sun. I still can't escape from the impression that something has taken a big bite out of that golden disc. In nine minutes, it will be gone and the Sun will be whole again.

Thirteen hours, seven minutes. Recorder on fast.

Earth has almost gone. There's just a shallow black dimple at the edge of the Sun. You could easily mistake it for a small spot, going over the limb.

Thirteen hours, eight.

Good-bye, beautiful Earth.

Going, going, going, good-bye, good—

I'm OK again now. The timings have all been sent home on the beam. In five minutes, they'll join the accumulated wisdom of mankind. And Lunacom will know that I stuck to my post.

But I'm not sending this. I'm going to leave it here for the next expedition – whenever that may be. It could be ten or twenty years before anyone comes here again; no point in going back to an old site when there's a whole world waiting to be explored.

So this capsule will stay here, as Scott's diary remained in his tent, until the next visitors find it. But they won't find me.

Strange how hard it is to get away from Scott. I think he gave me the idea. For his body will not lie frozen forever in the Antarctic, isolated from the great cycle of life and death. Long ago, that lonely tent began its march to the sea. Within a few years, it was buried by the falling snow and had become part of the glacier that crawls eternally away from the pole. In a few brief centuries, the sailor will have returned to the sea. He will merge once more into the pattern of living things – the plankton, the seals, the penguins, the whales, all the multitudinous fauna of the Antarctic Ocean.

There are no oceans here on Mars, nor have there been for at least five billion years. But there is life of some kind, down there in the badlands of Chaos II, that we never had time to explore. Those moving patches on the orbital photographs. The evidence that whole areas of Mars have been swept clear of craters by forces other than erosion. The long-chain optically active carbon molecules picked up by the atmospheric samplers.

And, of course, the mystery of Viking 6. Even now, no one has been able to make any sense of those last instrument readings before something large and heavy crushed the probe in the still, cold depths of the Martian night.

And don't talk to me about *primitive* life forms in a place like this! Anything that's survived here will be so sophisticated that we may look as clumsy as dinosaurs.

There's still enough propellant in the ship's tanks to drive the Marscar clear around the planet. I have three hours of daylight left – plenty of time to get down into the valleys and well out into Chaos. After sunset, I'll still be able to make good speed with the head lamps. It will be romantic, driving at night under the moons of Mars.

One thing I must fix before I leave. I don't like the way Sam's lying out there. He was always so poised, so graceful. It doesn't seem right that he should look so awkward now. I must do something about it.

I wonder if *I* could have covered 300 feet without a suit, walking slowly, steadily – the way he did to the very end.

I must try not to look at his face.

That's it. Everything shipshape and ready to go.

The therapy has worked. I feel perfectly at ease – even contented, now that I know exactly what I'm going to do. The old nightmares have lost their power.

It is true, we all die alone. It makes no difference at the end, being fifty million miles from home.

I'm going to enjoy the drive through that lovely painted landscape. I'll be thinking of all those who dreamed about Mars – Wells and Lowell and Burroughs and Weinbaum and Bradbury. They all guessed wrong – but the reality is just as strange, just as beautiful as they imagined.

I don't know what's waiting for me out there and I'll probably never see it. But on this starvelling world, it must be desperate for carbon, phosphorous, oxygen, calcium. It can use me.

And when my oxygen alarm gives its final ping, somewhere down there in that haunted wilderness, I'm going to finish in style. As soon as I have difficulty in breathing, I'll get off the Marscar and start walking – with a playback unit plugged into my helmet and going full blast.

For sheer, triumphant power and glory, there's nothing in the whole of music to match the *Toccata and Fugue in D Minor*. I won't have time to hear all of it; that doesn't matter.

Johann Sebastian, here I come.

9 – FRED HOYLE: Zoomen

Back in the early days of science fiction, Hugo Gernsback was anxious that the fiction he published would be informative and thus teach the readers basic science. Consequently many of the early writers were also scientists, and several of today's practitioners are also fully-fledged scientists, like Britain's Arthur Clarke, and America's Isaac Asimov. One of Britain's most renowned and respected practising scientists is the astronomer and mathematician Frederick Hoyle, FRS. Of Hoyle, Isaac Asimov has said: 'Hoyle . . . is perhaps the most eminent of those contemporary scientists who have written science fiction under their own names.' For his service to science Hoyle was knighted in 1972.

Fred Hoyle was born at Bingley, Yorkshire, on June 24th 1915. He was educated at St John's College, Cambridge, where he earned his MA. He is a staff member of both the Mount Wilson and Palomar Observatories, and has been the Plumian Professor of Astronomy and Experimental Philosophy at Cambridge University since 1958. Hoyle was responsible for the theory of continuous creation as regards the origins of the Universe, and put his theories into print in his book *The Nature of the Universe* (1950). He also wrote a valuable text book on astronomy in *Frontiers of Astronomy* (1955). He was thus a much respected name when in 1957 his science fiction novel, *The Black Cloud*, was published. It was well received. *Ossian's Ride* followed in 1959, but almost certainly his most famous work is *A For Andromeda*, doubtless due to its initial transmission as a seven part serial by the BBC in 1962.

Hoyle's shorter fiction is unfortunately less well known, although a collection of fifteen stories was published in 1967 as *Element 79*. From that collection comes the following intriguing piece, *Zoomen*.

ZOOMEN

Fred Hoyle

In the second half of July I was able to get away on a two week vacation. I decided to go off 'Munro-bagging' in the Scottish Highlands. Hotel accommodation being difficult in the Highlands in the summer, especially for a single person, I hired a caravan with a car to match. Driving north the first day, I got precisely to the Scottish border immediately south of Jedburgh. The evening was beautifully fine. I argued I didn't want to spend the whole of the morrow driving, if indeed the morrow was going to be as clear as this. The obvious tactic was to be away at the first light of dawn. By ten o'clock I could be well across the Lowlands. Then I could spend the afternoon 'doing' one of the southern peaks, perhaps in the Ben Lawers range.

It fell out as I had planned. I reached Killin not much after 10 am, found a caravan site, bought fresh meat and other provisions in the town, and set off for Glenlyon, with the intention of walking up Meall Ghaordie. The afternoon was as fine and beautiful as it could possibly be. I quitted the car at the nearest point to my mountain and set off across the lower bogland. I moved upward at a deliberately slow pace, in part because this was my first day on the hills, in part because the sun was hot. I remember the myriads of tiny coloured flowers under my feet. It took about two hours to reach the summit. I sat down there and munched a couple of apples. Then I laid myself flat on a grassy knoll, using my rucksack for a pillow. The early start and the warm day together had made me distinctly sleepy. It was not more than a minute, I suppose, before I nodded off.

I have fallen asleep quite a number of times on a mountain top. The wakening always produces a slight shock, presumably because one is heavily conditioned to waking indoors. There is always a perceptible moment during which you hunt for your bearings. It was so on this occasion, except the shock was deeper. There was a first moment when I expected to be in a normal bedroom, then a moment in which I remembered that by rights I should be on the summit of a mountain, then a moment when I had become aware of the place where I had in fact awakened and knew it was not at all the right place, not the summit of Meall Ghaordie.

The room I was in was a large rectangular box. I scrambled to my feet and started to inspect the place. Perhaps it may seem absurd to imply that a box-like room needed inspection, particularly when it was quite empty. Yet there were two very queer things about it. The light was artificial, for the box was wholly opaque and closed, except where a passageway opened out of one of the walls. The distribution of the light was strange. For the life of me I simply could not determine where it was coming from. There were no obvious bulbs or tubes. It almost seemed as if the walls themselves were aglow. They were composed of some material which looked to my inexpert eye merely like one of the many new forms of plastic. But in that case how could light be coming out of such a material?

The box was not nearly as large as I had at first thought. The dimensions in fact were roughly thirty by fifty, the height about twenty feet. The lighting produced the impression of a place the size of a cathedral, an effect I have noticed before in underground caves.

The second strange thing was my sense of balance. Not that I found it difficult to stand or anything as crude as that. When climbing a mountain, the legs quickly become sensitive to balance. If I had not just come off a mountain, it is likely the difference would have passed unnoticed. Yet I could feel a difference of some kind, slight but definite.

My explorations naturally led to the passageway, which didn't go straight for very far. Round a bend I came to a forking point. I paused to remember the division. There were more twists and turns, so that soon I had the strong impression of being in a maze. It gave me the usual moment of panic, of feeling I had lost my way. Then I reflected I had no 'way' to lose. Instantly I became calm again and simply strolled where my fancy dictated. The passage eventually brought me back to the large box-like room. There in the middle of it was my rucksack, the rucksack against which I had laid my head on the summit of Meall Ghaordie. I tried several times and always I came back to the box-like room. Although the passages had the semblance of a multitude of branches, this also was an illusion. In fact there were eight distinct ways through the system. I managed to get the time required for a single 'transit' of the passageways down to about ninety seconds, so the whole arrangement, if not actually poky, was not very large in size. It was just that it was made to seem large.

I did still another turn through the passageways and was startled on this occasion to hear running feet ahead of me. My heart thumped madly, for although I might have seemed calm outwardly, fear was never very far from my side. Around the corner ahead burst a girl of about eighteen or so clad in a dressing gown. At the sight of me, standing there blocking the passageway, she let out a nerve-shattering scream. She stood for twenty or thirty seconds and then flung herself with extreme violence into my arms. 'Where are we?' she sobbed, 'where are we?' She went on repeating her question, clutching me with a good, powerful muscular grip. Without in any way exceeding natural propriety, I held her closely; it was a natural enough thing to do in the circumstances. Suddenly I felt an acute nausea sweep through me, akin to the late stages of sea-sickness. The clinch between us dissolved in a flash, for the girl must have felt the same sickness, since she instantly burst out with a violent fit of vomiting.

We both stood there panting. I steadied myself against the wall of the passageway for my knees felt weak.

'And who might you be?'

'Giselda Horne,' she answered. The voice was American.

'You'd better take that thing off,' I said, indicating the dressing-gown, now the worse for wear from the sickness.

'I suppose so. I was in a room down here when I came to.'

The girl led the way to a box, precisely square as far as I could tell, opening out of the very passageway. I felt certain I must have passed this spot many times, but there had been no opening before. Giselda Horne staggered into the box, moaning slightly. I made to follow but soon stopped. I was only just inside when another wave of sickness hit me in the pit of the stomach. Some instinct prompted me to step back into the passage. As I did so, a panel slid silently and rapidly back, closing off the box. With the double attack I was hard put to take any action, but I did shout to the girl and bang my fist on the panel. If she made any answer I was unable to hear it.

I tried to walk off the sickness by touring through the system of passages, but to no avail. I felt just as rotten as before. At quite some length, for I must have gone through the system many times by other routes before I found it, I came on exactly such a square box as Giselda Horne had gone into. With some apprehension I stepped inside it. Two things happened. A similar panel slid closed behind me, and within thirty seconds the sickness had gone.

This box was a cube with sides of about twelve feet. It contained absolutely nothing except a heavy metal door let into one of the walls which opened to a moderate tug. Inside was a volume about the size of a fairish oven, in which I found a platter covered with stuff. Before I could examine it further the nausea started again. This time it seemed as if I too would reach the vomiting stage. Just in time the panel slid open and I staggered into the passage with the irrational thought that I must reach the toilet before my stomach hit the roof. Out in the passage the sickness dropped steeply away. In minutes I felt quite normal again. Then suddenly it started up once more; the panelling opened, as if to invite me back into the box, and once inside the sickness was gone. The process was repeated thrice more, in and out of the box. Long before the end of the lesson I knew exactly what it meant – move in, move out, to orders. From where? I had no idea, but the lesson had done one thing for me. My fears had quite gone. Manifestly I was under some kind of surveillance, a surveillance whose mode of operation I couldn't remotely guess. Yet instead of my fears being increased, the exact opposite happened. From this point on, I was not only outwardly calm but I was inwardly master of myself.

With the passing of the sickness I felt quite hungry. Apart from a light lunch on the slopes of Meall Ghaordie, my last meal had been at 5 am on the Scottish border. I tried the stuff on the platter in the oven. It was neither pleasant nor unpleasant, about like vegetable marrow. How nutritive it was I couldn't tell at all, so I simply ate until I was no longer hungry.

Next I noticed the floor was softer here than it was in the passage or than it was in the big rectangular box. It would be quite tolerable to sleep on. It was harder than the usual bed, but after the first two or three days it would seem comfortable enough. What about a toilet? There was nothing here in the box at all appropriate to a toilet. So how did one fare if taken short with the panel closed? I determined to put the matter to test. I made preparations to use the floor of the box itself. I didn't get very far, nor had I expected to do. The sickness came, the panel slid by, and within a minute I found a new box opening out off the passage. Stepping inside I discovered one large and one small compartment. The small compartment was obviously the privy, for it had a hole about a foot in diameter in its floor. I made the best use of it I could, wondering what I should do for toilet paper. My thoughts on this somewhat embarrassing subject were interrupted by a veritable deluge descending on my head from above. I hopped out of the smaller compartment into the larger one. Here the downpour was somewhat less intense, about the intensity of a good powerful shower. Within seconds I was soaked to the skin. The shower stopped and I began to peel off my sodden clothes. I had just about stripped when the shower started up again. Evidently it went off periodically, every three or four minutes in the fashion of a pissoir. Stripped naked, I was heartily glad of the downpour, for I had sweated fairly profusely in my walk up the mountain. Clearly the liquid coming down on my head was essentially water but it had a soapy feel about it. I stood up to about half a dozen bouts, in which I washed out my clothes as best I could. Then I carried the whole dripping caboodle back to my box. It would take several hours, I thought, for the heavier garments, particularly the trousers, to dry out, so I resolved to try for some sleep. As I dozed off I wondered what items I might lack for in this singular situation. I had no razor, but then why not grow a beard? By the greatest good fortune I always carry a small pair of scissors in my rucksack. At least I could eat, keep clean, and cut my nails.

I slept much longer than I intended, nearly ten hours. When I awoke I noticed that the box-door, cell-door if you like, was open. Before touring again through the passageways, or patronising the privy with its remarkable drenching qualities, I tested the metal oven door. A new platter was there, piled high with the same vegetable marrow stuff.

My clothes were snuff dry. So the humidity had to be quite low, as I had thought was probably the case. I trotted along to the showers in my underpants only, for these would easily be dried should I misjudge the pissoir. The panel fortunately was open, it remained open from that time on so far as I am aware, so I waited for the flush, then darted in and darted out before the thing fired itself for the next occasion. At the best of times my mountaineering clothes are distinctly rough. After their recent wetting and drying they were now baggy and down-at-heel in the extreme. I saw no point in putting on my boots and simply went barefoot, rather like a ship-wrecked mariner.

I padded along the passage knowing that sooner or later I would reach the 'cathedral', as I had come to think of the big rectangular box. Another box was open, different certainly from mine and different I thought from that of Giselda Horne. I was just on the point of stepping inside when a voice behind me said, 'hello,' in a foreign accent. I turned to find an Indian of uncertain middle-age standing there. He stared rather wildly for perhaps thirty seconds and reached for support against the wall. To my surprise he went on:

'It is not the stomach sickness. It is a matter of shock to

see you, Sir, for I attended a lecture you gave in Bombay last year. Professor Wycombe is it?'

'I did give a lecture in Bombay. You were in the audience?'

'Yes, but you will not remember me. It was a rather large audience. Daghri is my name, Sir.'

We shook hands, 'You have been in the big room, Sir?'

'Yes, many times.'

'Recently, Sir?'

'Yesterday. That's to say before I slept. Perhaps ten hours ago.'

'Then you will find it has changed.'

Daghri and I hurried along the passages until we emerged into the cathedral. On the walls now were a mass of points of light, stars obviously. The projection on to the flat surfaces introduced distortions of course, but this apart we were looking up at a complete representation of the heavens, both hemispheres.

'What does it mean, Sir?' whispered the Indian.

For the moment I made no attempt to answer this critical question. I asked Daghri to tell me how he came to be there. He said he remembered walking out in the evening in the Indian countryside. Then suddenly, in a flash it seemed, he was in this big cathedral room. It appeared almost as if he had walked around a corner in the road to find himself, not in the countryside anymore, but right there in the middle of this room, more or less at the exact spot where I myself had wakened.

Accepting that both Daghri and I were sane, there could only be one explanation:

'Daghri, it must be that we are in some enormous spaceship. This display here on the walls represents the view from the ship. We're seeing the pilot's view out into space.'

'My difficulty with that thought, Sir, is to find the Sun.' I pointed to the bright patch lighting the entrance to the passageway.

'That, I think, is the Sun.'

'Is there any way to make sure of this, Sir?'

'Quite easily. All we need do is sit and watch. The motion

of the ship, if we are in a ship, must produce changes in the planets. We only need to watch the brighter objects.'

Within half an hour we had it, the apparent motion of the Earth itself, for the Earth-Moon combination was easy to pick out, once you looked in the right direction. Within an hour or so we had Venus and Mars, and already we knew the rough direction we were travelling – toward the constellation of Scorpius. We also knew the approximate speed of the ship, something above two thousand miles an hour. Reckoning the ship to be accelerating smoothly, and trusting to time from my watch, I was able to check the acceleration itself. It was quite close to ordinary gravity, a bit larger than gravity as I calculated it. This might well be the difference I had noticed in my legs right at the beginning.

It was while we were thus watching the display on the walls of the cathedral that the others slowly filtered in, one by one over a period of about five hours. The first to appear was a sandy-haired man going a bit thin on top. He announced himself as being of the name Bill Bailey, a butcher from Rotherham, Yorkshire, and where the hell was he he'd like to know, and where was the bacon and eggs, and who was the bird he'd seen in the bloody showers, half-naked she was but he didn't object to that, the more naked the better so far as he was concerned. For a badly frightened man it was a good performance. Although I never took to Bill Bailey, the never-ending stream of ribald remarks which issued from his lips served in the months ahead to lighten a thoroughly grim situation, at any rate so far as I was concerned.

There were two other men and four women, making a total of nine captives. Of the whole nine of us only two had been acquainted before, Giselda Horne and Ernst Schmidt, a German industrialist. Schmidt and the girl's father were in the same line of business, meat-packing, and Schmidt had been visiting the Horne family in Chicago. He and Giselda had been swimming in the household pool when the 'snatch', as I liked to call it, had taken place. Schmidt had suddenly found himself in the central part of the 'cathedral', clad only in his swimming trunks. Giselda had found herself in one of the cell-like boxes attired in her dressing gown. Schmidt was pretty mad about the trunks, for obviously there was no chance of him acquiring any decent clothes here. Since we were not permitted to touch each other, since the temperature in the ship was a dry seventy degrees or thereabouts, there really wasn't any logical reason for clothes. Nevertheless I could see Schmidt's point. I gave him the anorak out of my rucksack. Although it was no doubt ludicrous, he was glad to wear it.

Jim McClay was a tall wiry Australian sheep farmer of about thirty-five. He had been snatched while out on his farm driving a Land Rover. Then he too was suddenly in the middle of the cathedral. The experience had very naturally knocked a good deal of the spring and bounce out of the man. But the confidence would soon return. I could see it would return by the way he was looking at Giselda Horne. She was a natural for the Australian, tall too and well muscled.

Bill Bailey greeted each of the four women in his own broad style. For Giselda Horne, in a cleaned dressing gown, it was no more than a terse 'Take it off, love, come in an' cool down.'

He didn't get far with Hattie Foulds, a farmer's wife from northern Lancashire. To his 'Come in, love, come right in 'ere by me. Come in to me lap an' smoulder,' she instantly retorted with 'Who's this bloody great bag of wind?'

Nevertheless it was clear from the beginning that Hattie Foulds and Bill Bailey made a 'right' pair. As the days and weeks passed they made every conceivable attempt to get into physical contact with each other. It became a part of our everyday existence to walk past some spot from which the sound of violent retching emerged. The other women affected disgust, but I suspect their lives would also have been the poorer without these strange sexio-gastronomic outbursts. Bailey never ceased to talk about it, 'Can't even match your fronts together before it hits you,' he would say, 'but we've got to keep on trying. Rome wasn't built in a day.'

The two remaining women were much the most interesting to me. One was an Englishwoman, a face I had seen before somewhere. When I asked her name, she simply said she had been christened 'Leonora Mary' and that we were to call her what we pleased. She came in that first day wearing a full length mink coat. She was moderately tall, slender, dark with fine nose and mouth. A long wolf whistle from Bailey was followed by 'Enjoy yer shower, baby?'

This must be the woman Bailey had seen. She must have got herself trapped in the deluge exactly as I had done. With most of her clothing wet she was using the mink coat as a covering.

The remaining woman was Chinese. She came in wearing a neat smock. She looked silently from one to another of us, her face like stone. Under her imperious gaze, Bailey cracked out with 'Eee, look what we've got 'ere. 'ad yer cherry plucked, love?'

They wanted to know about the stars, about the way Daghri and I figured out where we were going and so on and so forth. As the hours and days passed we watched the planets move slowly across the walls. We watched the inner planets getting fainter and fainter while Jupiter hardly seemed to change. But after three weeks even Jupiter was visibly dimming. The ship was leaving the solar system.

Of all these things everybody understood something. It was wonderful to see how suddenly acute the apparently ignorant became as soon as they realised the extent to which their fate depended on these astronomical matters. Throughout their lives the planets had been remote recondite things. Now they were suddenly as real to everybody as a sack of potatoes, more real I thought, for I doubted if any of us would ever see a potato again, erroneously as it turned out.

Of the Einstein time dilation they could make out nothing at all, however. It was beyond them to understand how in only a few years we could reach distant stars. I just had to tell them to accept it as a fact. Where were we going they all wanted to know. As if I could answer such a question! All I could say was that we had somehow been swept up by a raiding party, similar to our own parties rounding up animals for a zoo. It all fitted. Wasn't this exactly the kind of setup we ourselves provided for animals in a zoo? The boxes to sleep in, the regular food, the restrictions on mating, the passages and the cathedral hall to exercise in?

My longest conversations were with Daghri and with the aristocratic Mary. Mary and I found that so long as we kept about three feet apart we could go pretty well anywhere together at any time without falling into the troubles which were constantly afflicting Bill Bailey and Hattie Foulds. Quite early on, Mary wanted to know why we were so hermetically sealed inside this place. Animals in a terrestrial zoo can at least *see* their captors she pointed out. They breathe the same air, they glower at each other from opposite sides of the same bars. Not in the snake house or the fish tank I answered. *We* look in on snakes, we look in on fish, but it is doubtful if either look out on us in any proper sense. Only for birds and mammals is there much in the way of reciprocity in a terrestrial zoo. Mary burst out,

'But snakes are dangerous.'

'So may we be. Oh, not with poison like snakes, perhaps with bacteria. This place may be a veritable horror house so far as our captors are concerned.'

I was much worried about the Chinese girl, Ling was her name, for she had the problem of language to contend with as well as the actual situation. It was also very clear that Ling intended to be harshly uncooperative. I asked Mary to do what she could to break the ice. Mary reported that Ling 'read' English but didn't speak it, not yet. Gradually as the days passed we managed to thaw out the girl to some small degree. The basic trouble was that Ling had been a politician of quite exalted status in one of the Chinese provinces. She had been a person of real consequence, not in virtue of birth, but from her own determination and ability. She gave orders and she expected obedience from those around her. Her glacial attitude to us all was a general expression of contempt for the degenerate west.

Our clothes, while easily cleaned in the showers, became more and more battered and out of shape as time went on. We dressed as lightly as possible consistent with modesty, a commodity variable from person to person. One day Bill

Bailey, clad only in underpants, came into the cathedral, threw himself on the floor and said:

'Oo, what a bitch! A right bitch that. Used to run real cockfights back on the farm, illicit-like. She'd take on any half-dozen men after a fight. Says it used to key her up, put her in tone. That's what we need 'ere, Professor, a bloody great cockfight.'

Ling, who was standing nearby, looked down at Bailey.

'That is the sort of man who should be whipped, hard and long. In *my* town he would have been whipped for all the people to see.'

The girl's expression was imperious, although her voice was quiet. Because of this, because also of her curious accent and use of words – which I have not attempted to imitate – the others, particularly Bailey, did not realise what she had said. To me the girl's attitude demanded action. I took her firmly by the arm and marched her along the passages – until we came to the first open cell. Strangely enough this action induced no sense of sickness in either of us.

'Now see here, Ling, you're not in China anymore. We're all *captives* in this place. We've got to keep solidly together, otherwise we're lost. It's our only strength, to give support to each other. If it means putting up with a man like Bailey you've just got to do it.'

Even in my own ears this sounded flat and feeble, which is always the way with moderation and reason; it always sounds flat and feeble compared to an unrelenting fanatic or bigot. Certainly Ling was not impressed. She looked me over coolly, head-to-toe, and made the announcement, 'The time will come when it will be a pity you are not ten years younger.'

I was taking this as a left-handed compliment when she added another statement.

'I shall choose the Australian.'

'I think you'll have trouble from the American girl.' Ling laughed – I suppose it was a laugh. The eyes I noticed were an intense green, the teeth a shining white. The girl must be using the soapy solution in the shower baths. It tasted pretty horrible but it allowed one to clean away the vegetable marrow food on which we were obliged to subsist.

I gave it up. The best I could see in Ling's point of view was that her ideology represented a last link with Earth. Perhaps it was her way of keeping sane, but it was entirely beyond me to understand it. I was much more impressed at the way Ling always contrived to look neat, always in the same smock.

We were undereating, because unless you were actively hungry there was no point in consuming the tasteless vegetable marrow stuff. It was mushy with a lot of moisture in it. Even so, I was surprised we managed without needing to drink, for there was no possibility of drinking the one source of fluid, the liquid in the shower bath. I could only think we were generating a lot of water internally, through oxidising the vegetable marrow material. Every now and then we had an intense desire to chew something really hard. I used to bite away at the cord from my rucksack, often for an hour at a time.

The natural effect of the undereating was that we were nearly all losing weight. I had lost most of the excess ten pounds or so which I never seemed to get rid of back on Earth. Ernst Schmidt had lost a lot more, so much in fact that he had discarded my anorak. He went around now only in the bathing trunks, which he had tightened in quite a bit. Getting fit had become a passion with the German. He had taken to running through the passages according to a systematic schedule, ten laps from the cathedral and back again for every hour he was awake. Sometimes I accompanied him, to give my muscles a little exercise, but I could never be so regular about it. He commented on this one day.

'A strange difference of temperament, Professor. We often have these little runs together, but you can't quite keep them up. Of course I understand you have not the same need as I. But even if you had the need, you couldn't keep them up. No, I think not.'

'Personal temperament?'

'It is an interesting question. Both personal and national, I think. A misleading thing in politics – and in business – is the description given to your people. Anglo-Saxons, eh?

What is an Anglo-Saxon, Professor, a sort of German maybe?'

'We're always supposed to be a kind of first cousins. There's the similarity of language for one thing.'

'Accidental, imposed by a handful of conquerors. Look at me. I speak English. If you will pardon me, I speak it with an American accent. Does that make me an American? Obviously not. I speak this way because Americans have conquered my particular world, the business world.'

'Go on.'

'It is a pity we have no mirrors in this place. If we had a mirror, let me tell you how you would see yourself. You would see a tallish man, with a fair skin, a big red beard and blue eyes. You would see a Celt not a German. Your people are Celts, Professor, not Germans, and that is the true source of the difference in our temperaments, you and I.'

'So you think it goes a long way back?'

'Three thousand years or more, to the time when we Germans threw you Celts out of Europe. Yes, we understand a lot about each other, you and I, but we understand each other because we have fought each other for a long time now, not because we are the same.'

I was surprised at the turn of the conversation. Schmidt must have noticed something of this in my face.

'Ah, you wonder how I can tell you these things? Because these things are my real interest, not the packing of meat, for who should be interested in the packing of meat?'

'What does all this lead you to?'

'We Germans can pursue a goal relentlessly to the end. You Celts can never do so. You have what I think is called an easy going streak. It was this streak which made the Romans admire you so much in ancient times. But it was this weakness which very nearly cost you the whole of Europe, my friend.'

'To be easy going can mean reserve, you know, reserve energy in times of real crisis.'

'Ah, you are thinking of winning the last battle. It was like that in each of the wars of this century, wasn't it? You won the last battles, you won those wars. Yet from victory each time you emerged weaker than before. We Germans emerged each time stronger, even from defeat.'

'Because of a tenacity of purpose?'

'Correct, Professor.'

'What is it you are really telling me, Herr Schmidt? That in whatever should lie ahead of us you will come out best?'

'A leader will emerge among us. It will be a man, an intelligent man. This leaves the choice between the two of us. Of the others the one is a buffoon, the other a simple countryman. Which of us it will be, I am not sure yet.'

'Don't be too easy going, Herr Schmidt. You contradict yourself.'

Schmidt laughed. Then he became more serious.

'In a known situation a German will always win. He will win because all his energies are directed to a clear-cut purpose. In an unknown situation it is all much less sure.'

I mention these events in some detail because there were three points in them which came together. Hattie Foulds and her cockfights, Ling and the whipping she would have liked to administer on the person of Bill Bailey, and now Schmidt's reference to himself as a meat-packer. It made a consistent theory, except for one very big snag, Daghri. I had a long serious talk with the Indian. He denied all my suggestions with such poise and dignity that I felt I simply must believe his protestations of innocence. My theory just had to be wrong. I became depressed about it. Mary noticed the depression and wanted to know what it was all about. I decided to tell her of the things in my mind.

'Every one of us is affecting an attitude, or considering some problem,' I began.

'How do you know? About me for instance.'

'You are considering the moral problem of whether you should permit yourself to bear children into captivity.'

Mary looked me full in the face and nodded.

'My problem from the beginning,' I went on, 'has been to understand something of the psychology of the creatures running this ship. Zoomen, is the way I like to think of them. What the hell are they doing and why? Obviously taking samples of living creatures, perhaps everywhere throughout the Galaxy.'

'You mean there might be animals from other planets on this ship?'

'Quite certainly, I would think. Through the walls of this cathedral, through the passage walls there will be other "quarters", other rooms and passages with other specimens in them.'

'Literally, a zoo!'

'Literally. Yet my curiosity about those other compartments and their contents is less than my curiosity about the human content of this particular compartment. There are nine of us, four of us from the British Isles, an American girl, a Chinese girl, an Indian, a German and an Australian. What kind of a distribution is that? Seven out of nine white. Can you really believe interstellar zoomen have a colour prejudice?'

'Perhaps it wasn't easy to grab people, they took the first they could get.'

'Doesn't hold water. Geographically they snatched us from places as wide apart as Europe, America, India, Australia and China. They snatched McClay, Daghri and myself from the quiet countryside, they took you from the busy streets of London, Ling from a crowded town, Schmidt and Giselda Horne from the suburbs of Chicago. It doesn't seem as if the snatching process presented the slightest difficulty to them.'

'Have you any idea of how it was done?'

'Not really. I just visualise it like picking up bits of fluff with a vacuum cleaner. They simply held a nozzle over you and you disappeared into the works.'

'To come out in this place.'

'It must have been something like that. Where had we got to, this colour business. Differences in colour might seem very unimportant to these zoomen. We only see these differences, like the differences between you and Ling, because an enormous proportion of the human brain is given over to the analysis of what are really extremely fine distinctions. It could be the zoomen hardly notice these distinctions, and if they do they don't think them worth bothering about.'

'Then perhaps there was some other method of choice?'

'Must have been. If humans were snatched at random, a good half would be yellow or black. You'd only get a distribution as queer as this one if you had some system or other. But not a colour system.'

'Sounds like a contradiction.'

'Not necessarily. Right at the beginning it occurred to me that justice might be the criterion.'

'Justice!'

'Look, if *you* were taking a number of humans into lifelong captivity, it might occur to you to choose the very people who had themselves shown the least feeling for the captivity of other animals, or for the lives of other animals.'

'My coat!'

'Yes, your mink coat must have marked you out from the crowd in the street. The zoomen spotted it, and at the blink of an eye you were into their vacuum cleaner.'

Mary shuddered and then smiled wryly,

'I always thought of it as such a beautiful coat, warm and splendid to look at. You really believe it was the coat? I only use it for a pillow now.'

'A lot of things fit the same picture. Schmidt was a meat-packer. Giselda Horne's father was in the same business, stuffing bloody bits of animals into tins.'

Mary was quite excited, her own plight forgotten as the puzzle fitted into place.

'And McClay reared the animals, and Bailey was a butcher, an actual slaughterer.'

'And the cockfights for Hattie Foulds.'

'But what about you, and Ling, and Daghri?'

'Leave me out of it. I can make a good case against myself. Ling and Daghri are the critical ones. You see there isn't much animal-eating among Asiatic populations, really because they haven't enough in the way of feeding stuffs to be able to rear animals for slaughter. This seemed to me to be the reason why only two Asiatic people had been taken. It occurred to me that possibly even these two might have been chosen in some other way.'

'What about Ling?'

'Well, to Ling people are no more than animals. I've little doubt Ling has had many a person whipped at her immediate discretion, at her pleasure even for all I know.'

'And Daghri?'

'Daghri is the contradiction, the disproof of everything. Daghri is a Hindu. Hinduism is a complicated religion, but one important part of it forbids the eating of animals.'

'Perhaps Daghri doesn't have much use for that aspect of his religion.'

'Exactly what I thought. I charged him with it directly, more or less accusing him of some form of violence against either animals or humans. He denied it with the utmost dignity.'

'Maybe he was lying.'

'Why should he lie?'

'Perhaps because he's ashamed. You know, Daghri is different in another way. What odds would you give of taking nine people at random and of finding none with strong religious beliefs?'

'Very small, I would imagine.'

'Yet none of us has strong religious beliefs, except Daghri.'

I saw exactly what Mary meant. To Daghri, religion might be no more than a sham. Perhaps the Indian was no more than a gifted liar.

Not long after this conversation Daghri disappeared. For a while I thought he had retired, possibly in shame, to his box-like cell. In one of my runs with Schmidt I noticed all the cells open. Daghri was not to be found in any one of them. We searched high and low, but Daghri simply was not there. 'High and low' is an obvious exaggeration, for there wasn't any possible hiding place in our asceptic accommodations. It was rather that we looked everywhere many times. Daghri was gone. The general consensus was that the poor fellow has been abstracted by the zoomen for 'experiments'. I was of a similar mind at first, then it all clicked into place. I rushed into the cathedral. The others quickly followed, so we were assembled there, eight of us now. I studied the star pattern on the wall. We hadn't bothered with it of late, treating it more as a decoration than as a source of information.

What a fool I'd been! I should have noticed the slight shift of the patterns back to their original forms. Owing to the motion of the ship, the stars had moved very slightly, but now they had moved back. The planets were there too, the planets of our own solar system. The double Earth-Moon was there. So was the sunlight replacing artificial light at the entrance of the passageways – there was a small subtle difference.

'We're being taken back,' I heard someone say.

I knew we were not being taken back. Daghri had been taken back, the contradiction had been removed. My instinct had been right; Daghri had been telling the truth. Daghri had ill-treated no animal; Daghri was saved, but not so the rest of us. The planets moved across the wall, just as before. We were on our way out again.

The others couldn't believe it at first, then they didn't want to believe it, but at last, as the hours passed, they were forced to believe it. Disintegration set in quickly. Giselda Horne gave way badly. She seemed big and strong, but really she was only an overdeveloped kid. I thought she might be better alone, so I took her back to her own cell. She nodded and went in. Silently, from behind me, Ling glided after Giselda Horne. I shouted to Ling to come out and leave the girl alone. Ling turned with a look of haughty indifference on her face. At that very moment the panel of the cell closed. There was just a fleeting fraction of a second in which I saw the expression on Ling's face changed from indifference to triumph.

The others gathered outside the cell. We could hear nothing from inside, for the panel was completely sound proof. The Chinese girl had judged the situation quite exactly. Giselda Horne was near the edge of sanity. With cutting and sadistic words, and with the force of an intense personality, Ling would push her over that edge.

The panel slid open. Horror-stricken, I gazed inside. Horror dissolved to laughter. Gone was Ling's neat smock. Blood was oozing from long scratches on Giselda Horne's face. Ling had evidently fought cat-like, as I would have anticipated. Giselda Horne had fought in a different style. One swinging fist must have hit Ling on the mouth, for it was now puffy and bleeding. A fist had also whacked the Chinese girl a real beauty on the left eye. Ling staggered out, leaving Giselda Horne with a big smile on her face.

'Gee, that was real good,' said the American girl.

It was two days, two waking and sleeping periods, before I saw Ling again. She still contrived to appear reserved and haughty, even though the furious set-to had left her with the blackest eye I ever saw and with hardly any remnants of clothing.

'The American girl and I, we will share the Australian,' Ling said. 'It is a pity you are not five years younger,' she added.

Mary took it all with a great calmness.

'I'd become reconciled to it, captivity I mean. This really proves the zoomen have a sense of justice, to go back all that way to put Daghri home again.'

Somehow I couldn't tell Mary. I knew the zoomen hadn't made any mistake about Daghri. It was an experiment, done quite deliberately to see how we would react. The zoomen just couldn't have read me so accurately and Daghri so badly. With Daghri gone, we made eight, four couples – the animals came into the Ark. Another thing, choose a smallish number. Being an irrational creature a human might say, seven. A really rational creature would always choose a binary number, eight.

Mary put a hand lightly on my arm.

'You never said what it was *you* had done.'

'My sin was the worst of you all. My sin was that I was a consumer. I ate the poor creatures McClay reared on his farm, the animals Bailey slaughtered, the bloody bits Schmidt stuffed into tins.'

'But millions do the same. I did, everybody does!'

'Yes, but they know not what they do. *I* knew what I was

doing. For twenty years now I've been clear in my mind about it. Yet I've gone on taking the line of least resistance. I made minor adjustments, like eating more fish and less meat, but I never faced the real problem. I knew what I was doing.'

The weeks passed, then the months. For some time, Mary and I have shared the same cell for sleeping. We had no trouble with the sickness, even when we shared my rucksack for a pillow. The same favour was not immediately extended to the others. The favour perhaps was granted because I had kept my small scrap of knowledge about the zoomen strictly to myself.

The day did come, however, when the others were allowed into physical contact. There was no mistaking the day, for Bill Bailey appeared in the cathedral clad only in his now tattered underpants, shouting,

'Bloody miracle. We got on last night, real good and proper.' Then he was off, high stepping, knees up, like a boxer trotting along the road. Round and round the cathedral he went chanting,

'Raw eggs, raw eggs, mother. Oh, for a bloody basin of raw eggs.'

Giselda Horne was standing nearby.

'What does it mean?' she asked rather shyly.

'It means, my dear, that we're only nine months away from our destination,' I answered.

This narrative was discovered in curious circumstances many many years after it was written, indeed long long after it had become impossible to identify Meall Ghaordie, the mountain mentioned by its author.

Landing on a distant planetary system, the crew of the fifth deep interstellar mission was astonished to discover what seemed like a remarkable new species of humanoid. The language spoken by the creatures was quite unintelligible in its details but in the broad pattern of its sounds it was strikingly similar to an archaic human language.

The creatures lived a wild nomadic existence. Yet they

were imbued with a strong religious sense, a religion apparently centering around a 'covenant', guarded day and night in a remote stronghold. It was there, in a remote mountain valley, that the creatures assembled for their most solemn religious ceremonies. By a technologically-advanced subterfuge, access to the 'covenant' was at length obtained. It turned out to be the story of the 'Professor', reproduced above without amendations or omissions. It was written in a small book of the pattern of an ancient diary. This it was the creatures guarded with such abandoned ferocity, although not a word of it did they understand.

The manuscript has undoubtedly created many more problems than it has solved. What meaning can be attached to the fanciful, anatomical references? What was 'Munro-bagging'? These questions are still the subject of bitter debate among savants. Who were the sinister zoomen? Could it be that the Professor and his party turned out to be too hot to handle, in a biological sense of course, and that the zoomen were forced to dump them on the first vacant planet? The pity is that the 'Professor' did not continue his narrative. His writing materials must soon have become exhausted, for the above narrative almost fills his diary.

It was the appearance of the creatures which misled the fifth expedition into thinking they were dealing with humanoids, not humans. It was the unique combination of flaming red hair with intense green, mongoloid eyes. Did these characteristics become dominant in the mixed gene pool of the Professor's party, or was the true explanation more direct and elementary?

10 – KINGSLEY AMIS: Something Strange

Like J. B. Priestley, who was included in Volume one, Kingsley Amis involved himself in the negotiations over an Arts Council grant for the floudering *New Worlds* magazine in 1967, having already declared a life-long interest in science fiction.

Kingsley William Amis was born on April 16th, 1922, and was educated at the City of London school and St John's College, Oxford, where he earned his MA. Serving in the Army between 1942 and 1945, he later became a Lecturer in English at the University of Swansea from 1949 to 1961. He shot to fame in 1954 with the publication of his humorous novel *Lucky Jim*.

In the Spring of 1959 he was invited to give a series of lectures at Princeton University as part of the Christian Gauss Seminars in Criticism. Amis chose as his subject matter, science fiction. Reworked and lengthened these lectures were published in 1960 as *New Maps of Hell*. Whilst Amis classifies most early and much current sf as banal, he nevertheless champions the genre as a valuable vehicle for social comment which could never be attained in any other stream of literature.

Intent on proving himself within the field, Amis, in collaboration with fellow author and lecturer Robert Conquest (who has also written some science fiction), prepared a series of science fiction anthologies, *Spectrum*, annually from 1961 to 1966. He also turned his own pen to writing science fiction, with novels like *The Anti-Death League* (1966), *The Green Man* (1971), his recent alternate-Earth novel *The Alteration* (1976), and this earlier short story, *Something Strange*, which first appeared in *The Spectator* in 1960.

SOMETHING STRANGE

Kingsley Amis

Something strange happened every day. It might happen during the morning, while the two men were taking their readings and observations and the two women busy with the domestic routine: the big faces had come during the morning. Or, as with the little faces and the coloured fires, the strange thing would happen in the afternoon, in the middle of Bruno's maintenance programme and Clovis's transmission to Base, Lia's rounds of the garden and Myri's work on her story. The evening was often undisturbed, the night less often.

They all understood that ordinary temporal expressions had no meaning for people confined indefinitely, as they were, to a motionless steel sphere hanging in a region of space so empty that the light of the nearest star took some hundreds of years to reach them. The Standing Orders devised by Base, however, recommended that they adopt a twenty-four-hour unit of time, as was the rule on the Earth they had not seen for many months. The arrangement suited them well: their work, recreation and rest seemed to fall naturally into the periods provided. It was only the prospect of year after year of the same routine, stretching further into the future than they could see, that was a source of strain.

Bruno commented on this to Clovis after a morning spent repairing a fault in the spectrum analyser they used for investigating and classifying the nearer stars. They were sitting at the main observation port in the lounge, drinking the midday cocktail and waiting for the women to join them.

'I'd say we stood up to it extremely well,' Clovis said in answer to Bruno. 'Perhaps too well.'

Bruno hunched his fat figure upright. 'How do you mean?'

'We may be hindering our chances of being relieved.'

'Base has never said a word about our relief.'

'Exactly. With half a million stations to staff, it'll be a long time before they get round to one like this, where everything runs smoothly. You and I are a perfect team, and you have Lia and I have Myri, and they're all right together – no real conflict at all. Hence no reason for a relief.'

Myri had heard all this as she laid the table in the alcove. She wondered how Clovis could not know that Bruno wanted to have her instead of Lia, or perhaps as well as Lia. If Clovis did know, and was teasing Bruno, then that would be a silly thing to do, because Bruno was not a pleasant man. With his thick neck and pale fat face he would not be pleasant to be had by, either, quite unlike Clovis, who was no taller but whose straight, hard body and soft skin were always pleasant. He could not think as well as Bruno, but on the other hand many of the things Bruno thought were not pleasant. She poured herself a drink and went over to them.

Bruno had said something about its being a pity they could not fake their personnel report by inventing a few quarrels, and Clovis had immediately agreed that that was impossible. She kissed him and sat down at his side. 'What do you think about the idea of being relieved?' he asked her.

'I never think about it.'

'Quite right,' Bruno said, grinning. 'You're doing very nicely here. Fairly nicely, anyway.'

'What are you getting at?' Clovis asked him with a different kind of grin.

'It's not a very complete life, is it? For any of us. I could do with a change, anyway. A different kind of job, something that isn't testing and using and repairing apparatus. We do seem to have a lot of repairing to do, don't we? That analyser breaks down almost every day. And yet –'

His voice tailed off and he looked out of the port, as if to assure himself that all that lay beyond it was the familiar starscape of points and smudges of light.

'And yet what?' Clovis asked, irritably this time.

'I was just thinking that we really ought to be thankful

for having plenty to do. There's the routine and the fruits and vegetables to look after, and Myri's story. . . . How's that going, by the way? Won't you read us some of it? This evening, perhaps?'

'Not until it's finished, if you don't mind.'

'Oh, but I do mind. It's part of our duty to entertain one another. And I'm very interested in it personally.'

'Why?'

'Because you're an interesting girl. Bright brown eyes and a healthy glowing skin – how do you manage it after all this time in space? And you've more energy than any of us.'

Myri said nothing. Bruno was good at making remarks there was nothing to say to.

'What's it about, this story of yours?' he pursued. 'At least you can tell us that.'

'I have told you. It's about normal life. Life on Earth before there were any space stations, lots of different people doing different things, not this –'

'That's normal life, is it, different people doing different things? I can't wait to hear what the things are. Who's the hero, Myri? Our dear Clovis?'

Myri put her hand on Clovis's shoulder. 'No more, please, Bruno. Let's go back to your point about the routine. I couldn't understand why you left out the most important part, the part that keeps us busiest of all.'

'Ah, the strange happenings.' Bruno dipped his head in a characteristic gesture, half laugh, half nervous tremor. 'And the hours we spend discussing them. Oh yes. How could I have failed to mention all that?'

'If you've got any sense you'll go on not mentioning it,' Clovis snapped. 'We're all fed up with the whole business.'

'You may be, but I'm not. I want to discuss it. So does Myri, don't you, Myri?'

'I do think perhaps it's time we made another attempt to find a pattern,' Myri said. This was a case of Bruno not being pleasant but being right.

'Oh, not again.' Clovis bounded up and went over to the drinks table. 'Ah, hallo, Lia,' he said to the tall, thin, blonde woman who had just entered with a tray of cold dishes. 'Let me get you a drink. Bruno and Myri are getting philosophical – looking for patterns. What do you think? I'll tell you what I think. I think we're doing enough already. I think patterns are Base's job.'

'We can make it ours, too,' Bruno said. 'You agree, Lia?'

'Of course,' Lia said in the deep voice that seemed to Myri to carry so much more firmness and individuality in its tone than any of its owner's words or actions.

'Very well. You can stay out of this if you like, Clovis. We start from the fact that what we see and hear need not be illusions, although they may be.'

'At least that they're illusions that any human being might have, they're not special to us, as we know from Base's reports of what happens to other stations.'

'Correct, Myri. In any event, illusions or not, they are being directed at us by an intelligence and for a purpose.'

'We don't know that,' Myri objected. 'They may be natural phenomena, or the by-product of some intelligent activity not directed at us.'

'Correct again, but let us reserve these less probable possibilities until later. Now, as a sample, consider the last week's strange happenings. I'll fetch the log so that there can be no dispute.'

'I wish you'd stop it,' Clovis said when Bruno had gone out to the apparatus room. 'It's a waste of time.'

'Time's the only thing we're not short of.'

'I'm not short of anything,' he said, touching her thigh. 'Come with me for a little while.'

'Later.'

'Lia always goes with Bruno when he asks her.'

'Oh yes, but that's my choice,' Lia said. 'She doesn't want to now. Wait until she wants to.'

'I don't like waiting.'

'Waiting can make it better.'

'Here we are,' Bruno said briskly, returning. 'Right. . . . Monday. *Within a few seconds the sphere became encased in a thick brownish damp substance that tests revealed to be both impermeable and infinitely thick. No action by the staff suggested itself. After three hours and eleven minutes the substance disappeared.* It's the *infinitely thick* thing that's interesting. That must have been an illusion, or something would have happened to all the other stations at the same time, not to speak of the stars and planets. A total or partial illusion, then. Agreed?'

'Go on.'

'Tuesday. *Metallic object of size comparable to that of the sphere approaching on collision course at 500 kilometres per second. No countermeasures available. Object appeared instantaneously at 35 million kilometres' distance and disappeared instantaneously at 1500 kilometres.* What about that?'

'We've had ones like that before,' Lia put in. 'Only this was the longest time it's taken to approach and the nearest it's come before disappearing.'

'Incomprehensible or illusion,' Myri suggested.

'Yes, I think that's the best we can do at the moment. Wednesday: a very trivial one, not worth discussing. *A being apparently constructed entirely of bone approached the main port and made beckoning motions.* Whoever's doing this must be running out of ideas. Thursday. *All bodies external to the sphere vanished to all instruments simultaneously, reappearing to all instruments simultaneously two hours later.* That's not a new one either, I seem to remember. Illusion? Good. Friday. *Beings resembling terrestrial reptiles covered the sphere, fighting ceaselessly and eating portions of one another. Loud rustling and slithering sounds.* The sounds at least must have been an illusion, with no air out there, and I never heard of a reptile that didn't breathe. The same sort of thing applies to yesterday's performance. *Human screams of pain and extreme astonishment approaching and receding. No visual or other accompaniment.*' He paused and looked round at them. 'Well? Any uniformities suggest themselves?'

'No,' Clovis said, helping himself to salad, for they sat now at the lunch table. 'And I defy any human brain to devise any. The whole thing's arbitrary.'

'On the contrary, the very next happening – today's when it comes – might reveal an unmistakable pattern.'

'The one to concentrate on,' Myri said, 'is the approaching object. Why did it vanish before striking the sphere?'

Bruno stared at her. 'It had to, if it was an illusion.'

'Not at all. Why couldn't we have had an illusion of the sphere being struck? And supposing it wasn't an illusion?'

'Next time there's an object, perhaps it will strike,' Lia said.

Clovis laughed. 'That's a good one. What would happen if it did, I wonder? And it wasn't an illusion?'

They all looked at Bruno for an answer. After a moment or two, he said: 'I presume the sphere would shatter and we'd all be thrown into space. I simply can't imagine what that would be like. We should be . . . Never to see one another again, or anybody or anything else, to be nothing more than a senseless lump floating in space for ever. The chances of –'

'It would be worth something to be rid of your conver-ation,' Clovis said, amiable again now that Bruno was discomfited. 'Let's be practical for a change. How long will it take you to run off your analyses this afternoon? There's a lot of stuff to go out to Base and I shan't be able to give you a hand.'

'An hour, perhaps, after I've run the final tests.'

'Why run tests at all? She was lined up perfectly when we finished this morning.'

'Fortunately.'

'Fortunately indeed. One more variable and we might have found it impossible.'

'Yes,' Bruno said abstractedly. Then he got to his feet so abruptly that the other three started. 'But we didn't, did we? There wasn't one more variable, was there? It didn't quite happen, you see, the thing we couldn't handle.'

Nobody spoke.

'Excuse me, I must be by myself.'

'If Bruno keeps this up,' Clovis said to the two women, 'Base will send up a relief sooner than we think.'

Myri tried to drive the thought of Bruno's strange behaviour out of her head when, half an hour later, she sat down to work on her story. The expression on his face as he left the table had been one she could not name. Excitement? Dislike? Surprise? That was the nearest – a kind of persistent surprise. Well, he was certain, being Bruno, to set about explaining it at dinner. She wished he were more pleasant, because he did think well.

Finally expelling the image of Bruno's face, she began re-reading the page of manuscript she had been working on when the screams had interrupted her the previous afternoon. It was part of a difficult scene, one in which a woman met by chance a man who had been having her ten years earlier, with the complication that she was at the time in the company of the man who was currently having her. The scene was an eating alcove in a large city.

'Go away,' Volsci said, 'or I'll hit you.'

Norbu smiled in a not-pleasant way. 'What good would that do? Irmy likes me better than she likes you. You are more pleasant, no doubt, but she likes me better. She remembers me having her ten years ago more clearly than she remembers you having her last night. I am good at thinking, which is better than any amount of being pleasant.'

'She's having her meal with me,' Volsci said, pointing to the cold food and drinks in front of them. 'Aren't you, Irmy?'

'Yes, Irmy,' Norbu said. 'You must choose. If you can't let both of us have you, you must say which of us you like better.'

Irmy looked from one man to the other. There was so much difference between them that she could hardly begin to choose: The one more pleasant, the other better at thinking, the one slim, the other plump. She decided being pleasant was better. It was more important and more significant – better in every way that made a real difference. She said: 'I'll have Volsci.'

Norbu looked surprised and sorry. 'I think you're wrong.'

'You might as well go now,' Volsci said. 'Ila will be waiting.'

'Yes,' Norbu said. He looked extremely sorry now.

Irmy felt quite sorry too. 'Good-bye, Norbu,' she said.

Myri smiled to herself. It was good, even better than she

had remembered – there was no point in being modest inside one's own mind. She must be a real writer in spite of Bruno's scoffing, or how could she have invented these characters, who were so utterly unlike anybody she knew, and then put them into a situation that was so completely outside her experience? The only thing she was not sure about was whether she might not have overplayed the part about feeling or dwelt on it at too great length. Perhaps *extremely sorry* was a little heavy; she replaced it by *sorrier than before*. Excellent: now there was just the right touch of restraint in the middle of all the feeling. She decided she could finish off the scene in a few lines.

'Probably see you at some cocktail hour,' Volsci said, she wrote, then looked up with a frown as the buzzer sounded at her door. She crossed her tiny wedge-shaped room – its rear wall was part of the outer wall of the sphere, but it had no port – threw the lock and found Bruno on the threshold. He was breathing fast, as if he had been hurrying or lifting a heavy weight, and she saw with distaste that there were drops of sweat on his thick skin. He pushed past her and sat down on her bed, his mouth open.

'What is it?' she asked, displeased. The afternoon was a private time unless some other arrangement were made at lunch.

'I don't know what it is. I think I must be ill.'

'Ill? But you can't be. Only people on Earth get ill. Nobody on a station is ever ill: Base told us that. Illness is caused by –'

'I don't think I believe some of the things that Base says.'

'But who can we believe if we don't believe Base?'

Bruno evidently did not hear her question. He said: 'I had to come to you – Lia's no good for this. Please let me stay with you, I've got so much to say.'

'It's no use, Bruno. Clovis is the one who has me. I thought you understood that I didn't –'

'That's not what I mean,' he said impatiently. 'Where I need you is in thinking. Though that's connected with the other, the having. I don't expect you to see that. I've only just begun to see it myself.'

Myri could make nothing of this last part. 'Thinking? Thinking about what?'

He bit his lip and shut his eyes for a moment. 'Listen to this,' he said. 'It was the analyser that set my mind going. Almost every other day it breaks down. And the computer, the counters, the repellers, the scanners and the rest of them – they're always breaking down too, and so are their power supplies. But not the purifier or the fluid-reconstitutor or the fruit and vegetable growers or the heaters or the main power source. Why not?'

'Well, they're less complicated. How can a fruit grower go wrong? A chemical tank and a water tank is all there is to it. You ask Lia about that.'

'All right. Try answering this, then. The strange happenings. If they're illusions, why are they always outside the sphere? Why are there never any inside?'

'Perhaps there are,' Myri said.

'Don't. I don't want that. I shouldn't like that. I want everything in here to be real. Are you real? I must believe you are.'

'Of course I'm real.' She was now thoroughly puzzled.

'And it makes a difference, doesn't it? It's very important that you and everything else should be real, everything in the sphere. But tell me: whatever's arranging these happenings must be pretty powerful if it can fool our instruments and our senses so completely and consistently, and yet it can't do anything – anything we recognise as strange, that is – inside this puny little steel skin. Why not?'

'Presumably it has its limitations. We should be pleased.'

'Yes. All right, next point. You remember the time I tried to sit up in the lounge after midnight and stay awake?'

'That was silly. Nobody can stay awake after midnight. Standing Orders were quite clear on that point.'

'Yes, they were, weren't they?' Bruno seemed to be trying to grin. 'Do you remember my telling you how I couldn't account for being in my own bed as usual when the music woke us – you remember the big music? And – this is what I'm really after – do you remember how we all agreed at breakfast that life in space must have conditioned us in such a way that falling asleep at a fixed time had become an automatic mechanism? You remember that?'

'Naturally I do.'

'Right. Two questions, then. Does that strike you as a likely explanation? That sort of complete self-conditioning in all four of us after . . . just a number of months?'

'Not when you put it like that.'

'But we all agreed on it, didn't we? Without hesitation.'

Myri, leaning against a side wall, fidgeted. He was being not pleasant in a new way, one that made her want to stop him talking even while he was thinking at his best. 'What's your other question, Bruno?' Her voice sounded unusual to her.

'Ah, you're feeling it too, are you?'

'I don't know what you mean.'

'I think you will in a minute. Try my other question. The night of the music was a long time ago, soon after we arrived here, but you remember it clearly. So do I. And yet when I try to remember what I was doing only a couple of months earlier, on Earth, finishing up my life there, getting ready for this, it's just a vague blur. Nothing stands out.'

'It's all so remote.'

'Maybe. But I remember the trip clearly enough, don't you?'

Myri caught her breath. I feel surprised, she told herself. Or something like that. I feel the way Bruno looked when he left the lunch table. She said nothing.

'You're feeling it now all right, aren't you?' He was watching her closely with his narrow eyes. 'Let me try to describe it. A surprise that goes on and on. Puzzlement. Symptoms of physical exertion or strain. And above all a . . . a sort of discomfort, only in the mind. Like having a sharp object pressed against a tender part of your body, except that this is in your mind.'

'What are you talking about?'

'A difficulty of vocabulary.'

The loudspeaker above the door clicked on and Clovis's voice said: 'Attention. Strange happening. Assemble in the lounge at once. Strange happening.'

Myri and Bruno stopped staring at each other and hurried out along the narrow corridor. Clovis and Lia were already in the lounge, looking out of the port.

Apparently only a few feet beyond the steelhard glass, and illuminated from some invisible source, were two floating figures. The detail was excellent, and the four inside the sphere could distinguish without difficulty every fold in the naked skin of the two caricatures of humanity presented, it seemed, for their thorough inspection, a presumption given added weight by the slow rotation of the pair that enabled their every portion to be scrutinised. Except for a scrubby growth at the base of the skull, they were hairless. The limbs were foreshortened, lacking the normal narrowing at the joints, and the bellies protuberant. One had male characteristics, the other female, yet in neither case were these complete. From each open, wet, quivering toothless mouth there came a loud, clearly audible yelling, higher in pitch than any those in the sphere could have produced, and of an unfamiliar emotional range.

'Well, I wonder how long this will last,' Clovis said.

'Is it worth trying the repellers on them?' Lia asked. 'What does the radar say? Does it see them?'

'I'll go and have a look.'

Bruno turned his back on the port. 'I don't like them.'

'Why not?' Myri saw he was sweating again.

'They remind me of something.'

'What?'

'I'm trying to think.'

But although Bruno went on trying to think for the rest of that day, with such obvious seriousness that even Clovis did his best to help with suggestions, he was no nearer a solution when they parted, as was their habit, at five minutes to midnight. And when, several times in the next couple of days, Myri mentioned the afternoon of the caricatures to him, he showed little interest.

'Bruno, you are extraordinary,' she said one evening. 'What happened to those odd feelings of yours you were so eager to describe to me just before Clovis called us into the lounge?'

He shrugged his narrow shoulders in the almost girlish way he had. 'Oh, I don't know what could have got into me,' he said. 'I expect I was just angry with the confounded analyser and the way it kept breaking down. It's been much better recently.'

'And all that thinking you used to do.'

'That was a complete waste of time.'

'Surely not.'

'Yes, I agree with Clovis, let Base do all the thinking.'

Myri was disappointed. To hear Bruno resigning the task of thought seemed like the end of something. This feeling was powerfully underlined for her when, a little later, the announcement came over the loudspeaker in the lounge. Without any preamble at all, other than the usual click on, a strange voice said: 'Your attention, please. This is Base calling over your intercom.'

They all looked up in great surprise, especially Clovis, who said quickly to Bruno: 'Is that possible?'

'Oh yes, they've been experimenting,' Bruno replied as quickly.

'It is perhaps ironical,' the voice went on, 'that the first transmission we have been able to make to you by the present means is also the last you will receive by any. For some time the maintenance of space stations has been uneconomic, and the decision has just been taken to discontinue them altogether. You will therefore make no further reports of any kind, or rather you may of course continue to do on the understanding that nobody will be listening. In many cases it has fortunately been found possible to arrange for the collection of station staffs and their return to Earth: in others, those involving a journey to the remoter parts of the galaxy, a prohibitive expenditure of time and effort would be entailed. I am sorry to have to tell you that your own station is one of these. Accordingly, you will never be relieved. All of us here are confident that you will respond to this new situation with dignity and resource.

'Before we sever communication for the last time, I have one more point to make. It involves a revelation which may prove so unwelcome that only with the greatest reluctance can I bring myself to utter it. My colleagues, however, insisted that those in your predicament deserve, in your own interests, to hear the whole truth about it. I must tell you, then, that contrary to your earlier information we have had no reports from any other station whose content resembles in the slightest degree your accounts of the strange happenings you claim to have witnessed. The deception was considered necessary so that your morale might be maintained, but the time for deceptions is over. You are unique, and in the variety of mankind that is no small distinction. Be proud of it. Good-bye for ever.'

They sat without speaking until five minutes to midnight. Try as she would, Myri found it impossible to conceive their future, and the next morning she had no more success. That was as long as any of them had leisure to come to terms with their permanent isolation, for by midday a quite new phase of strange happenings had begun. Myri and Lia were preparing lunch in the kitchen when Myri, opening the cupboard where the dishes were kept, was confronted by a flattish, reddish creature with many legs and a pair of unequally sized pincers. She gave a gasp, almost a shriek, of astonishment.

'What is it?' Lia said, hurrying over, and then in a high voice: 'Is it alive?'

'It's moving. Call the men.'

Until the others came, Myri simply stared. She found her lower lip shaking in a curious way. *Inside* now, she kept thinking. Not just outside. *Inside.*

'Let's have a look,' Clovis said. 'I see. Pass me a knife or something.' He rapped at the creature, making a dry, bony sound. 'Well, it works for tactile and aural, as well as visual, anyway. A thorough illusion. If it is one.'

'It must be,' Bruno said. 'Don't you recognize it?'

'There is something familiar about it, I suppose.'

'You suppose? You mean you don't know a crab when you see one?'

'Oh, of course,' Clovis looked slightly sheepish. 'I remember now. A terrestrial animal, isn't it? Lives in the water. And so it must be an illusion. Crabs don't cross space as far as I know, and even if they could they'd have a tough time carving their way through the skin of the sphere.'

His sensible manner and tone helped Myri to get over her astonishment, and it was she who suggested that the crab be disposed of down the waste chute. At lunch, she said: 'It was a remarkably specific illusion, don't you think? I wonder how it was projected.'

'No point in wondering about that,' Bruno told her. 'How can we ever know? And what use would the knowledge be to us if we did know?'

'Knowing the truth has its own value.'

'I don't understand you.'

Lia came in with the coffee just then. 'The crab's back,' she said. 'Or there's another one there, I can't tell.'

More crabs, or simulacra thereof, appeared at intervals for the rest of the day, eleven of them in all. It seemed, as Clovis put it, that the illusion-producing technique had its limitations, inasmuch as none of them saw a crab actually materialize: the new arrival would be 'discovered' under a bed or behind a bank of apparatus. On the other hand, the depth of illusion produced was very great, as they all agreed when Myri, putting the eighth crab down the chute, was nipped in the finger, suffered pain and exuded a few drops of blood.

'Another new departure,' Clovis said. 'An illusory physical process brought about on the actual person of one of us. They're improving.'

Next morning there were the insects. Their main apparatus room was found to be infested with what, again on Bruno's prompting, they recognized as cockroaches. By lunch-time there were moths and flying beetles in all the main rooms, and a number of large flies became noticeable towards the evening. The whole of their attention became concentrated upon avoiding these creatures as far as possible. The day passed without Clovis asking Myri to go with him. This had never happened before.

The following afternoon a fresh problem was raised by Lia's announcement that the garden now contained no fruits or vegetables – none, at any rate, that were accessible to her senses. In this the other three concurred. Clovis put the feelings of all of them when he said: 'If this is an illusion, it's as efficient as the reality, because fruits and vegetables you can never find are the same as no fruits and vegetables.'

The evening meal used up all the food they had. Soon after two o'clock in the morning Myri was aroused by Clovis's voice saying over the loudspeaker: 'Attention, everyone. Strange happening. Assemble in the lounge immediately.'

She was still on her way when she became aware of a new quality in the background of silence she had grown used to. It was a deeper silence, as if some sound at the very threshold of audibility had ceased. There were unfamiliar vibrations underfoot.

Clovis was standing by the port, gazing through it with interest. 'Look at this, Myri,' he said.

At a distance impossible to gauge, an oblong of light had become visible, a degree or so in breadth and perhaps two and a half times as high. The light was of comparable quality to that illuminating the inside of the sphere. Now and then it flickered.

'What is it?' Myri asked.

'I don't know, it's only just appeared.' The floor beneath them shuddered violently. 'That was what woke me, one of those tremors. Ah, here you are, Bruno. What do you make of it?'

Bruno's large eyes widened further, but he said nothing. A moment later Lia arrived and joined the silent group by the port. Another vibration shook the sphere. Some vessel in the kitchen fell to the floor and smashed. Then Myri said: 'I can see what looks like a flight of steps leading down from the lower edge of the light. Three or four of them, perhaps more.'

She had barely finished speaking when a shadow appeared before them, cast by the rectangle of light on to a surface none of them could identify. The shadow seemed to them of a stupefying vastness, but it was beyond question that of a man. A moment later the man came into view, outlined by the light, and descended the steps. Another moment or two and he was evidently a few feet from the port, looking in on them, their own lights bright on the upper half of him. He was a well-built man wearing a grey uniform jacket and a metal helmet. An object recognizable as a gun of some sort was slung over his shoulder. While he watched them, two other figures, similarly accoutred, came down the steps and joined him. There was a brief interval, then he moved out of view to their right, doing so with the demeanour of one walking on a level surface.

None of the four inside spoke or moved, not even at the sound of heavy bolts being drawn in the section of outer wall directly in front of them, not even when that entire section swung away from them like a door opening outwards and the three men stepped through into the sphere. Two of them had unslung the guns from their shoulders.

Myri remembered an occasion, weeks ago, when she had risen from a stooping position in the kitchen and struck her head violently on the bottom edge of a cupboard door Lia had happened to leave open. The feeling Myri now experienced was similar, except that she had no particular physical sensations. Another memory, a much fainter one, passed across the far background of her mind: somebody had once tried to explain to her the likeness between a certain mental state and the bodily sensation of discomfort, and she had not understood. The memory faded sharply.

The man they had first seen said: 'All roll up your sleeves.'

Clovis looked at him with less curiosity than he had been showing when Myri first joined him at the port, a few minutes earlier. 'You're an illusion,' he said.

'No I'm not. Roll up your sleeves, all of you.'

He watched them closely while they obeyed, becoming impatient at the slowness with which they moved. The other man whose gun was unslung, a younger man, said: 'Don't be hard on them, Allen. We've no idea what they've been through.'

'I'm not taking any chances,' Allen said. 'Not after that crowd in the trees. Now this is for your own good,' he went on, addressing the four. 'Keep quite still. All right, Douglas.'

The third man came forward, holding what Myri knew to be a hypodermic syringe. He took her firmly by her bare arm and gave her an injection. At once her feelings altered, in the sense that, although there was still discomfort in her mind, neither this nor anything else seemed to matter.

After a time she heard the young man say: 'You can roll your sleeves down now. You can be quite sure that nothing bad will happen to you.'

'Come with us,' Allen said.

Myri and the others followed the three men out of the sphere, across a gritty floor that might have been concrete and up the steps, a distance of perhaps thirty feet. They entered a corridor with artificial lighting and then a room into which the sun was streaming. There were twenty or thirty people in the room, some of them wearing the grey uniform. Now and then the walls shook as the sphere had done, but to the accompaniment of distant explosions. A faint shouting could also be heard from time to time.

Allen's voice said loudly: 'Let's try and get a bit of order going. Douglas, they'll be wanting you to deal with the people in the tank. They've been conditioned to believe they're congenitally aquatic, so you'd better give them a shot that'll knock them out straight away. Holmes is draining the tank now. Off you go. Now you, James, you watch this lot while I find out some more about them. I wish those psycho chaps would turn up – we're just working in the dark.' His voice moved farther away. 'Sergeant – get these five out of here.'

'Where to, sir?'

'I don't mind where – just out of here. And watch them.'

'They've all been given shots, sir.'

'I know, but look at them, they're not human any more. And it's no use talking to them, they've been deprived of language. That's how they got the way they are. Now get them out right away.'

Myri looked slowly at the young man who stood near them: James. 'Where are we?' she asked.

James hesitated. 'I was ordered to tell you nothing,' he said. 'You're supposed to wait for the psychological team to get to you and treat you.'

'Please.'

'All right. This much can't hurt you, I suppose. You four and a number of other groups have been the subject of various experiments. This building is part of Special Wefare Research Station No. Four. Or rather it was. The government that set it up no longer exists. It has been removed by the revolutionary army of which I'm a member. We had to shoot our way in here and there's fighting still going on.'

'Then we weren't in space at all.'

'No.'

'Why did they make us believe we were?'

'We don't know yet.'

'And how did they do it?'

'Some new form of deep-level hypnosis, it seems, probably renewed at regular intervals. Plus various apparatus for producing illusions. We're still working on that. Now, I think that's enough questions for the moment. The best thing you can do is sit down and rest.'

'Thank you. What's hypnosis?'

'Oh, of course they'd have removed knowledge of that. It'll all be explained to you later.'

'James, come and have a look at this, will you?' Allen's voice called. 'I can't make much of it.'

Myri followed James a little way. Among the clamour of voices, some speaking languages unfamiliar to her, others speaking none, she heard James ask: 'Is this the right file? Fear Elimination?'

'Must be,' Allen answered. 'Here's the last entry. *Removal of Bruno V and substitution of Bruno VI accomplished, together with memory-adjustment of other three subjects. Memo to Preparation Centre: avoid repetition of Bruno V personality-type with strong curiosity-drives.* Started catching on to the set-up, eh? Wonder what they did with him.'

'There's that psycho hospital across the way they're still investigating; perhaps he's in there.'

'With Brunos I to IV, no doubt. Never mind that for the moment. Now. *Procedures: penultimate phase. Removal of all ultimate confidence: severance of communication, total denial of prospective change, inculcation of "uniqueness" syndrome, environment shown to be violable, unknowable crisis in prospect (food deprivation).* I can understand that last bit. They don't look starved, though.'

'Perhaps they've only just started them on it.'

'We'll get them fed in a minute. Well, all this still beats me, James. *Reactions. Little change. Responses poor. Accelerating impoverishment of emotional life and its vocabulary: compare portion of novel written by Myri VII with contributions of predecessors. Prognosis: further affective deterioration: catatonic apathy: failure of experiment.* That's comfort, anyway. But what has all this got to do with fear elimination?'

They stopped talking suddenly and Myri followed the direction of their gaze. A door had been opened and the man called Douglas was supervising the entry of a number of others, each supporting or carrying a human form wrapped in a blanket.

'This must be the lot from the tank,' Allen or James said.

Myri watched while those in the blankets were made as comfortable as possible on benches or on the floor. One of them, however, remained totally wrapped in his blanket and was paid no attention.

'He's had it, has he?'

'Shock, I'm afraid.' Douglas's voice was unsteady. 'There was nothing we could do. Perhaps we shouldn't have –'

Myri stooped and turned back the edge of the blanket. What she saw was much stranger than anything she had experienced in the sphere. 'What's the matter with him?' she asked James.

'Matter with him? You can die of shock, you know.'

'I can do what?'

Myri, staring at James, was aware that his face had become distorted by a mixture of expressions. One of them was understanding: all the others were painful to look at. They were renderings of what she herself was feeling. Her vision darkened and she ran from the room, back the way they had come, down the steps, across the floor, back into the sphere.

James was unfamiliar with the arrangement of the rooms there and did not reach her until she had picked up the manuscript of the novel, hugged it to her chest with crossed arms and fallen on to her bed, her knees drawn up as far as they would go, her head lowered as it had been before her birth, an event of which she knew nothing.

She was still in the same position when, days later, somebody sat heavily down beside her. 'Myri. You must know who this is. Open your eyes, Myri. Come out of there.'

After he had said this, in the same gentle voice, some hundreds of times, she did open her eyes a little. She was in a long, high room, and near her was a fat man with a pale skin. He reminded her of something to do with space and thinking. She screwed her eyes shut.

'Myri. I know you remember me. Open your eyes again.'

She kept them shut while he went on talking.

'Open your eyes. Straighten your body.'

She did not move.

'Straighten your body, Myri. I love you.'

Slowly her feet crept down the bed and her head lifted.

11 – BRIAN W ALDISS:
Manuscript Found in a Police State

The title to a story is all important, as not only must it encapsulate the intent of the fiction, but it must also capture a reader's interest. It's interesting therefore to find how often titles will become standards, almost *clichés*. The format of the above title, for instance, really owes its origin to the American genius Edgar Allan Poe, who won first-prize in a story contest in 1833 with his short sf-horror tale *Ms Found in a Bottle*. Ever since that date, that title format has been used by many authors to indicate a story wherein the fate of the narrator is unknown. A few recent examples are Cyril Kornbluth's *Ms Found in a Chinese Fortune Cookie* (1957), Hal Draper's *Ms Fnd in a Lbry* (1961), Gary Jennings' *Ms Found in an Oxygen Bottle* (1973) and Robert Silverberg's *Ms Found in an Abandoned Time Machine* (1973). And I very much doubt that will be the last of them.

The following story is a step outside what one might expect from Brian Aldiss – but then Aldiss's talents are so varied today that perhaps one should expect the unexpected from him. After all, his recent novels *Frankenstein Unbound* (1974) and *The Eighty-Minute Hour* (1974) are a far cry from earlier books like *Greybeard* (1964) and *The Dark Light Years* (1964). It is of course this versatility that makes Aldiss Britain's top sf writer.

As stated previously, Aldiss has a knack of appearing in the most unexpected places. Not too long ago, *Penthouse* carried his article on sex in sf magazine art; *The Saturday Book*, *Harpers Bazaar and Queen* and *Private Library* have also published Aldiss on art in sf. He has had poems published in such unlikely places as *The Daily Telegraph Colour Magazine* and *The Times*.

Similarly some of his fiction turns up where one wouldn't expect it, from *Punch* and *Penthouse* to picture post cards! His vignette *The Humming Heads* appeared in the June 8th

1969 *Solstice* and *The Oh in José* in the March 1966 *Cad.* Aldiss's second choice for this book, *Manuscript Found in a Police State* has appeared only once before, in *Winter's Tales 18* (1972) and for the bulk of the sf reading public this will be its first airing. Aldiss's comments about his fiction also cover his first choice *'Old Hundredth'* which was included in Volume one.

'Immensity is a part of us – the better part, I think, lying remote from the petty transactions of everyday like a moor beyond a mean town. It is something worth striving towards. Science fiction is one of the languages of immensity, although in many stories immensity is dwarfed by tiny ideas or silly psychology. You have to turn to the great grey master of British science fiction, Olaf Stapledon, to be confronted by Immensity, naked and unchained.

'There's little I can say about my stories included in the *Best of British SF* anthologies, except to point out that immensity lurks somewhere in the wings of both of them. *Manuscript Found in a Police State* incorporates some of the hidden symbols of Edgar Allan Poe; it may one day form the basis of a novel, although its reprinting here makes that possibility more remote.'

'When correcting the early drafts of stories, I go through them striking out adjectives. I have to be particularly firm about the word "vast". Both *Old Hundredth* and *Manuscript Found in a Police State* are the sort of story from which a number of "vasts" were probably struck.'

MANUSCRIPT FOUND IN A POLICE STATE

Brian W. Aldiss

A trail of prisoners wound slowly upwards along a mountain track until it reached the outer gates of Khernabhar Prison. There it waited in bright sunshine until the gates rolled open. Goaded on by their warders, the prisoners moved into the enclosure beyond.

The gates closed behind the prisoners, and were bolted. They stood in a courtyard formed between wall and cliff, the cliff of the great Mount Khernabhar. Offices stood in the courtyard, stern but dejected, their windows blank and dusty. A trough stood in one corner of the courtyard, against the rock; the prisoners were allowed to go over to it and drink.

Axel Mathers moved over with the other prisoners. He scooped up water and poured the first handful over his face; then he drank. As he sucked the water from his hands, he stared down into the trough, where water ran clear and deep.

The interior of the trough was rough. Pebbles and small plants could be seen, lucid under the water's disturbed surface. Although sun shone full on the trough, the liquid was brilliantly cold, cutting at a man's throat as it went down. It spurted into the trough from a fissure in the rock, spurted out of Khernabhar itself, spurted from the intestines of the great mountain. Because he knew the terrible legends of Khernabhar, Mathers found himself cocking an ear towards the fissure, half-expecting to hear human cries issue from it.

He still could not believe that the sentence of the Dictator Hener's courts was to be carried out – oh, yes, the others would serve their term, but surely for him some last minute reprieve would come! For him! He found that his every gesture was heavy with deliberation and that everywhere he cast his eye in that dreary courtyard he saw beauty. The very shards of rock tumbled from the mighty rock-face were miraculously cast and coloured. Everything was rare and beautiful – the dust, even the dust, because it would never be seen again!

He looked in the girl prisoner's face, reading there the same anxiety to draw in every memory of the world of light. He knew her first name: Joanna. Like him, she was sentenced for crimes against the State. She wore a ragged skirt that stretched down to her ankles, a long-sleeved blouse, and a poncho. Her thin face, her dark hair, were streaked with the dust that had accompanied them from the last ugly village on the plain. Yet she was attractive, the line of her nose, the line between her nose and mouth, the line of her mouth, possessing a mysterious and painful logic which was beyond words. It was easier to look at the trough, the dust, the stones, than at her face.

The party – it comprised twenty-one prisoners – was allowed to sit in the dirt and wait. Every minute spent here in the sunlight was precious. Mathers sat next to the girl while the guards who had made the trek up from the plain argued with the guards of the prison. Poor oafs – each side envied the other its job! The guards from the plain had brought drink to sell to the prison guards; the prison guards complained that the prices were too high. Slowly, cretinously, they bandied their dreary small change of language – and a minor language at that, hardly spoken outside the boundaries of the nation, not even universally spoken inside! Yet were the guards not to be envied? Would they not all, over the next years, be allowed their stupidities, their drunks, their randies, even their deaths, under the ever-changing sky?

The bargaining was concluded. Bottles and money changed hands. There was coarse laughter and most of the guards moved towards the guard room.

The guards remaining got the party to its feet again and moved it forward. Driven on by their curses, the prisoners pushed through inner gates, the mountainside moving in above them. Mathers looked up – saw a tribe of monkeys away above their heads, free to scamper over the slopes. He saw the shoulder of the mountain swing overhead, saw the sun, saw the sun eclipsed by mountain. He caught the expression on Joanna's face. Impulsively, they grasped each other's hands.

All the prisoners were clasping each other. No longer was there need for the guards to curse them. Shadow had fallen on them: they had no further will to resist. Now they heard the moan and grumble – rock itself complaining – of Khernabhar Prison!

That voice! It came from ahead, yet from all sides. They were moving in a tunnel now, and so had opportunity to note the sound well, to analyse – as the least intelligent among them must have done – how it seemed to comprise many of the noises of the animal kingdom, squeaks, squeals, moans, groans, bellows, chirps. They might have been entering some hideous underground farm in which everything from crickets and birds to sows and bullocks and still mightier animals were confined. yet there was no noise but rock moving on rock. Nothing lay ahead but rock. There was no destiny but rock.

The corridor widened into an underground chamber. No daylight reached this far: the darkness was broken by torchlight and by a long gutter which ran with a tarry substance that burned. This tarry substance dripped into a tank sunk in the floor of the chamber. Guards were dipping wooden brands into the tank.

Now the noise was louder; its full melancholy din beat upon them like the wings of some vast and weary creature in flight – some reptilian prehistoric bird that screamed as it pulled its weight over lands unknown.

With the noise came the odour . . . and that too seemed to move in from the reptilian distances of buried past-time. It was an ancient and dirty odour, trailing across the back of the throat a flavour of corrupt piscine flesh. yet so great were the other pressures on this doomed gathering, that it moved forward as if merely through a growing twilight.

Now it's coming – it's coming! I have no fear. This is not death for me, not death but a new chance. At last, I have this chance to be better – inwardly to be better. Whatever happens, an inner part of me can learn to be better. If I can stand it, for my own good, as well as the good of the revolution . . .

One of the guards thrust a torch into Mather's hand and pushed him forward. He noticed the girl took care to remain close to him. She evidently drew some reassurance from him, looking up now and then – but more with an air of appraisal than appeal, he noted. Many things he noted: all were subordinate, mere insignificant details glimpsed under the skirts of his black cloud of awareness.

What did overwhelm his attention was sight of the moving prison itself. The guards were prodding Joanna towards it, holding him back, holding the others back behind, separating them. The visible part of the prison loomed before the girl – they were thrusting her into a cell that had already half-disappeared into squealing, grunting darkness.

It was an open cell with no front wall. A cell, then a thick dividing wall, and then another cell. And then another dividing wall and another cell. Open cells: no doors, no front walls. She was pushed into the first cell and Mathers into the next one. The prisoner behind him was being readied for the following cell.

Clutching his torch, Mathers stood glaring out at his captors, at the dingy and muddled scene – but it was a scene from life, it existed, however precariously, on the fringes of the free world, it lay but a lung's breath away from open sky and running animals and the elaborate affairs of men. As he stood there, trying to memorise even the coarse faces of the guards, the cell gave a lurch and, with grinding slowness, moved a few inches to his right, reproducing all round him the noise of tortured animals.

To step into the cells, it was necessary to walk across a narrow gap which separated cells from cavern. The cells containing Mathers, the girl, and the next prisoner ground and bumped to one side. A pause, and then they moved again, an inch, half a dozen inches, a few more, stop . . . After another pause, this movement was repeated to the accompaniment of more anguished squeals of sandstone on sandstone. Already the cell containing Joanna had disappeared behind a wall of rock and could be seen no more from the underground chamber.

The cells had only another fifteen or so feet to move before Mathers too would find himself cut off from human view. He stood – crouched, rather, staring out, wondering if he should not spring forward and run for corridor and daylight. But the guards stared back, for once looking orderly and efficient, waiting for him to make a reckless move. He observed that further guards were herding the rest of the prisoners into a side-passage – perhaps to wait there until the slow progression of cells brought more empty ones into view. So he was cut off from the poor specimens of humanity with whom he had shared many painful days imprisonment in the town on the plains, with whom he had made the ascent to this more dreadful place; although he had no particular friends among them, regret leapt in him as they were driven from sight.

The cells lurched again, roaring cruelly as they moved. Only a few inches, painfully uncertain, but now on his right he saw protruding the edge of the cavern wall that would eventually cover his cell and eclipse him entirely from the outside world. He looked at it, reached out to touch it, saw how the rock had been reinforced with heavy stone blocks, making a pillar. As he touched it, the vibrations and squeals began again and the cells again jolted forward. When the movement and noise died, Mathers heard the man in the cell on his left weeping. He himself knew only paralysis, and could not weep or pray. As for the girl, whose cell had now disappeared into the rock, he heard not a sound from her.

There is still time. Someone will come forward. My friends will have managed to secure a reprieve. The guards will relent. Or I shall wake. . . . Wake, wake, damn you, out of this nightmare . . .

Again the lateral movement, the pause, the movement again. He roused partly out of his paralysis to take stock of his cell. It was carved from solid sandstone, even elaborately carved at its outer end, where pillars had been fashioned in the wall-ends between cells, chunky pillars with an archaic motif binding them. The cell held a wooden bed with a mattress on, and no other furniture. At the rear of the cell was a double trough, its two compartments, one below the other, filled with water that trickled in from a groove in the rear wall; the overflow of the water ran down into a hole in the floor evidently intended for sanitary purposes. The side walls, roughly carved from the rock, were covered with the graffiti of past incumbents of the cell.

Sandstone – weathered only by the hands of prisoners, hewn eternities ago. . . . And, if the rumours are true, a spell of imprisonment here means ten years. Ten years . . . Oh, Lord, ten years, where is Thy justice?

On one wall was carved the figure of an old stooped man with a long beard, beautifully picked out in an antique mode. Mathers glanced at it in cursory fashion, reflecting that all prisoners would look similarly stooped by the time they emerged into daylight once more. He ran his fingertips despairingly over the surface of the rock, feeling the very texture of injustice.

God knows, I should not be here – I have done no wrong. . . . Yet however false my conviction, all men are sinners. I'm guilty of many things. Perhaps we all deserve punishment. . . .

As he was setting his torch in a socket in the wall, the slow movement came again; his small world grated forward inch by inch, as if the whole mountain of Khernabhar were in action. The movement spoke of a vast and weary suffering, the last tremors of a dying man: while the negation of movement that followed spoke of death itself.

And now the fourth wall had moved across the front of his cell more than half way. His view of the cavern, the guards, the trough of pitch, was through a gap of less than six feet. He felt his spirit drifting out of him like smoke.

How much time passed, Mathers could not tell. After a long lethargic pause – the short lethargic movement, and a further narrowing of his view of the outer world. He sank down to await the stone eclipse. The vigil was punctuated by a guard coming and throwing him a bundle of food and an unlit torch, and by a struggle between the guards and the captive next door, who tried to break out; he was badly beaten about the head and kicked in the stomach before being dragged back into his cell. Mathers heard him groan occasionally.

Again the shuddering movement, the screams from the rock. Over Mathers, an annihilating numbness.

Why do I feel as I do? Nothing so terrible has even happened to me before, no, nothing ever approaching this. . . . It affronts the name of humanity. So why am I possessed by the idea that this pain is something I have suffered before? When, where, could I have suffered anything remotely as terrifying? My dear mother took such tender care of me in childhood that I was never suffered to be shut in a cupboard or chest. Darkness did not scare me. I had no fears – why, then, along with everything else, am I forced to bear this burden of an unmindful familiarity?

Hardly aware that he did so, he wept for his parents, now dead, and for the life they had given him, now to be stolen away. When he looked up, the cells had jarred on again in their journey into the rock, and only the narrowest gap permitted him to look at the world of the cavern. In anguish and surprise, he jumped up, threw himself at the gap, thrust his arm through, gesturing at the mean company of guards. He called to them, begging for mercy. They looked at each other and grinned almost enough to reveal their teeth.

The grinding began again, and the lurch forward. As the gap narrowed still further, he had to pull back his arm quickly or it would have been wrenched from him at the shoulder between outer wall and cell wall. He stopped his cries and stood quiet as the vibrating movement closed the space inch by inch. When the movement stopped, there was a gap here and there, at no place wider than an inch, to which he could apply his eye and see the guards still there in the cavern, talking among themselves, more casual now he had been carried from their view.

Later, the grinding began again, and this time it carried him and his cell completely into the rock and away from the world of men. Mathers collapsed against one wall, burying his face in his hands.

The revolution must come! Some day soon, it must come! Our country cannot bear this oppression much longer. . . . Help me to survive till then, oh Lord! The regime must be eradicated to the last man, and this hellish prison destroyed for ever.

Sinking into the well of his thoughts, he was a long time in realising that the tempo of movement and stillness had been broken. Now was only stillness. He jumped up in vague alarm, he stood there, he waited. Silence alone greeted him, pressed hard against his ears. The world of men was only a pace or so away – yet already it had sunk below the horizons of his awareness.

Movement had stopped. How long had it continued? Certainly not more than four hours, probably not less than two: for that sound as of animals being slaughtered had commenced only as Mathers and the others were ushered into the tunnel. From the legends he had heard of Khernabhar, he knew what this cessation meant, and his eyes turned instinctively to an object that had come into view on the outer wall, the rock face that cut him off from humanity.

The object consisted of an iron ring from which hung a length of chain. Mathers went over and lifted the heavy links. The boss that held the ring was firmly secured into the rock. He let the chain drop. The links clanked and hung still. He stood there motionless, his gaze locked to the dull length of chain. The horror of his situation was with him like a dark and invisible companion. His journey into the rock had begun.

At some featureless later moment in time, he came to himself again, his brain began to function along more normal channels, prompted by recognition of sound. When he turned his attention to it, a rush of small noise came to him, an underworld of sound that at first brought him only further terror.

Later, as the journey into the sandstone went deeper, after his torches had failed and died and he was alone in the dark of the mountain, he began to identify individual sounds, to force meaning from them, to hammer them into substitutes for those other senses of which he was bereft. Foremost among these were the sounds of water.

Mathers' water supply in the trough had its own collection of delicate noises. Its drips and splashes were close at hand, and generally as regular as clocks. They were busy and comforting noises, noises whose source he could verify by touch. Frivolous noises.

The next nearest water noises sprang from the first series.

They were deeper in tone, on the whole continuous, and solemn noises. They flowed in particular under the mobile floor of the cells, as if some deep groove ran there to bear the water further yet into the stone heart of Khernabhar. These were lazy noises, which sometimes sounded reassuring, sometimes menacing.

Distant noises came into two categories. Ever-present but intermittent were various drips and plops that stirred Mathers' imagination when he lay helpless in the dark, listening; by concentrating on these distant sounds, he could imagine that he was not incarcerated in a mountain but stood in one of the rain-forests which covered the northern half of his country. These watery messages gave him illusions of freedom, as did other distant sounds, for they became voices of brooks, waterfalls, and torrents – interior brooks, waterfalls, and torrents, cascading through the entrails of Khernabhar, similar enough acoustically to remind him of waters washing slopes of mountain-jungles which he had explored with his father in his youth.

This last category of water-sound came and faded, and Mathers grew familiar with it only as day succeeded day, and week week, and the cells moved further into the mountain.

With other subterranean noises, he was less comfortable. Along with the prisoners in their cells travelled other living things, mice, spiders, insects, possibly even snakes and bats – but chiefly rats, whose activities roused him from many an uneasy sleep.

Sometimes, patches of strange light would float before his eyes. He imagined himself to be going blind until he discovered that the outer wall was sometimes smeared with phosphorescence and gave off a phantom light. He would stand with his eyes almost touching it, trying to imagine it to be the blessed glare of daylight that bathed them.

By this time, routine – the iron and remorseless routine of Khernabhar – had gripped him. The one focal point of the day came every morning with a scattered tapping, rapidly growing in volume. Although he was generally prepared for the summons, Mathers would start up and begin to hammer on the wall himself with a piece of rock. This was the signal to begin the day's haul!

He would then feel in the dark for the chain hanging from the outer wall. The chains punctuated the outer wall. Wherever the cell stopped, somewhere there was a chain to haul on.

The haul began. No movement at first, then a jerky start. Unison was soon achieved. The prisoners heaved on their chains together, unseen and unknown to each other. With squeals of protest rock began to grind over rock. . . .

It was an enormously exhausting, an impossible task. Yet the cells moved. They moved only a few inches before rest was necessary. And then the effort had to be made again. And again. Over and over.

Being a methodical man, Mathers tried to keep track of time by counting. He came to believe that they generally worked for between two-and-a-half to three hours – nearer the latter mostly, but the strain varied according, he presumed, to the roughness of the ground underneath the cells.

The distance they moved was easier to compute, although it too varied. It was about twenty-two or twenty-three feet in one session. There was only one session a day: a morning's exhausting work.

When he had rested from the haul, Mathers habitually made an exploration of the newly exposed section of outer wall. He ran his fingers over the surface, arms outstretched. It was his way of mapping as best he could the dreadful journey inwards, and he worked his way along from end to end, from bottom to top, with methodical care.

The wall was by no means the smooth surface it had seemed at first casual glance. It had been scarred by numerous parallel lines, graphs of the moving walls, incised by small stone outcrops on the latter. There were other lines, too, and arabesques and patterns, carved by prisoners. Sometimes, a fault in the rock had caused part of the wall to crumble. In one place, the wall was extensively faulted, the fault extending over three days travel. Mathers was as excited as if he had discovered a new landscape. He noted that the fault had been carefully patched with stone, with smooth blocks ingeniously inserted into the wall. At the end of the fault, his fingers discovered what he believed to be flints. He pulled them from their ledge and discovered they were regularly shaped; the knowledge, for some reason, made him uneasy.

With the flints, he made sparks, cascading like stars from his fingers. Using straw and shavings from his mattress, he was able to create fire. The straw supply was limited. He rationed himself to a few wisps at a time, and these he lit only when rations arrived, until he could create a better lamp.

Food supplies were irregular. Above the groove from which his water supply trickled was a larger hole, into which a man could insert his head. The hole formed the lower end of a tube boring upward through solid rock. Somewhere distantly up there was a gallery and a nebulous world of men – an ear applied to the hole could detect, on occasion, their comings and goings, their voices distorted out of recognition. Every so often, they threw food down the tube – and no doubt down the countless other tubes under their care.

Considering the poverty and discomfort of all other arrangements in Khernabhar, the food was tolerable, though always insufficient. It reflected the ample and various local resources; hard round loaves of coarse oaten bread; various fruits – coconuts, mango, satsumas, the thick-rinded mangosteen – some of which arrived well pulverised; and bundles of rice with shreds of meat in, knotted into fabric squares for their downward journey.

Mathers made it his habit to conserve his tiny fires for meal-times, so that he could eat with a little light and feel he retained at least a shred of old civilized habit.

When I'm out of here, I will rejoin the guerrillas! I will lead a band on to Khernabhar itself. We will burst from its wooded defiles, destroy this vile machine, and release all the prisoners. This evil must be ended for all time. When I'm out of here . . .

He mused for hours at a time on the prison itself, hoping that he might be led to think of some way of escape. Escape was always in his mind, burning like a will-o'-the-wisp against the night of incarceration. He had to escape or go mad, and every day made the idea of getting free more urgent, because – yes, that was the supreme fiendishness of Khernabhar! – they were still – voluntarily, voluntarily – hauling themselves deeper into the great mountain.

Shredding the hempen squares that wrapped his deliveries of rice, soaking them in the oil of the coconut, Mathers made himself candles and lit one with the flints. A tiny flame grew, flickered, fluttered, became oval, and maintained itself. Mathers was kneeling on the floor over it. He sat up and looked about. There was his cell, his home – its walls, its roof, the shadows, banished to corners. How sane, even welcoming, it looked!

He scrambled up with his candle. His determination was to examine minutely the inner walls of his cell but curiosity first deflected him to the water trough. There, holding his candle before him, he stared down and saw his reflection staring up – or not his reflection surely, but that of a savage, a hermit, with ragged beard and ragged eyebrows, with protruding cheekbones, with sunken gleaming eyes and corrugated forehead! With a gasp of surprise, he started back and could not look again.

And how long had he been here? He went over to the record of days he had kept in the dark, a row of scratches scored on the wall with a stone. The scratches were muddled together and numbered thirty-three or thirty-five. So little more than a month had passed since he was exiled from the world of men! Time, down here in this infernal darkness, moved as protestingly as rock itself!

At last, he took his candle up and began a minute inspection of the past as recorded about him. He had, of course, made such an inspection when his torches burned; but his agony of mind then had been such that only general impressions had registered. What he wished to do was to match the information of the rock against the rumours he had heard of Khernabhar and see if they shed some new light on the situation which would give him a key towards escaping.

To his surprise, his memory of the cell walls was largely false. His mood had been such, to begin with, that he had had eyes only for messages carved by recent tenants of the cell – cries of misery, revolutionary slogans, and a proclamation of vivid obscenity. His attention was now directed to marks of past time – in many cases, long past.

By the dim flame, no larger than a human eye, he read the signs: the squinches or blind arches spanning the two inner corners and speaking, in their elaboration, of love rather than intentions of hatred: the sculpturing of the rock which showed no mark of the tools used to shape it; and the additions since, the mute voices of prisoners long dead! And how long dead? The earliest markings were in many cases obliterated by later additions, and the later additions by ones still later. It was noticeable that the most recent additions looked the roughest and least literate. Many of the earlier ones, faint though they were, were perfectly legible and perfectly formed.

Legible – but impossible to understand. For there was a script here that Mathers recognised but could not read. The Old Tongue! Men had written here using the Old Tongue as their natural language! Those prisoners must have died all of two thousand – perhaps as many as four thousand – years ago!

Many of the writings were records of individual lives. Where these were dated, Mathers saw that they went back many centuries. He read them marvelling, thinking how little life and consciousness had changed.

Frequently, the records were broken by the legend; CURSED BE THE NAME OF KHERN KAHZAA. This past tyrant, Emperor of the Eternal Wheel of Life and Death, had given his name to the mountain. His was the name most frequently invoked, until one got down to the present generation of scribbles, when the name of the hated dictator, Hener, and the beloved revolutionary leader, Reh – particularly the latter – predominated. The last occupant of the cell (so Mathers judged him to be) had scraped the revolutionary name everywhere. REH! REH! And on the rock of the trough was a large VICTORY TO REH!

That must have been carved at least ten years ago. Reh grows old. There are only white hairs in his beard. True, he survives, seems invincible. Yet victory is far from him. No doubt of it, new leaders are needed. Perhaps better leaders, perhaps better slogans. Perhaps better revolutionary material and better thought behind them. Perhaps our people are less than the men our ancestors were . . .

Only in one place had later scribblers been careful not to deface earlier writings. This was centrally, on the leading wall. Here an intricate figure had been engraved. Within a large circle, a double circle, slightly smaller, had been cut. Between these two inner circles were short radial lines, dividing the rim into a number of small partitions; the partitioners were not completed all round the circle. The outer circle was broken in two places. At the centre of the figure were smaller circles, some intersecting, cut to different depths. The whole figure was intersected by a grand line.

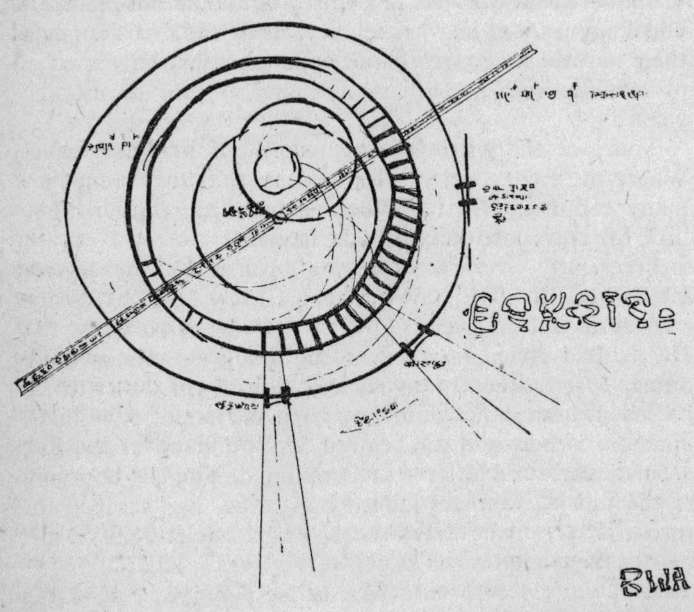

Against this design were written various figures and notations in a corrupt version of the Old Tongue, of which Mathers could understand little. But he did understand that he was looking at a representation of the prison of Khernabhar. This was confirmation of the rumours he had heard: that the prison was a great wheel, rotating in the fastnesses of rock, the cells being mere niches on its perimeter.

He could not interpret the measurements on the incised figure, but he had heard that the diameter of the wheel was as much as five miles, and that the array of cells along its perimeter numbered as many as three thousand, although they were not always continuous. The great central axle upon which the wheel revolved notated in the heart of the mountain. To this wheel of cells there was only one entrance, only one exit, as depicted in the design – the exit being sited somewhere on the mountainside before the entrance, so that those going in should not see the pitiful state of those emerging after their long ordeal.

That night – but in Khernabhar there was only night – Mathers lay down to sleep with his head full of the image of the great slow-grinding wheel, grinding men's lives away. The wheel moved every day, had perhaps moved every day since it was carved from the rock, for there were always wrongdoers in the eyes of the state. It could move only in one direction, and therein lay its monstrous paradox: that the captives holed like maggots in their cells were forced to propel themselves into the rock. Only by going deep into the mountain was it possible to re-emerge, only by going deep into the mountain was it possible to complete the revolution that meant freedom, only by going deep into the mountain could hope of survival be nourished.

So the prisoners hauled for almost three hours every day on the chains in the wall beyond the wheel, hauled till their sinews almost tore, to get the wheel through its long and grudging course!

Sandstone grinding past sandstone . . . Ten years to a

revolution – I'm sure that's what I heard at university. Ten years – about ten years, no matter who or what the prisoners are. It might as well be eternity. . . . How long is ten years?

And what minor paradoxes were involved! This daily collaboration was an unspoken one between rebels and outcasts of society. They were thrust down here precisely because they did not cooperate: and only in their co-operation could they drag their way through miles of rock.

Again: They cooperated even from the beginning, pulling themselves *voluntarily* from the outer world, when they were fresh and strong and healthy; yet at that period, inevitably, they would pull with less than a whole heart – might, in some cases, refuse to pull at all. Only later, when they could suppose that their call was half-way or more along the circumference of the prison – that, in other words, they were now *on their way out* – would they pull whole-heartedly; and by then, the evil regimen would have rendered them aged, feeble, and sick, incapable of real effort.

And again: many of the prisoners, because they were the victims of a warlike state, were men of peace. Yet they, as much as the fieriest revolutionary, must have echoed the eternal unspoken wish that dominated Khernabhar: LET THERE ALWAYS BE WAR!

Only when there was war was the supply of prisoners fully equal to the supply of cells. Only then was there full manpower to haul on the chains and drag the wheel round through eternal blackness. Only then was there a chance that the tons of rock might be speeded and long years of imprisonment thereby lessed by a few days or hours.

The things that Mathers read in the rock, shocking as they were, brought him a truer realisation of his situation. They and the presence of a little light for a few hours of the day permitted him to consider others beside himself. He thought with some horror of all the other prisoners who sweated and festered in their cells; but a gentler concern filled him when he turned his mind to the two people who had been incarcerated with him. Of the man who had been thrust into the cell behind his, he had heard nothing beyond the groans of the first day. From the girl's cell – yes, Joanna was her name – he had heard some noises, scuffles as if she had been throwing herself against the walls in an hysterical effort to escape, and even perhaps a cry or two.

He set himself to make contact with her, and investigated the walls afresh. The distance between the leading edge of the cell wall and the outer wall – that is, between wheel and solid mountain – was generally no more than an inch: which said a great deal for the superhuman abilities of the architect who had designed Khernabhar! But this distance did vary to some degree, as if the wheel had a slight eccentricity and, when Mathers began his new investigation, it was enlarging to something over two inches. Since the walls between cells were about four feet thick, there was no chance of making contact while circumstances remained as they were.

Yet, even in this static place, circumstances were not unalterable. On the first day of this new investigation, Mathers found part of the outer wall had crumbled. Almost by the roof, there was a fault in the rock, into which he could thrust his hand!

Shaking with excitement, he lit a precious candle and pushed his bed over to the wall. By climbing on the bed, he could look into the hole. The hole was the width of two hands spread wide, irregular inside, going back not much more than arm's length. And two objects lay inside the hole.

He pulled the objects out. One was a length of roughly carved wood, a cudgel perhaps. The other was a skull.

He sat on the side of his bed, nursing the skull and staring at it with delight. It was the skull, he supposed, of a wild cat, paper-thin but beautifully formed, the lower jaw still intact, the buttresses of the eye-sockets exquisite. He cupped it in his hands as if it were a jewel. The hours passed as his mind travelled all the meanings of the life that, fading at last among the shadows of Khernabhar, had built and utilised this shell.

It was only later, when he had placed the skull carefully

in a corner where he would not tread on it, that he turned his mind to the cudgel. It was more mysterious than the skull. He could accept that wild cats might be lured in from the mountainsides to hunt the rats living in the catacombs of the dark, scrambling in during the dry season down a water-hole. But where did the cudgel come from? Who had left it there?

In his solitude, he was making a mystery of nothing. The weapon had probably been tucked into the hole by another prisoner, tucked there and forgotten. What else?

Next morning, the signal came, the prisoners – each in the solitude of his cell – began their daily haul on the chains, six inches forward and pause, six inches forward a pause, repeated some forty-four times. And the hole in which the skull and cudgel had been cached slid away and was finally lost to view behind the following cell-wall.

But a new and more extensive fault appeared. This one was less high than the last, and extended raggedly sideways. It had some depth and, examining it closely, Mathers deduced that it had been artificially deepened. Some of the rock glistened; moisture seeped from one of the cracks.

It occurred to Mathers that faults like this might one day appear on a much larger scale. He would then be able to hide himself in the fault. On the following day, when the wheel moved on, he would stay where he was and find himself in the cell of the prisoner following him. But the notion of being walled into a narrow hole, even for no more than a couple of hours, was enough to make him break out in a chilly sweat. Nor did he want to set himself further from Joanna. He would have to wait until a fault appeared large enough for him to squeeze forward between his cell and hers.

As chance would have it, the rock faults now stopped. Although the gap between cell and wall continued slowly to widen, it was still scarcely enough to thrust an emaciated arm through. Day followed day, each swallowed up by silent sandstone.

A plague of rats came upon him. They came swarming down the food chute and milling through his cell. They easily slipped between wall and wheel, and were gone, came back, whisked by, vanished. A day later, he saw his first cat. It was an intimidating beast, mangey, long in the leg, and boardlike in the body, with the expression of ferocity on its face heightened by a rat hanging from its jaws, which it wore like a military moustache. Mathers called a welcome to it. It disappeared with a look of unalterable hatred.

The animals came and went according to their seasons. He began to detect and was presently overpowered by an odour of corruption. A prisoner had died near at hand, to add his peculiar stench to the atmosphere. This prolonged corruption doubtless accounted for the influx of the rats and their enemies. It was dismaying to think of a sightless face a few yards away, staring into the night of Khernabhar and being dismantled as it stared.

He devoted himself the more sedulously to plans to reach the girl. Since chance counted for so much, his plans soon degenerated into dreams of what he and she would do when they were together; in truth, imprisonment might then be tolerable. But he decided that he would be unable to forsake his cell permanently; it would be necessary to return frequently for food – two trying to live on one ration would starve; even love could not gainsay that. How could easy return be made possible? Clearly, only by breaking down a part of the wall between them.

The most vulnerable part of the wall was its outer edge. The chains dangling in the outer wall, by which the wheel was dragged round, were five feet in length. If Mathers could manage to prise a chain, boss and rivets and all, from the wall, then the chain could be used as a crude saw and, with him working at one end and the girl at another, it might be possible to wear a groove in the separating wall deep enough for them to be able to climb through uninterruptedly from one cell to another!

Now every afternoon (to himself, Mathers still used the diurnal terminology of the world outside) was spent with the cudgel, painfully attempting to prise a boss loose from the wall. Day after day, the bosses proved unmoving. The master-architect had had a skill that defied time.

Mathers' most terrifying day in Khernabhar began as wretchedly as any other. He woke from tantalising and instantly forgotten dreams of the world outside and paced round his cell as usual until the tapped summons brought him to his working position. With a rock, he tapped on the outer wall as heartily as anyone. Come on, you lazy swine! Get to those chains! Pull us to freedom! Since about two months had elapsed since his term of punishment began, there might be as many as ninety new captives behind him . . . little enough to set beside the three thousand-odd ahead, but at least a beginning.

The creaking, groaning, squealing progress was under way. How hateful the effort! How sickening, how weakening! How ill-matched was the human heart against the burden of night and sandstone! And yet . . . with cries of protest, the wheel turned slightly and the cells moved along.

When it was all over, Mathers threw himself on his bed. Exhaustion set in now, and he fell into one of those uneasy states between waking and sleeping which were a feature of his present life. A pair of rats chased themselves across his shoulder and stomach. He jumped up immediately, to sit shivering on the side of the bed.

Was there some faint light or suggestion of it about the cell?

Perhaps deliverance is here! Why not? The revolution has taken place. Reh has been successful! His men are in Khernabhar, slowly blowing the place up and reaching all the prisoners. . . . Or the evil Hener is dead, his henchmen killed, and liberty proclaimed from the palace! No, I'm just dreaming. But it could perhaps be a narrow shaft through the rock – too narrow even to climb through, let's say, but wide enough to let down a ray of light directly from the sun at a certain time of day!

He went to the outer wall. If there was light, it was uncertain, the feeblest glow. If there was light, it came from the direction of Joanna's cell. He called her name, louder and louder. The glimmer of light died. He pressed against the rock, still calling, and felt it faulted beneath his hands, ragged and recessed.

Although he had made a stern rule with himself to use his limited candles only in afternoon and evening, he decided this new factor warranted an exception to the rule. Kneeling, he struck his flints together, sending the sparks cascading until at last the hemp wick was touched and flickered into light. He cupped it lovingly in his hands until it grew strong. Then he carried it over to inspect the wall.

The fault in the rock was deep, tall, and lengthy; it extended behind the leading wall of his cell towards Joanna's, beyond the penetrating power of his illumination. It had been neatly patched with stones, beautifully squared cabbles, but they had been prised away and the depth of the hole increased. The hole was deep enough to hold a man!

I could get to her! Now! No need to return here until tomorrow morning, when the action signals start!

To carry the candle on what would probably be a difficult scramble seemed an unnecessary impediment. Mathers set it down on the edge of the cell floor and climbed into the fault.

The rock had broken along its veinings, and the veinings were irregular. There was plenty of room one moment, very little the next. He chose to work his way along with his back to the smooth inter-cell wall and his face to the ragged rock. The fault twisted, and he was forced to push his way forward lying virtually horizontal.

Progress became easier, the gap between wall and rock widened, he regained his feet, shuffled forward, and soon the edge of her cell wall met his knuckles.

He stepped out into her cell. Living darkness, strange smells.

'Joanna! Joanna!'

She flung herself on him out of the dark, kicking and screaming. Or for an awful moment he thought it was her. Then his hand, fighting to push her face away, met a bristling crop of beard! Almost at once, his hand was bitten.

He pulled it back and struck out wildly. Two hands closed around his throat and squeezed!

Electric colours punctured the blackness. Reaching forward, he linked his hands behind his opponent's skull, at the same time bringing his own skull violently forward. The bearded man fell back cursing unintelligibly and then charged in again. Mathers ducked, falling over with the enemy on top of him. He kicked out wildly and was lucky enough to connect his knee with something vital. As a howl of pain sounded, he staggered and almost fell back into the rock fault.

Before he could pull himself to safety, his assailant was at him again, this time poking a stick at him. It caught Mathers painfully in the ribs before he managed to grasp one end of it.

'What's the matter with you? I'm no enemy if you're an honest man. Where's the girl, where's Joanna?'

Savage growls and curses in a strange language were his answer.

The stick was wrenched from his grasp. He scrambled back to his own cell under a fusilade of blows. Never was refuge more welcome, or light more blessed, than his. He lay for a long while on his bed, trembling and gasping, clutching his wounds, and peering in dread at the rock fault.

All that night, he could not sleep for fear of his unknown attacker, for the pain of his wounds, and for wondering what had become of Joanna.

Next morning, he worried about trying to make contact with the prisoner on the other side of him. Perhaps they might form an alliance – Mathers suddenly felt the need of company. But, when the cells next moved on, the rock fault would lie, not between his cell and the next prisoner's, but between the next prisoner's and the cell following that. There was no way of getting in touch. At least he had the consolation of knowing that the unknown attacker would no longer be able to break in upon him after this morning's work.

His candle was almost at an end – he had been unwilling to extinguish it – when the working signal came. Never more gladly had Mathers gone over to take his position by the dangling chain.

In the brief fight, he had sustained nothing worse than bruises. Even in his weakened condition, it took Mathers only a few days to recover from them. His mental state required longer to stabilise, he was now victim of fears and suppositions that almost took on their own life. Night after night, he woke screaming from dreams in which terrible things with faces all hair and snout and teeth flung themselves at his throat in paroxysms of fury. Sometimes these dream attackers were gigantic, filling the cell; at other times, they were no larger than a finger-nail.

All were equally terrifying.

His hours of candle-light were necessarily rationed but, light or dark, he would crouch with every muscle tense, staring towards those cracks round his walls from which attack might come.

Gradually, however, his fears subsided. The plague of rats also died and, with it, the abominable stench that he imagined helped to distort his senses. The stench of Khernabhar was always permanent and corrosive; it ceased to be intolerable.

What has happened to me all these days? How is it I have been so preoccupied with myself? What about her? What has happened to Joanna? Is she still alive? She can't be dead, no . . .

One morning, he was his normal lucid self. The terror of the attack had vanished. He saw clearly, or imagined he saw, what had happened. That vile bearded creature was merely another prisoner, originally three cells ahead of Mathers, who had taken advantage of the rock fault to get back to Joanna's cell. He could be ousted if Mathers went prepared to fight. As for Joanna, Mathers had no proof that she was not still in her cell. He tried to avoid dwelling on the evils that might have befallen her.

What he needed was a weapon. Then he would be prepared for the next occasion on which it was possible to attack.

There were no metal objects available. But the cudgel was a fine solid affair, and one end could be sharpened into a point by the flints. By the time he had finished with it, it gave him added confidence.

But the grudging stone wheel of Khernabhar obeyed its own laws, turned at its own pace, unfolded its own possibilities when it would. Its rotation on its axis was like the slow turn of the centuries themselves, and its blind unchanging walls offered no chance of escape.

To divert himself, Mathers took to pacing the cell and to reciting such poetry and prose as he could recall at the top of his voice. By some insensible shift of his emotions, one poem in particular became his favourite:

Anna, thy beauty seems to bring
    Bewitchment of the world I know,
Spelling a change, till everything
    Is pale, impermanent, as though
    World were but rares-show.

O'er ravaged lands and prosperous,
    Countrysides of sun and shade,
Seascape or moonscape, without fuss
    Your dreaming eyes, your lips, have made
    Reality to fade.

So now before the bricks of town
    Palm trees advance or towers pace,
Wild mountains rise, breakers crash down!
    Unchanged alone where phantoms race –
    Thy love, thy face!

The Anna in the old poem became Joanna. The bricks of town became the walls of his cell. Then the poem was true, yes, yes, all else faded before the beauty of her face and all the intangible qualities her face stood for. No imprisonment could crush the budding of humanity's finer qualities. He forgot that the beauty of her face was something far more frail and transient than the beds of rock about him. Mathers was suddenly in love!

Over and over, he tried to trace all his memories of her.

Had I ever set eyes on her before we were assembled for the march up the mountain? Wait, yes, I saw her in the yard of the court on the day we were sentenced! Of course! She was standing in the cart as Hener's toughs thrust me down the steps! She in sunshine! Had she something round her head? A handkerchief . . . Her hands up to her hair? Why didn't I pay better attention? The sun was in my eyes.

So many times did he return to the few fragments of memory he had of her, that they became obliterated. He was left with nothing but a glimpse of her shoulder, the nape of her neck, a curl of hair on it, the sight of an ear-lobe. And that was all of Joanna that remained!

Through the days of progress and stillness through the rock, in which he sought her essence and waited to see her reality, Mathers paced his cell and kept himself exercised. He was at his exericses one day when a fresh aspect of the wheel design on his wall caught his eye. Holding the candle up close, he inspected it minutely.

It became apparent to him – and he wondered how he had failed to observe the fact before – that the design was etched over a much more ancient version of the same plan. What he had previously regarded as construction lines or markings in the rock were parts of a far older drawing, executed in a more fanciful and decorative way. Allegory had been used, and he realised that the old man with the beard, whose lineaments he had admired, was part of this archaic design, and supported the semi-obliterated wheel upon his shoulder.

Accompanying the design were hieroglyphs, faint, indecipherable, and certainly of great antiquity. Mathers, gazing at them, was taken back to a fine winter morning when he was a young man, riding on horseback early through the woods with his father. They cantered through a thicket of holly trees which cut at their legs, up to an eminence on which stood a dozen or so tall spruces, so old that they sprawled at angles, often leaning their trunks against each other for support. The hieroglyphs conjured up the intricate foliage of those spruces, glimpsed in freedom long ago. Mathers and his father rode up to the trees to enjoy the view and let the horses breathe. They jumped down onto the soft ground, peering through the mist across the valley.

'There's Khernabhar, the home of the ancient tyrant Khern Kahzaa!' Mathers Senior said. He pointed to a mountain that, from this distance, hardly looked bigger than others nearer at hand, up whose shaggy slopes the mists were drifting.

Leaning against one of the spruces, Mathers Senior spoke of the Saga of Cunais, which contained word of Khernabhar and its secrets. The Saga was of a great oral tradition, born long before the days even of Khern Kahzaa, before the days of written language; it contained legends that seemingly related to the coming of man on the planet. One legend spoke of a dynasty of terrible kings, father, son, and grandson, who imprisoned a whole nation in a mountainside because they were hairy and possessed six fingers on each hand.

. . . ther peltts
*Like fiber were up ta eye-pits * On befor-heds thankly as arm-pits*
*Sprooated while each furd' hand mounted extra furd' fingre **

Upon imprisonment, this strange nation was forced to build a great wheel of incarceration inside Khernabhar, to symbolise the eternity for which they would be sealed off from the world. The last king of the dynasty sealed up the entrances to the mountain; but the nation still survived inside and would one day emerge to overthrow the world. So claimed the saga.

'The Saga of Cunais has been banned from our libraries since Hener came to power,' said Mathers Senior to his son, looking across the valley. 'And perhaps before his day, too. Even very ancient and dead things can return to disrupt the present.'

The mist of that distant day faded into grainy sandstone; the sound of his father's voice changed back into the drip and boom of water; and the knot of trees became merely the hieroglyphs of Mathers' cell wall.

It's all older than anyone can guess at . . . Reh, do you know of this iniquity? The revolution must come! Or perhaps it has come, and we prisoners are abandoned here. Perhaps the revolution has been betrayed! Then there must be another revolution . . . I must get free!

Mathers stood for a long while, one shoulder against a wall, staring absently ahead, listening to the endless working of water all round. At university, he had joined one of the secret revolutionary societies, where he learned of another version of the story in the Saga of Cnnais. This version also claimed a dynasty of three kings, father, son, and grandson; but it presented the father as an upright and religious man, founder of a Holy Order for which the great subterranean wheel was designed. This saintly ruler intended the cells for monastic cells; and the holy penitents intended to occupy the cells would propel themselves, generation after generation, revolution after revolution, reverently through the deep earth until, at the time of the final Resurrection, they propelled themselves direct into the presence of the Lord Almighty. The son of the pious dynast had been a weak and dissolute man, who allowed construction to go forward without his personal interest. He was murdered by his son, who indeed took personal interest in the vast wheel but subverted its sacred intentions and turned it into combined prison and torture chamber, which usage had been maintained into historical times and ever since. The legend had it that the enslaved wheel-builders turned against this wicked king, and that he was the first to be set to work in his own instrument of terror.

Whatever version of the legend was nearest the facts – and the truth would now almost certainly never be established – this such was evident: however far one might cast one's mind back into the history of civilisation, the wheel would always be there, turning, groaning, every day on its axis.

As for the possibility that an ancient nation, hairy and six-fingered, had been incarcerated here, that was probably an embroidery. Unless – and an idea so paralysing came to Mathers that he dropped the candle. It rolled on the floor and went out. As he scrabbled for it on the floor, he tried to recall details of the hairy man who had assailed him in Joanna's cell, trembling to remember how many fingers the creature had on each hand . . .

Shakily, he felt for his flints and re-lit his candle, looking round fearfully at the swooping shadows.

Careful measurements of the outer wall revealed that the slight eccentricity of orbit was still gradually increasing the gap between wall and cell-end. Mathers was sure that the maximum gap would be small and, once maximum was reached, would dwindle again: so that when the gap was barely wide enough for him to struggle through, he resolved that go he must. He had his cudgel – if he met his old assailant, he would be ready.

As to that old assailant, Mathers had a new theory. It was mere supersition to imagine that any of a prehistoric race mentioned in a long-forgotten saga could survive below ground – wasn't it? There was a more practical explanation.

The wheel of Khernabhar could not continue without maintainance. He had seen how faults in the rock had been repaired, and rock debris would have to be cleared away. Very well: then, just as there were passages to allow for water and food to enter the cells from above, so there must be ways for humans – guards – to do the same thing. His assailant had probably been such a guard; which might well mean that a passage-way to the world above was near at hand. If he could find Joanna, they could escape by that route and find their way to Reh's headquarters, there to help fight for the revolution.

In his pockets were flints, a new candle, and some food. He went over to the water trough and took a last drink. He looked round the cell and counted the scratches he had made in the sandstone. His lifetime of imprisonment in the rock had in fact lasted only one hundred and two days so far. Something like one hundred and fifty three prisoners would have been thrown into the cells behind him – and the same number released far ahead of him – several miles and many years ahead of him!

He set his old candle down on the cell floor, since he would be sure to drop it in his struggle to reach the next cell. Taking up the cudgel, he pushed his way into the gap between cell wall and rock face. Thin though he was, there was scarcely room to edge forward but, inch by inch, he did it, cudgel in his leading hand, face forward into the darkness.

In the vacant cell, the candle continued to burn for some while. The marks of ancient occupancy stood on the walls, water continued to drip. Shadows fluttered occasionally against the roof of rock.

12 – J G BALLARD: Now: Zero

If any author is symbolic of the changing patterns in science fiction in the early 1960s, that author is J. G. Ballard. And, like any true revolutionary, Ballard had his origins firmly in the status quo.

James Graham Ballard was born on November 18th 1930, in Shanghai, the son of a Scottish doctor living in the American sector. Still in his mid-teens, Ballard was interned in a Japanese prisoner-of-war camp, and was eventually repatriated to England in 1946. He went to Cambridge University to read medicine, and there won the annual short story competition in 1951. Thus fortified, he launched himself into his first mainstream novel. Science fiction was still a few years away. He did some copywriting, and even flew with the RAF.

In the Summer of 1956 Ballard submitted a short story, *Escapement*, to John Carnell, who accepted it. The story is a new look at time travel, in that the protagonist finds himself out of synch with his surroundings. Ballard then visited Carnell and brought with him a beautiful fantasy, *Prima Belladonna*, which Carnell also bought. The two stories appeared concurrently in the December 1956 issues of *New Worlds* and *Science Fantasy*. Ballard was launched.

He had no trouble producing follow-ups. Every story had its own individual flavour: whether the emphasis of future society and its overpowering effects on man, as in *Build-Up* (*New Worlds*, January 1957), or his deft fantasies centred on Vermilion Sands, of which Prima Belladonna was the first.

Before the end of the 1950s it was obvious to everyone, that here was someone who had brought something new and original to sf. Writing in the November 1959 *New Worlds*, Carnell said:

'A sure sign of the present health of science fiction is the continued emergence of writers well outside the mainstream tradition, more interested in experimenting with the imaginative and stylistic possibilities offered by the medium than in the conventional story set against an interplanetary or futuristic background. Among these writers is J. G. Ballard . . ."

In the early 1960s Ballard utilised his talents in reshaping the catastrophe novel, starting with *The Wind From Nowhere* (1961), and then *The Drowned World* (1962) and *The Burning World* (1964). All showed his emphasis on people rather than events, and all proved highly successful.

His next novel, *The Crystal World*, grew from a serial, *Equinox*, published in *New Worlds*. The important factor though is that the first episode appeared in the first issue to be edited by Michael Moorcock, dated May–June 1964. Nova Publications had finally felt the pinch of the magazines' declining circulations, and the company folded. Carnell went on to edit his *New Writings* series, whilst *New Worlds* was handed to Moorcock, and *Science Fantasy* to Oxford art-dealer Kyril Bonfiglioli.

That first Moorcock *New Worlds* also carried an article by Ballard on the controversial William Burroughs. It was evident from the start that under new management *New Worlds* was already heading into other territory. The so-called 'new wave' was born. Ballard's fiction became more and more fantasy-orientated, bizarre, avant-garde. His stories would range from the highly readable and fascinating *Storm Bird, Storm Dreamer* (*New Worlds*, November 1966) to the apparently pointlessly symbolical *The Assassination of John Fitzgerald Kennedy Considered as a Downhill Motor Race*, reprinted in the first March 1967 *New Worlds*. I say 'first' because there were two issues bearing that date. They were the last paperback format *New Worlds*. The publishers encountered financial difficulty, but thanks to the efforts of stalwarts like Brian Aldiss, Marghanita Lhaski, J. B. Priestley, Kingsley Amis and the late Kenneth Allsop, *New Worlds* was reborn in a larger format with the aid of an

Arts Council grant. Moorcock now threw all caution to the winds and the Ballardian material came even more bizarre, reaching a peak of irrelevancy with *The Generations of America* and *Princess Margaret's Facelift*. These pieces will be remembered only as experiments in the flexibility of fiction, not for their entertainment value.

The stirrings of experimental Ballard are evident from the early days, and one of the best examples in his short story from the December 1959 *Science Fantasy* – *Now: Zero*.

NOW: ZERO

J G Ballard

You ask: how did I discover this insane and fantastic power? Like Dr Faust, was it bestowed upon me by the Devil himself, in exchange for the deeds to my soul? Did I, perhaps, acquire it with some strange talismaniac object – idol's eye-piece or monkey's paw – unearthed in an ancient chest or bequeathed by a dying mariner? Or, again, did I stumble upon it myself while researching into the obscenities of the Eleusian Mysteries and the Black Mass, suddenly perceiving its full horror and magnitude through clouds of sulphurous smoke and incense?

None of these. In fact, the power revealed itself to me quite accidentally, during the commonplaces of the everyday round, appearing unobtrusively at my finger-tips like a talent for embroidery. Indeed, its appearance was so unheralded, so gradual, that at first I failed to recognise it at all.

But again you ask: why should I tell you this, describe the incredible and hitherto unsuspected sources of my power, freely catalogue the names of my victims, the date and exact manner of their quietus? Am I so mad as to be positively eager for justice – arraignment, the black cap, and the hangman leaping onto my shoulders like Quasimodo, ringing the death-bell from my throat?

No, (consummate irony!) it is the strange nature of my power that I have nothing to fear from broadcasting its secret to all who will listen. I am the power's servant, and in describing it now I still serve it, carrying it faithfully, as you shall see, to its final conclusion.

However, to begin.

Rankin, my immediate superior at the Everlasting Insurance company, became the hapless instrument of the fate which was first to reveal power to me.

I loathed Rankin. He was bumptious and assertive, innately vulgar, and owed his position solely to an unpleasant cunning and his persistent refusal to recommend me to the directorate for promotion. He had consolidated his position as department manager by marrying a daughter of one of the directors (a dismal harridan, I may add) and was consequently unassailable. Our relationship was based on mutual contempt, but whereas I was prepared to accept my role, confident that my own qualities would ultimately recommend themselves to the directors, Rankin deliberately took advantage of his seniority, seizing every opportunity to offend and denigrate me.

He would systematically undermine my authority over the secretarial staff, who were tacitly under my control, by appointing others at random to the position. He would give me long-term projects of little significance to work on, so segregating me from the rest of the office. Above all, he sought to antagonise me by his personal mannerisms. He would sing, hum, sit uninvited on my desk as he made small talk with the typists, then call me into his office and keep me waiting pointlessly at his shoulder as he read silently through an entire file.

Although I controlled myself, my abomination of Rankin grew remorselessly. I would leave the office seething with anger at his viciousness, sit in the train home with my newspaper opened but my eyes blinded by rage. My evenings and weekends would be ruined, wastelands of anger and futile bitterness.

Inevitably, thoughts of revenge grew, particularly as I suspected that Rankin was passing unfavourable reports of my work to the directors. Satisfactory revenge, however, was hard to achieve. Finally I decided upon a course I despised, driven to it by desperation: the anonymous letter – not to the directors, for the source would have been too easily discovered, but to Rankin and his wife.

My first letters, the familiar indictments of infidelity, I never posted. They seemed naïve, inadequate, too obviously the handiwork of a paranoic with a grudge. I locked them away in a small steel box, later re-drafted them, striking out the staler crudities and trying to substitute something more subtle, a hint of perversion and obscenity, that would plunge deeper barbs of suspicion into the reader's mind.

It was while composing the letter to Mrs. Rankin, itemising in an old note-book the more despicable of her husband's qualities, that I discovered the curious relief afforded by the exercise of composition, by the formal statement, in the minatory language of the anonymous letter (which is, certainly, a specialised branch of literature, with its own classical rules and permitted devices) of the viciousness and depravity of the letter's subject and the terrifying nemesis awaiting him. Of course, this catharsis is familiar to those regularly able to recount unpleasant experiences to priest, friend or wife, but to me, who lived a solitary, friendless life, its discovery was especially poignant.

Over the next few days I made a point each evening on my return home of writing out a short indictment of Rankin's iniquities, analysing his motives, and even anticipating the slights and abuses of the next day. These I would cast in the form of narrative, allowing myself a fair degree of license, introducing imaginary situations and dialogues that served to highlight Rankin's atrocious behaviour and my own stoical forbearance.

The compensation was welcome, for simultaneously Rankin's campaign against me increased. He became openly abusive, criticised my work before junior members of the staff, even threatened to report me to the directors. One afternoon he drove me to such a frenzy that I barely restrained myself from assaulting him. I hurried home, unlocked my writing box and sought relief in my diaries. I wrote page after page, re-enacting in my narrative the day's events, then reaching forward to our final collision the following morning, culminating in an accident that intervened to save me from dismissal.

My last lines were:

... Shortly after two o'clock the next afternoon, spying from his usual position on the seventh floor stairway for any employees returning late from lunch, Rankin suddenly lost his balance, toppled over the rail and fell to his death in the entrance hall below.

As I wrote this ficitious scene it seemed scant justice, but little did I realise that a weapon of enormous power had been placed gently between my fingers.

Coming back to the office after lunch the next day I was surprised to find a small crowd gathered outside the entrance, a police car and ambulance pulled up by the curb. As I pushed forward up the steps several policemen emerged from the building, clearing the way for two orderlies carrying a stretcher across which a sheet had been drawn, revealing the outlines of a human form. The face was concealed, and I gathered from conversation around me that someone had died. Two of the directors appeared, their faces shocked and drawn.

'Who is it?' I asked one of the office boys who were hanging around breathlessly.

'Mr. Rankin,' he whispered. He pointed up the stairwell. 'He slipped over the railing on the seventh floor, fell straight down, completely smashed one of those big tiles outside the lift ...'

He gabbled on, but I turned away, numbed and shaken by

the sheer physical violence that hung in the air. The ambulance drove off, the crowd dispersed, the directors returned, exchanging expressions of grief and astonishment with other members of the staff, the janitors took away their mops and buckets, leaving behind them a damp red patch and the shattered tile.

Within an hour I had recovered. Sitting in front of Rankin's empty office, watching the typists hover helplessly around his desk, apparently unconvinced that their master would never return, my heart began to warm and sing. I became transformed, a load which had threatened to break me had been removed from my back, my mind relaxed, the tensions and bitterness dissipated. Rankin had gone, finally and irrevocably. The era of injustice had ended.

I contributed generously to the memorial fund which made the rounds of the office; I attended the funeral, gloating inwardly as the coffin was bundled into the sod, joining fulsomely in the expressions of regret. I readied myself to occupy Rankin's desk, my rightful inheritance.

My surprise a few days later can easily be imagined when Carter, a younger man of far less experience and generally accepted as my junior, was promoted to fill Rankin's place. At first I was merely baffled, quite unable to grasp the tortuous logic that could so offend all laws of precedence and merit. I assumed that Rankin had done his work of denigrating me only too well.

However, I accepted the rebuff, offered Carter my loyalty and assisted his reorganisation of the office.

Superficially these changes were minor. But later I realized that they were far more calculating than at first seemed, and transferred the bulk of power within the office to Carter's hands, leaving me with the routine work, the files of which never left the department or passed to the directors. I saw too that over the previous year Carter had been carefully familiarising himself with all aspects of my job and was taking credit for work I had done during Rankin's tenure of office.

Finally I challenged Carter openly, but far from being evasive he simply emphasised my subordinate role. From then on he ignored my attempts at a rapprochment and did all he could to antagonise me.

The final insult came when Jacobson joined the office to fill Carter's former place and was officially designated Carter's deputy.

That evening I brought down the steel box in which I kept record of Rankin's persecutions and began to describe all that I was beginning to suffer at the hands of Carter.

During a pause the last entry in the Rankin diary caught my eye:

. . . Rankin suddenly lost his balance, toppled over the rail and fell to his death in the entrance hall below.

The words seemed to be alive, they had strangely vibrant overtones. Not only were they a remarkably accurate forecast of Rankin's fate, but they had a distinctly magnetic and compulsive power that separated them sharply from the rest of the entries. Somewhere within my mind a voice, vast and sombre, slowly intoned them.

On a sudden impulse I turned the page, found a clean sheet and wrote:

The next afternoon Carter died in a street accident outside the office.

What childish game was I playing? I was forced to smile at myself, as primitive and irrational as a Haitian witch doctor transfixing a clay image of his enemy.

I was sitting in the office the following day when the squeal of tyres in the street below riveted me to my chair. Traffic stopped abruptly and there was a sudden hubbub followed by silence. Only Carter's office overlooked the street; he had gone out half an hour earlier so we pressed past his desk and leaned out through the window.

A car had skidded sharply across the pavement and a group of ten or a dozen men were lifting it carefully back onto the roadway. It was undamaged but what appeared to be oil was leaking sluggishly into the gutter. Then we saw the body of a man outstretched beneath the car, his arms and head twisted awkwardly.

The colour of his suit was oddly familiar.

Two minutes later we knew it was Carter.

That night I destroyed my notebook and all records I had made about Rankin's behaviour. Was it coincidence, or in some way had I willed his death, and in the same way Carter's? Impossible – no conceivable connection could exist between the diaries and the two deaths, the pencil marks on the sheets of paper were arbitrary curved lines of graphite, representing ideas which existed only in my mind.

But the solution to my doubts and speculations was too obvious to be avoided.

I locked the door, turned a fresh page of the notebook and cast round for a suitable subject. I picked up my evening paper. A young man had just been reprieved from the death penalty for the murder of an old woman. His face stared from a photograph: coarse, glowering, conscienceless.

I wrote:

Frank Taylor died the next day in Pentonville Prison.

The scandal created by Taylor's death almost brought about the resignations of both the Home Secretary and the Prison Commissioners. During the next few days violent charges were levelled in all directions by the newspapers, and it finally transpired that Taylor had been brutally beaten to death by his warders. I carefully read the evidence and findings of the tribunal of enquiry when they were published, hoping that they might throw some light on the extraordinary and malevolent agency which linked the statements in my diaries with the inevitable deaths on the subsequent day.

However, as I feared, they suggested nothing. Meanwhile I sat quietly in my office, automatically carrying out my work, obeying Jacobson's instructions without comment, my mind elsewhere, trying to grasp the identity and import of the power bestowed on me.

Still unconvinced, I decided on a final test, in which I

would give precisely detailed instructions, to rule out once and for all any possibility of coincidence.

Conveniently, Jacobson offered himself as my subject.

So, the door locked securely behind me, I wrote with trembling fingers, fearful lest the pencil wrench itself from me and plunge into my heart:

Jacobson died at 2-43 p.m. the next day after slashing his wrists with a razor blade in the second cubicle from the left in the men's washroom on the third floor.

I sealed the notebook into an envelope, locked it into the box and lay awake through a sleepless night, the words echoing in my ears, glowing before my eyes like jewels of Hell.

After Jacobson's death – exactly according to my instructions – the staff of the department were given a week's holiday (in part to keep them away from curious newspapermen, who were beginning to scent a story, and also because the directors believed that Jacobson had been morbidly influenced by the deaths of Rankin and Carter). During those seven days I chafed impatiently to return to work. My whole attitude to the power had undergone a considerable change. Having to my own satisfaction verified its existence, if not its source, my mind turned again towards the future. Gaining confidence, I realised that if I had been bequeathed the power it was my obligation to restrain any fears and make use of it. I reminded myself that I might be merely the tool of some greater force.

Alternatively, was the diary no more than a mirror which revealed the future, was I in some fantastic way twenty-four hours ahead of time when I described the deaths, simply a recorder of events that had already taken place?

These questions exercised my mind ceaselessly.

On my return to work I found that many members of the staff had resigned, their places being filled only with difficulty, news of the three deaths, particularly Jacobson's suicide, having reached the newspapers. The directors' appreciation of those senior members of the staff who remained with the firm I was able to turn to good account in consolidating my position. At last I took over command of the department – but this was no more than my due, and my eyes were now set upon a directorship.

All too literally, I would step into dead men's shoes.

Briefly, my strategy was to precipitate a crisis in the affairs of the firm which would force the board to appoint new executive directors from the ranks of the department managers. I therefore waited until a week before the next meeting of the board, and then wrote out four slips of paper, one for each of the executive directors. Once a director I should be in a position to propel myself rapidly to the chairmanship of the board, by appointing my own candidates to vacancies as they successively appeared. As chairman I should automatically find a seat on the board of the parent company, there to repeat the process, with whatever variations necessary. As soon as real power came within my orbit my rise to absolute national, and ultimately global, supremacy would be swift and irreversible.

If this seems naïvely ambitious, remember that I had as yet failed to appreciate the real dimensions and purpose of the power, and still thought in the categories of my own narrow world and background.

A week later, as the sentences on the four directors simultaneously expired, I sat calmly in my office, reflecting upon the brevity of human life, waiting for the inevitable summons to the board. Understandably, the news of their deaths, in a succession of motor-car accidents, brought general consternation upon the office, of which I was able to take advantage by retaining the only cool head.

To my amazement the next day I, with the rest of the staff, received a month's pay in lieu of notice. Completely flabbergasted – at first I feared that I had been discovered – I protested volubly to the chairman, but was assured that although everything I had done was deeply appreciated, the firm was nonetheless no longer able to support itself as a viable unit and was going into enforced liquidation.

A farce indeed! So a grotesque justice had been done. As I left the office for the last time that morning I realised that in future I must use my power ruthlessly. Hesitation, the exercise of scruple, the calculation of niceties – these merely made me all the more vulnerable to the inconstancies and barbarities of fate. Henceforth I would be brutal, merciless, bold. Also, I must not delay. The power might wane, leave me defenceless, even less fortunately placed than before it revealed itself.

My first task was to establish the power's limits. During the next week I carried out a series of experiments to assess its capacity, working my way progressively up the scale of assassination.

It happened that my lodgings were positioned some two or three hundred feet below one of the principal airlanes into the city. For years I had suffered the nerve-shattering roar of airliners flying in overhead at two-minute intervals, shaking the walls and ceiling, destroying thought. I took down my notebooks. Here was a convenient opportunity to couple research with redress.

You wonder: did I feel no qualms of conscience for the seventy-five victims who hurtled to their deaths across the evening sky twenty-four hours later, no sympathy for their relatives, no doubts as to the wisdom of wielding my power indiscriminately?

I answer: No! Far from being indiscriminate I was carrying out an experiment vital to the furtherance of my power.

I decided on a bolder course. I had been born in Stretchford, a mean industrial slum that had done its best to cripple my spirit and body. At last it could justify itself by testing the efficacy of the power over a wide area.

In my notebook I wrote the short flat statement:

Every inhabitant of Stretchford died at noon the next day.

Early the following morning I went out and bought a radio, sat by it patiently all day, waiting for the inevitable interruption of the afternoon programmes by the first horrified reports of the vast Midland holocaust.

Nothing, however, was reported! I was astonished, the orientations of my mind disrupted, its very sanity threatened. Had my power dissipated itself, vanishing as quickly and unexpectedly as it had appeared?

Or were the authorities deliberately suppressing all mention of the cataclysm, fearful of national hysteria?

I immediately took the train to Stretchford.

At the station I tactfully made enquiries, was assured that the city was firmly in existence. Were my informants, though, part of the government's conspiracy of silence, was it aware that a monstrous agency was at work, and was somehow hoping to trap it?

But the city was inviolate, its streets filled with traffic, the smoke of countless factories drifting across the blackened rooftops.

I returned late that evening, only to find my landlady importuning me for my rent. I managed to postpone her demands for a day, promptly unlocked my diary and passed sentence upon her, praying that the power had not entirely deserted me.

The sweet relief I experienced the next morning when she was discovered at the foot of the basement staircase, claimed by a sudden stroke, can well be imagined.

So my power still existed!

During the succeeding weeks its principal features disclosed themselves. Firstly, I discovered that it operated only within the bounds of feasibility. Theoretically the simultaneous deaths of the entire population of Stretchford might have been effected by the coincident explosions of several hydrogen bombs, but as this event was itself apparently impossible (hollow, indeed, are the boastings of our militarist leaders) the command was never carried out.

Secondly, the power entirely confined itself to the passage of the sentence of death. I attempted to control or forecast the motions of the stock market, the results of horse races, the behaviour of my employers at my new job – all to no avail.

As for the sources of the power, these never revealed themselves. I could only conclude that I was merely the agent, the willing clerk, of some macabre nemesis struck like an arc between the point of my pencil and the vellum of my diaries.

Sometimes it seemed to me that the brief entries I made were cross-sections through the narrative of some vast book of the dead existing in another dimension, and that as I made them my handwriting overlapped that of a greater scribe's along the narrow pencilled line where our respective planes of time crossed each other, instantly drawing from the eternal banks of death a final statement of account onto some victim within the tangible world around me.

The diaries I kept securely sealed within a large steel safe and all entries were made with the utmost care and secrecy, to prevent any suspicion linking me with the mounting catalogue of deaths and disasters. The majority of these were effected solely for purposes of experiment and brought me little or no personal gain.

It was therefore all the more surprising when I discovered that the police had begun to keep me under sporadic observation.

I first noticed this when I saw my landlady's successor in surreptitious conversation with the local constable, pointing up the stairs to my room and making head-tapping motions, presumably to indicate my telepathic and mesmeric talents. Later, a man whom I can now identify as a plainclothes detective stopped me in the street on some flimsy pretext and started a wandering conversation about the weather, obviously designed to elicit information.

No charges were ever laid against me, but subsequently my employers also began to watch me in a curious manner. I therefore assumed that the possession of the power had invested me with a distinct and visible aura, and it was this that stimulated curiosity.

As this aura became detectable by greater and greater numbers of people – it would be noticed in bus queues and cafes – and the first oblique, and for some puzzling reason, amused references to it were made openly by members of the public, I knew that the power's period of utility was ending. No longer would I be able to exercise it without fear of detection. I should have to destroy the diary, sell the safe which so long had held its secret, probably even refrain from ever thinking about the power lest this alone generate the aura.

To be forced to lose the power, when I was only on the threshold of its potential, seemed a cruel turn of fate. For reasons which still remained closed to me, I had managed to penetrate behind the veil of commonplaces and familiarity which masks the inner world of the timeless and the preternatural. Must the power, and the vision it revealed, be lost forever?

This question ran through my mind as I looked for the last time through my diary. It was almost full now, and I reflected that it formed one of the most extraordinary texts, if unpublished, in the history of literature. Here, indeed, was established the primacy of the pen over the sword!

Savouring this thought, I suddenly had an inspiration of remarkable force and brilliance. I had stumbled upon an ingenious but simple method of preserving the power in its most impersonal and lethal form without having to wield it myself and itemise my victims' names.

This was my scheme: I would write and have published an apparently fictional story in conventional narrative in which I would describe, with complete frankness, my discovery of the power and its subsequent history. I would detail precisely the names of my victims, the mode of their deaths, the growth of my diary and the succession of experiments I carried out. I would be scrupulously honest, holding nothing back whatsoever. In conclusion I would tell of my decision to abandon the power and publish a full and dispassionate account of all that had happened.

Accordingly, after a considerable labour, the story was written and published in a magazine of wide circulation.

You show surprise? I agree; as such I should merely have been signing my own death warrant in indelible ink and delivering myself straight to the gallows. However, I omitted a single feature of the story: its denouement, or surprise ending, the twist in its tail. Like all respectable stories, this one too had its twist, indeed one so violent as to throw the earth itself out of its orbit. This was precisely what it was designed to do.

For the twist in this story was that it contained my last command to the power, my final sentence of death.

Upon whom? Who else, but upon the story's reader!

Ingenious, certainly, you willingly admit. As long as issues of the magazine remain in circulation (and their proximity to victims of this extraordinary plague guarantees that) the power will continue its task of annihilation. Its author alone will remain unmolested, for no court will hear evidence at second-hand, and who will live to give it at first-hand?

But where, you ask, was the story published, fearful that you may inadvertently buy the magazine and read it.

I answer: Here! It is the story that lies before you now. Savour it well, its finis is your own. As you read these last few lines you will be overwhelmed by horror and revulsion, then by fear and panic. Your heart seizes, its pulse falling . . . your mind clouds . . . your life ebbs . . . you are sinking, within a few seconds you will join eternity . . . three . . . two . . . one . . .

Now!

Zero.

13 – MICHAEL MOORCOCK: Pale Roses

One of the biggest-selling fantasy authors in Britain today is Michael Moorcock, with his heroic sword-and-sorcery adventures involving the various incarnations of the Eternal Champion – Elric, Erekosë, Corum and Dorian Hawkmoon. The Corum and Hawkmoon series in particular are centred upon science fictional ideas, whereas Elric and Erekosë originally started their days as straight fantasy. Moorcock has however long since mapped out his Champion Mythos, and written as much into the network as possible – even his science fiction finds its way into the threads. All his books are interlinked in some way, including his mainstream fiction, like the humorous spy novel *The Chinese Agent* (1970).

Moorcock was born in London on December 18th 1939. He graduated to sf via the works of Edgar Rice Burroughs. Naturally this led to him writing for and editing the juvenile comic *Tarzan Adventures*, to which he had sold his first professional story, *Sojan The Swordsman* for the June 1957 issue. Before he was twenty he was turning out all manner of thrillers, westerns, air stories, historicals for Fleetway's publications. Teaming with sf writer Barrington J Bayley, he sold a story to *New Worlds, Peace on Earth*, which appeared in the December 1959 issue credited to Michael Barrington. His career really got under way as far as fantasy was concerned with the first Elric story, *The Dreaming City* in the June 1961 *Science Fantasy*. This and subsequent stories formed his first hardcover book, *The Stealer of Souls* (1963). Ten years later his books number over forty, and the end is far from sight.

In 1964 Moorcock accepted the editorial position with *New Worlds*, and instantly began to steer it into new directions, gambling with experiments, and to some extent succeeding. New authors emerged who had an adept capability at instilling sf with fresh ideas – Langdon Jones, Charles Platt, George Collyn, whilst from America he attracted Thomas Disch, Roger Zelazny and later Norman Spinrad. So was born the notorious 'new-wave' of sf, which by and large had a far better effect on the field than readers at the time imagined. For a while science fiction went mad with its new liberation. It was the mid-1960s, with 'Swinging London' and England suddenly the centre for art and fashion. 'Underground' magazines appeared, and by 1968 *New Worlds* had itself become something of an underground publication. And Michael Moorcock's fictional character Jerry Cornelius had become a 'cult' figure. The first Cornelius novel, *The Final Programme*, written in 1964/5 was not published until an American edition came out in 1968. It has subsequently been successfully filmed.

By 1970 the new wave had splashed into a myriad ripples, but it had left behind much in its wash. Many American writers, including those mentioned above and Harlan Ellison and Robert Silverberg, Barry Malzberg and Samuel Delany had capitalised on the gateway Moorcock and Ballard had opened. Once again, after some sixty years in the sf wilderness, Britain was again dictating the trends. Sf had been revolutionised. True, writers had led their followers down some murky cul-de-sacs, but ultimately they constructed a pathway through from old style to new style. Now, like motorways and railways they exist, compatibly, side by side, each supplying the other with style and themes like some symbiotic service station!

Moorcock quite naturally works on all levels. Despite the intricacy of his fantasy, much of it is little more than standard, swashbuckling adventure. At the other extreme have been works like the Nebula-award winning *Behold The Man* (1967) and the moralistic *Breakfast in the Ruins* (1971), or the frightening *The Black Corridor* (1969) written in collaboration with his wife, Hilary Bailey.

When *New Worlds* as a magazine died in 1970, Moorcock was able to revive it as a regular paperback series, editing the first six volumes. Hilary Bailey has since taken over that task to enable Moorcock to concentrate more fully on his writing, although he still turns a hand to editing occasionally such as his series of Victorian science fiction which began with *Before Armageddon* (1975). This aside Moorcock finds time to write screenplays for films, make record albums, and perform occasionally with the rock group Hawkwind.

New Worlds 7 (1974) carried a novelette by Moorcock, *Pale Roses*, which forms part of his series about the Dancers at the End of Time. (The novels are *An Alien Heat, The Hollow Lands*, and *The End of All Songs*.) It will be best appreciated by readers well acquainted with Moorcock's fiction, but can still be read as the satirical romp that it is by those not conversant. Note for instance the reference to Eric of Marylebone, a reincarnation of Elric of Melniboné! Moorcock chose *Pale Roses* as his favourite after much deliberation. He comments:

> 'My tendency these days is to move increasingly from fantasy to comedy. Comedy can supply the element which is otherwise supplied by fantastic imagery. I chose *Pale Roses* as my favourite (at the time I was asked) *sf* story – I don't for instance count my Cornelius stories as sf (or my fantasy stories either).'

PALE ROSES

A Tale of the Dancers at the End of Time

Michael Moorcock

Short summer-time and then, my heart's desire.
The winter and the darkness: one by one
The roses fall, the pale roses expire
Beneath the slow decadence of the sun.
Ernest Dowson, *Transition*

I

In Which Werther Is Inconsolable

'You can still *amuse* people, Werther, and that's the main thing,' said Mistress Christia, lifting her skirts to reveal her surprise.

It was rare enough for Werther de Goethe to put on an entertainment (though this one was typical – it was called 'Rain') and rare, too, for the Everlasting Concubine to think in individual terms to please her lover of the day.

'Do you like it?' she asked as he peered into her thighs.

Werther's voice in reply was faintly, unusually, animated. 'Yes.' His pale fingers traced the tattoos which were primarily on the theme of Death and the Maiden but corpses also coupled, skeletons entwined in a variety of extravagant carnal embraces – and at the centre, in bone-white, her pubic hair had been fashioned in the outline of an elegant and somehow quintessentially feminine skull. 'You alone know me, Mistress Christia.'

She had heard the phrase so often and it always delighted her. 'Cadaverous Werther!'

He bent to kiss the skull's somewhat elongated lips.

His rain rushed through dark air, each drop a different gloomy shade of green, purple or red. And it was actually wet so that when it fell upon the small audience (The Duke of Queens, Bishop Castle, My Lady Charlotina, and one or two recently arrived, absolutely bemused, time-travellers from the remote past) it soaked their clothes and made them shiver as they stood on the shelf of glassy rock overlooking Werther's Romantic Precipice (below, a waterfall foamed through fierce, black rock.)

'Nature,' exclaimed Werther. 'The only verity!'

The Duke of Queens sneezed. He looked about him with a delighted smile, but nobody else had noticed. He coughed to draw their attention, tried to sneeze again, but failed. He looked up into the ghastly sky; fresh waves of black cloud boiled in: there was lightning now, and thunder. The rain became hail. My Lady Charlotina, in a globular dress of pink veined in soft blue, giggled as the little stones fell upon her gilded features with an almost inaudible ringing sound.

But Bishop Castle, in his nodding, crenellated *téte* (from which he derived the latter half of his name and which was twice his own height) turned away, saturnine and bored, plainly noting a comparison between all this and his own entertainment of the previous year which had also involved rain, but with each drop turning into a perfect manikin as it touched the ground. There was nothing in his temperament to respond to Werther's rather innocent recreation of a Nature long-since departed from a planet which could be wholly re-modelled at the whim of any one of its inhabitants.

Mistress Christia, ever quick to notice such responses, eager for her present lover not to lose prestige, cried: 'But there is more, is there not, Werther? A finale?'

'I had thought to leave it a little longer . . .'

'No! No! Give us your finale now, my dear!'

'Well, Mistress Christia, if it is for you.' He turned one of his power rings, disseminating the sky, the lightning, the thunder, replacing them with pearly clouds, radiated with golden light through which silvery rain still fell.

'And now,' he murmured, 'I give you Tranquillity, and in Tranquillity – Hope . . .'

A further twist of the ring and a rainbow appeared, bridging the chasm, touching the clouds.

Bishop Castle was impressed by what was an example of elegance rather than spectacle, but he could not resist a minor criticism. 'Is black exactly the shade, do you think? I should have supposed it expressed your Idea, well, perhaps not perfectly . . .'

'It is perfect for me,' answered Werther a little gracelessly.

'Of course,' said Bishop Castle, regretting his impulse. He drew his bushy red brows together and made a great show of studying the rainbow. 'It stands out so well against the background.'

Emphatically (causing a brief, ironic glint in the eye of the Duke of Queens) Mistress Christia clapped her hands. 'It is a beautiful rainbow, Werther. I am sure it is much more as they used to look.'

'It takes a particularly original kind of imagination to invent such – simplicity.' The Duke of Queens, well-known for a penchant in the direction of vulgarity, fell in with her mood.

'I hope it does more than merely represent.' Satisfied both with his creation and with their responses, Werther could not resist indulging his nature, allowing a tinge of hurt resentment in his tone.

All were tolerant. All responded, even Bishop Castle. There came a chorus of consolation. Mistress Christia reached out and took his thin, white hand, inadvertently touching a power ring.

The rainbow began to topple. It leaned in the sky for a few seconds while Werther watched; his disbelief gradually turning to miserable reconciliation; then, slowly, it fell, shattering against the top of the cliff, showering them with shards of jet.

Mistress Christia's tiny hand fled to the rosebud of her mouth; her round, blue eyes expressed horror already becoming laughter (checked when she noted the look in Werther's dark and tragic orbs). She still gripped his hand; but he slowly withdrew it, kicking moodily at the fragments of the rainbow. The sky was suddenly a clear, soft grey, actually lit, one might have guessed, by the tired rays of the fading star about which the planet continued to circle, and the only clouds were those on Werther's noble brow. He pulled at the peak of his bottle-green cap, he stroked at his long, auburn hair, as if to comfort himself. He sulked.

'Perfect!' praised My Lady Charlotina, refusing to see error.

'You have the knack of making the most of a single symbol, Werther.' The Duke of Queens waved a brocaded arm in the general direction of the now disseminated scene, 'I envy you your talent, my friend.'

'It takes the product of panting lust, of pulsing sperm and eager ovaries, to offer us such brutal originality!' said Bishop Castle, in reference to Werther's birth (he was the product of sexual union, born of a womb, knowing childhood – a rarity, indeed). 'Bravo!'

'Ah,' sighed Werther, 'how cheerfully you refer to my doom: To be such a creature, when all others came into this world as mature, uncomplicated adults!'

'There was also Jherek Carnelian,' said My Lady Charlotina. Her globular dress bounced as she turned to leave.

'At least he was not born malformed,' said Werther.

'It was the work of a moment to re-form you properly, Werther,' the Duke of Queens reminded him. 'The six arms (was it?) removed, two perfectly fine ones replacing them. After all, it was an unusual exercise on the part of your mother. She did very well, considering it was her first attempt.'

'And her last,' said My Lady Charlotina, managing to have her back to Werther by the time the grin escaped. She snapped her fingers for her air-car. It floated towards her, a great, yellow rocking horse. Its shadow fell across them all.

'It left a scar,' said Werther, 'nonetheless.'

'It would,' said Mistress Christia, kissing him upon his black velvet shoulder.

'A terrible scar.'

'Indeed!' said the Duke of Queens in vague affirmation, his attention wandering. 'Well, thank you for a lovely afternoon, Werther. Come along, you two!' He signed to the time-travellers who claimed to be from the eighty-third millenium and were dressed in primitive transparent 'exoskin' which was not altogether stable and was inclined to writhe and make it seem that they were covered in hundreds of thin, excited snakes. The Duke of Queens had acquired them for his menagerie. Unaware of the difficulties of returning to their own time (temporal travel had, apparently, only just been re-invented in their age) they were inclined to treat the Duke as an eccentric who could be tolerated until it suited them to do otherwise. They smiled condescendingly, winked at each other, and followed him to an air-car in the shape of a cube whose sides were golden mirrors decorated with white and purple flowers. It was for the pleasure of enjoying the pleasure they enjoyed seemingly at his expense, that the Duke of Queens had brought them with him today. Mistress Christia waved at his car as it disappeared rapidly into the sky.

At last they were all gone, save herself and Werther de Goethe. He had seated himself upon a mossy rock, his shoulders hunched, his features downcast, unable to speak to her when she tried to cheer him.

'Oh, Werther,' she cried at last, 'what would make you happy?'

'Happy?' his voice was a hollow echo of her own. 'Happy?' He made an awkward, dissmissive gesture. 'There is no such thing as happiness for such as I!'

'There must be some sort of equivalent, surely?'

'Death, Mistress Christia, is my only consolation!'

'Well, die, my dear! I'll resurrect you in a day or two, and then . . .'

'Though you love me, Mistress Christia – though you know me best – you do not understand. I seek the inevitable, the irreconcilable, the unalterable, the inescapable! Our ancestors knew it. They knew Death *without* Resurrection; they knew what it was to be Slave to the Elements. Incapable of choosing their own destinies, they had no responsibility for choosing their own actions. They were tossed by tides. They were scattered by storms. They were wiped out by wars, decimated by disease, ravaged by radiation, made homeless by holocausts, lashed by lightnings . . .'

'You could have lashed yourself a little today, surely?'

'But it would have been *my* decision. We have lost what is Random, we have banished the Arbitrary, Mistress Christia. With our power rings and our gene banks we can, if we desire, change the courses of the planets, populate them with any kind of creature we wish, make our old sun burst with fresh energy or fade completely from the firmament. We control All. Nothing controls us!'

'There are our whims, our fancies. There are our *characters*, my moody love.'

'Even those can be altered at will.'

'Except that it is a rare nature which would wish to

change itself. Would you change yours? I, for one, would be disconsolate if, say, you decided to be more like the Duke of Queens or the Iron Orchid.'

'Nonetheless, it is *possible*. It would merely be a matter of decision. Nothing is impossible, Mistress Christia. Now do you realise why I should feel unfulfilled?'

'Not really, dear Werther. You can be anything you wish, after all. I am not, as you know, intelligent – it is not my choice to be – but I wonder if a love of Nature could be, in essence, a grandiose love of oneself – with Nature identified, as it were, with one's ego?' She offered this without criticism.

For a moment he showed surprise and seemed to be considering her observation. 'I suppose it could be. Still, that has little to do with what we were discussing. It's true that I can be anything – or, indeed, anyone – I wish. That is *why* I feel unfulfilled!'

'Aha,' she said.

'Oh, how I pine for the pain of the past! Life has no meaning without misery!'

'A common view, then, I gather. But what sort of suffering would suit you best, dear Werther? Enslavement by Esquimaux?' She hesitated, her knowledge of the past being patchier than most people's, 'The beatings with thorns? The barbed-wire trews? The pits of fire?'

'No, no – that is primitive. Psychic, it would have to be. Involving – um– morality.'

'Isn't that some sort of wall-painting?'

A large tear welled and fell. 'The world is too tolerant. The world is too kind. They all – you most of all – *approve* of me! There is nothing I can do which would not amuse you – even if it offended your taste – because there is no danger, nothing at stake. There are no *crimes*, inflamer of my lust. Oh, if I could only *sin*!'

Her perfect forehead wrinkled in the prettiest of frowns. She repeated his words to herself. Then she shrugged, embracing him.

'Tell me what sin is,' she said.

II

In Which Your Auditor Interposes

Our time-travellers, once they have visited the future, are only permitted (owing to the properties of Time itself) brief returns to their present. They can remain for any amount of time in their future, where presumably they can do no real damage to the course of previous events, but to come back at all is difficult; to make a prolonged stay has been proved impossible. Half an hour with a relative or a loved one, a short account to an auditor, such as myself, of life, say, in the seventy-fifth century, a glimpse at an artefact allowed to some interested scientist – these are the best the time-traveller can hope for, once he has made his decision to leap into the mysterious future.

As a consequence our knowledge of the future is sketchy, to say the least: we have no idea of how civilisations will grow up or how they will decline; we do not know why the number of planets in the Solar System seems to vary drastically between, say, half a dozen to almost a hundred; we cannot explain the popularity in a given age for certain fashions striking us as singularly bizarre or perverse: are beliefs which we consider fallacious or superstitious based on an understanding beyond our comprehension?

The stories we hear are often partial, hastily recounted, poorly observed, perhaps misunderstood by the traveller. We cannot question him closely, for he is soon whisked away from us (Time insists upon a certain neatness, to protect her own nature, which is essentially of the practical, ordering sort, and should that nature ever be successfully altered, then we might, in turn, successfully alter the terms of the human condition) and it is almost inevitable that we shall never have another chance of meeting him.

Resultantly, the stories brought to us of the Earth's future assume the character of legends rather than history and tend, therefore, to capture the imagination of artists, for serious scientists need permanent, verifiable evidence with which to work and precious little of that is permitted them (some refuse to believe in the future, save as an abstraction, some believe firmly that returning time-travellers' accounts are accounts of dreams and hallucinations and that they have not actually travelled in time at all!). It is left to the Romancers, childish fellows like myself, to make something of these tales. While I should be delighted to assure you that everything I have set down in this story is based closely on the truth, I am bound to admit that while the outline comes from an account given me by one of our greatest and most famous temporal adventuresses, Miss Una Persson, the conversations and many of the descriptions are of my own invention, intended hopefully to add a little colour to what would otherwise be a somewhat spare, a rather dry, recounting of an incident in the life of Werther de Goethe.

That Werther will exist, only a few entrenched sceptics can doubt. We have heard of him from many sources, usually quite as reliable as the admirable Miss Persson, as we have heard of other prominent figures of that Age we choose to call 'the End of Time'. If it is this Age which fascinates us more than any other, it is probably because it seems to offer a clue to our race's ultimate destiny.

Moralists make much of this period and show us that on the one hand it describes the pointlessness of human existence or, on the other, the whole point. Romancers are attracted to it for less worthy reasons; they find it colourful, they find its inhabitants glamorous, attractive; their imagination is sparked by the paradoxes, the very ambiguities which exasperated our scientists, by the idea of a people possessing limitless power and using it for nothing but their own amusement, like gods at play. It is pleasure enough for the Romancer to describe a story; to colour it a little, to fill in a few details where they are missing, in the hope that, by entertaining himself, he entertains others.

Of course, the inhabitants at the End of Time are not the creatures of our past legends, not mere representations of our ancestors' hopes and fears, not mere metaphors, like Siegfried or Zeus or Krishna, and this could be why they fascinate us so much. Those of us who have studied this Age (as best it can be studied) feel on friendly terms with the

Iron Orchid, with the Duke of Queens, with Lord Jagged of Canaria and the rest, and even believe that we can guess something of their inner lives.

Werther de Goethe, suffering from the *knowledge* of his, by the standards of his own time, unusual entrance into the world, doubtless felt himself apart from his fellows, though there was no objective reason why he should feel it. (I trust the reader will forgive my abandoning any attempt at a clumsy future tense.) In a society where eccentricity is encouraged, where it is celebrated no matter how extreme its realisation, Werther felt, we must assume, uncomfortable: – wishing for peers who would demand some sort of conformity from him. He could not retreat into a repressive past age; it was well-known that it was impossible to remain in the past (the phenomenon had a name at the End of Time: it was called the Morphail Effect), and he had an ordinary awareness of the futility of recreating such an environment for himself – for *he* would have created it; the responsibility would still ultimately be his own. We can only sympathise with the irreconcilable difficulties of leading the life of a gloomy fatalist when one's fate is wholly decisively, in one's own hands!

Like Jherek Carnelian, whose adventures I have recounted elsewhere, he was particularly liked by his fellows for his vast and often naïve enthusiasm for whatever he did. Like Jherek, it was possible for Werther to fall completely in love – with Nature, with an Idea, with Woman (or Man, for that matter).

It seemed to the Duke of Queens (from whom we have it on the excellent authority of Miss Persson herself) that one with such a capacity must love themselves enormously and such love is enviable. The Duke, needless to say, spoke without disapproval when he made this observation: 'To shower such largesse upon the Ego! He kneels before his soul in awe – it is a moody king, in constant need of gifts which must always seem rare!' And what is Sensation, our Moralists might argue, but Seeming Rarity? Last year's gifts regilded.

It might be true that young Werther (in years no more

than half a millenium) loved himself too much and that his tragedy was his inability to differentiate between the self-gratifying sensation of the moment and what we would call a lasting and deeply-felt emotion. We have a fragment of poetry, written, we are assured, by Werther for Mistress Christia:

At these times, I love you most when you are sleeping;
Your dreams internal, unrealised to the world at large:
And do I hear you weeping?

Most certainly a reflection of Werther's views, scarcely a description, from all that we know of her, of Mistress Christia's essential being.

Have we any reason to doubt her own view of herself? Rather, we should doubt Werther's view of everyone, including himself. Possibly this lack of insight was what made him so thoroughly attractive in his own time – *le Grand Náif*!

And, since we have quoted one, it is fair to quote the other, for happily we have another fragment, from the same source, of Mistress Christia's verse:

To have my body moved by other hands;
Not only those of Man,
But Woman, too!
My Liberty in pawn to those who understand:
That Love, alone, is True.

Surely this displays an irony entirely lacking in Werther's fragment. Affectation is also here, of course, but affectation of Mistress Christia's sort so often hides an equivalently sustained degree of self-knowledge. It is sometimes the case in our own age that the greater the extravagant outer show the greater has been the plunge by the showman into the depths of his private conscience: Consequently, the greater the effort to hide the fact, to give the world not what one is, but what it wants. Mistress Christia chose to reflect with consummate artistry the desires of her lover of the day; to fulfil her ambition as subtly as did she, reveals a person of exceptional perspicacity.

I intrude upon the flow of my tale with these various bits of explanation and speculation only, I hope, to offer credibility for what is to follow – to give a hint at a natural reason for Mistress Christia's peculiar actions and poor Werther's extravagant response. Some time has passed since we left our lovers. For the moment they have separated. We return to Werther . . .

III

In Which Werther Finds a Soul Mate

Werther de Goethe's pile stood on the pinnacle of a black and mile-high crag about which, in the permanent twilight, black vultures swooped and croaked. The rare visitor to Werther's crag could hear the vulture's voices as he approached. 'Never more!' and 'Beware the Ides of March!' and 'Picking a Chicken With You' were three of the least cryptic warnings they had been created to caw.

At the top of the tallest of his thin, dark towers, Werther de Goethe sat in his favourite chair of unpolished quartz, in his favourite posture of miserable introspection, wondering why Mistress Christia had decided to pay a call on My Lady Charlotina at Lake Billy the Kid.

'Why should she wish to stay here, after all?' He cast a suffering eye upon the sighing sea below. 'She is a creature of light – she seeks colour, laughter, warmth, no doubt to try to forget some secret sorrow – she needs all the things I cannot give her. Oh, I am a monster of selfishness!' He allowed himself a small sob. But neither the sob nor the preceding outburst produced the usual satisfaction; self-pity eluded him. He felt adrift, lost, like an explorer without chart or compass in an unfamiliar land. Manfully, he tried again:

'Mistress Christia! Mistress Christia! Why do you desert me? Without you I am desolate! My pulsatile nerves will sing at your touch only! And yet it must be my doom forever to be betrayed by the very things to which I give my fullest loyalty. Ah, it is hard! It is hard!'

He felt a little better and rose from his chair of unpolished quartz, turning his power ring a fraction so that the wind blew harder through the unglazed windows of the tower and whipped at his hair, blew his cloak about, stung his pale, long face. He raised one jackbooted foot to place it on the low sill and stared through the rain and the wind at the sky like a dreadful, spreading bruise overhead, at the turbulent, howling sea below.

He pursed his lips, twisting his power ring to darken the scene a little more, to bring up the wind's wail and the ocean's roar. He was turning back to his previous preoccupation when he perceived that something alien tossed upon the distant waves; an artefact not of his own design, it intruded upon his careful conception. He peered hard at the object, but it was too far away from him to identify it. Another might have shrugged it aside, but he was painstaking, even prissy, in his need for artistic perfection. Was this some vulgar addition to his scene made, perhaps, by the Duke of Queens in a misguided effort to please him?

He took his parachute (chosen as the only means by which he could leave his tower) from the wall and strapped it on, stepping through the window and tugging at the ripcord as he fell into space. Down he plummeted and the scarlet balloon soon filled with gas, the nacelle opening up beneath him, so that by the time he was hovering some feet above the sombre waves, he was lying comfortably on his chest, staring over the rim of his parachute at the trespassing image he had seen from his tower. What he saw was something resembling a great shell, a shallow boat of mother-of-pearl, floating on that dark and heaving sea.

In astonishment he now realised that the boat was occupied by a slight figure, clad in filmy white, whose face was pale and terrified. It could only be one of his friends, altering their appearance for some whimsical adventure. But which? Then he caught, through the rain, a better glimpse and he heard himself saying:

'A child? A child? Are you a child?'

She could not hear him; perhaps she could not even see him, having eyes only for the watery walls which threatened to engulf her little boat and carry her down to the land of Casey Jones. How could it be a child? He rubbed his eyes. He must be projecting his hopes – but there, that movement, that whimper! It *was* a child! Without doubt!

He watched, open-mouthed, as she was flung this way and that by the elements – *his* elements. She was powerless; actually powerless! He relished her terror; he envied her her fear. Where had she come from? Save for himself and Jherek Carnelian there had not been a child on the planet for thousands upon thousands of years.

He leaned further out, studying her smooth skin, her lovely rounded limbs. Her eyes were tight shut now as the waves crashed upon her fragile craft; her delicate fingers, unstrong, courageous, clung hard to the side! her white dress was wet, outlining her new-formed breasts; water poured from her long, auburn hair. She panted in delicious impotence.

'It *is* a child!' Werther exclaimed. 'A sweet, frightened child!'

And in his excitement he toppled from his parachute with an astonished yell, and landed with a crash, which winded him, in the sea-shell boat beside the girl. She opened her eyes as he turned his head to apologise. Plainly she had not been aware of his presence overhead. For a moment he could not speak, though his lips moved. But she screamed.

'My dear . . .' The words were thin and high and they faded into the wind. He struggled to raise himself on his elbows. 'I apologise . . .'

She screamed again. She crept as far away from him as possible. Still she clung to her flimsy boat's side as the waves played with it: a thoughtless giant with too delicate a toy; inevitably, it must shatter. He waved his hand to indicate his parachute, but it had already been borne away. His cloak was caught by the wind and wrapped itself around his arm; he struggled to free himself and became further entangled;

he heard a new scream and then some demoralised whimpering.

'I will save you!' he shouted, by way of reassurance, but his voice was muffled even in his own ears. It was answered by a further pathetic shriek. As the cloak was saturated it became increasingly difficult for him to escape its folds. He lost his temper and was deeper enmeshed. He tore at the thing. He freed his head.

'I am not your enemy, tender one. But your saviour,' he said. It was obvious that she could not hear him. With an impatient gesture he flung off his cloak at last and twisted a power ring. The volume of noise was immediately reduced. Another twist, and the waves became calmer. She stared at him in wonder.

'Did you do that?' she asked.

'Of course. It is my scene, you see. But how you came to enter it, I do not know!'

'You are a wizard, then?' she said.

'Not at all. I have no interest in sport.' He clapped his hands and his parachute re-appeared, perhaps a trifle reluctantly as if it had enjoyed its brief independence, and drifted down until it was level with the boat. Werther lightened the sky. He could not bring himself, however, to dismiss the rain, but he let a little sun shine through it.

'There,' he said. 'The storm has passed, eh? Did you like your experience?'

'It was horrifying! I was so afraid. I thought I would drown.'

'Yes? And did you like it?'

She was puzzled, unable to answer as he helped her aboard the nacelle and ordered the parachute home.

'You *are* a wizard!' she said. She did not seem disappointed. He did not quiz her as to her meaning. For the moment, if not for always, he was prepared to let her identify him however she wished.

'You are actually a child?' he asked hesitantly. 'I do not mean to be insulting. A time-traveller, perhaps? Or from another planet?'

'Oh, no. I am an orphan. My father and mother are now

dead. I was born on Earth some fourteen years ago.' She looked in mild dismay over the side of the craft as they were whisked swiftly upward. '*They* were time-travellers. We made our home in a forgotten menagerie – underground, but it was pleasant. My parents feared recapture, you see. Food still grew in the menagerie. There were books, too, and they taught me to read – and there were other records through which they were able to present me with a reasonable education. I am not illiterate. I know the world. I was taught to fear wizards.'

'Ah,' he crooned, 'the world! But you are not a part of it, just as I am not a part.'

The parachute reached the window and, at his indication, she stepped gingerly from it to the tower. The parachute folded itself and placed itself upon the wall. Werther said: 'You will want food, then? I will create whatever you wish!'

'Fairy food will not fill mortal stomachs, sir,' she told him.

'You are beautiful,' he said. 'Regard me as your mentor, as your new father. I will teach you what this world is really like. Will you oblige me, at least, by trying the food?'

'I will.' She looked about her with a mixture of curiosity and suspicion. 'You lead a spartan life.' She noticed a cabinet. 'Books? You read, then?'

'In transcription,' he admitted. 'I listen. My enthusiasm is for Ivan Turgiditi, who created the Novel of Discomfort and remained its greatest practitioner. In, I believe, the 900th (though they could be spurious, invented, I have heard) . . .'

'Oh, no, no! I have read Turgiditi.' She blushed. 'In the original. *Wet Socks* – four hours of discomfort, every second brought to life, and in less than a thousand pages!'

'My favourite,' he told her, his expression softening still more into besotted wonderment. 'I can scarcely believe – in this Age – one such as you! Innocent of device. Uncorrupted! Pure!'

She frowned. 'My parents taught me well, sir. I am not . . .'

'You cannot know! And dead, you say? Dead! If only I

could have witnessed – but no, I am insensitive. Forgive me. I mentioned food.'

'I am not really hungry.'

'Later then. That I should have so recently mourned such things as lacking in this world. I was blind. I did not look. Tell me everything. Whose was the menagerie?'

'It belonged to one of the lords of this planet. My mother was from a period she called the October Century, but recently recovered from a series of interplanetary wars and fresh and optimistic in its rediscoveries of ancestral technologies. She was chosen to be the first into the future. She was captured upon her arrival and imprisoned by a wizard like yourself.'

'The word means little. But continue.'

'She said that she used the word because it had meaning for her and she had no other short description. My father came from a time known as the Preliminary Structure, where human kind was rare and machines proliferated. He never mentioned the nature of the transgression he made from the social code of his day, but as a result of it he was banished to this world. He, too, was captured for the same menagerie and there he met my mother. They lived originally, of course, in separate cages, where their normal environments were recreated for them. But the owner of the menagerie became bored, I think, and abandoned interest in his collection . . .'

'I have often remarked that people who cannot look after their collections have no business keeping them,' said Werther. 'Please continue, my dear child.' He reached out and patted her hand.

'One day he went away and they never saw him again. It took them some time to realise that he was not returning. Slowly the more delicate creatures, whose environments required special attention, died.'

'No one came to resurrect them?'

'No one. Eventually my mother and father were the only ones left. They made what they could of their existence, too wary to enter the outer world in case they should be recaptured, and, to their astonishment, conceived me. They had heard that people from different historical periods could not produce children.'

'I have heard the same.'

'Well, then, I was a fluke. They were determined to give me as good an upbringing as they could and to prepare me for the dangers of your world.'

'Oh, they were right! For one so innocent, there are many dangers. I will protect you, never fear.'

'You are kind.' She hesitated. 'I was not told by my parents that such as you existed.'

'I am the only one.'

'I see. My parents died in the course of this past year, first my father, then my mother (of a broken heart, I believe). I buried my mother and at first made an attempt to live the life we had always led, but I felt the lack of company and decided to explore the world, for it seemed to me I, too, could grow old and die before I had experienced anything!'

'Grow old,' mouthed Werther rhapsodically, 'and die!'

'I set out a month or so ago and was disappointed to discover the absence of ogres, of malevolent creatures of any sort – and the wonders I witnessed, while a trifle bewildering, did not compare with those I had imagined I would find. I had fully expected to be snatched up for a menagerie by now, but nobody has shown interest, even when they have seen me.'

'Few follow the menagerie fad, at present.' He nodded. 'They would not have known you for what you were. Only I could recognise you. Oh, how lucky I am. And how lucky *you* are, my dear, to have met me when you did. You see, I, too, am a child of the womb. I, too, made my own hard way through the utereal gloom to breathe the air, to find the light of this faded, this senile globe. Of all those you could have met, you have met the only one who understands you, who is likely to share your passions, to relish your education. We are soul mates, child!'

He stood up and put a tender arm about her young shoulders.

'You have a new mother, a new father now! His name is Werther!'

IV

In Which Werther Finds Sin At Last

Her name was Catherine Lily Marguerite Natasha Dolores Beatrice Machineshop-Seven Flambeau Gratitude (the last two names but one being her father's and her mother's respectively).

Werther de Goethe continued to talk to her for some hours. Indeed, he became quite carried away as he described all the exciting things they would do, how they would live lives of the purest poetry and simplicity from now on, the quiet and tranquil places they would visit, the manner in which her education would be supplemented, and he was glad to note, he thought, her wariness dissipating, her attitude warming to him.

'I will devote myself entirely to your happiness,' he informed her, and then, noticing that she was fast asleep, he smiled tenderly: 'Poor child. I am a worm of thoughtlessness. She is exhausted.'

He rose from his chair of unpolished quartz and strode to where she lay curled upon the iguana-skin rug; stooping, he placed his hands under her warm-smelling, her yielding body, and somewhat awkwardly lifted her. In her sleep she uttered a tiny moan, her cherry lips parted and her newly budded breasts rose and fell rapidly against his chest once or twice until she sank back into a deeper slumber.

He staggered, panting with the effort, to another part of the tower and then he lowered her with a sigh to the floor. He realised that he had not prepared a proper bedroom for her.

Fingering his chin, he inspected the dank stones, the cold obsidian which had suited his mood so well for so long and now seemed singularly offensive. Then he smiled.

'She must have beauty,' he said, 'and it must be subtle. It must be calm.'

An inspiration, a movement of a power ring, and the walls were covered with thick carpets embroidered with scenes from his own old book of fairy tales. He remembered how he had listened to the book over and over again – his only consolation in the lonely days of his extreme youth.

Here, Man Shelley, a famous harmonican, ventured into Odeon (a version of Hell) in order to be re-united with his favourite three-headed dog Omnibus. The picture showed him with his harmonica (or 'harp') playing 'Blues for a Nightingale' – a famous lost piece. There, Casablanca Bogard, with his single eye, in the middle of his forehead, wielded his magic spade, Sam, in his epic fight with that ferocious bird, the Malted Falcon, to save his love, the Acrilan Queen, from the power of Big Sleepy (a dwarf who had turned himself into a giant) and Mutinous Caine, who had been cast out of Hollywood (or paradise) for the killing of his sister, the Blue Angel.

Such scenes were surely the very stuff to stir the romantic, delicate imagination of this lovely child, just as his had been stirred when – he felt the *frisson* – he had been her age. He glowed. His substance was suffused with delicious compassion for them both as he recalled, also, the torments of his own adolescence.

That she should be suffering as he had suffered filled him with the pleasure all must feel when a fellow spirit is recognised, and at the same time he was touched by her plight, determined that she should not know the anguish of his earliest years. Once, long ago, Werther had courted Jherek Carnelian, admiring him for his fortitude, knowing that locked in Jherek's head were the memories of bewilderment, misery and despair which would echo his own; but Jherek, pampered progeny of that most artificial of all creatures, the Iron Orchid, had been unable to recount any suitable experiences at all, had, whilst cheerfully eager to please Werther, recalled nothing but pleasurable times, had reluctantly admitted, at last, to the possession of the happiest of childhoods. That was when Werther had concluded that Jherek Carnelian had no soul worth speaking of and he had never altered his opinion (now he secretly doubted Jherek's origins and sometimes believed that Jherek merely pretended to have been a child – merely one more of his boring and superficial affectations).

Next, a bed – a soft, downy, bed, spread with sheets of silver silk, with posts of ivory and hangings of precious perspex, antique and yellowed, and on the floor the finely-tanned skins of albino hamsters and marmalade cats.

Werther added gorgeous lavs of intricately patterned red and blue ceramic, their bowls filled with living flowers: with whispering toadflax, dragonsnaps, goldilocks and shanghai lilies, with blooming scarlet margravines (his adopted daughter's name-flower, as he knew to his pride), with soda-purple poppies and tea-green roses, with iodine and cerise and crimson hanging johnny, with golden cynthia and sky-blue true-lips, calomine and creeping larrikin, until the room was saturated with their intoxicating scents.

Placing a few bunches of hitler's balls in the corners near the ceiling, a toy fish-tank (capable of firing real fish), which he remembered owning as a boy, under the window, a trunk (it could be opened by pressing the navel) filled with clothes near the bed, a full set of bricks and two bats against the wall close to the doorway, he was able, at last, to view the room with some satisfaction.

Obviously, he told himself, she would make certain changes according to her own tastes. That was why he had shown such restraint. He imagined her naïve delight when she wakened in the morning. And he must be sure to produce days and nights of regular duration, because at her age routine was the main thing a child needed. There was nothing like the certainty of a consistently glorious sunrise! This reminded him to make an alteration to a power ring on his left hand, to spread upon the black cushion of the sky crescent moons and stars and starlets in profusion. Bending carefully, he picked up the vibrant youth of her body and lowered her to the bed, drawing the silver sheets up to her vestal chin. Chastely he touched lips to her forehead and crept from the room, fashioning a leafy door behind him, hesitating for a moment, unable to define the mood in which he found himself. A rare smile illumined features set so long in lines of gloom. Returning to his own quarters, he murmured:

'I believe it is Contentment!'

A month swooned by. Werther lavished every moment of his time upon his new charge. He thought of nothing but her youthful satisfactions. He encouraged her in joy, in idealism, in a love of Nature. Gone were his blizzards, his rocky spires, his bleak wastes and his moody forests, to be replaced with gentle landscapes of green hills and merry, tinkling rivers, sunny glades in copses of poplars, rhododendrons, redwoods, laburnums, banyans and good old amiable oaks. When they went on a picnic large-eyed cows and playful gorillas would come and nibble scraps of food from Catherine Gratitude's palm. And when it was day, the sun always shone and the sky was always blue, and if there were clouds, they were high, hesitant puffs of whiteness and soon gone.

He found her books so that she might read. There was Turgiditi and Uto, Pett Ridge and Zakka, Pyat Sink – all the ancients. Sometimes he asked her to read to him, for the luxury of dispensing with his usual translators. She had been fascinated by a picture of a typewriter she had seen in a record, so he fashioned an air-car in the likeness of one, and they travelled the world in it, looking at scenes created by Werther's peers.

'Oh, Werther,' she said one day, 'you are so good to me. Now that I realise the misery which might have been mine (as well as the life I was missing underground) I love you more and more.'

'And I love you more and more,' he replied, his head a-swim. And for a moment he felt a pang of guilt at having forgotten Mistress Christia so easily. He had not seen her since Catherine had come to him and he guessed that she was sulking somewhere. He prayed that she would not decide to take vengeance on him.

They went to see Jherek Carnelian's famous 'London, 1896' and Werther manfully hid his displeasure at her admiration for his rival's buildings of white marble, gold and sparkling quartz. He showed her his own abandoned tomb, which he privately considered in better taste, but it was plain that it did not give her the same satisfaction.

They saw the Duke of Queens' latest, 'Ladies and Swans', but not for long, for Werther considered it unsuitable. Later they paid a visit to Lord Jagged of Canaria's somewhat abstract 'War and Peace in Two Dimensions' and Werther thought it too stark to please the girl, judging the experiment 'successful', but Catherine laughed with glee as she touched the living figures and found that somehow it was true – Lord Jagged had given them length and breadth but not a scrap of width – when they turned aside, they disappeared.

It was on one of these expeditions, to Bishop Castle's 'A Million Angry Wrens' (an attempt in the recently revised art of Aesthetic Loudness), that they encountered Lord Mongrove, a particular confidante of Werther's until they had quarrelled over the method of suicide adopted by the natives of Uranus during the period of the Great Sodium Breather. By now they would, if Werther had not found a new obsession, have patched up their differences and Werther felt a pang of guilt for having forgotten the one person on this planet with whom he had, after all, shared something in common.

In his familiar dark green robes, with his leonine head hunched between his massive shoulders, the giant, apparently disdaining an air-carriage, was riding home upon the back of a monstrous snail.

The first thing they saw, from above, was its shining trail over the azure rocks of some abandoned, half-created scene of Argonheart Po's (who believed that nothing was worth making unless it tasted delicious and could be eaten and digested). It was Catherine who saw the snail itself first and exclaimed at the size of the man who occupied the swaying howdah on its back.

'He must be ten feet tall, Werther!'

And Werther, knowing whom she meant, made their typewriter descend, crying:

'Mongrove! My old friend!'

Mongrove, however, was sulking. He had chosen not to forget whatever insult it had been which Werther had levelled at him when they had last met. 'What? Is it Werther? Bring freshly sharpened dirks for the flesh between my shoulder blades? It is that Cold Betrayer himself, whom I befriended when a bare boy, pretending carelessness, feigning insouciance, as if he cannot remember, with relish, the exact degree of bitterness of the poisoned wine he fed me when we parted. Faster, steed! Bear me away from Treachery! Let me fly from further Insult! No more shall I suffer at the hands of Calumny!' And, with his long, jewelled stick, he beat upon the shell of his molluscuIoid mount. The beast's horns waved agitatedly for a moment, but it did not really seem capable of any greater speed. In good-humoured puzzlement, it turned its slimy head towards its master.

'Forgive me, Mongrove! I take back all I said,' announced Werther, unable to recall a single sour syllable of the exchange. 'Tell me why you are abroad. It is rare for you to leave your doomy dome.'

'I am making my way to the Ball,' said Lord Mongrove, 'which is shortly to be held by My Lady Charlotina. Doubtless I have been invited to act as a butt for their malice and their gossip, but I go in good faith.'

'A Ball? I know nothing of it.'

Mongrove's countenance brightened a trifle. 'You have not been invited? Ah!'

'I wonder . . . But, no – My Lady Charlotina shows unsuspected sensitivity. She knows that I now have responsibilities – to my little Ward, here. To Catherine – to my Kate.'

'The child?'

'Yes, to my child. I am privileged to be her protector. Fate favours me as her new father. This is she. Is she not lovely? Is she not innocent?'

Lord Mongrove raised his great head and looked at the slender girl beside Werther. He shook his huge head as if in pity for her.

'Be careful, my dear,' he said. 'To be befriended by de Goethe is to be embraced by a viper!'

She did not understand Mongrove; questioningly, she looked up at Werther. 'What does he mean?'

Werther was shocked. He clapped his hands to her pretty ears.

'Listen no more! I regret the overture. The movement, Lord Mongrove, shall remain unresolved. Farewell, spurner of good-intent. I had never guessed before the level of your cynicism. Such an accusation! Goodbye, for ever, most malevolent of mortals, despiser of altruism, hater of love! She shall know me no longer!'

'You have known yourself not at all,' snapped Mongrove spitefully, but it was unlikely that Werther, already speeding skyward, heard the remark.

And thus it was with particular and unusual graciousness that Werther greeted My Lady Charlotina when, a little later, they came upon her.

She was wearing the russett ears and eyes of a fox, riding her yellow rocking horse through the patch of orange sky left over from her own turbulent 'Death of Neptune'. She waved to them. 'Cock-a-loodle-do!'

'My dear Lady Charlotina. What a pleasure it is to see you. Your beauty continues to rival Nature's mightiest miracles.'

It is with such unwonted effusion that one will greet a person, who has not hitherto aroused our feelings, when we are in a position to compare them against another, closer, acquaintance who had momentarily earned our contempt or anger.

She seemed taken aback, but received the compliment equably enough.

'Dear Werther! And is this that rarity, the girl-child I have heard so much about and whom, in your goodness, you have taken under your wing? I could not believe it! A child! And how lucky she is to find a father in yourself – of all our number the one best suited to look after her.'

It might also be said that Werther preened himself beneath the golden shower of her benediction, and if he detected no irony in her tone, perhaps it was because he still smarted from Mongrove's dash of vitriol.

'I have been chosen, it seems,' he said modestly, 'to lead this waif through the traps and illusions of our weary world. The burden I shoulder is not light . . .'

'Valiant Werther!'

'. . . but it is shouldered willingly. I am devoting my life to her upbringing, to her peace of mind.' He placed a bloodless hand upon her auburn locks and, winsomely, she shook his other one.

'You are tranquil, my dear?' asked Lady Charlotina kindly, arranging her blue skirts over the saddle of her rocking horse. 'You have no doubts?'

'At first I had,' admitted the sweet child, 'but gradually I learned to trust my new father. Now I would trust him in anything!'

'Ah,' sighed My Lady Charlotina, 'trust!'

'Trust,' said Werther. 'It grows in me, too. You encourage me, charming Charlotina, for a short time ago I believed myself doubted by all.'

'Is it possible? When you are evidently so reconciled – so – happy!'

'And I am happy, also, now that I have Werther,' carolled the commendable Catherine.

'Exquisite!' breathed My Lady Charlotina. 'And you will, of course, both come to my Ball.'

'I am not sure . . .' began Werther, 'perhaps Catherine is too young . . .'

But she raised her tawny hands. 'It is your duty to come. To show us all that simple hearts are the happiest.'

'Possibly . . .'

'You must. The world must have examples, Werther, if it is to follow your Way.'

Werther lowered his eyes shyly. 'I am honoured,' he said. 'We accept.'

'Splendid! Then come soon. Come now, if you like. A few arrangements, and the Ball begins.'

'Thank you,' said Werther, 'but I think it best if we return to my castle for a little while.' He caressed his ward's fine, long tresses. 'For it will be Catherine's first Ball and she must choose her gown.'

And he beamed down upon his radiant protégée as she clapped her hands in joy.

My Lady Charlotina's Ball must have been at least a mile in circumference, set against the soft tones of a summer twilight, red-gold and transparent so that, as one approached, the guests who had already arrived could be seen standing upon the inner wall, clad in creations extravagant even at the End of Time.

The Ball itself was inclined to roll a little, but those inside it were undisturbed; their footing was firm, thanks to My Lady Charlotina's artistry. The Ball was entered by means of a number of sphincterish openings, placed more or less at random in its outer wall. At the very centre of the Ball, on a floating platform, sat an orchestra comprising the choicest musicians, out of a myriad ages and planets, from My Lady's great menagerie (she specialised, currently, in artists).

When Werther de Goethe, a green-gowned Catherine Gratitude upon his blue velvet arm, arrived, the orchestra was playing some primitive figure of My Lady Charlotina's own composition. It was called, she claimed as she welcomed them. 'On the Theme of Childhood', but doubtless she thought to please them, for Werther believed he had heard it before, under a different title.

Many of the guests had already arrived and were standing in small groups chatting to each other. Werther greeted an old friend Li Pao, of the 27th century, and such a kill-joy that he had never been wanted for a menagerie. While he was forever criticising their behaviour, he never missed a party. Next to him stood the Iron Orchid, mother of Jherek Carnelian, who was not present. In contrast to Li Pao's faded blue overalls, she wore rags of red, yellow and mauve, thousands of sparkling bracelets, anklets and necklaces, a head-dress of woven peacock's wings, slippers which were moles and whose beady eyes looked up from the floor.

'What do you mean – waste?' she was saying to Li Pao. 'What else could we do with the energy of the universe? If our sun burns out, we create another. Doesn't that make us conservatives? Or is it preservatives?'

'Good evening, Werther,' said Li Pao in some relief. He bowed politely to the girl. 'Good evening, miss.'

'Miss?' said the Iron Orchid. 'What?'

'Gratitude.'

'For whom?'

'This is Catherine Gratitude, my ward,' said Werther, and the Iron Orchid let forth a peal of luscious laughter.

'The girl-bride, eh?'

'Not at all,' said Werther. 'How is Jherek?'

'Lost, I fear, in Time. We have seen nothing of him recently. He still pursues his paramour. Some say you copy him, Werther.'

He knew her bantering tone of old and took the remark in good part. 'His is a mere affectation,' he said. 'Mine is Reality.'

'You were always one to make that distinction, Werther,' she said. 'And I will never understand the difference!'

'I find your concern for Miss Gratitude's upbringing most worthy,' said Li Pao somewhat unctuously. 'If there is any way I can help. My knowledge of twenties' politics, for instance, is considered unmatched – particularly, of course, where the 26th and 27th centuries are concerned . . .'

'You are kind,' said Werther, unsure how to take an offer which seemed to him overeager and not entirely selfless.

Gaf the Horse in Tears, whose clothes were real flame, flickered towards them, the light from his burning, unstable face almost blinding Werther. Catherine Gratitude shrank from him as he reached out a hand to touch her, but her expression changed as she realised that he was not at all hot – rather, there was something almost chilly about the sensation on her shoulder. Werther did his best to smile. 'Good evening, Gaf.'

'She is a dream!' said Gaf. 'I know it, because only I have such a wonderful imagination. Did I create her, Werther?'

'You jest.'

'Ho, ho! Serious old Werther.' Gaf kissed him, bowed to the child, and moved away, his body erupting in all directions as he laughed the more. 'Literal, literal Werther!'

'He is a boor,' Werther told his charge. 'Ignore him.'

'I thought him sweet,' she said.

'You have much to learn, my dear.'

The music filled the Ball and some of the guests left the floor to dance, hanging in the air around the orchestra, darting streamers of coloured energy in order to weave complex patterns as they moved.

'They are very beautiful,' said Catherine Gratitude. 'May we dance soon, Werther?'

'If you wish. I am not much given to such pastimes as a rule.'

'But tonight?'

He smiled. 'I can refuse you nothing, child.'

She hugged his arm and her girlish laughter filled his heart with warmth.

'Perhaps you should have made yourself a child before, Werther?' suggested the Duke of Queens, drifting away from the dance and leaving a trail of green fire behind him. He was clad all in soft metal which reflected the colours in the Ball and created other colours in turn. 'You are a perfect father. Your métier.'

'It would not have been the same, Duke of Queens.'

'As you say.' His darkly handsome face bore its usual expression of benign amusement. 'I am the Duke of Queens, child. It is an honour.' He bowed, his metal booming.

'Your friends are wonderful,' said Catherine Gratitude. 'Not at all what I expected.'

'Be wary of them,' murmured Werther. 'They have no conscience.'

'Conscience? What is that?'

Werther touched a ring and led her up into the air of the Ball. 'I am your conscience, for the moment, Catherine. You shall learn in time.'

Lord Jagged of Canaria, his face almost hidden by one of his high, quilted collars, floated in their direction.

'Werther, my boy! This must be your daughter. Oh! Sweeter than honey! Softer than petals! I have heard so much – but the praise was not enough! You must have poetry written about you. Music composed for you. Tales must be spun with you as the heroine.' And Lord Jagged made a deep and elaborate bow, his long sleeves sweeping the air below his feet. Next, he addressed Werther:

'Tell me, Werther, have you seen Mistress Christia? Everyone else is here, but not she.'

'I have looked for the Everlasting Concubine without success.' Werther told him.

'She should arrive soon. In a moment My Lady Charlotina announces the beginning of the masquerade – and Mistress Christia loves the masquerade.'

'I suspect she pines,' said Werther.

'Why so?'

'She loved me, you know.'

'Aha! Perhaps you are right. But I interrupt your dance. Forgive me.'

And Lord Jagged of Canaria floated, stately and beautiful, towards the floor.

'Mistress Christia?' said Catherine. 'Is she your Lost Love?'

'A wonderful woman,' said Werther. 'But my first duty is to you. Regretfully I could not pursue her, as I think she wanted me to do.'

'Have I come between you?'

'Of course not. Of course not. That was infatuation – this is a sacred duty.'

And Werther showed her how to dance – how to notice a gap in a pattern which might be filled by the movements from her body. Because it was a special occasion he had given her her very own power ring – only a small one, but she was proud of it, and she gasped so prettily at the colours her train made that Werther's fears that his gift might corrupt her precious innocence were plainly unfounded. It was then that he realised with a shock how deeply he had fallen in love with her.

At the realisation, he made an excuse, leaving her to dance with first Sweet Orb Mace, feminine tonight, with a latticed face, and then with O'Kala Incarnadine who, with his usual preference for the bodies of beasts, was currently a bear. Although he felt a pang as he watched her stroke O'Kala's ruddy fur, he could not bring himself just then to interfere. His immediate desire was to leave the Ball, but to do that would be to disappoint his ward, to raise questions he would not wish to answer. After a while he began to feel a certain satisfaction from his suffering and remained, miserably, on the floor while Catherine danced on and on.

And then My Lady Charlotina had stopped the orchestra and stood on the platform calling for their attention.

'It is time for the masquerade. You all know the theme, I hope.' She paused, smiling. 'All, save Werther and Catherine. When the music begins again, please reveal your creations of the evening.'

Werther frowned, wondering her reasons for not revealing the theme of the masquerade to him. She was still smiling at him as she drifted towards him and settled beside him on the floor.

'You seem sad, Werther. Why so? I thought you at one with yourself at last. Wait. My surprise will flatter you, I'm sure!'

The music began again. The Ball was filled with laughter – and there was the theme of the masquerade!

Werther cried out in anguish. He dashed upward through the gleeful throng, seeing each face as a mockery, trying to reach the side of his girl-child before she could realise the dreadful truth.

'Catherine! Catherine!'

He flew to her. She was bewildered as he folded her in his arms.

'Oh, they are monsters of insincerity! Oh, they are grotesque in their aping of all that is simple, all that is pure!' he cried.

He glared about him at the other guests. My Lady Charlotina had chosen 'Childhood' as her general theme. Sweet Orb Mace had changed himself into a gigantic single sperm, his own face still visible at the glistening tail; the Iron Orchid had become a monstrous new-born baby with a red and bawling face which still owed more to Paint than to Nature; the Duke of Queens, true to character, was three-year-old Siamese twins (both the faces were his own, softened); even Lord Mongrove had deigned to become an egg.

'What ith it, Werther?' lisped My Lady Charlotina at his feet, her brown curls bobbing as she waved her lollipop in the general direction of the other guests. 'Doeth it not pleathe you?'

'Ugh! This is agony! A parody of everything I hold most perfect!'

'But, Werther . . .'

'What is wrong, dear Werther?' begged Catherine. 'It is only a masquerade.'

'Can you not see? It is you – everything you and I mean – that they mock. No – it is best that you do not see. Come, Catherine. They are insane; they revile all that is sacred!' And he bore her bodily towards the wall, rushing through the nearest doorway and out into the darkened sky.

He left his typewriter behind, so great was his haste to be gone from that terrible scene. He fled with her willy-nilly through the air, through daylight, through pitchy night. He fled until he came to his own tower, flanked now by green lawns and rolling turf, surrounded by song-birds, swamped in sunshine. And he hated it – landscape, larks and light – all were hateful.

He flew through the window and found his room full of comforts – of cushions and carpets and heady perfume – and with a gesture he removed them. Their particles hung gleaming in the sun's beams for a moment. But the sun, too, was hateful. He blacked it out and night swam into that bare chamber. And all the while, in amazement, Catherine Gratitude looked on, her lips forming the question, but never uttering it. At length, tentatively, she touched his arm.

'Werther?'

His hands flew to his head. He roared in his mindless pain.

'Oh, Werther!'

'Ah! They destroy me! They destroy my ideals!'

He was weeping when he turned to bury his face in her hair.

'Werther!' She kissed his cold cheek. She stroked his shaking back. And she led him from the ruins of his room and down the passage to her own apartment.

'Why should I strive to set up standards,' he sobbed, 'when all about me they seek to pull them down. It would be better to be a villain!'

But he was quiescent; he allowed himself to be seated upon her bed; he felt suddenly drained. He sighed. 'They hate innocence. They would see it gone forever from this globe.'

She gripped his hand. She stroked it. 'No, Werther. They meant no harm. I saw no harm.'

'They would corrupt you. I must keep you safe.'

Her lips touched his and his body came alive again. Her fingers touched his skin. He gasped.

'I must keep you safe.'

In a dream, he took her in his arms. Her lips parted, their tongues met. Her young breasts pressed against him – and for perhaps the first time in his life Werther understood the meaning of physical joy. His blood began to dance to the rhythm of a sprightlier heart. And why should he not take what they would take in his position? He placed a hand upon a pulsing thigh. If cynicism called the tune, then he would show them he could pace as pretty a measure as any. His kisses became passionate, and passionately they were returned.

'Catherine!'

A motion of a power ring and their clothes were gone, the bed hangings drawn.

And your auditor not being of that modern school which salaciously seeks to share the secrets of others' passions (secrets familiar, one might add, to the great majority of us) retires from this scene.

But when he woke the next morning and turned on the sun, Werther looked down at the lovely child beside him, her auburn hair spread across the pillows, her little breasts rising and falling in tranquil sleep, and he realised that he had used his reaction to the masquerade to betray his trust. A madness had filled him; he had raised an evil wind and his responsibility had been borne off by it, taking Innocence and Purity, never to return. His lust had lost him everything.

Tears reared in his tormented eyes and ran cold upon his

heated cheeks. 'Mongrove was perceptive indeed,' he murmured. 'To be befriended by Werther is to be embraced by a viper. She can never trust me – anyone – again. I have lost my right to offer her protection. I have stolen her childhood.'

And he got up from the bed, from the scene of that most profound of crimes, and he ran from the room and went to sit in his old chair of unpolished quartz, staring listlessly through the window at the paradise he had created outside. It accused him; it reminded him of his high ideals. He was astonished by the consequences of his actions: he had turned his paradise to hell.

A great groan reverberated in his chest. 'Oh, now I know what sin is!' he said. 'And what terrible tribute it exacts from the one who tastes it!'

And he sank almost luxuriously into the deepest gloom he had ever known.

V

In Which Werther Finds Redemption Of Sorts

He avoided Catherine Gratitude all that day, even when he heard her calling his name, for if the landscape could fill him with such agony, what would he feel under the startled inquisition of her gaze? He erected himself a heavy dungeon door so that she could not get in, and, as he sat contemplating his poisoned paradise, he saw her once, walking on a hill he had made for her. She seemed unchanged, of course, but he knew in his heart how she must be shivering with the chill of lost innocence. That it should have been himself, of all men, who had introduced her so young to the tainted joys of carnal love! Another deep sigh and he buried his fists savagely into his eyes.

'Catherine! Catherine! I am a thief, an assassin, a despoiler of souls. The name of Werther de Goethe becomes a synonym for Treachery!'

It was not until the next morning that he thought himself able to admit her to his room, to submit himself to a judgement which he knew would be worse for not being spoken. Even when she did enter, his shifty eye would not focus on her for long. He looked for some outward sign of her experience, somewhat surprised that he could detect none.

He glared at the floor, knowing his words to be inadequate. 'I am sorry,' he said.

'For leaving the Ball, darling Werther! The epilogue was infinitely sweeter.'

'Don't!' He put his hands to his ears. 'I cannot undo what I have done, my child, but I can try to make amends. Evidently you must not stay here with me. You need suffer nothing further on that score. For myself, I must contemplate an eternity of loneliness. It is the least of the prices I must pay. But Mongrove would be kind to you, I am sure.' He looked at her. It seemed that she had grown older. Her bloom was fading now that it had been touched by the icy fingers of that most sinister, most insinuating, of libertines, called Death. 'Oh,' he sobbed, 'how haughty was I in my pride! How I congratulated myself on my high-mindedness. Now I am proved the lowliest of all my kind!'

'I really cannot follow you, Werther dear,' she said. 'Your behaviour is rather odd today, you know. Your words mean very little to me.'

'Of course they mean little,' he said. 'You are unworldly, child. How can you anticipate . . . ah, ah . . .' and he hid his face in his hands.

'Werther, please cheer up. I have heard of *le petit mal*, but this seems to be going on for a somewhat longer time. I am still puzzled . . .'

'I cannot, as yet,' he said, speaking with some difficulty through his palms, 'bring myself to describe in cold words the enormity of the crime I have committed against your spirit – against your childhood. I had known that you would – eventually – wish to experience the joys of true love – but I had hoped to prepare your soul for what was to come – so that when it happened it would be beautiful.'

'But it *was* beautiful, Werther.'

He found himself experiencing a highly inappropriate impatience with her failure to understand her doom.

'It was not the right *kind* of beauty,' he explained.

'There are certain correct kinds for certain times?' she asked. 'You are sad because we have offended some social code?'

'There is no such thing in this world, Catherine – but you, child, could have known a code. Something I never had when I was your age – something I wanted for you. One day you will realise what I mean.' He leaned forward, his voice thrilling, his eye hot and hard, 'And if you do not hate me now, Catherine, oh, you will hate me then. Yes! You will hate me then.'

Her answering laughter was unaffected, unstrained. 'This is silly, Werther. I have rarely had a nicer experience.'

He turned aside, raising his hands as if to ward off blows. 'Your words are darts – each one draws blood in my conscience.' He sank back into his chair.

Still laughing, she began to stroke his limp hand. He drew it away from her. 'Ah, see! I have made you lascivious. I have introduced you to the drug called lust!'

'Well, perhaps to an aspect of it!'

Some change in her tone began to impinge on Werther, though he was still deep-trapped in the glue of his guilt. He raised his head, his expression bemused, refusing to believe the import of her words.

'A wonderful aspect,' she said. And she licked his ear.

He shuddered. He frowned. He tried to frame words to ask her a certain question, but he failed.

She licked his cheek and she twined her fingers in his lacklustre hair. 'And one I should love to experience again, most passionate of anachronisms. It was as it must have been in those ancient days – when poets ranged the world, stealing what they needed, taking any fair maiden who pleased them, setting fire to the towns of their publishers, laying waste the books of their rivals: ambushing their readers. I am sure you were just as delighted, Werther. Say that you were!'

'Leave me!' he gasped. 'I can bear no more.'

'If it is what you want.'

'It is.'

With a wave of her little hand, she tripped from the room.

And Werther brooded upon her shocking words, deciding that he could only have misheard her. In her innocence she had seemed to admit an understanding of certain inconceivable things. What he had half-interpreted as a familiarity with the carnal world was doubtless merely a child's romantic conceit. How could she have had previous experience of a night such as that which they had shared?

She had been a virgin. Certainly she had been that.

He wished that he did not then feel an ignoble pang of pique at the possibility of another having also known her. Consequently this was immediately followed by a further wave of guilt for entertaining such thoughts and subsequent emotions. A score of conflicting glooms warred in his mind, sent tremors through his body.

'Why,' he cried to the sky, 'was I born! I am unworthy of the gift of life. I accused My Lady Charlotina, Lord Jagged and the Duke of Queens of base emotions, cynical motives, yet none are baser or more cynical than mine! Would I turn my anger against my victim, blame her for my misery, attack a little child because she tempted me? That is what my diseased mind would do. Thus do I seek to excuse myself my crimes. Ah, I am vile! I am vile!'

He considered going to visit Mongrove, for he dearly wished to abase himself before his old friend, to tell Mongrove that the giant's contempt had been only too well-founded; but he had lost the will to move; a terrible lassitude had fallen upon him. Hating himself, he knew that all must hate him, and while he knew that he had earned every scrap of their hatred, he could not bear to go abroad and run the risk of suffering it.

What would one of his heroes of Romance have done? How would Casablanca Bogard or Eric of Marylebone have exonerated themselves, even supposing they could have committed such an unbelievable deed in the first place?

He knew the answer.

It drummed louder and louder in his ears. It was implacable and grim. But still he hesitated to follow it. Perhaps some other, more original act of contrition would occur to him? He racked his writhing brain. Nothing presented itself as an alternative.

At length he rose from his chair of unpolished quartz. Slowly, his pace measured, he walked towards the window, stripping off his power rings so that they clattered to the flagstones.

He stepped upon the ledge and stood looking down at the rocks a mile below at the base of the tower. Some jolting of a power ring as it fell had caused a wind to spring up and to blow coldly against his naked body. 'The Wind of Justice,' he thought.

He ignored his parachute. With one final cry of 'Catherine! Forgive me!' and an unvoiced hope that he would be found long after it proved impossible to resurrect him, he flung himself, unsupported, into space.

Down he fell and death leapt to meet him. The breath fled from his lungs, his head began to pound, his sight grew dim, but the spikes of black rock grew larger until he knew that he had struck them, for his body was a-flame, broken in a hundred places, and his sad, muddled, doom-clouded brain was chaff upon the wailing breeze. Its last coherent thought was: *Let none say Werther did not pay the price in full.* And thus did he end his life with a proud negative.

VI

In Which Werther Discovers Consolation

'Oh, Werther, what an adventure!'

It was Catherine Gratitude looking down on him as he opened his eyes. She clapped her hands. Her blue eyes were full of joy.

Lord Jagged stood back with a smile. 'Re-born, magnificent Werther, to sorrow afresh!' he said.

He lay upon a bench of marble in his own tower. Surrounding the bench were My Lady Charlotina, the Duke of Queens, Gaf the Horse in Tears, the Iron Orchid, Li Pao, O'Kala Incarnadine, and many others. They all applauded.

'A splendid drama!' said the Duke of Queens.

'Amongst the best I have witnessed,' agreed the Iron Orchid (a fine compliment from her).

Werther found himself warming to them as they poured their praise upon him; but then he remembered Catherine Gratitude and what he had meant himself to be to her, what he had actually become, and although he felt much better for having paid his price, he stretched out his hand to her, saying again: 'Forgive me.'

'Silly Werther! Forgive such a perfect rôle? No, no! If anyone needs forgiving, then it is I.' And Catherine Gratitude touched one of the many power rings now festooning her fingers and returned herself to her original appearance.

'It is you!' He could make no other response as he looked upon the Everlasting Concubine. 'Mistress Christia?'

'Surely you suspected towards the end?' she said. 'Was it not everything you told me you wanted? Was it not a fine "sin", Werther?'

'I suffered . . .' he began.

'Oh, yes! *How* you suffered! It was unparalleled. It was equal, I am sure, to anything in History. And, Werther, did you not find the "guilt" particularly exquisite?'

'You did it for me?' He was overwhelmed. 'Because it was what I said I wanted most of all?'

'He is still a little dull,' explained Mistress Christia, turning to their friends. 'I believe that is often the case after a resurrection.'

'Often,' intoned Lord Jagged, darting a sympathetic glance at Werther. 'But it will pass, I hope.'

'The ending, though it could be anticipated,' said the Iron Orchid, 'was absolutely right.'

Mistress Christia put her arms around him and kissed him. 'They are saying that your performance rivals Jherek Carnelian's,' she whispered. He squeezed her hand. What a wonderful woman she was, to be sure, to have added to his experience and to have increased his prestige at the same time.

He sat up. He smiled a trifle bashfully. Again they applauded.

'I can see that this was where "Rain" was leading,' said Bishop Castle. 'It gives the whole thing point, I think.'

'The exaggerations were just enough to bring out the essential mood without being too prolonged,' said O'Kala Incarnadine, waving an elegant hoof (he had come as a goat).

'Well, I had not . . .' began Werther, but Mistress Christia put a hand to his lips.

'You will need a little time to recover,' she said.

Tactfully, one by one, still expressing their most fulsome congratulations, they departed, until only Werther de Goethe and the Everlasting Concubine were left.

'I hope you did not mind the deception, Werther,' she said. 'I had to make amends for ruining your rainbow and I had been wondering for ages how to please you. My Lady Charlotina helped a little, of course, and Lord Jagged – though neither knew too much of what was going on.'

'The real performance was yours,' he said. 'I was merely your foil.'

'Nonsense. I gave you the rough material with which to work. And none could have anticipated the wonderful, consummate use to which you put it!'

Gently, he took her hand. 'It was everything I have ever dreamed of,' he said. 'It is true, Mistress Christia, that you alone know me.'

'You are kind. And now I must leave.'

'Of course.' He looked out through his window. The comforting storm raged again. Familiar lightnings flickered; friendly thunder threatened; from below there came the sound of his old consoler the furious sea flinging itself, as always, at the rock's black fangs. His sigh was contented. He knew that their liaison was ended; neither had the bad taste to prolong it and thus produce what would be, inevitably, an anti-climax, and yet he felt regret, as evidently did she.

'If death were only permanent,' he said wistfully, 'but it cannot be. I thank you again, granter of my deepest desires.'

'If death,' she said, pausing at the window, 'were permanent, how would we judge our successes and our failures? Sometimes, Werther, I think you ask too much of the world.' She smiled. 'But you are satisfied for the moment, my love?'

'Of course.'

It would have been boorish, he thought, to have claimed anything else.

14 – KEITH ROBERTS: The Signaller

And so we come up to date. Science fiction in Britain today has at last become accepted by the general readership as a literature worthy of attention rather than something to hide away and read in plain wrappers. To close this anthology I decided to choose a writer who has become particularly accepted by a wide cross-section of the reading public, both in Britain and the United States, plus one who belongs to the new generation of sf writers that first appeared in the 1960s. To my mind the most appropriate author was Keith Roberts, and there could be no better story than his favourite *The Signaller*. This episode forms part of his fascinating and perceptive novel of an alternate England, *Pavane* (1968), and it shows perfectly the range of British sf following in particular the brash satire of Moorcock's *Pale Roses*.

Keith John Kingston Roberts was born at Kettering, Northamptonshire, on September 20th, 1935. He trained as a book illustrator, and later spent some years in an animation studio. Then, after a period in the advertising business, he broke free as a freelance visualiser and copywriter.

In 1964 he sent some stories to John Carnell, but they proved too short for Carnell's new project – that of *New Writings*. Roberts was encouraged to write longer stories, and the result was *Boulter's Canaries*, his first sale. But his first appearance was in *Science Fantasy*. What Carnell could not use he passed on to Kyril Bonfiglioli, who found Roberts's fiction fascinating, in particular his tales about the young witch Anita and her grandmother. As a result the September-October 1964 issue of *Science Fantasy* carried three stories by Roberts – *Escapism* (a time travel story) and two Anita adventures. Roberts appeared regularly in *Science Fantasy* thereafter, including several under the Alistair Bevan alias. His *New Writings* sales also kept his name in the public eye, particularly *Sub-Lim* and *The Inner Wheel* (later reworked into a novel).

In the meantime Roberts was working on a novel set in an alternate England wherein Queen Elizabeth I had been assassinated. The completed work was purchased by Bonfiglioli, and the first episode appeared in the first issue of the new *Science Fantasy*, retitled *Impulse*, dated March 1966. That first episode was *The Signaller* and set perfectly the mood for the rest of the series. It obviously satisfied Keith Roberts. He recalls:

> 'I'm difficult to satisfy where my own work's concerned and usually finish a job feeling I've lost out somewhere or other, but *The Signaller* was one that just flowed. I had the idea on a Friday, and finished the rough draft by Sunday night following; whereas most of my stuff gets four, five or more drafts it went through largely unchanged. It seems to have a good balance between strong personal storyline and technical invention, and I wish to God I could do it again.'

THE SIGNALLER

Keith Roberts

On either side of the knoll the land stretched in long, speckled sweeps, paling in the frost smoke until the outlines of distant hills blended with the curdled milk of the sky. Across the waste a bitter wind moaned, steady and chill, driving before it quick flurries of snow. The snow squalls flickered and vanished like ghosts, the only moving things in a vista of emptiness.

What trees there were grew in clusters, little coppices that leaned with the wind, their twigs meshed together as if for protection, their outlines sculpted into the smooth, blunt shapes of ploughshares. One such copse crowned the summit of the knoll; under the first of its branches, and sheltered by them from the wind, a boy lay face down in the snow. He was motionless but not wholly unconscious; from time to time his body quivered with spasms of shock. He was maybe sixteen or seventeen, blond-haired, and dressed from head to feet in a uniform of dark green leather. The uniform was slit in many places; from the shoulders down the back to the waist, across the hips and thighs. Through the rents could be seen the cream-brown of his skin and the brilliant slow twinkling of blood. The leather was soaked with it, and the long hair matted. Beside the boy lay the case of a pair of binoculars, the Zeiss lenses without which no man or apprentice of the Guild of Signallers ever moved, and a dagger. The blade of the weapon was red-stained; its pommel rested a few inches beyond his outflung right hand. The hand itself was injured, slashed across the backs of the fingers and deeply through the base of the thumb. Round it blood had diffused in a thin pink halo into the snow.

A heavier gust rattled the branches overhead, raised from somewhere a long creak of protest. The boy shivered again and began, with infinite slowness, to move. The outstretched hand crept forward, an inch at a time, to take his weight beneath his chest. The fingers traced an arc in the snow, its ridges red-tipped. He made a noise half-way between a grunt and a moan, levered himself onto his elbows, waited gathering strength. Threshed, half turned over, leaned on the undamaged left hand. He hung his head, eyes closed; his heavy breathing sounded through the copse. Another heave, a convulsive effort, and he was sitting upright, propped against the trunk of a tree. Snow stung his face, bringing back a little more awareness.

He opened his eyes. They were terrified and wild, glazed with pain. He looked up into the tree, swallowed, tried to lick his mouth, turned his head to stare at the empty snow round him. His left hand clutched his stomach; his right was crossed over it, wrist pressing, injured palm held clear of contact. He shut his eyes again briefly; then he made his hand go down, grip, lift the wet leather away from his thigh. He fell back, started to sob harshly at what he had seen. His hand, dropping slack, brushed tree bark. A snag probed the open wound below the thumb; the disgusting surge of pain brought him round again.

From where he lay the knife was out of reach. He leaned forward ponderously, wanting not to move, just stay quiet and be dead, quickly. The knife was still beyond his grip. He lunged sideways. His fingers touched the blade; he worked his way back to the tree, made himself sit up again. He rested, gasping; then he slipped his left hand under his knee, drew upward till the half-paralysed leg was crooked. Concentrating, steering the knife with both hands, he placed the tip of its blade against his trews, forced down slowly to the ankle cutting the garment apart. Then round behind his thigh till the piece of leather came clear.

He was very weak now; it seemed he could feel the strength ebbing out of him, faintness flickered in front of his eyes like the movements of a black wing. He pulled the leather toward him, got its edge between his teeth, gripped, and began to cut the material into strips. It was slow, clumsy work; he gashed himself twice, not feeling the extra pain. He finished at last and began to knot the strips round his leg, trying to tighten them enough to close the long wounds in the thigh. The wind howled steadily; there was no other sound but the quick panting of his breath. His face, beaded with sweat, was nearly as white as the sky.

He did all he could for himself, finally. His back was a bright torment, and behind him the bark of the tree was streaked with red, but he couldn't reach the lacerations there. He made his fingers tie the last of the knots, shuddered at the blood still weeping through the strappings. He dropped the knife and tried to get up.

After minutes of heaving and grunting his legs still refused to take his weight. He reached up painfully, fingers exploring the rough bole of the tree. Two feet above his head they touched the low, snapped-off stump of a branch. The hand was soapy with blood; it slipped, skidded off, groped back. He pulled, feeling the tingling as the gashes in the palm closed and opened. His arms and shoulders were strong, ribboned with muscle from hours spent at the semaphores; he hung tensed for a moment, head thrust back against the trunk, body arced and quivering; then his heel found a purchase in the snow, pushed him upright.

He stood swaying, not noticing the wind, seeing the blackness surge round him and ebb back. His head was pounding now, in time with the pulsing of his blood. He felt fresh warmth trickling on stomach and thighs, and the rise of a deadly sickness. He turned away, head bent, and started to walk, moving with the slow ponderousness of a diver. Six paces off he stopped, still swaying, edged round clumsily. The binocular case lay on the snow where it had fallen. He went back awkwardly, each step requiring now a separate effort of his brain, a bunching of the will to force the body to obey. He knew foggily that he daren't stoop for the case; if he tried he would fall headlong, and likely never move again. He worked his foot into the loop of the shoulder strap. It was the best he could do; the leather tightened as he moved, riding up round his instep. The case bumped along behind him as he headed down the hill away from the trees.

He could no longer lift his eyes. He saw a circle of snow, six feet or so across, black-fringed at its edges from his impaired vision. The snow moved as he walked, jerking toward him, falling away behind. Across it ran a line of faint impressions, footprints he himself had made. The boy followed them blindly. Some spark buried at the back of his brain kept him moving; the rest of his consciousness was gone now, numbed with shock. He moved draggingly, the leather case jerking and slithering behind his heel. With his left hand he held himself, low down over the groin; his right waved slowly, keeping his precarious balance. He left behind him a thin trail of bloodspots; each drop splashed pimpernel-bright against the snow, faded and spread to a wider pink stain before freezing itself into the crystals. The bloodmarks and the footprints reached back in a ragged line to the copse. In front of him the wind skirled across the land; the snow whipped at his face, clung thinly to his jerkin.

Slowly, with endless pain, the moving speck separated itself from the trees. They loomed behind it, seeming through some trick of the fading light to increase in height as they receded. As the wind chilled the boy the pain ebbed fractionally; he raised his head, saw before him the tower of a semaphore station topping its low cabin. The station stood on a slight eminence of rising ground; his body felt the drag of the slope, reacted with a gale of breathing. He trudged slower. He was crying again now with little whimperings, meaningless animal-noises, and a sheen of saliva showed on his chin. When he reached the cabin the copse was still visible behind him, grey against the sky. He leaned against the plank door gulping, seeing faintly the texture of the wood. His hand fumbled for the lanyard of the catch, pulled; the door opened, plunging him forward onto his knees.

After the snow light outside, the interior of the hut was dark. The boy worked his way on all fours across the board floor. There was a cupboard; he searched it blindly, sweeping glasses and cups aside, dimly hearing them shatter. He found what he needed, drew the cork from the bottle with his teeth, slumped against the wall and attempted to drink. The spirit ran down his chin, spilled across chest and belly. Enough went down his throat to wake him momentarily. He coughed and tried to vomit. He pulled himself to his feet, found a knife to replace the one he'd dropped. A wooden chest by the wall held blankets and bed linen; he pulled a sheet free and haggled it into strips, longer and broader this time, to wrap round his thigh. He couldn't bring himself to touch the leather tourniquets. The white cloth marked through instantly with blood; the patches elongated, joined and began to glisten. The rest of the sheet he made into a pad to hold against his groin.

The nausea came again; he retched, lost his balance and sprawled on the floor. Above his eye level, his bunk loomed like a haven. If he could just reach it, lie quiet till the sickness went away . . . He crossed the cabin somehow, lay across the edge of the bunk, rolled into it. A wave of blackness lifted to meet him, deep as a sea.

He lay a long time; then the fragment of remaining

will reasserted itself. Reluctantly, he forced open gummy eyelids. It was nearly dark now; the far window of the hut showed in the gloom a vague rectangle of greyness. In front of it the handles of the semaphore seemed to swim, glinting where the light caught the polished smoothness of wood. He stared, realising his foolishness; then he tried to roll off the bunk. The blankets, glued to his back, prevented him. He tried again, shivering now with the cold. The stove was unlit; the cabin door stood ajar, white crystals fanning in across the planking of the floor. Outside, the howling of the wind was relentless. The boy struggled; the efforts woke pain again and the sickness, the thudding and roaring. Images of the semaphore handles doubled, sextupled, rolled apart to make a glistening silver sheaf. He panted, tears running into his mouth; then his eyes slid closed. He fell into a noisy void shot with colours, sparks and gleams and washes of light. He lay watching the lights, teeth bared, feeling the throb in his back where fresh blood pumped into the bed. After a while, the roaring went away.

The child lay couched in long grass, feeling the heat of the sun strike through his jerkin to burn his shoulders. In front of him, at the conical crest of the hill, the magic thing flapped slowly, its wings proud and lazy as those of a bird. Very high it was, on its pole on top of its hill; the faint wooden clattering it made fell remote from the blueness of the summer sky. The movements of the arms had half hypnotised him; he lay nodding and blinking, chin propped on his hands, absorbed in his watching. Up and down, up and down, *clap* . . . then down again and round, up and back, pausing, gesticulating, never staying wholly still. The semaphore seemed alive, an animate thing perched there talking strange words nobody could understand. Yet words they were, replete with meanings and mysteries like the words in his Modern English Primer. The child's brain spun. Words made stories; what stories was the tower telling, all alone there on its hill? Tales of kings and shipwrecks, fights and pursuits, Fairies, buried gold . . . It was talking, he knew that without a doubt; whispering and clacking, giving messages and taking them from the others in the lines, the great lines that stretched across England everywhere you could think, every direction you could see.

He watched the control rods sliding like bright muscles in their oiled guides. From Avebury, where he lived, many other towers were visible; they marched southwards across the Great Plain, climbed the westward heights of the Marlborough Downs. Though those were bigger, huge things staffed by teams of men whose signals might be visible on a clear day for ten miles or more. When they moved it was majestically and slowly, with a thundering from their jointed arms; these others, the little local towers, were friendlier somehow, chatting and pecking away from dawn to sunset.

There were many games the child played by himself in the long hours of summer; stolen hours usually, for there was always work to be found for him. School lessons, home study, chores about the house or down at his brothers' smallholding on the other side of the village; he must sneak off, evenings or in the early dawn, if he wanted to be alone to dream. The stones beckoned him sometimes, the great gambolling diamond-shapes of them circling the little town. The boy would scud along the ditches of what had been an ancient temple, climb the terraced scarps to where the stones danced against the morning sun; or walk the long processional avenue that stretched eastward across the fields, imagine himself a priest or a god come to do old sacrifice to rain and sun. No one knew who first placed the stones. Some said the Fairies, in the days of their strength; others the old gods, they whose names it was a sin to whisper. Others said the Devil.

Mother Church winked at the destruction of Satanic relics, and that the villagers knew full well. Father Donovan disapproved, but he could do very little; the people went to it with a will. Their ploughs gnawed the bases of the markers, they broke the megaliths with water and fire and used the bits for patching drystone walls; they'd been doing it for centuries now, and the rings were depleted and showing gaps. But there were many stones; the circles remained, and barrows crowning the windy tops of hills, *hows* where the old dead lay patient with their broken bones. The child would climb the mounds, and dream of kings in fur and jewels; but always, when he tired, he was drawn back to the semaphores and their mysterious life. He lay quiet, chin sunk on his hands, eyes sleepy, while above him Silbury 973 chipped and clattered on its hill.

The hand, falling on his shoulder, startled him from dreams. He tensed, whipped round and wanted to bolt; but there was nowhere to run. He was caught; he stared up gulping, a chubby little boy, long hair falling across his forehead.

The man was tall, enormously tall it seemed to the child. His face was brown, tanned by sun and wind, and at the corners of his eyes were networks of wrinkles. The eyes were deep-set and very blue, startling against the colour of the skin; to the boy they seemed to be of exactly the hue one sees at the very top of the sky. His father's eyes had long since bolted into hiding behind pebble-thick glasses; these eyes were different. They had about them an appearance of power, as if they were used to looking very long distances and seeing clearly things that other men might miss. Their owner was dressed all in green, with the faded shoulder lacings and lanyard of a Serjeant of Signals. At his hip he carried the Zeiss glasses that were the badge of any Signaller; the flap of the case was only half-secured and beneath it the boy could see the big eye-pieces, the worn brassy sheen of the barrels.

The Guildsman was smiling; his voice when he spoke was drawling and slow. It was the voice of a man who knows about Time, that Time is for ever and scurry and bustle can wait. Someone who might know about the old stones in the way the child's father did not.

'Well,' he said, 'I do believe we've caught a little spy. Who be you, lad?'

The boy licked his mouth and squeaked, looking hunted. 'R-Rafe Bigland, sir . . .'

'And what be 'ee doin'?'

Rafe wetted his lips again, looked at the tower, pouted miserably, stared at the grass beside him, looked back to the Signaller and quickly away. 'I . . . I . . .'

He stopped, unable to explain. On top of the hill the tower creaked and flapped. The Serjeant squatted down, waiting patiently, still with the little half-smile, eyes twinkling at the boy. The satchel he'd been carrying he'd set on the grass. Rafe knew he'd been to the village to pick up the afternoon meal; one of the old ladies of Avebury was contracted to supply food to the Signallers on duty. There was little he didn't know about the working of the Silbury station.

The seconds became a minute, and an answer had to be made. Rafe drew himself up a trifle desperately; he heard his own voice speaking as if it was the voice of a stranger, and wondered with a part of his mind at the words that formed themselves on his tongue without it seemed the conscious intervention of thought. 'If you please, sir,' he said pipingly, 'I was watching the t-tower . . .'

'Why?'

'I . . .'

Again the difficulty. How explain? The mysteries of the Guild were not to be revealed to any casual stranger. The codes of the Signallers and other deeper secrets handed down, jealously, through the families privileged to wear the Green. The Serjeant's accusation of spying had had some truth to it; it had sounded ominous.

The Guildsman helped him. 'Canst thou read the signals, Rafe?'

Rafe shook his head, violently. No commoner could read the towers. No commoner ever would. He felt a trembling start in the pit of his stomach but again his voice used itself without his will. 'No, sir,' it said in a firm treble. 'But I would fain learn . . .'

The Serjeant's eyebrows rose. He sat back on his heels, hands lying easy across his knees, and started to laugh. When he had finished he shook his head. 'So you would learn . . . Aye, and a dozen kings, and many a highplaced gentleman, would lie easier abed for the reading of the towers.' His face changed itself abruptly into a scowl. 'Boy,' he said, 'you mock us . . .'

Rafe could only shake his head again, silently. The Serjeant stared over him into space, still sitting on his heels. Rafe wanted to explain how he had never, in his most secret dreams, ever imagined himself a Signaller; how his tongue had moved of its own, blurting out the impossible and absurd. But he couldn't speak any more; before the Green, he was dumb. The pause lengthened while he watched inattentively the lurching progress of a rain beetle through the stems of grass. Then, 'Who's thy father, boy?'

Rafe gulped. There would be a beating, he was sure of that now; and he would be forbidden ever to go near the towers or watch them again. He felt the stinging behind his eyes that meant tears were very close, ready to well and trickle. 'Thomas Bigland of Avebury, sir,' he said. 'A clerk to Sir William M-Marshall.'

The Serjeant nodded. 'And thou wouldst learn the towers? Thou wouldst be a Signaller?'

'Aye, sir . . .' The tongue was Modern English of course, the language of artisans and tradesmen, not the guttural clacking of the landless churls; Rafe slipped easily into the old-fashioned usage of it the Signallers employed sometimes among themselves.

The Serjeant said abruptly, 'Canst thou read in books, Rafe?'

'Aye, sir . . .' Then falteringly, 'If the words be not too long . . .'

The Guildsman laughed again, and clapped the boy on the back. 'Well Master Rafe Bigland, thou who would be a Signaller, and can read books if the words be but short, my book learning is slim enough as God he knows; but it may be I can help thee, if thou hast given me no lies. Come.' And he rose and began to walk away toward the tower. Rafe hesitated, blinked, then roused himself and trotted along behind, head whirling with wonders.

They climbed the path that ran slantingly round the hill. As they moved, the Serjeant talked. Silbury 973 was part of the C class chain that ran from near Londinium, from the great relay station at Pontes, along the line of the road to Aquae Sulis. Its complement . . . but Rafe knew the complement well enough. Five men including the Serjeant; their cottages stood apart from the main village, on a little rise of ground that gave them seclusion. Signallers' homes were always situated like that, it helped preserve the Guild mysteries. Guildsmen paid no tithes to locals demesnes, obeyed none but their own hierarchy; and though in theory they were answerable under Common Law, in practice they were immune. They governed themselves according to their own high code; and it was a brave man, or a fool, who squared with the richest Guild in England. There had been deadly accuracy in what the Serjeant said; when kings waited on their messages as eagerly as commoners they had little need to fear. The Popes might cavil, jealous of their independence, but Rome herself leaned too heavily on the continent-wide networks of the semaphore towers to do more than adjure and complain. In so far as such a thing was possible in a hemisphere dominated by the Church Militant, the Guildsmen were free.

Although Rafe had seen the inside of a signal station often enough in dreams he had never physically set foot in one. He stopped short at the wooden step, feeling awe rise in him like a tangible barrier. He caught his breath. He had never been this close to a semaphore tower before; the rush and thudding of the arms, the clatter of dozens of tiny joints, sounded in his ears like music. From here only the tip of the signal was in sight, looming over the roof of the hut. The varnished wooden spars shone orange like the masts of a boat; the semaphore arms rose and dipped, black against the sky. He could see the bolts and loops near their tips where in bad weather or at night when some message of vital importance had to be passed, cressets could be attached to them. He'd seen such fires once, miles out over the Plain, the night the old King died.

The Serjeant opened the door and urged him through it. He stood rooted just beyond the sill. The place had a clean smell that was somehow also masculine, a compound of polishes and oils and the fumes of tobacco; and inside too it had something of the appearance of a ship. The cabin was airy and low, roomier than it had looked from the foot of the hill. There was a stove, empty now and gleaming with blacking, its brasswork brightly polished. Inside its mouth a sheet of red crêpe paper had been stretched tightly; the doors were parted a little to show the smartness. The plank walls were painted a light grey; on the breast that enclosed the chimney of the stove duty rosters were pinned neatly. In one corner of the room was a group of diplomats, framed and richly coloured; below them an old Daguerreotype, badly faded, showing a group of men standing in front of a very tall signal tower. In one corner of the cabin was a bunk, blankets folded into a neat cube at its foot; above it a hand-coloured pinup of a smiling girl wearing a cap of Guild green and very little else. Rafe's eyes passed over it with the faintly embarrassed indifference of childhood.

In the centre of the room, white-painted and square, was the base of the signal mast; round it a little podium of smooth, scrubbed wood, on which stood two Guildsmen. In their hands were the long levers that worked the semaphore arms overhead; the control rods reached up from them, encased where they passed through the ceiling in white canvas grommets. Skylights, opened to either side, let in the warm July air. The third duty signaller stood at the eastern window of the cabin, glasses to his eyes, speaking quietly and continuously. 'Five . . . eleven . . . thirteen . . . nine . . .' The operators repeated the combinations, working the big handles, leaning the weight of their bodies against the pull of the signal arms overhead, letting each downward rush of the semaphores help them into position for their next cypher. There was an air of concentration but not of strain; it all seemed very easy and practised. In front of the men, supported by struts from the roof, a telltale repeated the positions of the arms, but the Signallers rarely glanced at it. Years of training had given a fluidness to their movements that made them seem almost like the steps and posturings of a ballet. The bodies swung, checked, moved through their arabesques; the creaking of wood and the faint rumbling of the signals filled the place, as steady and lulling as the drone of bees.

No one paid any attention to Rafe or the Serjeant. The Guildsman began talking again quietly, explaining what was happening. The long message, that had been going through now for nearly an hour, was a list of current grain and fatstock prices from Londinium. The Guild system was invaluable for regulating the complex economy of the country; farmers and merchants, taking the Londinium prices as a yardstick, knew exactly what to pay when buying and selling for themselves. Rafe forgot to be disappointed; his mind heard the words, recording them and storing them away, while his eyes watched the changing patterns made by the Guildsmen, so much a part of the squeaking, clacking machine they controlled.

The actual transmitted information, what the Serjeant called the payspeech, occupied only a part of the signalling; a message was often almost swamped by the codings necessary to secure its distribution. The current figures for instance had to reach certain centres, Aquae Sulis among them, by nightfall. How they arrived, their routing on the way, was very much the concern of the branch Signallers through whose stations the cyphers passed. It took years of experience coupled with a certain degree of intuition to route signals in such a way as to avoid lines already congested with information; and of course while a line was in use in one direction, as in the present case with a complex message being moved from east to west, it was very difficult to employ it in reverse. It was in fact possible to pass two messages in different directions at the same time, and it was often done on the A Class towers. When that happened every third cypher of a northbound might be part of another signal moving south; the stations transmitted in bursts, swapping the messages forward and back. But co-axial signalling was detested even by the Guildsmen. The line had to be cleared first, and a suitable code agreed on; two lookouts were employed, chanting their directions alternately to the signallers, and even in the best-run station total confusion could result from the smallest slip, necessitating re-clearing of the route and a fresh start.

With his hands, the Serjeant described the washout signal a fouled-up tower would use; the three horizontal extensions of the semaphores from the sides of their mast. If that happened he said, chuckling grimly, a head would roll somewhere; for a Class A would be under the command of a Major of Signals at least, a man of twenty or more years experience. He would be expected not to make mistakes, and to see in turn that none were made by his subordinates. Rafe's head began to whirl again; he looked with fresh respect at the worn green leather of the Serjeant's uniform. He was beginning to see now, dimly, just what sort of thing it was to be a Signaller.

The message ended at last, with a great clapping of the semaphore arms. The lookout remained at his post but the operators got down, showing an interest in Rafe for the first time. Away from the semaphore levers they seemed far more normal and unfrightening. Rafe knew them well; Robin Wheeler, who often spoke to him on his way to and from the station, and Bob Camus, who'd split a good many heads in his time at the Feast-day cudgel playing in the village. They showed him the code books, all the scores of cyphers printed in red on numbered black squares. he stayed to share their meal; his mother would be concerned and his father annoyed, but home was almost forgotten. Toward evening another message came up from the west; they told him it was police business, and sent it winging and clapping on its way. It was dusk when Rafe finally left the station, head in the clouds, two unbelievable pennies jinking in his pocket. It was only later, in bed and trying to sleep, he realised a long-submerged dream had come true. He did sleep finally, only to dream again of signal towers at night, the cressets on their arms roaring against the blueness of the sky. He never spent the coins.

Once it had become a real possibility, his ambition to be a Signaller grew steadily; he spent all the time he could at the Silbury station, perched high on its weird prehistoric hill. His absences met with his father's keenest disapproval. Mr Bigland's wage as an estate clerk barely brought in enough to support his brood of seven boys; the family had of necessity to grow most of its own food, and for that every pair of hands that could be mustered was valuable. But nobody guessed the reason for Rafe's frequent disappearance; and for his part he didn't say a word.

He learned, in illicit hours, the thirty-odd basic positions of the signal arms, and something of the commonest sequences of grouping; after that he could lie out near Silbury Hill and mouth off most of the numbers to himself, though without the codes that informed them he was still dumb. Once Serjeant Gray let him take the observer's place for a glorious half hour while a message was coming in over the Marlborough Downs. Rafe stood stiffly, hands sweating on the big barrels of the Zeiss glasses, and read off the cyphers as high and clear as he could for the signallers at his back. The Serjeant checked his reporting unobtrusively from the other end of the hut, but he made no mistakes.

By the time he was ten Rafe had received as much formal education as a child of his class could expect. The great question of a career was raised. The family sat in conclave; father, mother and the three eldest sons. Rafe was unimpressed; he knew, and had known for weeks, the fate they had selected for him. He was to be apprenticed to one of the four tailors of the village, little bent old men who sat like crosslegged hermits behind bulwarks of cloth bales and stitched their lives away by the light of penny dips. He hardly expected to be consulted on the matter; however he was sent for, formally, and asked what he wished to do. That was the time for the bombshell. 'I know exactly what I want to be,' said Rafe firmly. 'A Signaller.'

There was a moment of shocked silence; then the laughing started, and swelled. The Guilds were closely guarded; Rafe's father would pay dearly even for his entry into the tailoring trade. As for the Signallers . . . No Bigland had ever been a Signaller, no Bigland ever would. Why, that . . . it would raise the family status! The whole village would have to look up to them, with a son wearing the Green. Preposterous . . .

Rafe sat quietly until they were finished, lips compressed, cheekbones glowing. He'd known it would be like this, he knew just what he had to do. His composure discomfited the family; they quietened down enough to ask him, with mock seriousness, how he intended to set about achieving his ambition. It was time for the second bomb. 'By approaching the Guild with regard to a Common Entrance Examination,' he said, mouthing words that had been learned by rote. 'Serjeant Gray, of the Silbury Station, will speak for me.'

Into the fresh silence came his father's embarrassed coughing. Mr Bigland looked like an old sheep, sitting blinking through his glasses, nibbling at his thin moustache. 'Well,' he said. 'Well, I don't know . . . *Well* . . .' But Rafe had already seen the glint in his eyes at the dizzying prospect of prestige. That a son of his should wear the Green . . .

Before their minds could change Rafe wrote a formal letter which he delivered in person to the Silbury Station; it asked Serjeant Gray, very correctly, if he would be kind enough to call on Mr Bigland with a view to discussing his son's entry to the College of Signals in Londinium.

The Serjeant was as good as his word. He was a widower, and childless; maybe Rafe made up in part for the son he'd never had, maybe he saw the reflection of his own youthful enthusiasm in the boy. He came the next evening, strolling quietly down the village street to rap at the Biglands' door; Rafe, watching from his shared bedroom over the porch, grinned at the gaping and craning of the neighbours. The family was all a-flutter; the household budget had been scraped for wine and candles, silverware and fresh linen were laid out in the parlour, everybody was anxious to make the best possible impression. Mr Bigland of course was only too agreeable; when the Serjeant left, an hour later, he had his signed permission in his belt. Rafe himself saw the signal originated asking Londinium for the necessary entrance papers for the College's annual examination.

The Guild gave just twelve places per year, and they

were keenly contested. In the few weeks at his disposal Rafe was crammed mercilessly; the Serjeant coached him in all aspects of Signalling he might reasonably be expected to know about while the village dominie, impressed in spite of himself, brushed up his bookwork, even trying to instil into his aching head the rudiments of Norman French. Rafe won admittance; he had never considered the possibility of failure, mainly because such a thought was unbearable. He sat the examination in Sorviodunum, the nearest regional centre to his home; a week later a message came through offering him his place, listing the clothes and books he would need and instructing him to be ready to present himself at the College of Signals in just under a month's time. When he left for Londinium, well muffled in a new cloak, riding a horse provided by the Guild and with two russet-coated Guild servants in attendance, he was followed by the envy of a whole village. The arms of the Silbury tower were quiet; but as he passed they flipped quickly to Attention, followed at once by the cyphers for Origination and Immediate Locality. Rafe turned in the saddle, tears stinging his eyes, and watched the letters quickly spelled out in plaintalk. *'Good luck . . .'*

After Avebury, Londinium seemed dingy, noisy and old. The College was housed in an ancient, ramshackle building just inside the City walls; though Londinium had long since overspilled its former limits, sprawling south across the river and north nearly as far as Tyburn Tree. The Guild children were the usual crowd of brawling, snotty-nosed brats that comprised the apprentices of any trade. Hereditary sons of the Green, they looked down on the Common Entrants from the heights of an unbearable and largely imaginary eminence; Rafe had a bad time till a series of dormitory fights, all more or less bloody, proved to his fellows once and for all that young Bigland at least was better left alone. He settled down as an accepted member of the community.

The Guild, particularly of recent years, had been tending to place more and more value on theoretical knowledge, and the two year course was intensive. The apprentices had to become adept in Norman French, for their further training would take them inevitably into the houses of the rich. A working knowledge of the other tongues of the land, the Cornish, Gaelic and Middle English, was also a requisite; no Guildsman ever knew where he would finally be posted. Guild history was taught too, and the elements of mechanics and coding, though most of the practical work in those directions would be done in the field, at the training stations scattered along the south and west coasts of England and through the Welsh Marches. The students were even required to have a nodding acquaintance with thaumaturgy; though Rafe for one was unable to see how the attraction of scraps of paper to a polished stick of amber could ever have an application to Signalling.

He worked well none the less, and passed out with a mark high enough to satisfy even his professors. He was posted directly to his training station, the A Class complex atop Saint Adhelm's Head in Dorset. To his intense pleasure he was accompanied by the one real friend he had made at College; Josh Cope, a wild, black-haired boy, a Common Entrant and the son of a Durham mining family.

They arrived at Saint Adhelm's in the time-honoured way, thumbing a lift from a road train drawn by a labouring Fowler compound. Rafe never forgot his first sight of the station. It was far bigger than he'd imagined, sprawling across the top of the great blunt promontory. For convenience, stations were rated in accordance with the heaviest towers they carried; but Saint Adhelm's was a clearing centre for B, C and D lines as well, and round the huge paired structures of the A Class towers ranged a circle of smaller semaphores, all twirling and clacking in the sun. Beside them, establishing rigs displayed the codes the towers spoke in a series of bright-coloured circles and rectangles; Rafe, staring, saw one of them rotate, displaying to the west a yellow Bend Sinister as the semaphore above it switched in mid-message from plaintalk to the complex Code Twenty-Three. He glanced sidelong at Josh, got from the other lad a jaunty thumbs-up; they swung their satchels onto their shoulders and headed up toward the main gate to report themselves for duty.

For the first few weeks both boys were glad enough of each other's company. They found the atmosphere of a major field station very different from that of the College; by comparison the latter, noisy and brawling as it had been, came to seem positively monastic. A training in the Guild of Signallers was like a continuous game of ladders and snakes; and Rafe and Josh had slid back once more to the bottom of the stack. Their life was a near-endless round of canteen fatigues, of polishing and burnishing, scrubbing and holystoning. There were the cabins to clean, gravel paths to weed, what seemed like miles of brass rail to scour till it gleamed. Saint Adhelm's was a show station, always prone to inspection. Once it suffered a visit from the Grand Master of Signallers himself, and his Lord Lieutenant; the spitting and polishing before that went on for weeks. And there was the maintenance of the towers themselves; the canvas grommets on the great control rods to renew and pipeclay, the semaphore arms to be painted, their bearings cleaned and packed with grease, spars to be sent down and re-rigged, always in darkness when the day's signalling was done and generally in the foulest of weathers; while the semi-military nature of the Guild made necessary sidearms practice and shooting with the longbow and crossbow, obsolescent weapons now but still occasionally employed in the European wars.

The station itself surpassed Rafe's wildest dreams. Its standing complement including the dozen or so apprentices always in training was well over a hundred, of whom some sixty or eighty were always on duty or on call. The big semaphores, the Class A's, were each worked by teams of a dozen men, six to each great lever, with a Signalmaster to control coordination and pass on the cyphers from the observers. With the station running at near capacity the scene was impressive; the lines of men at the controls, as synchronised as troupes of dancers; the shouts of the Signalmasters, scuffle of feet on the white planking, rumble and creak of the control rods, the high thunder of the signals a hundred feet above the roofs.

Though according to the embittered Officer in Charge that was not Signalling but 'unscientific bloody timber-hauling.' Major Stone had spent most of his working life on the little Class C's of the Pennine Chain before an unlooked-for promotion had given him his present position of trust.

The A messages short-hopped from Saint Adhelm's to Swyre Head and from thence to Gad Cliff, built on the high land overlooking Warbarrow Bay. From there along the coast to Golden Cap, the station poised six hundred sheer feet above the fishing village of Lyme, to fling themselves in giant strides into the West, to Somerset and Devon and far-off Cornwall, or northwards again over the heights of the Great Plain *en route* for Wales. Up there Rafe knew they passed in sight of the old stone rings of Avebury. He often thought with affection of his parents and Serjeant Gray; but he was long past homesickness. His days were too full for that.

Twelve months after their arrival at Saint Adhelm's, and three years after their induction into the Guild, the apprentices were first allowed to lay hands on the semaphore bars. Josh in fact had found it impossible to wait and had salved his ego some months before by spelling out a frisky message on one of the little local towers in what he hoped was the dead of night. For that fall from grace he had made intimate and painful contact with the buckle on the end of a green leather belt, wielded by none other than Major Stone himself. Two burly Corporals of Signals held the miner's lad down while he threshed and howled; the end result had convinced even Josh that on certain points of discipline the Guild stood adamant.

To learn to signal was like yet another beginning. Rafe found rapidly that a semaphore lever was no passive thing to be pulled and hauled at pleasure; with the wind under the great black sails of the arms an operator stood a good chance of being bowled completely off the rostrum by the backwhip of even a thirty foot unit, while to the teams on the A Class towers lack of co-ordination could prove, and had proved in the past, fatal. There was a trick to the thing, only learned after bruising hours of practice; to lean the weight of the body against the levers rather than just using the muscles of back and arms, employ the jounce and swing of the semaphores to position them automatically for their next cypher. Trying to fight them instead of working with the recoil would reduce a strong man to a sweat-soaked rag within minutes; but a trained Signaller could work half the day and feel very little strain. Rafe approached the task assiduously; six months and one broken collarbone later he felt able to pride himself on stery of his craft. It was then he first encountered the murderous intricacies of co-axial signalling.

After two years on the station the apprentices were finally deemed ready to graduate as full Signallers. Then came the hardest test of all. The site of it, the arena, was a bare hillock of ground some half mile from Saint Adhelm's Head. Built onto it, and facing each other, about forty yards apart, were two Class D towers with their cabins. Josh was to be Rafe's partner in the test. They were taken to the place in the early morning, and given their problem; to transmit to each other in plaintalk the entire of the Book of Nehemiah in alternate verses, with appropriate Attention, Acknowledgement and End-of-Message cyphers at the head and tail of each. Several ten-minute breaks were allowed, though they had been warned privately it would be better not to take them; once they left the rostrums they might be unable to force their tired bodies back to the bars.

Round the little hill would be placed observers who would check the work minute by minute for inaccuracies and sloppiness. When the messages were finished to their satisfaction the prentices might leave, and call themselves Signallers; but not before. Nothing would prevent them deserting their task if they desired before it was done. Nobody would speak a word of blame, and there would be no punishment; but they would leave the Guild the same day, and never return. Some boys, a few, did leave. Others collapsed; for them, there would be another chance.

Rafe neither collapsed nor left, though there were times when he longed to do both. When he started, the sun had barely risen; when he left it was sinking toward the western rim of the horizon. The first two hours, the first three, were nothing; then the pain began. In the shoulders, in the back, in the buttocks and calves. His world narrowed; he saw neither the sun nor the distant sea. There was only the semaphore, the handles of it, the text in front of his eyes, the window. Across the space separating the huts he could see Josh staring as he engaged in his endless, useless task. Rafe came by degrees to hate the towers, the Guild, himself, all he had done, the memory of Silbury and old Serjeant Gray; and to hate Josh most of all, with his stupid white blob of a face, the signals clacking above him like some absurd extension of himself. With fatigue came a trance-like state in which logic was suspended, the reasons for actions lost. There was nothing to do in life, had never been anything to do but stand on the rostrum, work the levers, feel the jounce of the signals, check with the body, feel the jounce . . . His vision doubled and trebled till the lines of copy in front of him shimmered unreadably; and still the test ground on.

At any time in the afternoon Rafe would have killed his friend had he been able to reach him. But he couldn't get to him: his feet were rooted to the podium, his hands glued to the levers of the semaphore. The signals grumbled and creaked; his breath sounded in his ears harshly, like an engine. His sight blackened; the test and the opposing semaphore swam in a void. He felt disembodied; he could sense his limbs only as a dim and confused burning. And somehow, agonisingly, the transmission came to an end. He clattered off the last verse of the book, signed End of Message, leaned on the handles while the part of him that could still think realised dully that he could stop. And then, in black rage, he did the thing only one other apprentice had done in the history of the station; flipped the handles to Attention again, spelled out with terrible exactness and letter by letter the message *'God Save the Queen.'* Signed End of Message, got no acknowledgement, swung the levers up and locked them into position for Emergency-Contact Broken. In a signalling chain the alarm would be flashed back to the originating station, further information re-routed and a squad sent to investigate the breakdown.

Rafe stared blankly at the levers. He saw now the puzzling

bright streaks on them were his own blood. He forced his raw hands to unclamp themselves, elbowed his way through the door, shoved past the men who had come for him and collapsed twenty yards away on the grass. He was taken back to Saint Adhelm's in a cart, and put to bed. He slept the clock round; when he woke it was with the knowledge that Josh and he now had the right to put aside the cowled russet jerkins of apprentices for the full green of the Guild of Signallers. They drank beer that night, awkwardly, gripping the tankards in both bandaged paws; and for the second and last time, the station cart had to be called into service to get them home.

The next part of training was a sheer pleasure. Rafe made his farewells to Josh and went home on a two month leave; at the end of his furlough he was posted to the household of the Fitzgibbons, one of the old families of the south-west, to serve twelve months as Signaller-Page. The job was mainly ceremonial, though in times of national crisis it could obviously carry its share of responsibility. Most well-bred families, if they could afford to do so, bought rights from the Guild and erected their own tiny stations somewhere in the grounds of their estate; the little Class E towers were even smaller than the Class D's on which Rafe had graduated.

In places where no signal line ran within easy sighting distance, one or more stations might be erected across the surrounding country and staffed by Journeyman-Signallers without access to coding; but the Fitzgibbons' great aitch-shaped house lay almost below Swyre Head, in a sloping coombe open to the sea. Rafe, looking down on the roofs of the place the morning he arrived, started to grin. He could see his semaphore perched up among the chimney stacks; above it a bare mile away was the A repeater, the shorthop tower for his old station of Saint Adhelm's just over the hill. He touched heels to his horse, pushing it into a canter. He would be signalling direct to the A Class, there was no other outroute; he couldn't help chuckling at the thought of its Major's face when asked to hurl to Saint Adhelm's or Golden Cap requests for butter, six dozen eggs or the services of a cobbler. He paid his formal respects to the station, and rode down into the valley to take up his new duties.

They proved if anything easier than he had anticipated. Fitzgibbon himself moved in high circles at Court and was rarely home, the running of the house being left to his wife and two teenage daughters. As Rafe had expected, most of the messages he was required to pass were of an intensely domestic nature. And he enjoyed the privileges of any young Guildsman in his position; he could always be sure of a warm place in the kitchen at nights, the first cut off the roast, the prettiest serving-wenches to mend his clothes and trim his hair. There was sea bathing within a stone's throw, and Feast day trips to Durnovaria and Bourne Mouth. Once a little fair established itself in the grounds, an annual occurrence apparently; and Rafe spent a delicious half hour signalling the A Class for oil for its steam engines, and honey for a dancing bear.

The year passed quickly; in late autumn the boy, promoted now to Signaller-Corporal, was re-posted, and another took his place. Rafe rode west, into the hills that crowd the southern corner of Dorset, to take up what would be his first real command.

The station was part of a D Class chain that wound west over the high ground into Somerset. In winter, with the short days and bad seeing conditions, the towers would be unused; Rafe knew that well enough. He would be totally isolated; winters in the hills could be severe, with snow making travel next to impossible and frosts for weeks on end. He would have little to fear from the *routiers*, the footpads who legend claimed haunted the West in the cold months; the station lay far from any road and there was nothing in the cabins, save perhaps the Zeiss glasses carried by the Signallers, to tempt a desperate man. He would be in more danger from wolves and Fairies, though the former were virtually extinct in the south and he was young enough to laugh at the latter. He took over from the bored Corporal just finishing his term, signalled his arrival back through the chain and settled down to take stock of things.

By all reports this first winter on a one-man station was a worse trial than the endurance test. For a trial it was, certainly. At some time through the dark months ahead, some hour of the day, a message would come along the dead line, from the west or from the east; and Rafe would have to be there to take it and pass it on. A minute late with his acknowledgement and a formal reprimand would be issued from Londinium; that might peg his promotion for years, maybe for good. The standards of the Guild were high, and they were never relaxed; if it was easy for a Major in charge of an A Class station to fall from grace, how much easier for an unknown and untried Corporal! The duty period of each day was short, a bare six hours, five through the darkest months of December and January; but during that time, except for one short break, Rafe would have to be continually on the alert.

One of his first acts on being left alone was to climb to the diminutive operating gantry. The construction of the station was unusual. To compensate for its lack of elevation a catwalk had been built across under the roof; the operating rostrum was located centrally on it, while at each end double-glazed windows commanded views to west and east. Between them, past the handles of the semaphore, a track had been worn half an inch deep in the wooden boards. In the next few months Rafe would wear it deeper, moving from one window to the other checking the arms of the next towers in line. The matchsticks of the semaphores were barely visible; he judged them to be a good two miles distant. He would need all his eyesight, plus the keenness of the Zeiss lenses, to make them out at all on a dull day; but they would have to be watched minute by minute through every duty period because sooner or later one of them would move. He grinned and touched the handles of his own machine. When that happened, his acknowledgement would be clattering before the tower had stopped calling for Attention.

He examined the stations critically through his glasses. In the spring, riding out to take up a new tour, he might meet one of their operators; but not before. In the hours of daylight they as well as he would be tied to their gantries, and on foot in the dark it might be dangerous to try to reach them. Anyway it would not be expected of him; that was an unwritten law. In case of need, desperate need, he could call help through the semaphores; but for no other reason. This was the true life of the Guildsman; the bustle of Londinium, the warmth and comfort of the Fitzgibbons' home, had been episodes only. Here was the end result of it all; the silence, the desolation, the ancient, endless communion of the hills. He had come full circle.

His life settled into a pattern of sleeping and waking and watching. As the days grew shorter the weather worsened; freezing mists swirled round the station, and the first snow fell. For hours on end the towers to east and west were lost in the haze; if a message was to come now, the Signallers would have to light their cressets. Rafe prepared the bundles of faggots anxiously, wiring them into their iron cages, setting them beside the door with the paraffin that would soak them, make them blaze. He became obsessed by the idea that the message had in fact come, and he had missed it in the gloom. In time the fear ebbed. The Guild was hard, but it was fair; no Signaller, in winter of all times, was expected to be a superman. If a Captain rode suddenly to the station demanding why he had not answered this or that he would see the torches and the oil laid ready and know at least that Rafe had done his best. Nobody came; and when the weather cleared the towers were still stationary.

Each night after the light had gone Rafe tested his signals, swinging the arms to free them from their wind-driven coating of ice; it was good to feel the pull and flap of the thin wings up in the dark. The messages he sent into blackness were fanciful in the extreme; notes to his parents and old Serjeant Gray, lurid suggestions to a little girl in the household of the Fitzgibbons to whom he had taken more than a passing fancy. Twice a week he used the lunchtime break to climb the tower, check the spindles in their packings of grease. On one such inspection he was appalled to see a hairline crack in one of the control rods, the first sign that the metal had become fatigued. He replaced the entire section that night, breaking out fresh parts from store, hauling them up and fitting them by the improvised light of a handlamp. It was an awkward, dangerous job with his fingers freezing and the wind plucking at his back, trying to tug him from his perch onto the roof below. He could have pulled the station out of line in daytime, signalled Repairs and given himself the benefit of light, but pride forbade him. He finished the job two hours before dawn, tested the tower, made his entry in the log and went to sleep, trusting in his Signaller's sense to wake him at first light. It didn't let him down.

The long hours of darkness began to pall. Mending and laundering only filled a small proportion of his off-duty time; he read through his stock of books, re-read them, put them aside and began devising tasks for himself, checking and re-checking his inventories of food and fuel. In the blackness, with the long crying of the wind over the roof, the stories of Fairies and werethings on the heath didn't seem quite so fanciful. Difficult now even to imagine summer, the slow clicking of the towers against skies bright blue and burning with light. There were two pistols in the hut; Rafe saw to it their mechanisms were in order, loaded and primed them both. Twice after that he woke to crashings on the roof, as if some dark thing was scrabbling to get in; but each time it was only the wind in the skylights. He padded them with strips of canvas; then the frost came back, icing them shut, and he wasn't disturbed again.

He moved a portable stove up onto the observation gallery and discovered the remarkable number of operations that could be carried out with one eye on the windows. The brewing of coffee and tea were easy enough; in time he could even manage the production of hot snacks. His lunch hours he preferred to use for things other than cooking. Above all else he was afraid of inaction making him fat; there was no sign of it happening but he still preferred to take no chances. When snow conditions permitted he would make quick expeditions from the shack into the surrounding country.

On one of these the hillock with its smoothly shaped crown of trees attracted his eye. He walked toward it jauntily, breath steaming in the air, the glasses as ever bumping his hip. In the copse, his Fate was waiting.

The catamount clung to the bole of a fir, watching the advance of the boy with eyes that were slits of hate in the vicious mask of its face. No one could have read its thoughts. Perhaps it imagined itself about to be attacked; perhaps it was true what they said about such creatures, that the cold of winter sent them mad. There were few of them now in the West; mostly they had retreated to the hills of Wales, the rocky peaks of the far north. The survival of this one was in itself a freak, an anachronism.

The tree in which it crouched leaned over the path Rafe must take. He ploughed forward, head bent a little, intent only on picking his way. As he approached the catamount drew back its lips in a huge and silent snarl, showing the wide pink vee of its mouth, the long needle-sharp teeth. The eyes blazed; the ears flattened, making the skull a round, furry ball. Rafe never saw the wildcat, its stripes blending perfectly with the harshness of branches and snow. As he stepped beneath the tree it launched itself onto him, landed across his shoulders like a spitting shawl; his neck and back were flayed before the pain had travelled to his brain.

The shock and the impact sent him staggering. He reeled, yelling; the reaction dislodged the cat but it spun in a flash, tearing upward at his stomach. He felt the hot spurting of blood, and the world became a red haze of horror. The air was full of the creature's screaming. He reached his knife but teeth met in his hand and he dropped it. He grovelled blindly, found the weapon again, slashed out, felt the blade strike home. The cat screeched, writhing on the snow. He forced himself to push his streaming knee into the creature's back, pinning the animal while the knife flailed down, biting into its mad life; until the thing with a final convulsion burst free, fled limping and splashing blood, died maybe somewhere off in the trees. Then there was the time of blackness, the hideous crawl back to the signal station; and now he lay dying too, unable to reach the semaphore, knowing that finally he had failed. He wheezed hopelessly, settled back farther into the crowding dark.

In the blackness were sounds. Homely sounds. A regular *scrape-click, scrape-click*; the morning noise of a rake being drawn across the bars of a grate. Rafe tossed muttering, relaxed in the spreading warmth. There was light now, orange and flickering; he kept his eyes closed, seeing the glow of it against the insides of the lids. Soon his mother would call. It would be time to get up and go to school, or out into the fields.

A tinkling, pleasantly musical, made him turn his head. His body still ached, right down the length of it, but somehow the pain was not quite so intense. He blinked. He'd expected to see his old room in the cottage at Avebury; the curtains stirring in the breeze perhaps, sunshine coming through open windows. It took him a moment to readjust to the signal hut; then memory came back with a rush. He stared; he saw the gantry under the semaphore handles, the rods reaching out through the roof; the whiteness of their grommets, pipeclayed by himself the day before. The tarpaulin squares had been hooked across the windows, shutting out the night. The door was barred, both lamps were burning; the stove was alight, its doors open and spreading warmth. Above it, pots and pans simmered; and bending over them was a girl.

She turned when he moved his head and he looked into deep eyes, black-fringed, with a quick nervousness about them that was somehow like an animal. Her long hair was restrained from falling round her face by a band or ribbon drawn behind the little pointed ears; she wore a rustling dress of an odd light blue, and she was brown. Brown as a nut, though God knew there had been no sun for weeks to tan her skin like that. Rafe recoiled when she looked at him, and something deep in him twisted and needed to scream. He knew she shouldn't be here in this wilderness, amber-skinned and with her strange summery dress; that she was one of the

Old Ones, the half-believed, the Haunters of the Heath, the possessors of men's souls if Mother Church spoke truth. His lips tried to form the word 'Fairy' and could not. Blood-smeared, they barely moved.

His vision was failing again. She walked toward him lightly, swaying, seeming to his dazed mind to shimmer like a flame; some unnatural flame that a breath might extinguish. But there was nothing ethereal about her touch. Her hands were firm and hard; they wiped his mouth, stroked his hot face. Coolness remained after she had gone away and he realised she had laid a damp cloth across his forehead. He tried to cry out to her again; she turned to smile at him, or he thought she smiled, and he realised she was singing. There were no words; the sound made itself in her throat, goldenly, like the song a spinning wheel might hum in the ears of a sleepy child, the words always nearly there ready to well up through the surface of the colour and never coming. He wanted badly to talk now, tell her about the cat and his fear of it and its paws full of glass, but it seemed she knew already the things that were in his mind. When she came back it was with a steaming pan of water that she set on a chair beside the bunk. She stopped the humming, or the singing, then and spoke to him; but the words made no sense, they banged and splattered like water falling over rocks. He was afraid again, for that was the talk of the Old Ones; but the defect must have been in his ears because the syllables changed of themselves into the Modern English of the Guild. They were sweet and rushing, filled with a meaning that was not a meaning, hinting at deeper things beneath themselves that his tired mind couldn't grasp. They talked about the Fate that had waited for him in the wood, fallen on him so suddenly from the tree. *'The Norns spin the Fate of a man or of a cat,'* sang the voice. *'Sitting beneath Yggdrasil, great World Ash, they work; one Sister to make the yarn, the next to measure, the third to cut it at its end . . .'* And all the time the hands were busy, touching and soothing.

Rafe knew the girl was mad, or possessed. She spoke of Old

things, the things banished by Mother Church, pushed out for ever into the dark and cold. With a great effort he lifted his hand, held it before her to make the sign of the Cross; but she gripped the wrist, giggling, and forced it down, started to work delicately on the ragged palm, cleaning the blood from round the bases of the fingers. She unfastened the belt across his stomach, eased the trews apart; cutting the leather, soaking it, pulling it away in little twitches from the deep tears in groin and thighs. *'Ah . . .'* he said. *'Ah . . .'* She stopped at that, frowning, brought something from the stove, lifted his head gently to let him drink. The liquid soothed, seeming to run from his throat down into body and limbs like a trickling anaesthesia. He relapsed into a warmness shot through with little coloured stabs of pain, heard her crooning again as she dressed his legs. Slid deeper, into sleep.

Day came slowly, faded slower into night that turned to day again, and darkness. He seemed to be apart from Time, lying dozing and waking, feeling the comfort of bandages on his body and fresh linen tucked round him, seeing the handles of the semaphores gleam a hundred miles away, wanting to go to them, not able to move. Sometimes he thought when the girl came to him he pulled her close, pressed his face into the mother-warmth of her thighs while she stroked his hair, and talked, and sang. All the time it seemed, through the sleeping and the waking, the voice went on. Sometimes he knew he heard it with his ears, sometimes in fever dreams the words rang in his mind. They made a mighty saga; such a story as had never been told, never imagined in all the lives of men.

It was the tale of Earth; Earth and a land, the place her folk called Angle-Land. Only once there had been no Angle-Land because there had been no planets, no sun. Nothing had existed but Time; Time, and a void. Only Time was the void, and the void was Time itself. Through it moved colours, twinklings sudden shafts of light. There were hummings, shoutings perhaps, musical tones like the notes of organs that thrummed in his body until it shook with them and became a melting part. Sometimes in the dream he wanted to cry out; but still he couldn't speak, and the beautiful blasphemy ground on. He saw the brown mists lift back waving and whispering, and through them the shine of water; a harsh sea, cold and limitless, ocean of a new world. But the dream itself was fluid; the images shone and altered, melding each smoothly into each, yielding place majestically, fading into dark. The hills came, rolling, tentative, squirming, pushing up dripping flanks that shuddered, sank back, returned to silt. The silt, the sea bed, enriched itself with a million-year snowstorm of little dying creatures. The piping of the tiny snails as they fell was a part of the chorus and the song, a thin, sweet harmonic.

And already there were Gods; the Old Gods, powerful and vast, looking down, watching, stirring with their fingers at the silt, waving the swirling brownness back across the sea. It was all done in a dim light, the cold glow of dawn. The hills shuddered, drew back, thrust up again like golden, humped animals, shaking the water from their sides. The sun stood over them, warming, adding steam to the fogs, making multiple and shimmering reflections dance from the sea. The Gods laughed; and over and again, uncertainty, unsurely, springing from the silt, sinking back to silt again, the hills writhed, shaping the shapeless land. The voice sang, whirring like a wheel; there was no 'forward', no 'back'; only a sense of continuity, of massive development, of the huge Everness of Time. The hills fell and rose; strange creatures slithered on them and flopped and barked; tree leaves brushed away the sun, their reflections waved in water, the trees themselves sank, rolled and heaved, were thrust down to rise once more dripping, grow afresh. The rocks formed, reformed, became solid, melted again until from the formlessness somehow the land was made; Angle-Land, nameless still, with its long pastures, its fields and silent hills of grass. Rafe saw the endless herds of animals that crossed it, wheeling under the wheeling sun; and the first shadowy Men. Rage possessed them; they hacked and hewed, rearing their stone circles in the wind and emptiness, finding again the bodies of the Gods in the chalky flanks of downs. Until all ended, the Gods grew tired; and the ice came flailing and crying from the north, the sun sank dying in its blood and there was coldness and blackness and nothingness and winter.

Into the void. He came; only He was not the Christos, the God of Mother Church. He was Balder, Balder the Lovely, Balder the Young. He strode across the land, face burning bright as the sun, and the Old Ones grovelled and adored. The wind touched the stone circles, burning them with frost; in the darkness men cried for spring. So he came to the Tree Yggdrasil – *What Tree*, Rafe's mind cried despairingly, and the voice checked and laughed and said without anger, *'Yggdrasil, great World Ash, whose branches pierce the layers of Heaven, whose roots wind through all Hells . . .'* Balder came to the Tree, on which he must die, for the sins of Gods and Men; and to the Tree they nailed him, hung him by the palms. And there they came to adore while his blood ran and trickled and gouted bright, while he hung above the Hells of the Trolls and of the Giants of Frost and Fire and Mountain, below the Seven Heavens where Tiw and Thunor and old Wo-Tan trembled in Valhalla at the mightiness of what was done.

And from his blood sprang warmth again and grass and sunlight, the meadow flowers and the calling, mating birds. And the Church came at last, stamping and jingling, out of the east, lifting the brass wedding cakes of her altars while men fought and roiled and made the ground black with their blood, while they raised their cities and their signal towers and their glaring castles. The Old Ones moved back, the Fairies, the Haunters of the Heath, the People of the Stones, taking with them their lovely bleeding Lord; and the priests called despairingly to Him, calling Him the Christos, saying he did die on a tree, at the Palace Golgotha, the Place of the Skull. Rome's navies sailed the world; and England woke up, steam jetted in every tiny hamlet, and clattering and noise; while Balder's blood, still raining down, made afresh each spring. And so after days in the telling, after weeks, the huge legend paused, and turned in on itself, and ended.

The stove was out, the hut smelled fresh and cool. Rafe lay quiet, knowing he had been very ill. The cabin was a place of browns and clean bright blues. Deep brown of woodwork, orange-brown of the control handles, creamy-brown of planking. The blue came from the sky, shafting in through windows and door, reflecting from the long-dead semaphore in pale spindles of light. And the girl herself was brown and blue; brown of skin, frosted blue of ribbon and dress. She leaned over him smiling, all nervousness gone. *'Better,'* sang the voice. *'You're better now. You're well.'*

He sat up. He was very weak. She eased the blankets aside, letting the air tingle like cool water on his skin. He swung his legs down over the edge of the bunk and she helped him stand. He sagged, laughed, stood again swaying, feeling the texture of the hut floor under his feet, looking down at his body, seeing the pink criss-crossing of scars on stomach and thighs, the jaunty penis thrusting from its nest of hair. She found him a tunic, helped him into it laughing at him, twitching and pulling. She fetched him a cloak, fastened it round his neck, knelt to push sandals on his feet. He leaned against the bunk panting a little, feeling stronger. His eye caught the semaphore; she shook her head and teased him, urging him toward the door. *'Come,'* said the voice. *'Just for a little while.'*

She knelt again outside, touched the snow while the wind blustered wetly from the west. Round about, the warming hills were brilliant and still. *'Balder is dead,'* she sang. *'Balder is dead . . .'* And instantly it seemed Rafe could hear the million chuckling voices of the thaw, see the very flowers pushing coloured points against the translucency of snow. He looked up at the signals on the tower. They seemed strange to him now, like the winter a thing of the past. Surely they too would melt and run, and leave no trace. They were part of the old life and the old way; for the first time he could turn his back on them without distress. The girl moved from him, low shoes showing her ankles against the snow; and Rafe followed, hesitant at first then more surely, gaining strength with every step. Behind him, the signal hut stood forlorn.

The two horsemen moved steadily, letting their mounts pick their way. The younger rode a few paces ahead, muffled in his cloak, eyes beneath the brim of his hat watching the horizon. His companion sat his horse quietly, with an easy slouch; he was grizzled and brown-faced, skin tanned by the wind. In front of him, over the pommel of the saddle, was hooked the case of a pair of Zeiss binoculars. On the other side was the holster of a musket; the barrel lay along the neck of the horse, the butt thrust into the air just below the rider's hand.

Away on the left a little knoll of land lifted its crown of trees into the sky. Ahead, in the swooping bowl of the valley, was the black speck of a signal hut, its tower showing thinly above it. The officer reined in quietly, took the glasses from their case and studied the place. Nothing moved, and no smoke came from the chimney. Through the lenses the shuttered windows stared back at him; he saw the black vee of the semaphore arms folded down like the wings of a dead bird. The Corporal waited impatiently, his horse fretting and blowing steam, but the Captain of Signals was not to be hurried. He lowered the glasses finally, and clicked to his mount. The animal moved forward again at a walk, picking its hooves up and setting them down with care.

The snow here was thicker; the valley had trapped it, and the day's thaw had left the drifts filmed with a brittle skin of ice. The horses floundered as they climbed the slope to the hut. At its door the Captain dismounted, leaving the reins hanging slack. He walked forward, eyes on the lintel and the boards.

The mark. It was everywhere, over the door, on its frame, stamped along the walls. The circle, with the crab pattern inside it; rebus or pictograph, the only thing the People of the Heath knew, the only message it seemed they had for men. The Captain had seen it before, many times; it had no power left to surprise him. The Corporal had not. The older man heard the sharp intake of breath, the click as a pistol was cocked; saw the quick, instinctive movement of the hand, the gesture that wards off the Evil Eye. He smiled faintly, almost absentmindedly, and pushed at the door. He knew what he would find, and that there was no danger.

The inside of the hut was cool and dark. The Guildsman looked round slowly, hands at his sides, feet apart on the boards. Outside a horse champed, jangling its bit, and snorted into the cold. He saw the glasses on their hook, the swept floor, the polished stove, the fire laid neat and ready on the bars; everywhere, the Fairy mark danced across the wood.

He walked forward and looked down at the thing on the bunk. The blood it had shed had blackened with the frost; the wounds on its stomach showed like leaf-shaped mouths. The eyes were sunken now and dull; one hand was still extended to the signal levers eight feet above.

Behind him the Corporal spoke harshly, using anger as a bulwark against fear. 'The . . . People that were here. They done this . . .'

The Captain shook his head. 'No,' he said slowly. ''Twas a wildcat.'

The Corporal said thickly, 'They were here though . . .' The anger surged again as he remembered the unmarked snow. 'There weren't no tracks, sir. *How could they come . . .*'

'How comes the wind?' asked the Captain, half to himself. He looked down again at the corpse in the bunk. He knew a little of the history of this boy, and of his record. The Guild had lost a good man.

How did they come? The People of the Heath . . . His mind twitched away from using the name the commoners had for them. What did they look like, when they came? What did they talk of, in locked cabins to dying men? Why did they leave their mark . . .

It seemed the answers shaped themselves in his brain. It was as if they crystallised from the cold, faintly sweet air of the place, blew in with the soughing of the wind. *All this would pass*, came the thoughts, *and vanish like a dream. No more hands would bleed on the signal bars, no more children freeze in their lonely watchings. The Signals would leap continents and seas, winged as thought. All this would pass, for better or for ill . . .*

He shook his head, bear-like, as if to free it from the clinging spell of the place. He knew, with a flash of inner sight, that he would know no more. The People of the Heath, the Old Ones; they moved back, with their magic and their lore. Always back, into the yet remaining dark. Until one day they themselves would vanish away. They who were, and yet were not . . .

He took the pad from his belt, scribbled, tore off the top sheet. 'Corporal,' he said quietly. 'If you please . . . Route through Golden Cap.'

He walked to the door, stood looking out across the hills at the matchstick of the eastern tower just visible against the sky. In his mind's eye a map unrolled; he saw the message flashing down the chain, each station picking it up, routing it, clattering it on its way. Down to Golden Cap, where the great signals stood gaunt against the cold crawl of the sea; north up the A line to Aquae Sulis, back again along the Great West Road. Within the hour it would reach its destination at Silbury Hill; and a grave-faced man in green would walk down the village street of Avebury, knock at a door.

The Corporal climbed to the gantry, clipped the message in the rack, eased the handles forward lightly testing against the casing ice. He flexed his shoulders, pulled sharply. The dead tower woke up, arms clacking in the quiet. *Attention, Attention* . . . Then the signal for Origination, the cypher for the eastern line. The movements dislodged a little cloud of ice crystals; they fell quietly, sparkling against the greyness of the sky.

EPILOGUE TO VOLUME TWO

It was *Pavane* that really cemented Keith Robert's name into the science fiction hierarchy. And although he temporarily vanished from the scene in the late 1960s after *Impulse* (which he edited for a few issues) ceased in 1967, he has lately returned with a vengeance with a collection of his short stories, *Machines and Men* (1973), plus a new novel *The Chalk Giants* (1974), as well as a breathtaking historical novel about the fall of the Roman Empire, *The Boat of Fate* (1971). Without a doubt Keith Roberts will be one of the new British sf writers to follow in the future.

And what of others? Again, had this anthology been larger I would liked to have squeezed in many other British writers; not only those that made their initial impact under John Carnell, such as Dan Morgan, Don Malcolm or Ed Mackin, but also the new authors who have come to the fore in the 1970s. To close this second volume therefore I would like to look briefly at some of those writers who are currently keeping sf alive in Britain and laying the foundations for the next generation.

Scores of names spring to mind immediately, but it would seem that the current new name leading writer is Christopher Priest. Priest has recently produced some startling novels, starting with *Indoctrinaire* (1971), followed by *Fugue For a Darkening Island* which came third in the voting for the John W Campbell Memorial award for best sf novel of 1972, *Inverted World* (1974), and the recent extravaganza, *The Space Machine* (1976), set on the Mars of Wells's *War of the Worlds*. Like most professional sf writers, Priest firmly has his feet in science fiction fandom, having edited his own fanzines, like *Con* back in 1964. His first professional sf story in print was *The Run* in the third issue of *Impulse* dated May 1966, and he hasn't looked back since. Ironically back in those fannish days many fans took

Chris Priest to task over an article he wrote for the first issue of a fanzine called *Fusion*. The article was on how to write science fiction, and since Priest had not written any, some fans felt he had no right to give his opinions. I am sure everyone will agree he has sufficient justification to answer them now.

Ian Watson has made a colossal impact with his first novel *The Embedding* (1973) which is sure to go down in sf history as one of the most impressive first novels ever. Watson first appeared on the sf scene during the last experimental days of *New Worlds* with three stories beginning with *Roof Garden Under Saturn* in the November 1969 issue. He still appears in the *New Worlds* anthologies, and was a regular contributor to *Science Fiction Monthly*. A second novel, *The Jonah Kit*, was published in 1975, and his most recent, *The Martian Inca*, in 1977.

A writer better known in America than Britain is Yorkshireman Brian M Stableford. He has had over a dozen novels published, starting with *Cradle of the Sun* (1969), and including the most inventive space opera series to see print, concerning the starship *Hooded Swan*. Stableford also had his fannish apprenticeship, although he severed all connections when studying at University so that he could also concentrate on writing. He too appeared originally in magazines, starting with a novelette, *Beyond Time's Aegis* in the November 1965 *Science Fantasy*. Written with his friend Craig Mackintosh it appeared under the alias Brian Craig. His first solo sale was the brief *The Man Who Came Back* (*Impulse*, October 1966). Recent story sales in America resulted in *The Sun's Tears* (*Amazing*, October 1974) being chosen for one of that country's annual anthologies of the year's best sf.

Mark Adlard is unique in that he began writing sf without realising that was what it was, and only looked into the genre after his annoyance with friends calling his stories science fiction. Since then he has become one of Britain's most stylistic sf writers, as well as an accepted critic and authority on the field. He has had three sf novels published so far, all centred on a massive future city on an Earth where plastic and steel has given way to an all-purpose stahlex. The novels are *Interface* (1971). *Volteface* (1972) and *Multiface* (1975). Adlard writes from experience as he is in real life an executive in the steel industry.

The lack of female writers in this anthology is quite apparent because, alas, on proportion there are few British female sf writers. The leading British female sf writer today is almost certainly Josephine Saxton who first appeared in the November 1965 *Science Fantasy* with a short puzzler, *The Wall*. Most of her subsequent sales though have been to the American magazine market, and she has established herself firmly in the sf field with novels like *The Hieros Gamos of Sam and An Smith* (1969) and *Vector For Seven* (1970), though has yet to receive just recognition in this country.

Other authors who spring to mind are Michael G Coney, Charles Partington, David I Masson, and M John Harrison, all of whom have started to establish themselves in the last decade and will almost certainly be amongst the names to follow in the ensuing years. But alas, space precludes but a passing mention of them and their colleagues.

With all this talent brimming over the science fiction barrel in Britain it is sad to realise that the majority of them have first to establish themselves in the United States before they can begin to make a name in Britain. This is solely due to the lack of suitable markets for sf in Britain. It is true that at last several paperback publishers are now making science fiction a leading part of their output, especially Futura with its specialist Orbit imprint. But these prefer to publish novels, and whilst that is fine for a seasoned writer, it is no easy thing for an untrained writer to launch himself straight into a novel. Also sf is ideally suited to the short story form and yet there are few outlets for original short fiction in Britain.

At the time I'm writing this, March 1977, there are four markets, only one of which is a magazine. That is *Vortex*, which first appeared in January 1977 and has yet to establish itself. It sets itself an ambitious target, wishing to publish the whole range of scientific and speculative fiction and fantasy, but only publishes about three new stories a month, say forty a year. The other outlets are all original anthology series. *New Writings in SF*, edited by Ken Bulmer, *New Worlds* edited by Hilary Bailey, and the most recent *Andromeda* from Orbit, edited by Peter Weston. All three appear only twice yearly, and at the very most will not include more than ten stories per volume, which would be sixty in a year. All in all then there is a possible market for about one hundred new stories a year in Britain. Since the bulk of that can easily be absorbed by the regular professionals, what chance do new writers have of making an impact except by sending to America. Since few American magazines are freely distributed in this country it means that only a minimal number of home readers will be able to enjoy the fruits of their country's bright and imaginative minds. Most will have to wait several years until the stories appear in a British anthology, such as this (take *The Teacher* for example), or in an author's collection.

Britain needs more regular sf magazines. During the 1950s when interest in sf was nothing compared to today's enthusiastic fans, Britain was able to support four leading magazines: *New Worlds*, *Nebula*, *Science Fantasy*, and *Authentic*, producing about forty issues a year, a market for over two hundred stories annually. They were the magazines that produced today's Aldiss, Ballard, Shaw, White and Kapp but where will the next generation of sf writers owe their origins?

In this anthology I have traced both the development of science fiction in Britain and the number of talented writers Britain has produced. I hope that in the not too distant future I shall be able to produce a third volume containing the writers omitted from these two books, and I would like to think that by then I would be able to discuss the growth of many new markets for science fiction in Britain. This country desperately needs them.

THE HOT-BLOODED DINOSAURS

Adrian J. Desmond

For 150 million years dinosaurs stalked and ruled the earth. Then, 70 million years ago, the greatest empire the world has ever seen disappeared without trace. What they looked like, how they lived, why they vanished, has absorbed and perplexed man almost more than any other single issue concerning the animal kingdom. Now, in THE HOT-BLOODED DINOSAURS, Adrian J. Desmond challenges nearly every accepted theory.

'Likely to become the definitive work for a reader who wants an account of the most astounding episode so far in the entire history of the earth . . . There is no doubt that the dinosaurs represented the most successful order of creation so far achieved by whatever achieves such things . . . beside them the whole of human history to date is contained in an eyeblink. Mr. Desmond has given us a fascinating glimpse into an unimaginable world.' *Bernard Levin, The Observer*

MYSTERIES OF THE EARTH

Jacques Bergier

What was the point of building a skyscraper in the desert?

Why did the dinosaur suddenly become extinct?

Can the giant drawings on the plateau in Peru only be seen from the air because they were done for people who could fly?

Who could have made sophisticated metal cylinders long before civilized man ever existed?

Jacques Bergier, co-author of the bestselling MORNING OF THE MAGICIANS, has become famous in France through his belief that 'Intelligences' in outer space are watching us and interfering in our affairs. THE MYSTERIES OF THE EARTH is his unique and startling explanation of the phenomena of our universe: a terrifying demonstration that the science fiction of today may be the reality of tomorrow.

LIGHTNING IN MAY

Gordon Parker

'FINE WRITING, VIVID STORYTELLING . . . Those who have had the privilege of reading Gordon Parker's first novel, THE DARKNESS OF THE MORNING, will need no recommendation from me'. *Ted Willis.*

LIGHTNING IN MAY is the story of one mining village involved in the drama of the General Strike, and of families incited by a vicious rabble-rouser to a deed of vengeance that threatens the safety of the entire community. It is also the story of John Kinghorn, a young doctor who chooses the bleak, sordid mining village for his first practice and finds himself drawn inexorably into its tragedy through his love for a miner's daughter.

'Compels the reader's attention right from the beginning until the tense climax is reached'. *British Book News.*

THE ULTRA SECRET

F. W. Winterbotham

'The greatest British Intelligence coup of the Second World War has never been told till now'
Daily Mail

For thirty-five years the expert team of cryptanalysts who worked at Bletchley Park have kept the secret of how, with the help of a Polish defector, British Intelligence obtained a precise copy of the highly secret and complex German coding machine known as Enigma, and then broke the coding system to intercept all top-grade German military signals. Group-Captain Winterbotham was the man in charge of security and communication of this information. Now he is free to tell the story of that amazing coup and what it uncovered.

'A story as bizarre as anything in spy fiction . . . the book adds a new dimension to the history of World War II'
New York Times

'Military historians, like the general reader, will be astonished by this book . . . Group-Captain Winterbotham cannot be too highly commended'
The Listener

'Superbly told'
Daily Express